9/23

THE STARS ENTWINED

BOOK ONE OF THE ARYSHAN WAR

JON DEL ARROZ

9|23

COPYRIGHT INFO

PART I

PROLOGUE

Alarms blared. Warning lights flashed from the side of the cockpit. Regus Jackson shook his head to purge the grogginess from his eyes. He sat up straight, gripping the arms of his chair.

"What the hell is going on?" How long had he been asleep? He glanced to the sidewall chrono—over two hours.

"We have an incoming ship gaining on us." Ellund tapped controls. An overlay window opened on the screen. A plot-point map projected the other ship's trajectory in relation to the *Sunflower*. "They'll overtake us in five minutes."

"What kind of ship?" Regus asked. His palm slipped on the metal armrest. He wiped his sweat on his pant leg. It wasn't hot in here. Nerves were getting the best of him.

"What do you think?" Ellund asked, irritation seeping into his voice. This crew never handled tense situations well. They'd had shouting matches in the past, usually over foolish matters. It would do no good to shout now.

"Aryshans," Regus muttered under his breath. He had made the decision to take the shorter trade route through this sector to make up for lost time spent at their last port. It had been a calculated risk, but there shouldn't have been any other ships this far into open space. "Bill, can we shake them?"

Bill shook his head. "I don't know anything about Aryshans, but we got a piece of junk here that's barely spaceworthy. We do have an incoming communication, text only."

"Display it."

Another window layered on the screen, this time with text: *Human vessel. Turn around. Return to your space.*

A simple enough demand, but they were now two hours of fuel into the journey and a return trajectory would set them even further back if they had to go around. He had to think quickly. "Tell them... Hmm," Bill said, stroking his chin. He snapped his fingers. "I got it. Tell them our crystal drive is stuck engaged. It's going to take some time for us to fix."

Bill typed into his keyboard and sent the message.

The three men stared at the screen, waiting. Hopefully, the Aryshans bought the story.

"Another message," Bill said.

The display on the screen changed. *Reverse course. No further delays.*

"I think we should do as they say, boss," Ellund said.

The *Sunflower* jolted forward as if it had collided with something. Regus dug his feet into the metal plating on the floor to stay in his chair. On his armrest display, the crystal drive schematic blinked red. They had a real problem.

"Now what?" Regus asked.

"Drive failure. We're going to need a reboot and... Oh, damn."

The screen switched to a view of a massive Aryshan ship only just avoiding collision with the *Sunflower*. It would look to them as if the *Sunflower* had intentionally tried to hit them. This couldn't be good.

"Send apologies, quickly!" Regus said.

"I'm working on it," Bill said, typing frantically. Alarms blared again.

"They fired on us!" Ellund shouted. He jumped from his seat, ready to flee, but there was nowhere to go. Like a trapped animal, he stared at Regus.

Crossing into Aryshan space had been a terrible decision. He should never have pressed his luck like this. The incoming projectiles loomed on the map, taunting him, seeming to take an eternity to reach the *Sunflower*. It was the last thing Regus Jackson would ever see.

1

An assignment like this could make or break a career. Those were rarities in Internal Affairs, with most cases dealing with petty theft, embezzlement, or matters requiring a few interviews and some paperwork to settle. Lieutenant Sean Barrows had been good at that job, keeping his head down and getting his work done. He'd never had such a high-profile case as his investigation on Palmer Station.

The transport shuttle hatch descended onto the station's flight deck. Its passengers crowded the exit, bottlenecking through the hatch to exit one at a time. Sean stood at the back of the line, ducking under the short hatch frame to accommodate his six feet in height. The line paused. Up ahead, security ran individual body scans on each passenger present.

"What's going on?" Sean asked a station security guard who walked along the line of travelers.

"Heightened security sweep. Commodore V'bosh's orders," the guard said.

That didn't give him too much new information. His assignment had been to interview Captain Jemile Grayson, someone from the fleet proper who had been investigating recent attacks in this sector of space. "I'm from INIA," Sean said to the guard, craning his neck to see the line of people extending in front of him. At this rate, it would take him hours to get through. "Any way I could bypass this?"

"Ident crystal please," the guard said, holding out his hand.

Sean reached into the pocket of his gray uniform and produced the crystal. The guard took it, stepping away to place the crystal in a scanner. He reviewed the information and called someone on a comm unit. Several moments later, he stepped forward. "You've been authorized. The commodore would like you to go directly to the scene of the latest incident. If you'd follow me, sir?"

Sean nodded. Though he had been hoping for a brief introduction to Captain Grayson, and an evening of settling in to adjust to local station time, it did appear as if some new emergency had created the need for additional security at the shuttle bay. Station personnel seemed tense, acting more formal than in his usual first encounters.

The guard led the way, and Sean followed without a word. They took a liftcar through several of the station's sections that led to a series of apartment quarters. The corridor they entered had been cordoned off, guards standing at the entrance. Those guards scanned Sean's escort's ident crystal before letting them pass.

They moved down the corridor until they reached an open door. Several members of station security swept the room with various equipment. Captain Grayson stood at the entryway, dressed in an Interplanetary Navy gray uniform, with a rank patch over his right breast pocket that signaled his captaincy. He looked exactly like his dossier: an aged face with dark skin, along with salt and pepper hair and beard. He had his hands on his hips, and he tapped the toe of his boot on the floor. "Any idea how long this is going to be?" he asked the men inside. "This is going to slow down the investigation another day or two at this rate."

The guard with Sean cleared his throat, stood at attention, and then saluted Captain Grayson. "Sir," he said.

Sean saluted as well, even though protocol from Internal Affairs technically kept him outside of the chain of command. It was better to be polite, especially to someone of such an advanced rank.

Captain Grayson turned, his face tight and lips clamped together. He gave them a once-over. "At ease," he said. "What's going on? Did Commodore V'bosh send you to escort me to new quarters? I already told the last group, I'm not going without my belongings."

"No, sir," the guard said. "We have a visitor here from IA, Lieutenant Sean Barrows." He motioned toward Sean.

Grayson's glare was so strong it could have cut through the station hull. "I'm sorry you traveled all this way. At this point, you're probably not needed."

Sean tried to remain impassive. It wasn't unusual for the subject of his investigations to be hostile to him. After all, it was their career on the line. But information from someone like Grayson was as useful as anyone else. It would be best to keep a cordial relationship if he could manage it. That required de-escalation. "Why's that?" Sean asked in as polite a tone as possible.

Grayson pointed to the scene in front of him. "You see station forensics in there?"

"Yes," Sean said.

"I heard a strange beeping sound coming from the air vents in my quarters about an hour ago. Thankfully, I have sensitive hearing. It turns out it was a timed explosive device," Grayson said. "They keep scanning the room to make sure there's not another one, but I need my space." He raised the volume of his voice with the end of that statement, as if to be sure the men inside heard his frustration.

Sean watched the crew do their work. They covered every nook and cranny of the room, going through drawers, files, and everything. He could see why Grayson must have been frustrated with such an invasion of his privacy. By the same token, they couldn't risk another problem.

He had been ordered to look into Grayson's work in the sector. A few weeks had gone by, and there'd been little progress in confirming an increase in Aryshan activity in this area. More than that, a series of strange incidents had occurred around Grayson. The Senate back on

Earth requested that IA get involved in bringing further evidence that the Aryshans were becoming aggressive and to monitor Captain Grayson's work thus far. His report could determine far more than just the fate of this captain's career.

"I see you have your hands full here," Sean said, trying to be careful with what he said. "Has security made any headway as to who may have planted the explosive?"

Grayson grumbled and shook his head. "Not yet. They've been hovering in my quarters for hours."

"I see," Sean said. There was the possibility that Grayson planted it himself, but that seemed unlikely. Despite the coincidental nature of the recent incidents occurring around Grayson, he wasn't truly suspected of any wrongdoing beyond mismanagement of a case. That, and he had been accused of a propensity to lash out at his subordinates in inappropriate ways. Sean could see how there might be some truth to that.

"But you can bet it's the Aryshans," Grayson said.

There was something Sean could use. He quirked a brow at the Captain. "Why do you say that?"

Grayson took a couple of paces away from the door. His steps were hurried, his eyes cast to the floor. Concern filled his face. "I'm sure you've heard a great deal about the trader ship that disappeared inside Aryshan space. They were last seen on the scanners by my ship on a routine border patrol. We couldn't keep that one out of the media when it was so public."

"Yes, sir," Sean said. The incident had been one he'd studied on the transport flight over to the station. What he'd found interesting was that after the ship had disappeared, communications with the Aryshans had ground to a halt. Almost nothing had come across the border from them. Even the usual merchant channels had slowed compared to normal. "Then, there was the other incident, which occurred while you patrolled this sector, correct?"

Grayson frowned. "The disappearance of the *Hong Kong*. I was on station at the time, though it was during night cycle hours. Alarms went crazy throughout this place. I've never seen so many people rushing into the hallways in various stages of undress. By the time I reached main ops, the ship was long gone."

"Did they see which way it went?" Sean asked, somewhat jokingly. He wanted to alleviate some of Grayson's stress.

Grayson gave him a look like he was an idiot child. "Space doesn't work that way, Lieutenant. You have to realize, when a ship engages their crystal drive to go into FTL, it sends out energy patterns in several directions with little to no dissipation since there's no friction in the vacuum. Not only that but when your options are in three dimensions, it makes tracking routes much more difficult. Little details like that are why I suggested to the commodore against bringing out life-long dirtside personnel for investigations. Spatial experience matters."

Sean didn't want to argue that he had past experience on ships, stations, and planets with dome structures. His last assignment had been on Mars, but it wasn't relevant to the discussion. "What you say doesn't implicate Aryshans. Any number of groups could find value in one of our battleships. I know the outer colonies and worlds are plagued by raiders."

Grayson gestured wildly to his quarters. "An explosive was planted here, Lieutenant. I've been investigating the Aryshan involvement. It's not a coincidence." He took a deep breath to collect himself. "Have you heard of pirates operating this close to Aryshan space? Come now, Lieutenant. It's obvious who would benefit most from having that kind of intelligence, and the Aryshans have grown odder and more xenophobic over the last several years. Now, they have all the specs on my ship."

Sean didn't know much about the geopolitical situations with the Aryshans, and though Captain Grayson was biased and hostile, he was inclined to take his word on the matter.

Before he could ask another question, the forensics investigators came to the door, holding their equipment in their hands. "We're all wrapped up here, Captain," one of the investigators said.

"About time," Grayson muttered. He stepped aside to allow the investigators to pass. Then he moved into his quarters' doorway and turned to Sean. "If you'll excuse me, Lieutenant. It's been a rough day, and I'd like to have a bit of peace and quiet so I can get back to work on this." His eyes softened. "One more thing, though. Commodore V'bosh has told me you have interest in a command track. Even when you're the captain, you're never in command. All of our orders come down from government bureaucrats, whether the civilian board of directors for Palmer Station or the Earth senate. If I were allowed some leeway to profile them, rattle a few Aryshan feathers, we wouldn't be sitting here, and these cases would be solved. But procedures and politics dictate everything. And so, we have to work together."

This was the first indication that Grayson perceived him as anything but an enemy. Some might describe his behavior as erratic, but Sean wasn't ready to put something like that down in a report. "I'll keep that in mind."

"Good day, Lieutenant, Ensign," Grayson said, inclining his head to the guard who had brought Sean there. He tapped his door control panel, and it slid shut a moment later.

Sean had almost forgotten the guard existed, with him having been so quiet in the conversation. He turned to the man. "You don't say much."

The guard smirked. "I know better than to interrupt a conversation with Captain Grayson, sir. Would you like me to escort you to guest quarters?"

"Please," Sean said. He followed the guard down the corridor once more. They stayed silent along the walk. All he could do was think about the immense amount of work ahead of him.

2

Tamar stood outside the arched doorway of the *Issiana's* committee chambers. She had just arrived on the ship, leaving her belongings with enlisted crew in the shuttle bay. Her instructions had been to come here immediately upon arrival.

Cool air dumped into the hallway from the vent above her head. When she entered, she would make her first impression on the rest of the committee, where they doubtless already knew far more about her than she did of them. Everyone in the Aryshan Fleet seemed to know her name. It often was more of a burden than a boon, being recognized as the person hand-groomed by First Speaker Ny'aet. It resulted in her being under constant watch, pressured to perform.

As much as that pressure brought tension to her crown ridges, she thrived on it. Without the drive it brought her, would she have been pushed into a commanding committee at such a young age? She couldn't be certain. But now was the time to make her mark. That meant exuding confidence and quiet and ensuring her nervousness didn't trickle through the bondsense with her tribemates.

Tamar raised her wrist to the scanner, which granted her access to the chamber beyond.

The doors opened to reveal a circular room with four crescent-shaped stations with tall stools, allowing the committee to surround those who entered its center and look down upon them. Three of the four stations had occupants. The empty fourth station would be hers.

The chamber glowed in a light green color that reflected off the metal walls, with lights at a low level to allow for a three-dimensional holographic schematic of the *Issiana* hovering in the center of the room. At a cursory glance of the hologram, all systems appeared to be functioning normally, and all crew stations were filled and accounted for. A well-run ship. On the opposite side of the room was an emergency exit that led to the commanding committee's personal escape pods.

"Commander Chavi Tamar di Aresh?" A man said with a deep, booming voice. He had short black hair over his crown ridges and a small scar under his left eye. His hardened face said it had seen battle, up close and personal.

Tamar inclined her head toward him while the other two fixed their eyes on her. The first was an older woman with darker, silver skin who showed her more advanced age. The second was another man, perhaps a few years older than Tamar herself, who she knew as another of Ny'aet's protégés.

"Safely arrived, that I might continue in duty to the Aryshan Empire and my Aresh tribe," Tamar said, the words rote at this point for whenever she entered into duty.

"Enter into our chamber and take your rightful place." The older man motioned to her station. "I am Dentrai Tendell di Aresh, commander with a specialty in ship systems and operations."

Tamar moved toward her station and slid onto the stool. The station came to life, controls lighting up as she settled. The configuration had been ported from her last assignment to provide a familiar sight to an unfamiliar space.

Tendell glanced at the woman to his left. "Perhaps the other two should introduce themselves."

The older woman offered a soft smile. "Dentrai Intrei di Aresh, commander of requisitions and deployments."

To the right of Tendell, the younger man inclined his own head. "Tamar, good to see you again." He looked toward Tendell. "We've met in the past. I handle personnel and controls on this current posting."

"Neyral," Tamar said coolly in reply. They had worked together when interning directly for the Ruling Committee under First Speaker Ny'aet. He had shown more than enough interest in her at the time, and she hoped that wouldn't continue in this current post, where she would handle mission briefings and strategic decisions. It was odd that she'd be assigned such a critical role at her newly-minted rank, but it showed the faith the Aresh had in her. She had to be perfect, and that left no time for personal distractions.

"Ah, good," Tendell said, either not catching her tone or ignoring it. "You've worked together before. This should be a smooth transition. We do have a first order of business, which will be to have a vote as to who will serve as Speaker, in keeping with regulations in a change in commanding committee. This must be first before we can discuss new divisions of labor so we all may work in unity in command. I am open to suggestions."

"I motion for Commander Tamar to be named Speaker," Neyral said, his dark eyes fixed on her.

Was he trying to curry favor? Tamar herself was taken aback at the suggestion. Her post already held deep weight, but to be Speaker as well?

Intrei leaned forward. "I motion Tendell, as he is the most senior among us." Her eyes flicked toward Neyral with the end of that statement, as if to admonish him.

Tendell shifted. His emotions, both of pride and fear, hit her strong through the tribal bond. Judging from the projected nerves, the others in the room must have sensed it as well.

Tamar tried to keep herself calm. "Project calm, and those around you will follow suit," First Speaker Ny'aet himself had told her on her first day of her internship with him. She'd been nervous then, as she was now. No good came from panicking. Those emotional reverberations were vestigial links from a time past when the Aryshan people didn't have technology to warn them of danger. They'd had to rely on each other for everything. Modern times made such abilities a nuisance rather than a help, in most situations.

Tendell finally broke the protracted silence resulting from the odd sense of emotion that filled the room. "I thank you, Commander Intrei. However, my speakership has been one of necessity, for when there were three and not the whole of four. You may recall the last Speaker was removed from this very vessel because his lack of self-control created a crisis for our people. I am not saying I have similar lack of control, but urgent emotions through the bond do have an impact on me." His eyes fell upon Tamar. "Much more than it appears to affect our new colleague."

The crisis he spoke of was the rising tension with the humans, caused by a commander who panicked when a human freighter captain violated Aryshan space. What was the human thinking? All the same, the Aryshan commander should not have reacted so hastily. Anyone in command of a warship had to remain calm and to be careful about projecting too much panic through the bondsense. It could cause a feedback loop of emotions from others, compounding the possibility of overreactions. Tamar had a reputation for not being affected by the bond in that way.

"If you are confident, Commander Tamar, to cast this vote for yourself, then I will back Neyral's motion that you be named Speaker."

Was she ready? Tamar couldn't be certain. Though she'd taken over command in an emergency before, she had very little record of making command decisions. She wouldn't be alone. There would always be the vote of the rest of the commanding committee, but the tie-break vote would be hers and hers alone.

The mere fact she was being considered was an honor. She hadn't heard of anyone so young being granted a speakership in all the Aryshan fleet. "Yes, I will accept that responsibility."

"Then it is settled," Tendell said. He tapped several commands into his station. "I am transferring the Speaker designation to your terminal, for recorded votes and agenda setting purposes."

"She will need time to acclimate to the *Issiana* and the command station," Dentrai said. Though she didn't add anything else about Tamar's inexperience, her bond projected uneasiness.

"Of course, which is why she has us to rely upon. We are but a unit together within the whole that is Arysha," Neyral said, citing their naval motto dutifully.

"I'll rely on all of you for advice, and to steer me back to course if I should fall astray," Tamar said, offering a small smile to the other three. Her limbs felt light, and she couldn't help but tingle with pride at the new appointment. "What are our next orders?"

Tendell changed the image on the center display to a star map, one that held a trajectory of the *Issiana's* future course. It led into human space. "We have a mission from the Ruling Committee. We will officially be escorting one of our own trade vessels across the border to Palmer Station, the first venture into human space since the crisis. That's our official task. We also have a separate information-gathering mission. I presume you understand classified mission information cannot leave this room beyond those directly involved?"

Tamar raised a brow, intrigued. This wouldn't be some simple patrol mission. Speaker Ny'aet had thrown her directly into the storm. "Of course. You can count on me."

3

The commodore's office was on the top level, which held a panoramic view of space through its exterior viewports. A middle-aged woman in Interplanetary Navy garb, with a Lieutenant's rank insignia, stopped him before he could enter.

"I'm here to see the commodore," Sean said.

"You must be the one from IA? I'm Lieutenant Carrabba," the woman said, giving him an easy salute.

"Lieutenant Barrows. A pleasure." Sean returned the gesture.

"Let me see if the commodore is available." Lieutenant Carrabba produced a datapad and hailed Commodore V'bosh. A green glow came from the screen. "He says he's been expecting you," she said, motioning toward the office door.

The door hissed when it opened. Sean stepped into the office, about twice the size of his quarters. The opposite wall had a floor-to-ceiling window to space beyond it. More classic wooden cabinets and bookshelves lined the interior wall to its right. The office would make an incredible location for formal receptions, allowing guests a breathtaking view.

Sean almost missed Commodore V'bosh pushing himself up

from his belly to his four webbed feet. There was no way to hide his Tralos origin as a giant reptilian quadruped. Commodore V'bosh had a distinguished tail slithering behind him, almost the size of his torso. His Interplanetary Navy uniform was modified for his form. He stood atop a flattened floor computer display tailored for the species. Another pad behind him broadcasted tri-D images within his side-long line of sight. A much more powerful light than the rest of the room shone over the display, creating warmth in addition to a bright room.

"Lieutenant Barrows," Commodore V'bosh said. His vocal intonations sounded like a lisp. His face held what appeared to be a perpetual grin, sharp teeth protruding from his jaws. "Welcome to Palmer Station. I'm pleased your travels were safe."

"It's been a long time," Sean said.

"Not long, by the molt. Have you met with Captain Grayson yet?"

Sean nodded. "That's why I'm here, sir."

Commodore V'bosh's forearm stretched like rubber, his hand sticking to a large glass of water to bring it closer. His tongue slithered out and snapped against the liquid. "Your hesitancy registers in your vibrations. Are you troubled by your assignment? I don't think it's anything you can't handle."

Sean glanced out the window, seeing a pale reflection of himself faded against the vastness of space. He had to be direct when speaking with a Tralos. They didn't always understand human nuances, any more than humans understood theirs. If a Tralos detected subterfuge, they could explode into anger. The vibrations, as they called it, often caused by deceit, threw Tralos heads for a spin. Thankfully, Sean had never experienced much of the rage they'd become infamous for. He took that as a sign that Commodore V'bosh liked him. "Thank you, sir," Sean said. "I appreciate your kindness."

"It is no matter of kindness. You've voiced your wish to move up the ranks to command. I sense you have the skills to do it. But with responsibility comes difficult and important assignments. Any new sunder-brother must reflect in the light and find his way."

"I'm wondering," Sean said, "if there is anything else I should be reading into this assignment. I presume if Captain Grayson had ill will, you would have detected something malicious about him?"

"Ahh, Jemile," V'bosh said. "He has spent too much time in the shade. The cold and darkness colors his thoughts. A reflection in the light is what he requires. Perhaps you can provide such light?" The Tralos paused in his speech to focus his black eyes on Sean. "Did you know that two molts ago, my grandself was the first Tralos to make high rank within the Interplanetary Navy?"

Sean nodded as he listened to the story.

"The humans had such bad vibrations. I see it clearly. Not ones to quickly accept that which is different, humans. When you have spent as much time in the cosmos as the Tralos, you may understand, may see the light in all. The labels 'traitor' or 'lizard-man'—they stung like the tail of a venomite. This I did not understand, and it led to many bad vibrations. I was unsure about my path, much as I see you are now."

"What's that got to do with this assignment?"

"You understand more than you know. Very few have the ability to see and have clarity in vision. I believe that will lead you to command, as you seek." His tail slid to his left side. "But know also the resources of this station are at your disposal. Though the vibrations caused by death in humans are foreign to me, I understand they pull humans into the shade. Call Lieutenant Carrabba at any time. She will be your guide."

"Thank you." The talk of command unsettled Sean. Was that what he truly wanted? He had talked with Commodore V'Bosh in the past about the prospect, but now, years later, it seemed like a foreign dream, the kind of unrealistic reaching one had as a child. His career track in Internal Affairs wouldn't take him that route, despite V'bosh's compliments.

"You're dismissed, Lieutenant."

Sean left Commodore V'bosh's office with more questions than he had answers. In fact, he hadn't even delved into what he'd hoped to learn in the conversation. The Tralos had an odd way of thinking —and leading, for that matter. So much weight rested on Sean's shoulders, but at least the commodore had faith in him. He wished that brought the comfort it should.

4

_____

Stars loomed in the distance beyond the curved edges of the *Issiana's* hull. All it would take to end Tamar's life would be for one rogue asteroid to pierce through the ship's deflector field, striking anywhere on the long window. What a morbid thought. It was unlike her.

She glanced up from her lone table by the cold window of the mess lounge. Translucent insulation still kept it warmer than it would have been, so close to space, and the window itself was made of a material as strong as anything else on the ship's hull, but that knowledge didn't help Tamar's uneasiness. Perhaps it was someone else in the crew, influencing her with negative projections through the bond-sense. She scanned the room to find one of her crewmen seated alone.

It was a man, tall, with dark features and a crease on either side of his eyes from smile lines. He wasn't smiling now. Tamar tried to recall who it was. Mynoan. That was his name. He held the position of intelligence officer in the lower officer corps.

Mynoan inclined his head ever so slightly before standing from his seat. "Commander," he said, acknowledging her rank with stiff attention. "May I assist you?"

"Nothing so formal. We're close to arriving at Palmer Station. The crew is on edge," Tamar said, coaxing what she could from him. She didn't want to accuse him directly of a negative aura, but she did want him aware of his emotions.

The bondsense dimmed in intensity, and the fear disappeared. "That's correct. I was about to prepare a briefing based on what we've learned from our informants," he said, turning back to his table and picking up a datapad from it. He returned to her and handed her the device. "We may have to change our tactics soon, with how Earth is stirring."

Tamar took it, giving a cursory glance over the opening contents of his report. "The humans already brought in a dedicated investigator under the guise of their Internal Affairs. I wonder what the Earth government is planning," Tamar said.

"I don't have enough data to reach that conclusion as of yet," Mynoan said, taking back the datapad when she offered it to him. "I know that our plans are in flux, but we are ready to act with proportionate force to deter any future aggression into our space."

Tamar couldn't help but laugh. "Are you trying to start a war?"

"I wouldn't try to do anything without direct orders," Mynoan said, his face deadly serious. "The orders I do have while aboard the station come directly from the Ruling Committee, and they are classified."

"Classified?"

"Correct," Mynoan said. "I should not have said what I did. The less you know, the better."

The intelligence officer was faithful, Tamar would give him that. Once committed to a tribe, going against the good of the whole would be near impossible. An officer wouldn't be prone to violating any orders the Ruling Committee gave. Not without someone sensing it. "It's odd that the Ruling Committee would get directly involved in a lower officer's orders," Tamar said, trying to sound as casual as possible, keeping her emotions in check. She wanted more information, but couldn't give the impression of prying.

Mynoan shrugged. "Is that all?" he asked.

Tamar considered, moistening her bottom lip. Speaker Ny'aet had placed her in this assignment through his machinations. It made it likely that there were others working toward his ends. What could he have been up to? "Yes, that is all. Thank you for informing me. I will be vigilant when aboard the station and act with care. I trust you will do the same."

Mynoan nodded. "Of course, Commander. Enjoy your drink. We will have no taste but human food for a while, I fear." He smirked, as if trying to crack a joke.

Tamar gave him a light laugh out of courtesy and motioned his dismissal.

Mynoan took his datapad and returned to his seat, and to his report.

Tamar picked up her drink. Curiosity had the best of her at this point. She needed her own direction from Ny'aet. It would do no good for her to be in the dark this far out among the stars.

With a quick step, she exited the mess, crossing to her quarters. When she arrived, Tamar allowed her automatic entry, tapping the door to ensure it was locked behind her.

As Speaker, she had been assigned the largest quarters on the ship. This included an open area with a view of the stars. Beyond the reception room was her bedroom, one sealed completely with the thick walls that adorned the rest of the ship. The bedroom had minimalistic features: a small desk with a chair, a holoscreen, a bed, a chest, a closet for clothing, and a piece of serene art on the wall for her to focus on in meditations. She moved to the chest by her bed, kneeling on the floor and opening it. The top shelf of the chest opened to reveal a private comm unit with a small screen. "Scramble transmission. Encrypt. Call First Speaker Ny'aet's private line," she ordered.

The comm unit flickered to life, displaying a moving graphic as it established a connection into Aryshan space. To Tamar's surprise, Ny'aet answered quickly. The connection gave audio only. "Commander Tamar. I'm surprised to hear from you. Did you need something?"

Something about the way he said her name made Tamar smile. His tone reassured her. Ny'aet never did anything without purpose. He was a shrewd and cautious man, which is what gained him his position. Even if she couldn't sense his emotional aura from this distance, she had to trust that. "First Speaker," Tamar said, "Lieutenant Mynoan told me he had been given a mission direct from the Ruling Committee. Are you planning something else with this visit to Palmer Station? If I am to represent our people, I should have some awareness as to the functions of my crew."

The comm unit went silent. With a scrambled signal crossing so much space, it would take some time for each transmission to go through. "You haven't been privy to the plans this far up the chain of command for good reason. You'll be aboard the station soon. If something goes awry, you will have deniability."

"Deniability? Of what?"

"I won't make the same mistakes as the Anwii, this I vow. You're doing well by all accounts, Commander. I am watching, as is the committee. Do your best for Arysha. That is all I can say."

"I don't understand," Tamar said, unable to help sounding like a youth with her words.

"Trust. For the good of the Aresh."

Why was he speaking to her so cryptically? What could it mean? That logo on the comm unit twisted and turned, mocking her. If only she could sense something through the bond, or see him. Tamar was good at reading other people. But that was a crutch. She wouldn't be able to rely on the bondsense among the humans. Perhaps First Speaker Ny'aet meant this as a test. "One more thing. Is the Ruling Committee all on board with your course of action?"

"I can't say more, but you need not worry. I know this prospect is difficult, but no more questions. Not for now," Ny'aet said.

The logo stopped spinning and the comm unit went dark before Tamar could protest. Ny'aet had ended the transmission. His words didn't make any sense and gave her no clarity. It made her angry. She wasn't used to working this way. Until this point, fleet orders had been clear, with purpose. Ever since this incident with the human traders, everyone had gone crazy, including granting her a promotion.

Could the *Issiana* be a victim of bad luck? This was the ship that opened fire on those traders, a dangerous overreaction even if they had violated Aryshan space. Its walls held a strange aura. But everyone here wanted what was best for the Aresh tribe, didn't they?

A chime came through on her main comm. "Tamar here," she said.

"Speaker," Tendell's voice came through. "I wanted to alert you that we're about to drop from FTL on our approach to Palmer Station."

Tamar wanted time to meditate, to reflect on everything she'd just heard from Ny'aet, but that would have to wait. She took a deep breath to compose herself. "I'll be in the chamber momentarily. Tamar out."

5

The kitchenette in Palmer Station's guest quarters didn't make for the best working office. It was cramped, with a small cooking unit, a refrigerator, and cabinets filled with necessities for guest workers. Sean spent two evenings hunched over the countertop, poring over files of the tactical incidents in this sector. The more he delved into them, the more he couldn't deny that the sum of the incidents benefited Aryshan interests.

Each report had been separated into individual files on his datapad, cross referenced and annotated from hours of study. Still, he had found nothing beyond circumstantial evidence. Sean didn't think that Captain Grayson could be implicated in anything other than being at the wrong place at the wrong time. That much should be a relief, and perhaps he could win the man over to his side after explaining the finding.

Time slipped from Sean while he studied. When he looked up again, the chrono on the wall read 0300, and he'd still made no progress other than glazing over the same lines several times. Where should he start? What did he need to uncover? What did Palmer Station have to offer that he couldn't review from a desk somewhere in the Sol system?

Station security cameras hadn't captured anything of use, though privacy laws required quarters to remain off limits unless the occupant requested them. The third incident, the bomb discovered in Captain Grayson's own quarters, was an interesting one. The only way someone could have gone in or out, assuming the whole station's security system hadn't been tampered with, would have been through the air ducts. Security later placed impenetrable grills over the outlets in each quarters. Sean could hardly believe they were constructed in an insecure manner to begin with.

That incident left Sean nothing to work with, but the *Hong Kong's* theft was much more interesting. Someone didn't march through the docking tubes or latch another ship onto it. That would have been detected. It wasn't an inside job, as no station or ship personnel went missing after the event. A person in a pressure suit could have been a possibility. Depending on the size and their movements, objects that size wouldn't trip external station sensors, not with all the asteroids and debris floating around space.

But could one person have stolen an Interplanetary Navy ship from a space station? How inept could station and ship personnel be? Sean supposed that was why Internal Affairs had been called in to investigate. Anyone in the senate back home who read into the reports to this depth probably had the same red flags in their head.

Sean glanced at the chrono one more time. 0330. Still too early to wake appropriate station personnel to ask about guard shifts and retrofitting schedules of docked ships. However, his lack of sleep and anticipation had his body tingling for action. What could he do in the meantime to pursue his new thoughts? Could he retrace the steps of the alleged ship thief?

That wasn't a bad idea. He tapped his comm unit to activate it. "Call Lieutenant Carrabba." Dots passed along the holographic display as it tried to connect.

A still image of Lieutenant Carrabba appeared on the screen—no live video feed. "Hello?" a raspy, weary voice asked.

"Good morning," Sean said as cheerfully as possible. "Lieutenant Barrows from Internal Affairs. I know it's early, but Commodore

V'bosh asked that I call you if I needed anything. Is it possible I could get access to a p-suit and an airlock for a jaunt outside?"

"At this hour?"

"Early bird gets the worm, so they say," Sean said. "Sorry to wake you."

"It's okay," Lieutenant Carrabba grumbled. A couple moments passed. "Try Flight Deck Manager Sophia Reyna in cargo bay B-17. Civilian shipping. She can probably assist you."

"B-17. Got it. Thanks. I owe you one," Sean said, trying to let his gratefulness show in his voice.

"Yeah, you do. Goodnight."

"WE'RE GOOD TO GO. You can decompress the compartment now," Sean said through his pressure suit comm.

The cargo bay was empty, and Reyna gave two thumbs up from where she stood behind a thick wall of transparent plasteel.

Reyna was athletic, strong in every good way, with shoulder length brown hair that fell into a soft curl. In addition to being pleasant to look at, she was one of the more genuinely nice people Sean had met since coming to the station. Though to be fair, his experiences so far with station personnel had been a bad sample of meeting someone hostile to him, dealing with a strange alien, and then bothering someone in the middle of the night.

Reyna tapped in her commands and the exterior doors opened. The vacuum of space sucked out the cargo bay atmosphere, carrying Sean along with it.

Stars filled Sean's field of vision, twinkling lights in a vast darkness. Sean took a deep breath, suppressing the anxiety that came with losing his local vertical. Up and down meant nothing now. His body floated helplessly, deprived of the sense of weight it always carried. His stomach churned.

He had never become used to free fall, and he hoped he would never spend enough time in it to have to. "Calm down. Everything is fine," he said to himself. Sean hit his suit thrusters on his left side to turn, and Palmer Station came into view. A focal point.

"Did you say something?" Reyna's voice came through the comm. He'd forgotten about the live signal.

"Nothing. Everything's normal so far. They have a civilian crew manning the flight deck?"

"Yeah," Reyna said. "Cestus Shipping Incorporated. From what I hear, the colony's primary trading company invested in the station when it first came online, and the contract went with it. We've done such a good job ever since that they keep us on."

The conversation served as a pleasant distraction from the reality of floating through space. That distraction broke the moment he could feel the tug of his tether. "Stand by," Sean said. He adjusted his pack thrusters to change his direction now that he'd found the limits of distance the tether allowed him.

He turned, and the station towered in front of him like an unending wall of metal. Glancing upward, he could see Captain Grayson's ship, the *Avery*, attached to its docking port. The oblong-shaped destroyer ship paled in comparison to the vastness of Palmer Station. Several terminals jutted from the station and connected with the ship at different points.

The ebb and flow of the *Avery's* metallic design gave Sean no logical place to start looking for clues as to the *Hong Kong's* disappearance. The idea of tracing the culprit's steps had only come to him hours ago. He hadn't planned this vacuum adventure out as well as he should have, but, jumped at the idea too soon. If there was one failing of his he needed to work on, better planning would be it. He'd had the same problems back on Mars when he dug a little too deeply into his mission before obtaining a search warrant.

This exercise might have been fruitless even with proper planning. The idea of someone floating through space to steal a ship seemed fanciful in retrospect. The fatigue of not having slept set in, now that his adrenaline had worn off.

No sense in second-guessing now, though. He was out in space for better or worse. Sean thrust closer to the ship, and it soon encompassed his field of vision. Staring at landmarks settled his stomach, giving his brain the perception of a distinct up and down to mitigate some of his natural vertigo.

Sean spent several minutes traversing the bottom of the *Avery's* hull. What would a potential attacker look for in an Earth destroyer? The systems that were most volatile were probably the weapons, the atmospheric converters, and then the engines. "Reyna, you still there?" he asked.

"Of course. You need something, Lieutenant?"

"Can you tell me where the *Avery's* crystal drive is housed?"

"One moment. I have to look it up." The transmitter went silent, leaving Sean with a distinct lack of sound. Only his breathing kept him from a complete sensory deprivation. A moment later, her reassuring voice returned. "It says here aft, toward the bottom. It's about two hundred meters below your feet and to your right."

He adjusted the course of his thrusters and saw an indentation about the length of five commercial transports in a row, four decks deep. A hatch was open in the dead center. "What's this hatch for?" Sean asked.

"I'm not sure, but I've seen engineering crews moving parts through there before."

"Thanks." He tweaked his thrusters to set his course for the hatch. It was three meters by four in diameter, enough to allow for a medium-sized cargo crate's passage. Sean looked inside to see the silhouette of complicated machinery. If he had a few months, he could learn every part and its function, but his assignment wouldn't allow that much time to study.

Pistons pumped and gears turned inside the assembly. Even at rest, the *Avery's* systems breathed life into the ship, powering its artificial gravity and life support systems. Emergency lighting allowed a glimmer of what rested beyond, but Sean's lifeline tugged him to a halt, reaching its taut end.

"Dammit," he said, frustrated. He tried to tap the command to extend it again, but no more line came. This was his maximum range.

"What's that?" Reyna asked.

"Sorry, talking to myself again." Sean shook his head. He'd formed some bad social habits while on so many assignments alone, having to ask questions and answer them himself. Those questions helped him do his job better than most in Internal Affairs.

He titled his head for a better view, looking for anything that might be of use to the investigation. Nothing stood out. As he already concluded, his space jaunt had only wasted time.

Sean tugged on the lifeline to ease himself from the *Avery's* open hatch, and came to a halt.

Something moved in the darkness of space, in the periphery of Sean's vision.

The object came into dim view as Sean passed some of the *Avery's* emergency lights. Another person in a pressure suit. This person, not bound by a tether, struggled with a large valve by the hatch. "Is there a tech performing maintenance on the *Avery* right now?" Sean asked.

"Checking," Reyna said, pausing to retrieve the data. "No, you should be the only person out there."

"Well, I'm not." Sean hit his thrusters to try to keep out of view. Someone unauthorized to be working on the *Avery*, at the very least, meant that his plan to go out in a pressure suit himself hadn't been for naught. Station security would be happy he spotted someone doing something amiss. But what was this person doing?

The other figure turned before Sean could fully conceal himself. The person froze, his tinted black mask reflecting emergency lights into Sean's eyes.

"I checked again. You're the only person scheduled outside of the airlock for another hour. We should report this." Reyna sounded concerned. It did nothing to ease Sean's nerves.

Sean tugged at his tether, and he floated back toward the station. Either a maintenance tech was out in a pressure suit without clearing the records, or someone was sabotaging the ship exactly in the manner he imagined happened with the *Hong Kong*. Sean wasn't prepared for a confrontation with the latter. His counterpart obviously had far more experience with zero-g, moving without a tether like an old pro.

The other figure thrust from the hatch, speeding toward him. That ruled out a maintenance tech. No, this person meant to attack.

The two pressure suits smashed together, knocking Sean off course. The intruder grappled Sean and brought his thrusters to full strength. They sped toward the station.

Sean flailed, glancing back toward the growing Palmer Station. He was about to get smashed into the hull. The impact would crack his pressure suit and release his atmosphere. The prospect of vacuum crushing his head made him gasp for air. If he survived this, he swore he would never go into space again.

Sean tugged at his tether, pulling all of the slack toward him. The attacker looked down at Sean's not-so-sly attempt to free himself and grabbed onto his arm, ripping Sean's hand away from the tether with considerable strength. Inhuman strength.

At that moment, Sean remembered his own suit's thrusters. "Stupid, should have used those to begin with."

"Used what?" Reyna asked through the comm.

Right, Reyna. "Not talking to you, again. Sorry! Ah, contact security. We've got a saboteur out here."

"A what? Are you okay?"

"No time! Find me some back up!" With his other hand free, he set his thrusters to fire at full capacity.

The attacker adjusted thrust to match, but their velocity toward the station had already slowed. Two equal forces from both pressure suit thrusters canceled each other out with no friction to tip the balance. The prior momentum carried them toward the station, but it wasn't fast enough to smash Sean's suit open.

Sean bounced against Palmer Station's hull like a rubber ball. "Ugh!" Something popped in his shoulder. Pain flared all the way down his arm. At least he didn't hear the hissing of decompression.

Their trajectory shifted away from the station, both suits still engaged in full thrust toward each other. Momentum was the only difference. A second wave of pain shot through Sean's spine, sending an unnatural jolt all the way up through his neck. While he was focused on his injuries, the attacker gripped his shoulders hard.

A surge of adrenaline jolted him like a crystal drive entering FTL. Pain didn't matter if the alternative meant breathing vacuum. He couldn't die. Not now.

Sean focused all of his strength and chopped at his assailant's arms, dislodging both of the other man's hands from his suit's collar. He fought hard for control of the grapple, squirming to dodge the grip. His back throbbed and pain pulsed with each labored breath into his lungs.

The longer the fight went on, the more Sean would be at a disadvantage. The attacker was so strong, so fast. The attrition of pain would overwhelm Sean soon enough.

In a last-ditch attempt to free himself, Sean curled up his legs, using his feet as pincers against his assailant's torso. He twisted the attacker's direction, and by default the trajectory of the thrusters. Then he gave his best kick to the attacker's thigh.

If the fight had occurred in gravity, his maneuver would have done little to impact the outcome, but momentum meant everything in space. When Sean set his enemy into motion, the thrusters took over. The two separated and veered off in opposite directions.

Sean took advantage of his freedom by adjusting his own thrusters to give him a push back toward the station's cargo bay. He grabbed onto the lifeline and tugged until it was tight. *Go, go, go!* If his assailant could catch him again, Sean would never make it.

His shoulder burned, but he peered back over it, stretching the muscles and tendons anyway. His body protested, shooting deep pain all the way up his spine. He needed to gauge his assailant's position.

The attacker was in his peripheral vision, nearly a hundred meters away. The distance between them would be insurmountable at this juncture. He'd lucked out.

The attacker disappeared behind the *Avery,* and a moment later, gravity tugged on Sean. He'd moved much closer to the cargo bay than he realized. Before he could react to slow his thrusters, the bay's gravity plates sucked him in.

Sean tumbled to the floor, and his suit thrusters cut out upon detecting the gravity field. All he could see was the nauseating, spinning view of the floor and ceiling of the cargo bay. His body jolted with each additional roll. The impact knocked the wind out of him, leaving him unable to cry out. He skidded across the docking bay floor and crashed hard into the wall.

Reyna stood wide-eyed in the control room beyond. She must have sealed the bay, as Sean heard the room pressurize. He was in no condition to move, let alone remove his helmet. His eyes were heavy, and it took all of his energy to keep them half-open.

Two station techs ran over to assist him, helping him undo his helmet's clamps. Yet another wave of pain reverberated up Sean's spine as the motion shook him. He coughed.

"Lieutenant Barrows, are you all right?" Reyna asked, crouching in front of him.

"Medical," he mouthed, and then lost consciousness.

6

"Thank you for taking the time in our brief respite from duty to dine with me," Neyral said, slurping a stringy substance. "I find I seldom get to enjoy these delicacies back home. It's difficult to import human cuisine."

Tamar looked down at her own plate with a small frown. Whatever he enjoyed in these...noodles, they had been called—she found them repulsive. The texture was like that of dirt-dwelling tube creatures, and the taste reminded her of storm water. No, she wouldn't eat this dross. It required a special enzyme to be able to digest at all anyway. Far more trouble than it was worth.

The *Issiana* had docked with Palmer Station several hours before, and the Aryshan personnel had to acclimate to more than just the cuisine. The time clock for the station had a strange system based on twelves, the open atmosphere of the station design was nerve-racking, and, more than that, she had knowledge of a secret mission here that could only get her people into trouble.

Neyral stopped eating, setting down his utensils. He focused on her. "You're on edge."

She must have projected more through the bondsense than she had realized. Tamar took in a breath, dampening her emotions the best she could. A focus on nothingness, on the void of space. That's what it took to keep herself in check. Few could do that to the degree she could, or so she'd been told as she rose through the ranks. "I dislike being on a foreign station," she admitted.

"I know what you mean. I enjoy the cuisine, but their people...you can almost feel their xenophobia," Neyral said. "I've heard they spent years portraying other species as some evil, unthinking hive mind in their literature and films. They must still think that of us now."

"I wouldn't presume to know what they think," Tamar said.

"We can't presume much with so limited interaction, this is true. Such unpredictability leads to our own volatility. It's why we shouldn't be anywhere near them." Neyral lowered his voice to a near whisper. "Certain missions will ensure that."

Tamar nearly choked on her food. More cryptic words. Was everyone in on these classified plans except for her? "You are aware of a...secondary mission?" She had to be careful about how this was phrased.

"I noticed the outbound transmission from a personal comm unit. I didn't intrude; I wouldn't invade your privacy as such." He studied her. "It led back to the Ruling Committee."

His words sounded casual enough, but Tamar could sense he wanted more information from her. "You are aware of my connections," she said.

"I am. Mine are similar, but I don't share as close a connection with the Ruling Committee as you. That's why I proposed you for Speaker. It would serve our ship. All of our careers. That connection." He reached across the table, his hand lightly grazing hers. "Those connections could bring us far."

Tamar drew back her hand, keeping her eyes on Neyral. Ulterior motives on top of ulterior motives. He had too much ambition, and though his overture was inappropriate, it almost made it worse that she understood his true motives. She had to keep her own emotions firmly concealed around him. He was dangerous. "Those connections aren't as strong as one might imagine."

Neyral laughed. "You're a smart woman. You should be aware of the situation here on the station. We believe the humans are trying to implicate the Aryshan Empire in all sorts of crimes to justify further advancement into our territory. Watch out who you interact with while here. It could lead to trouble that even strong connections might not cure."

Tamar inclined her head. An odd deflection from his prior move. "Thank you. I'll be careful." She'd experienced enough discomfort for one evening, and found herself standing, ready to be out of this place, and out of Neyral's company. "I should get back to work, ensuring that our people stay together and out of trouble."

Neyral nodded. "I'll finish up here and take yours to go for later if you're not going to eat it." He motioned to her still-full plate.

Tamar shook her head. "It's all yours. Good day, Commander Neyral." She walked away, but felt his eyes drilling into her backside. It made her skin crawl.

7

"He's waking up." Sean heard Reyna's voice before his eyes could adjust to the surroundings. The world seemed hazy, overly bright, and his head felt fuzzy as if he'd taken too long of a nap.

The room smelled of sterilization, some cheap chemicals, and a faint perfume that Reyna was wearing. This wasn't the cargo bay. Instruments cluttered the walls and cabinets, and he lay on a plastic-covered bed.

He remembered skidding to the floor in the cargo bay. He must have hurt himself more than he had thought. He'd awoken in the station's medical center.

Sean tried to sit up.

"No, no!" said a doctor he didn't recognize, storming into the room. She approached and gave him a gentle touch to his sternum, halting his progress upward. "You're just waking up from a concussion. You need to keep from moving, or you're risking permanent damage."

Sean relaxed back into the bio-bed. "I can't think."

Something pricked his right arm. "I'm administering you a

painkiller, one safe for your condition. Please, take it easy for a moment."

The room was somewhat larger than Sean expected. A curtain divided where he was from another bio-bed. The door was open, and another figure made its way in, close enough to the floor below that Sean barely noticed it.

"Doctor," came Commodore V'bosh's distinct whisper. His tail slid across the floor, then paused. "The vibrations coming from him are wrong. Very wrong. What is the projected recovery time?"

"It's difficult to say," the doctor said. "Perhaps it would be best if you came back later, Commodore."

Sean closed his eyes again, his head pounding from all the sound. "I'm sorry," he said. "But I'll talk. Don't leave." He instinctively tried to sit up again and allowed his eyes to reopen.

The doctor's hand stopped him once more, this time before he moved a centimeter. "I told you to stay still, Lieutenant Barrows."

Reyna smirked from the corner of the room, and then crossed her arms.

"I'm afraid Lieutenant Barrows is right, doctor," Commodore V'bosh said. "We must bring all to center, to the light. This is a security matter. If you might give us a moment?"

With that, both the doctor and Reyna moved toward the exit.

"Perhaps Reyna should stay," Sean suggested. "She witnessed the events as much as I."

"Agreed," Commodore V'bosh said.

Reyna stopped, allowing the doctor to continue. "Whatever I can do to help," she said.

"What happened, Lieutenant Barrows? Why were you outside the station?" Commodore V'bosh asked.

Sean tried to recount the story as well as he could, though his memories proved fuzzy. He mentioned the idea about the missing *Hong Kong*, and how he wanted to get a different perspective, one that might correlate to the criminal's own. He paused after mentioning the attack on his person. "All I saw was a tinted mask. I couldn't tell you anything else about my attacker even if my head didn't feel like it was about to fall off. Whoever came after me was about the strongest person I'd ever met. I'm lucky I made it back. I wish I could tell you more."

"Reflect in the light, Lieutenant," V'bosh said. "If not for your intuition, we might have lost another destroyer. When we checked on the *Avery,* our technicians uncovered explosives in the ship's crystal drive housing."

Reyna cocked her head. "Sorry to interrupt. But, Barrows, you said you were following a person who stole that starship a few weeks back, right?"

"Yeah," Sean said. He almost nodded but stopped himself prior to hurting his head again.

"Sounds like they're related. I bet whoever did this learned where the ship's critical systems are because of the first theft," Reyna said.

Commodore V'bosh shifted his tail. "A good hypothesis. The places the explosives were planted would have required detailed knowledge. This is of the light. Fortuitous that you joined us."

"Glad to help." Reyna smiled brightly.

"It might be confirmation bias, but with the strength of the person, it might be another clue toward Aryshan involvement," Sean said.

"Other species, such as myself, the Drenites, or Xy, would require a different pressure suit. Only Aryshans share similar body structures to humans," Commodore V'bosh said.

"It's not conclusive, though," Sean said, considering the facts once more. "It could be someone who's genetically modified."

V'bosh blinked his beady eyes. "It could be. I will have Captain Grayson search records to see if anyone with such talents might be aboard. Clarity will prevail." He tilted his head toward Reyna. "Thank you. We should leave Lieutenant Barrows to regenerate."

Reyna glanced to Sean with some concern. "Let me know when you're up and about, okay?"

Sean forced a small smile. "I will. Thanks."

Commodore V'bosh took his time to turn around, his tail moving with precision around the furniture in the room. Reyna followed the commodore out, leaving Sean to the sterile and quiet environment. The more he thought about it, the more he doubted there would be any genetically modified humans in this sector. People like that had lucrative contracts with larger corporations back home or were rumored to be involved in some of the black ops military departments. Explaining that sort of person's presence on Palmer Station required much more evidence than they had. Captain Grayson was right. All clues pointed to the Aryshans. But why? What did they have to gain?

8

_____

"You did _what?_" Tamar nearly fell over the ledge of her lodging's balcony which overlooked the open travel section of the station. A liftcar zoomed on its tracks while people busily walked to wherever their business required. Tamar couldn't help but allow anger to flash through the bondsense.

Mynoan paced the balcony behind her. He projected something akin to jumping out of his skin. "I followed through with my orders to act based on what I observed of the humans," he said in a cool tone.

Tamar inhaled slowly, using her meditative breaths to keep calm, or at least to dampen what she projected. She didn't want to alert anyone and cause a scene. She turned away from the busy station. "Let's start over so I might better understand. Didn't we discuss you not acting until after I had deliberated with Speaker Ny'aet?"

Mynoan inclined his head. "I waited until you contacted the Speaker. Commander Neyral told me you had."

"You didn't check the result of the conversation," Tamar said, reeling, but doing her best not to let her temper get the best of her. She hated when her subordinates used technicalities to justify disobeying. But that was her problem. She hadn't had time to gain her crew's trust. Her rank pips still had that new sheen to them. Or perhaps her crew would never see her as their true Speaker.

"My orders came from the Ruling Committee. I've told you as much." Mynoan shrugged, as if to say, *It's not as if you could have overridden them.*

Tamar turned back to him. None of his actions could willfully be done to hurt the Aresh. It would physically tear him apart if that were the case. He truly believed what he did was the best for the tribe. She lowered her voice. "This could be construed as an act of war if this is traced back to you. Sabotaging an Earth destroyer on the station? It's insanity."

"The fewer ships on the border with our space, the less we will have to worry about incursion when this escalates," Mynoan said.

He sounded much like Tamar remembered First Speaker Ny'aet in casual conversation. The First Speaker had always thought that the humans had long-term designs on enveloping Aryshan space. The way they folded the Tralos into their budding empire, not to mention the overtures they'd made toward the Drenites... she had to admit it was bothersome.

Did Ny'aet have more radical plans? Was this recent encroachment of a human trade vessel something that truly worried him this much? Each incident would escalate, one after another, until there would be no option but war. The deaths that would be involved would be enormous. The bondsense would be a liability with so many tribemates perishing in such a conflict. It could be worse than the Great Death. There had to be another way.

"I think this is a terrible plan, Mynoan. It cannot end well for us," she said.

"When we are victorious, when the humans understand there is only attrition gained by their relentless expansion, my sacrifice will be remembered. It will ensure our people live in peace for another thousand years, just as the last great dynasty did."

"What about the bloodshed?"

"Some bloodshed is better than the alternative." Mynoan looked out beyond the balcony, motioning to the people below. "They don't understand what it's like to be connected, to have a bond as we do. They're isolated, barely sentient in their decisions. They don't protect themselves or each other from the storms ahead. It's here-and-now, short-term thinking." His face hardened, and anger flared through the bondsense. "They nearly bankrupted our entire world before we were born, and caused how many to starve and die? We're warned in every school not to repeat those mistakes. Humanity is not compatible with the needs of our factions." Mynoan tightened his grip on the balcony railing. "I've fought one of them myself. Their strength is no match for us. Nor is their cunning. Our engineers have already analyzed their ships, and they have a weakness. Our next steps will send them away from this part of the galaxy."

"And just what steps would those be?"

Mynoan's eyes widened as he turned back to her. The bondsense closed off tight. He did have some ability to control himself after all. "I've said far too much. Again."

He didn't wait for her to reply, but stormed through the quarters and out the door.

Tamar watched. She wouldn't cause a scene or threaten a member of her own tribe. Not even to get the answers she so desired, or to put a stop to whatever he was planning. She didn't like this course of action, but she didn't have the authority of the Ruling Committee either. What could she do other than watch this play out?

She turned back to the open travel section of the station once more. These humans were isolated, and it did produce the small thinking that Mynoan had warned about. If Speaker Ny'aet had a plan to manipulate that, these poor souls had no idea what was coming for them. In some ways, she pitied the humans as much as she feared for her own people.

9

"What you did was reckless," Captain Grayson said. The older man swirled a small glass of what appeared to be a dark whiskey. The ice cubes clinked against one another. He took a sip.

Sean wasn't sure what to say. He wanted to explain how his space jaunt, even with the danger of the saboteur, had more or less proved that Captain Grayson didn't deserve an Internal Affairs investigation. He wouldn't state something that could backfire if there was future evidence that could implicate the captain, however. Sean had too much experience to bite at the bait, or even to defend himself. "I'm sorry you feel that way," Sean said. He glanced around the restaurant.

The place had quite a crowd to it, and it made him wonder why Captain Grayson invited him here in the first place. The old "keep your enemies close" adage? If that were the case...

Then the potential enemies might be closer than they first appeared. Two Aryshans were engrossed in conversation at a table not too distant from them. A man and a woman. A rather striking woman at that. Black hair that weaved through and around the ridges of her distinctly Aryshan crown, and silver skin that gave her an exotic flare. Sean found himself searching for breath.

"What're you looking at, *Lieutenant*?" Captain Grayson asked, bringing Sean right back to reality. He scowled, then his eyes went wide, and he lowered his voice. "I see. I didn't think they'd be here. It's a local stationer hangout—not too many transients come here."

Sean saw an opportunity to shift Captain Grayson's ire without impacting the investigation. "All the same, it looks like they're here now. Should be careful what we say, no?"

Captain Grayson nodded to that. He looked into his whiskey glass again, appearing conflicted. "It seems I haven't given you a fair shake, Lieutenant. There's a lot of tension going on at the higher ranks, not knowing if war is imminent, and with the investigation, I may have taken my anxiety out on you."

That was unexpected. Sean lifted his chin, and did his best to keep eye contact with the man. He didn't want to deviate his attention to the captivating Aryshan woman out of the corner of his eye. "My job is a tough one. I'm used to not being liked." Sean gave a half-smile to the captain. "Maybe I should get my own drink. We're both off duty right now, hmm?"

Captain Grayson's comm rang before he could reply, and he held up a single finger to Sean. He produced his comm card and tapped the button. "Grayson here." The signal must have transmitted to a flesh-toned ear insert.

Sean watched, unable to hear the other end.

Captain Grayson stepped back, sliding from his chair. "What? Really? No, not busy at all. I'll be there right away, and I'm going to bring the IA guy with me."

Sean mouthed, "What?" to him before looking around. No one else seemed to be paying any heed to their conversation. The decibel level held high, with the whole room socially engaged.

Captain Grayson hit his comm button once more and leaned in toward Sean. "Station security reviewed the cargo bay workers' union camera footage." His eyes flicked over to the Aryshan table, then back again.

"Yeah?" Sean asked.

A group of security personnel entered the restaurant. They spoke with the hostess at the front, who pointed in Sean and Grayson's direction. The security team moved on, brushing past tables, causing no shortage of commotion as they passed.

Captain Grayson's eyes went wide when he saw security close in. "This might be our lucky day. Do you think your friends over there might be...? That'd be too easy."

Sure enough, the security team moved to the table where the two Aryshans were seated. The woman stood up, her expression incensed. Sean had a full view of her–even more striking than she had been while seated. Tall, slender, and with a dark Aryshan uniform that fit her curves. She might have been one of the most beautiful women Sean had ever seen. The anger she displayed almost suited her. She argued with one of the security personnel, who stepped past her, isolating the Aryshan man from her.

The Aryshan male stood to confront the security officer. He turned his head toward Sean and Captain Grayson, as if he sensed they were watching him. His face was eerily calm, and the glance put Sean on edge.

A moment later, two of the security guards had apprehended him, grabbing him by the arms and tugging them back to slap on handcuffs.

The woman yelled something in the Aryshan language. The words she used sounded angry, the language staccato, and hiss-like. She seemed as if she were protesting for her rights, gesturing wildly.

The security personnel ignored her, dragging the man away from the table. The Aryshan man stumbled, but didn't resist, walking with them. The woman followed, all of them heading past Sean and Captain Grayson's table.

Captain Grayson leaned over the table toward Sean, dropping his voice. "That's our attacker. Good work, Lieutenant. We'll be interrogating him later."

Sean nodded, still watching as security moved through the restaurant. The rest of the patrons rubbernecked along with them, their quiet conversations inquisitive to the situation. When the security detail had gone, normal conversation resumed.

Sean stood. "I should probably see what Commodore V'bosh has in mind for the prisoner, and make sure he's in the loop. Catch up on conversation later?" he asked.

With a gruff nod, Captain Grayson agreed. "Don't worry about the tab. It's on me."

10

Tamar seethed. Had she been on the *Issiana*, she would have called an immediate inspection and brought her wrath down on the crew. However, she was among humans, on their station, in a crowded promenade of shops. The station security personnel had taken Mynoan and, after very little discussion, ignored her. There had to be rules against this sort of arrest of Aryshan personnel. If word of this reached the Ruling Committee...

...there would be war. Had that been the plan all along? Had this classified mission with Mynoan been meant to escalate the conflict? As much as her thoughts kept returning to that scenario, Tamar couldn't believe it. The practical elements, removing human warships from the area, made much more sense as an objective.

Regardless, Tamar had to figure out what to do here and now. Unable to follow security any longer, she'd been left standing alone in the middle of this busy intersection. Civilians buzzed past her, as did station personnel. One passerby, even though humans had such similar faces to them, stood out to her. This one had been seated at the restaurant where she'd been talking to Mynoan, and more, Mynoan had commented on how the human seemed to have been watching them. He might have been the one to tip off security in the first place.

The human moved through the crowd, and Tamar followed, though she did her best to make sure he didn't pay attention to her. He entered a liftcar, and she moved after him, standing far enough away as to appear as another passenger. He didn't seem to notice her, but she kept her head facing away so her Aryshan features wouldn't single her out. After the car reached its destination, the man traveled down a corridor. Tamar kept with him, but as she did, her anger subsided to her better senses.

What did she intend to do if she did catch up with him? Would she attack him? Confront him? And then what? He likely was following orders, as Mynoan had been, unable to exert any real authority. A threat from her wouldn't give her the result she wanted. She stopped in her tracks, letting him go wherever he intended.

This had been the wrong course to pursue. In fact, she began to doubt whether coming onto this station had been a good idea at all. Backtracking, Tamar made her way to her quarters. She was supposed to oversee supply shipments and trade, but the trip had not allowed her to perform much of that duty. It didn't require much active oversight anyhow.

She planted herself in front of her bedroom terminal, activating the comm system and privacy encryption. What she should do would be to contact the Ruling Committee and inform them that their operative had been captured. Receiving orders was a much better alternative to reacting on one's own initiative out of emotion. The latter was what caused the problems with the *Issiana* in the first place.

The screen flickered with the word "connecting," and Tamar waited. Several minutes went by with no answer. It could be hard to get ahold of the Ruling Committee, but usually First Speaker Ny'aet, at least, had an aide speak with her. The silence didn't comfort Tamar at all.

11

An hour after the Aryshan man's capture, Sean received a message from Commodore V'bosh that the prisoner had been processed, and he could commence interrogations at his leisure. He hurried from his quarters and made his way to the detention facility, where Captain Grayson stood outside waiting for him.

They entered through two large doors engraved with a representation of planet Earth. There, they stopped at a counter, where a female guard sat behind glass. "Captain, Lieutenant," the guard said. "You're here to see the Aryshan prisoner?" Both men nodded, and the guard stood, tapping her badge against the wall. The lock deactivated and a light on the side of the door flashed green. The guard opened the door for them. "This way, sirs."

Behind the doors was a hallway that led to five cells, two on each side and one larger cell at the end. Each had a transparent face with a force field maintaining security.

The Aryshan prisoner sat on a bench in the end cell, facing Captain Grayson and Sean. His hands lay folded across his lap, and he leaned against the back wall. Squared crown ridges on his head betrayed his species. The prisoner didn't dignify them with an acknowledgement.

"His name is Mynoan, according to our customs records," the security guard said. She saluted Captain Grayson, and upon his acknowledgement, she returned to her desk down the hall.

Captain Grayson sized up the Aryshan. "Mynoan," he said. "Which Aryshan tribe do you serve?"

Mynoan kept his eyes straight ahead, down on the ground, and remained silent.

Captain Grayson lowered the force field with a tap of his hand to a wall control panel. He entered Mynoan's cell, and in a sudden move, grabbed Mynoan by the shirt to force him to look him in the eye. "That was my ship you were screwing around with. You could have killed several of my colleagues. If you don't think I'm going to make this painful when you don't cooperate, you're fooling yourself."

Sean froze, startled at Captain Grayson's aggressiveness. Imagining himself in Mynoan's position, he was glad he didn't push Captain Grayson when they first met. The uneasiness almost made him forget he was standing across from a dangerous Aryshan who came close to killing him days earlier.

Mynoan spat on Captain Grayson's face.

Grayson wiped the spit off with his free arm's sleeve and pressed his grip on Mynoan. "I'll ask one more time."

Mynoan's voice was strained by the compression on his windpipes, though he didn't appear worried. "You're violating Earth's ethics declaration on prisoner treatment."

As much as Sean wanted to see the Aryshan beat to a pulp, and as much as that desire amplified when the prisoner took such a mocking tone to Earth's laws, Mynoan was right. The Interplanetary Navy had strict rules regarding prisoner treatment. But what Mynoan forgot was—who was going to vouch for his account of events?

The words didn't deter Captain Grayson. He delivered a blow to Mynoan's jaw that landed with a crack. "You answer what I ask and nothing else!"

Mynoan's head whipped to the side. He took a moment to recover, and then met Captain Grayson's gaze with narrow eyes. He showed no indications of pain. Did Aryshans even have the capability to register pain? "I am of the Aresh, though I am sure you have that information in your files already."

Sean crossed his arms, leaning his weight to one side against the cell's frame. Captain Grayson was much better at intimidation tactics than he was, enough so that it frightened him. He made a mental note to get him a gift along with Lieutenant Carrabba after this ordeal was over. "Sabotage is a serious charge. If you cooperate with us, you may even see your people again," Sean said, more than happy to take the role of the good cop.

Mynoan raised a brow at Sean and shrugged, again refusing verbal response. He touched his jaw where Captain Grayson had struck him.

Captain Grayson threw another punch, this time at Mynoan's gut.

Even with air being knocked from him, Mynoan maintained a stoic face. Captain Grayson's interrogation tactics were leading nowhere. How was this Aryshan so smug? Didn't he care about surviving?

"Captain, may I speak with you privately?" Sean asked.

Captain Grayson released Mynoan and backed out of the cell. Sean followed, and they stopped further down the hallway where Mynoan wouldn't be able to overhear. "What's the matter, Lieutenant?"

"With all due respect, the aggressive tactics don't seem to be working, sir." Captain Grayson's eyes lit up in anger, but Sean held up a hand to calm him. "I don't think that's your fault, sir. Something feels off with the Aryshan. The more I think about it, there's no way this case or his capture could be so simple. It wouldn't make sense for it to be so easy to find this guy after there was little to no trace left at the other crime scenes."

"You're right. He should be scared out of his wits after I'd shown a willingness to break rules and get violent. But he's not. What could he be thinking? I still don't understand what the motives are," Captain Grayson said.

Events connected in Sean's head. This was bad. Very bad. "He wanted to get caught."

"Go on."

"What if we're thinking about this wrong? What if the first few attacks were to shake us up, give them a tactical advantage while the Aryshans, all this time, prepared for war? I'm just thinking aloud."

"No, Lieutenant, you're the first person who's made any sense during this entire investigation. I've been saying for weeks that the Aryshans—"

Hard footsteps clanked in the corridor. Sean looked to see Mynoan darting from his cell. Captain Grayson hadn't sealed the door before moving for their private conversation. That had been a mistake.

Mynoan shoved Sean to the side and leapt atop Captain Grayson. Oddly, his first move wasn't to strike the captain but to bring his hand behind his own ear instead, pinching it as if it bothered him. Captain Grayson tried to put his hands up to guard himself, but the Aryshan was too fast. Mynoan struck, and rubbed his hands rapidly over Captain Grayson's face.

Sean wished he had a weapon, but Palmer Station regulations didn't allow anyone other than active security personnel to carry anything that could discharge. It was a precaution to ensure no one accidentally misfired and poked a hole in the station's hull.

They'd been overconfident in presuming that the two men could handle a lone Aryshan prisoner. Considering Mynoan's strength from the zero-g encounter, he should have been more careful. Sean reacted as fast as he could, kicking Mynoan in the side, causing the Aryshan to fall off Captain Grayson.

Mynoan scrambled to his feet and jumped back.

Sean turned to Captain Grayson, who had been pushed against the wall and struggled to right himself. "Sir, are you okay?"

"Call..." Captain Grayson coughed out the word, but didn't complete his sentence. His hand shook, and his jaw hung open as if he'd lost control of it. He stumbled.

Mynoan charged toward them. Sean ducked out of the way.

Captain Grayson collapsed face-first onto the floor, his body falling in Mynoan's path. The Aryshan tripped over him and fell to the floor.

Sean hopped over his companion and bolted for the security entrance. "Guard!" He wondered what had happened to Captain Grayson. It looked like some sort of poison.

Mynoan gripped Sean by the pant leg to stop his progress. Sean attempted to break free, but Mynoan's grip was too strong. He kicked at Mynoan's hand with his free leg, which caused his release, but Sean lost his balance as a result.

Sean hit the floor, landing on his ass. He backpedaled across the floor to try to scoot himself out of Mynoan's reach.

Mynoan recovered as if he were never struck, back on his feet before Sean had time to plan his next move. "About time you die, human. You've caused enough problems for our plans already," Mynoan said. He scratched behind his ears again. The movement left an orange resin on his fingertips.

That's where he had the poison. It must have been a solution that activated to touch. The compound had to be safe for Aryshans but toxic to humans. Invisible and dangerous. It made even more sense now. His purpose had been to get captured, bring in the investigators, and remove them from the equation. That would have kept the Earth senate from receiving a report until another investigator could reach the station and delay any action Earth might take. The Aryshans might even be able to claim he acted alone, without their government's knowledge.

Sean shuffled on his rear, away from Mynoan, but the Aryshan advanced much faster than Sean could move away. He'd suffer the same fate as Captain Grayson at any moment. He didn't want to die. He wasn't ready. The fear froze him.

Two shots from a plasma gun rang in the corridor, the high-pitched frequency blasting in Sean's ears. The plasma bolts whizzed past Sean's head.

Mynoan staggered back, but no blood splattered. He stared at Sean, and as he turned, Sean could see two singed holes in his side. Mynoan's eyes rolled back, and he fell to the floor, dead.

Sean spun to see the security guard who had ushered them in earlier, plasma gun still trained on Mynoan's body.

"You got him," Sean said, and then laughed until he couldn't breathe, the stress of nearly dying—for the second time in the past few days—overwhelming him.

The security guard holstered her plasma gun and offered him a hand up. "I see that. I don't see what's funny though." She peered over him to the Aryshan body. "No blood. That's odd."

Sean took the hand up and glanced at Mynoan. "I read about their physiology on the trip to the station. The only way you'd get blood would be if you pierced the bone structure. What's more important is Captain Grayson, though. The Aryshan used some sort of fast-acting poison." He crouched down to Captain Grayson's body and grabbed his wrist. There was no pulse. Sean frowned.

"Is he?" the security guard asked.

Sean frowned. Despite having seen many dead bodies over his career, it never became easier when it was someone he knew. The man had been with him for almost his entire duration on the station. Though he was hard on Sean at first, he was beginning to like working with the captain. The way that poison reacted had looked so painful. His face was covered in boils and burns. "Why don't you call medical and get some more security down here. I'll stay here and make sure no one contaminates the scene."

As the security guard turned to leave, the station alarms sounded, red lights flashing everywhere. Sean had a feeling the dead captain wasn't the worst of his problems.

12

Tamar quickened her pace through the crowded docking area. All too many pedestrians shot dirty looks at her, and even though humans didn't have the same bondsense Aryshans did, she could tell she was in danger. Their ire was strong, and who could blame them? Mynoan's actions had already generated enough rumors she'd heard through the idle whispers of market promenade shoppers. No one felt safe on Palmer Station anymore, and they blamed that on Aryshans.

Which was why the docking bay had such a crowd rushing to get to their vessels. It was like a storm of humans about to swallow her, and she had to run for safety.

When she reached the transit tube that connected to the *Issiana*, she could sense her fellow tribemates through the bondsense. That connection brought her comfort, safety. Being out, alone, away from her tribe, was far too dangerous. She should have brought an escort besides Mynoan.

The station's emergency alarm sounded. Red lights flashed through the tube.

Neyral stood with a couple of the *Issiana*'s cargo technicians, talking logistics. He looked up, no doubt feeling Tamar's presence. "Speaker," he said, bowing his head toward her.

Tamar stopped in front of him. He didn't have an aura of fear or annoyance to him, like her own. Instead, he projected confidence, almost smugness. With alarms sounding, and so many angry people around, how did it not impact him? "You knew about Mynoan," Tamar said.

He had the look of someone who had done something wrong and been caught in the act, but that faded into a hardened, stoic expression. Neyral turned to the technicians with him. "Proceed to load all you can on my authority. We'll be departing in short order." He turned back to Tamar. "I'm sorry, Speaker. We had strict orders from the Ruling Committee to inform as few as possible so that this mission could progress as intended. Since you had to be our face on the station, you required deniability."

"So I've been told before. I knew something was wrong. Who else was in on this?" Tamar was more irritated than she should have been, but deceit was rare between tribesmen. The bondsense made sure of that. What it didn't protect from was omission of information.

"Only Mynoan and myself. He will go down as a hero to our people."

"Don't you see this is a tragedy for our people?" Tamar couldn't help but vent. "The other tribes will see us as overly-aggressive, incompetent. We'll lose our status." They had worked so hard to build an image as the strongest, most efficient tribe in the empire. That's how they managed to maintain not just the speakership, but two seats upon the Ruling Committee—something unheard of since the height of the Anwii's rule. It gave them unchecked power; Tamar was beginning to wonder if that was a good thing.

"Calm yourself, Speaker. Your projections influence others. The reason you were chosen among the rest of the commanders was partially because of how well you shield your emotional aura. The tribe perceives you as steady and logical. We should maintain that image. Besides, all went according to plan. Better, even," Neyral said. He smiled at her.

She wanted to wipe that smile right off his face, but his overconfident tone was not directed at her. He believed in this course of action. His words about her emotional aura rang true. She focused her mind, concentrating on the void of space. Her projections settled, and the passing crew didn't appear to notice anything amiss. "What was this plan, now that it's over?"

"Ah, you haven't heard?" He flicked his eyes up to the flashing lights in the tube. "Mynoan was successful in hiding an explosive aboard the human battleship. The schematics from the stolen ship revealed its weaknesses perfectly. There is one less threat so close to our border."

No wonder the alarms sounded. Palmer Station was preparing for war. "We have to leave the system as soon as we possibly can," Tamar said.

"I know. I've recalled all our personnel. We'll be ready to depart within the hour."

"If security doesn't come for us."

"They are preoccupied at the moment. By the time they're ready, we'll be long departed."

This whole situation still felt rotten to Tamar. Mynoan had sacrificed himself in a foolish effort, and because of what? Earth would send more ships to the border because of this. Arysha would be more encroached upon, not less. All of this was so short-sighted, so unlike Ny'aet. His work had been so subtle when he rose to power, when he'd trained her. What had happened to him?

Tamar told herself Ny'aet was committed to the Aresh, a loyal and bonded member of the tribe. She had to trust the direction that the tribe went. No one could try to hurt the Aresh without the others being aware and putting a stop to it. That was the secret that made Aryshans so superior to the other nearby races. The thought comforted her. For now, she had a job to do.

"Okay," Tamar said. "Let's return to the committee chambers and oversee the rest of this process. Are the other commanders aware of our situation?"

"Only that we'll be departing soon. We can brief them on the rest together. Thank you, Speaker. I knew that nominating you would be the right choice. With you and me working as a team, we'll ensure good, decisive leadership for our crew and tribe," Neyral said.

Tamar nodded, though she wasn't certain she agreed with him. He led the way into the crescent-shaped ship and through its corridors. At least these walls felt like home. Despite her not agreeing with the hidden mission, she would be happy to be back among her people.

13

Palmer Station's senior staff gathered in a big conference room on the station's main operations level. Sean and a couple of members of security were the only outsiders invited. Commodore V'bosh and several members of his staff huddled around a conference table. Lights still flashed with alarms outside, though the sound dampened when the door shut behind them.

"By the light, it's well you're all here," Commodore V'bosh said. He situated on a platform at the end of the table, designed for the Tralos to maintain similar height to human eye contact while seated. "I am sorry to report that Captain Jemile Grayson was poisoned by an Aryshan prisoner, but that's not the reason for the alarm or the negative vibrations." He paused to survey the others. "Captain Grayson's ship, the *Avery*, had an explosion in its engine room. The Aryshans detonated a device that was linked to its crystal drive, causing a cascade failure. Despite early warning that the ship was being tampered with, we weren't able to find the device."

Those words caused a stir around the conference room. "Is anyone safe on the station?" one of V'bosh's staff members asked.

It didn't feel like it. Sean could have sworn he was being followed earlier, and even though he didn't think much of it at the time, now it bothered him. His job had been to act as an Internal Affairs investigator, but that ran parallel with finding the truth of what was happening in this sector. Now he had an answer, and if he delivered his report to the Earth senate, war would be coming—or at the very least, an intense militarization of the border. If the Aryshans didn't want that, removing him from the equation would be the best option. The more he thought about matters, the more certain he felt that there had to be more conspirators involved, perhaps even Aryshan spies among them.

Lieutenant Carrabba raised her hand to speak. "What we need to do is make sure that this station remains a safe place to conduct business and for civilians to gather. If we can't ensure that, we won't be able to operate."

"That is why I've brought all of you in to deliberate on the matter," Commodore V'bosh said. "We must ensure that vibrations are brought back into tune. My first concern is everyone's safety. After speaking with Lieutenant Carrabba, we've found three conditions to help. One—non-essential personnel will be moved to safe zones while we investigate. Two—engineering will conduct a sweep of the station for any potential explosives, sabotage, or biohazards. Three— all Aryshan personnel are to be removed from the station."

"Is that legal?" someone asked. Concern echoed across the conference room.

"By the molt, it is not an easy decision. It is the safe one. It is in the light of the law," Commodore V'bosh said.

Sean couldn't help but think of the political implications. Earth had had an open arms foreign policy until this point, and removing Aryshans from the station went against that sentiment. Even during the Drenite War, civilian populations had been allowed to interact on Earth colony worlds and installations. The thought had been that continued commerce would shorten the war and remind the Drenites that the resources they gained benefited them.

The Aryshans had a different psychology, but Sean couldn't help but think there had to be another way.

"We will be implementing these policies immediately. It is my understanding that the lone Aryshan naval ship has broken dock. We shouldn't have any problem with remaining transport. You are dismissed. Reflect in the light," Commodore V'Bosh said.

Everyone gathered around the table stood and headed for the exits. Sean stood, but Commodore V'bosh motioned for him to stay.

Commodore V'bosh waited for the room to clear before he spoke. "By the molt, these conditions send the worst of vibrations. It is not in my nature to implement such, but it is correct."

"You made the right choice, sir," Sean said.

"Let us hope so. I will leave you to make your report. It's a darkness what occurred with Captain Grayson," Commodore V'Bosh said.

Sean frowned. "I enjoyed working with him. He was a good officer."

"That he was. Take care in your report, Lieutenant. Your words to the Earth senate will dictate the next course in your history, perhaps the history of all the species of this arm of the galaxy."

No pressure. Sean could feel the lump in his throat growing. "Aye, sir," he said.

"You did well in your investigation. I will be making my own report to command about both your ingenuity and your clarity in the light. Perhaps something good will come out of this, more than Internal Affairs, hmm?"

Sean nodded. "I would appreciate that, sir. There's one thing I wanted to talk to you about, as I think about it. There were incidents before this Aryshan vessel came aboard the station. This isn't over."

"Your clarity is strong. We are aware of this, but our next investigative team on this matter will be from the shadows, not in the direct light." Commodore V'bosh made what could only be described as a purring noise, but Sean was unsure what that meant, coming from a Tralos. "Go and reflect. You are dismissed, Lieutenant."

14

The committee chambers had been quiet for some time. The four members were deep into composing their reports of the recent mission. Tamar had received a communication from the Ruling Committee as to where they were headed to next. She read the orders transmitted, which were short.

"We have our next mission," Tamar said. Her words garnered the attention of the other commanders in the room. "We are to return to Aryshan space, to sector four-four-nine by three-five, where we will begin a month-long patrol that ends in sector four-five-eight by three-three." Border patrol. Long days, monitoring, waiting, doing very little. The *Issiana* had a long history of such assignments, though Tamar had hoped with her being given the commander position that they would be involved with fewer procedural duties.

"Very good," Tendell said. "It was nerve-racking to be in human space. It'll be good to get back to something more routine. I will adjust ship schedules to accommodate the mission and create a program for system checks to ensure we are running efficiently."

Intrei, the older woman of the four, frowned at her screen. "I'm not sure we have supplies to accommodate the length of that mission.

Sirdanse Station is not far from our starting point. Will we be able to make a detour?"

Tamar tapped her console and brought up star maps onto the center holodisplay. The mission was set to commence in one week's time, which gave them enough leeway for a supplies detour. "The Ruling Committee appears to have factored that into the schedule."

Intrei relaxed. "I will make a list of supplies needed, then."

"We should also put in for a replacement for Mynoan," Neyral said.

That comment made Tamar frown. It wasn't as if she didn't want to replace him, but she still had misgivings about their mission in the first place, and the fact that he was used as a sacrifice with an end result that had been dubious. Even though they'd left the human station hours ago, the reminder made her uncomfortable. "His skills will be missed. Write the request, and I will present it to the Ruling Committee, though I cannot guarantee they will respond in time for us to take on a new crewman."

Neyral took note of her, scrutinizing her almost too intensely. He didn't project anything odd through the bondsense, however.

Tamar tried to ignore his gaze. "If that's all, we'll have piloting set a course for Sirdanse Station," she said.

The other three commanders muttered their agreements, a unanimous decision for the ship's course. That was always a good way to start a mission. Tamar appreciated the symbolic unity they held together.

With their orders logged, the ship's pilots in the operations chamber executed the transition to FTL. The *Issiana* moved toward Sirdanse Station. Even though Tamar knew the gravitational dampeners prevented any effects of the acceleration, she still couldn't help but feel like the ship's sudden acceleration tugged at her.

"Personnel transfer request sent," Neyral said, and sure enough, the message appeared on Tamar's display. "I also added general requests to shore up our piloting corps and medical team."

Tamar forced herself not to visibly react, though Neyral overstepped in his additional requests. She hated going to the Ruling

Committee for more than was necessary. Even so, with this much danger looming from the humans, it probably was right to have some redundancies aboard. Their patrol was supposed to be routine, but strange things could happen. She approved the message and forwarded it to the Ruling Committee.

15

A week passed as Sean worked from his guest quarters to produce his final report for the Earth senate. He had been listed as one of the nonessential personnel for Commodore V'bosh's lockdown, confined to quarters with the civilians and other transient members of the Interplanetary Navy. His temporary status as special investigator from Internal Affairs had ended with the proof of Aryshan involvement in attacks.

Though the lockdown had ended, security remained at a heightened level. Guards patrolled the corridors with scanning devices to detect explosives. It created an atmosphere of tension on Palmer Station, though even the media declared Commodore V'bosh's actions a success. Safety had been restored.

Merchants in the promenade had returned to their jovial talk, and restaurants and bars had come back to life over the last couple of days. Even the maintenance engineers seemed more at ease than they had before, no longer worried that one of their consoles might explode while they work. Civilians still buzzed with worry. It would only be a matter of time before the Earth senate announced their intended course of action with the Aryshans. It wasn't a question of whether there would be some form of retaliation, only of how severe that retaliation would be.

Sean flipped through news reports. Many centered on the mysterious Aryshan culture. Pundits discussed whether they could truly be considered as sentient as humans, Drenites or Tralos. As Aryshans held such a similar appearance to humans comparatively, further speculation mounted in sociological circles. Several interspecies psychologists published net commentary, most concluding the obvious—that it couldn't be presumed Aryshan thought patterns or processes were the same as humans'.

One dissident pundit went so far as to claim that humanity's actions in economic policies created the isolationist fear in Aryshans, justifying their actions. This wouldn't have had traction, but popular North American Governor Antony Lemkin quoted the article in a speech.

Though Sean had as many questions about the future as anyone else, he had more personal considerations. What was he going to do next? Commodore V'bosh had hinted at a new assignment in their last meeting, but he had been too busy with station operations since that time to meet with Sean.

As if his thoughts had been heard by others on the station, Lieutenant Carrabba sent a message that Sean was to meet with Commodore V'bosh as soon as possible to discuss his reassignment. What was it that Captain Grayson had told him? He couldn't recall the exact words, but it had been something to do with the military bureaucracy making all decisions. They were just cogs in a wheel. With nothing else in his way, Sean made the trek to the commodore's office.

On his way there, he came across a familiar face—Flight Deck Manager Reyna. Sean stopped, politely nodding to her.

"Lieutenant Barrows, I didn't realize you were still aboard the station," Reyna said. She had a faint twinkle to her eyes.

"Yeah, I've been confined to quarters. Nonessential, you know," Sean said.

Reyna frowned. "Your security clearance didn't get around that?"

"My clearance was rescinded. In all honesty, it was relaxing."

"Well, if you have some time, maybe we could share a meal after my shift?" She ran a finger through a strand of her hair, eyes darting to the side.

Sean wasn't oblivious to the way people acted when attraction was involved. She meant to ask him on a date. While flattered, the last thing Sean wanted to do would be to get close with someone and have it ripped apart when he had to leave. He'd been through that wringer before. No matter how charming Reyna was, he didn't want to do it again. "I'm on my way to see Commodore V'bosh now, actually. I'm about to be reassigned. I'd hate to...you know..." Sean said.

Her face became long with disappointment. "Yeah, I understand," she said. "Good luck, wherever the stars may take you."

"Thanks," Sean said. With an awkward smile, he continued on his way to see the commodore.

Once he arrived, Lieutenant Carrabba ushered him in and closed the door behind her.

Commodore V'bosh was on his platform, eyeing a display of statistical graphs hovering in front of him. "Thank you for coming so quickly," he said. "Please, sit."

Sean helped himself to one of the guest chairs. "You mentioned a new assignment, sir?"

"Your vibrations have slowed. It doesn't suit you. Discussing with my colleagues in command, however, we determined it was best to allow you rest, to reflect in the light and allow your vibrations to sync."

"I appreciate that. I'm ready for whatever comes next," Sean said.

"I do see this to be correct." Commodore V'bosh's tail flopped behind him. "Your work was good, and I have passed along my recommendations. Tell me, do you know the reason I chose you to handle this investigation?"

"You said you needed an outside perspective."

"Yes, but there are thousands of people I could have placed on the assignment."

Sean wasn't sure how he should respond. He had an acute attention for details and came up with creative solutions. Commodore V'bosh had understood that. If he wanted to be flippant, he could say because there were so few Internal Affairs men to choose from who were worth a salt. Sean certainly had that opinion of his department from time to time, but he didn't want to risk sounding unprofessional. "I don't know. Why me?"

"Do you remember when you first reported to me on Mars?"

"Vividly," Sean said.

When he first arrived on the red planet, it was intimidating to see what amounted to a giant lizard-person, staring him down with unreadable black eyes. Little did he know that that cold-blooded, monstrous looking creature would be one of the easiest people to work with, once he had the hang of the way he spoke.

"Most base commanders keep distance from their crew. My human counterparts worried so much, as if they will lose everything by imparting knowledge. Tralos do not worry. You humans lack the molt, and do not comprehend. But I understand that your light is not received through molt, and therefore must be fostered."

Sean nodded, listening.

"You are one of the few humans who listen. It's a rare skill, listening. When you have been through as many molts as I have, it becomes easier, but to learn that in such youth?—it's precious."

"Thank you, sir." Sean couldn't help but smile.

"As I said before, I wasn't the only one who noticed your performance in this case. I have the opportunity to present you something rare in this service, a choice in your next assignments."

A choice? That was intriguing. Returning to the IA grind was a tough pill to swallow after all he had experienced on Palmer Station. Sean hoped for something greater. "What are my options, then?"

"First would be continuing in your prior post. You'd have a commendation, which would assist in your route to command— likely of the Internal Affairs office when it becomes available."

That would be a boring desk job, dispatching the Seans of the universe out to the various investigations. This choice wouldn't be much of one at all. Whatever Commodore V'bosh had saved would be his option. Sean tried not to react, but Tralos were too in tune to other creatures to mask emotion.

Commodore V'bosh made the regurgitating noise that the Tralos considered laughter. "Your vibrations are all wrong. All wrong!" He sounded all too amused. "The second option is unique, dangerous, and classified. No word of it may be breathed outside this room, by the molt."

"Of course, sir."

"Your report showed an ability to act in the light, and to communicate in a clear manner. I have not told you of my dual role, not only as commander of this station, but as head of Earth Intelligence Forces in this sector. I would be honored if you would join our division."

"Intelligence," Sean said under his breath, "Wow." He imagined decoding different ciphers, analyzing the information, and delivering reports. Palmer Station wouldn't make a bad place for a permanent home, and he did enjoy working for Commodore V'bosh. "I think I'd like that."

"You may wish to temper your vibrations. The assignment I speak of is unique, as I said. As of now, we don't have the data we need to ascertain the Aryshan military's strength. We know very little of their capabilities."

"You need an analyst for information on defensive capabilities?" Sean asked.

The Tralos shook his long head. "No, Lieutenant. What we need is an undercover informant to provide the information."

Sean could barely keep his jaw from dropping. He considered the proposition. "Wouldn't it be better to employ an actual Aryshan for this?"

"Given the physiological nature of Aryshans, impossible. Allegiance to tribe is engrained in the Aryshans, so firmly it cannot be broken, more so than a sunder-brother. Their bonds have been studied, but we do not fully understand it. The theory is that Arysha as a planet had such vicious predators that they formed a pack. Safety in numbers became imperative."

Sean had read a little about the bond in his briefing. They had actual psychological ties to their various tribes that were said to be impossible to break. In theory, it created perfect loyalty. He understood why one would be hard to conscript. "How would I pass as one?"

"Genetic surgery specialists would make you indistinguishable. In our division, you would learn. They can give more clarity than I." Commodore V'bosh turned off his display. He focused on Sean. "I know it is not easy. You must reflect in the light. I know not more of Aryshan evolution or culture, but our team at our training facility on Cestus III will bring you the light. If you accept."

He had the chance to be an honest-to-goodness spy. Outside of commanding a starship, that had to be the most appealing assignment possible, even with the danger involved. Seeing the Aryshans, learning about them as no other human had—that was appealing on its own. If he took the time to consider it, though, he would find reasons not to. He had to make a decision. "I'll do it," Sean said. "Do you know when I'll ship out?"

"Immediately. Your training must be expedient."

"I meant to Aryshan space."

Commodore V'bosh made what sounded like a sighing noise. "We can't wait for many cycles, by the molt, but we've allowed for three of your months as training and readjustment. You are dismissed, Lieutenant. Pack your belongings."

Sean stood, then gave a salute to Commodore V'bosh. "Thank you, sir."

"We are grateful for all you have done, Lieutenant. May your new work bring you closer to the light," Commodore V'bosh said.

PART II

16

———————

Tamar lost her focus long ago. The display at the center of the chambers had shown the darkness of space for hours. Nothing was there. No star system. No planets. Nothing. The patrol duty had started by the colony world of Gennis, but since then, the *Issiana* had flown on a trajectory of open space. And open it was.

Since travelling this course, Tamar had seen no sign of human activity. Others had reported the same. There had been one false alarm where the sensors produced what looked like a human vessel, but that, in actuality, had been degradation in one of the sensor cells. The engineering department replaced the sensor within hours. It had put the ship on full alert all the same, a good drill to get the crew into action in a timely fashion. They succeeded in battle-appropriate measurements, but did have room for improvement.

Over the next week, the committee planned daily battle preparedness drills. The crew responsiveness impressed Tamar, and it became clear why they had been chosen for her ship. Tendell had especially impressed her, noting operations procedures and recommending programming to automate several key system startups that the computer corps estimated would increase efficiency by fifteen percent. Though Tamar had not seen combat herself, she understood the small improvement could mean life or death in space.

After a week of daily drills, the crew all seemed as prepared as they would be, and with the drills being so repetitive, they were seeing diminishing returns on their efforts. Tamar elected then to end the regular drills and return to random spot drills every few days.

Those few days came and went, and yet she still saw no human activity on their flight path, which took them close enough to the actual border with human space that it aroused Tendell's suspicions.

"Perhaps there's something wrong with the course the Ruling Committee sent to us. There doesn't appear to be any danger of human contact here, and we are veering toward uncontested territory."

Tamar checked into the coordinates, placing them up on the center display for all the commanders to see. Sure enough, the trajectory looked strange for a border patrol. She had Neyral send a request to the Ruling Committee for order confirmation, but they received no reply.

At the end of the shift, Tamar couldn't help but feel that there had been something wrong with their patrol orders. Even so, she didn't dare bring up the prospect of insubordination and changing the path. Getting the Ruling Committee to respond and clarify would be the only way to rectify the situation.

Tired from a long day of doldrums, and far too much paperwork, Tamar left the chambers alone, slipping away without a word. She moved through the corridors of the vessel, never failing to appreciate the work of art in design that the ship held. This was the life she chose, the one that she wanted, to follow in First Speaker Ny'aet's footsteps. She needed a robust military record for that, and a spotless one. What good would assignments like this accomplish for that?

A couple of the crewmen passed by, tensing as they saw her. Being off duty, she did her best to project calm and a sense of relaxation. She didn't want to get caught up in procedures right now. Something about the ship's orders bothered her beyond the mere strange trajectory, just as it had when the *Issiana* had gone into human space. This felt the same, yet different.

Hard footsteps pounded down the hall behind her, and Tamar turned to see who came. Neyral jogged toward her. "Speaker," he said. He exuded confidence through the bondsense, as he typically did.

Tamar inclined her head to greet him. "Commander. Surprised to see you so soon," she said, trying to keep her want for solitude pressed downward and out of the bondsense.

"I know your shift just ended, but I thought you might want to hear this," Neyral said.

"Go on."

"We received a transmission from the Ruling Committee. It was simple: stay on course," he said.

Tamar grimaced. "It makes no sense. Did it say who it came from?"

Neyral shook his head. "One of their aides, but it came on official command frequency."

No explanation. First Speaker Ny'aet could be maddening sometimes. He typically had a purpose for what he did, but he wasn't often forthcoming as to why he chose particular plans. His lack of trust in her grated on her nerves and, for a moment, she forgot to shield that from her projections.

Neyral noticed. He cocked his head. "Do you want to talk, Speaker?"

Tamar did want to vent, and to have someone to talk with about her concerns, but Neyral wasn't a person she trusted. How could she politely tell him so? She didn't sense any maliciousness through the bond, and she didn't want to make him question his faith in her speakership. He was the one who nominated her, and she owed him to some extent. On the other hand, his interest in her was far from professional. That sense had grown stronger over the last several days. He hadn't said anything or acted inappropriately, but sometimes the tribal bond betrayed more than one bargained for. By the same token, he was of her tribe, and she could trust him to some extent. There was no tactful way to turn him down. "Sure. Shall we go to the mess?"

"Good by me."

The mess happened to follow the same path as the walk to her quarters. Tamar continued along with Neyral beside her. "Something about these orders gives me a bad feeling, like I'm not being told everything that's going on here. It's just like our last mission. We had our orders, but the intention was something completely different. Except this time, it can't be about plausible deniability."

Neyral listened as he walked along. "Perhaps because of your import to the Aryshan people, the Ruling Committee put you on a course that would keep you from combat."

Tamar stopped, nearly tripping over her own feet. That she hadn't considered. But important to the Aryshan people? She may have been in training under the First Speaker but, so far, she was untested and not worthy of such a consideration. Was he coddling her? The prospect infuriated her. "If I'm worth anything to the Aryshan people, then I should be serving as much as anyone else would in my position."

Neyral held his hands up in front of her. He lowered his voice. "Speaker, you're projecting intense negativity. It was just a thought, and not one to get offended over. You should be honored. Everyone knows you are being groomed for the Ruling Committee. Keeping you out of danger is in everyone's best interests."

"I will not have special treatment from the First Speaker or anyone else," Tamar said through her teeth. Neyral was right, however. She did have to calm herself. Her anger could pass through the bondsense and influence far too many people. She took a deep breath, trying to focus on the void of space. "On second thought, I should probably retire to my quarters. If you're right, I have a lot of thinking to do on how not to waste the capabilities of this warship because someone thinks it's a good idea to protect me."

Neyral's eyes flickered with a tinge of disappointment, but he recovered quickly. "Very well. I appreciate your confiding in me."

Tamar nodded. "Thank you," she said, and turned back down the hall for the junction toward the crew quarters. She could feel Neyral's eyes on her as she drew distance between them.

17

The flitter descended into the spaceport outside of Cestus III's premier city, Vortselas. Several other ships and warehouses lined the landing pad and workers guided the ships into individual bays. The city itself had millions of residents on the terraformed world—a bustling skyline filled with hovercars and illuminated by dozens of tall buildings.

The flitter door opened, and Sean stepped out, along with his pilot. One man stopped and saluted him, wearing the commander rank patch. "Lieutenant Barrows. My name's David McCleever. I'm the Aryshan intelligence specialist assigned to get you up to speed on the alien culture and mannerisms. I know it's been a long flight, so if you'll come with me, we'll get you settled."

Sean returned the salute and slung his bag over his shoulder. "Nice to meet you," he said. It brought back memories of first arriving on Palmer Station, though this Commander McCleever already seemed much more amiable than Captain Grayson had been when he arrived.

Unlike Palmer Station, the Cestus III intelligence facility was a strict military base. Sean followed McCleever through the landing bay and into a pod that led to a secure warehouse. Inside was a wide corridor of conference rooms, private offices, a sealed vault, and a door labeled *Scenario Room*. Past that were the crew and guest quarters, all neatly in a line. They arrived at Sean's quarters. McCleever stopped at the access pad. "Thumb print."

Sean placed his thumb on the scanner. It lit green.

McCleever nodded. "You're good for access now, both to here and to the rooms you'll be utilizing during your stay."

"Do you know how long a training like this takes?"

"Usually months or years. We don't have that option, given the crisis situation. Latest reports say there's a buildup of Aryshan warships along the border. We'll need to get you deployed before it gets too hot for any civilian vessels to travel through their space." McCleever motioned for Sean to enter.

The room was smaller than his quarters on Palmer Station: a cot that lined the wall, some storage space for his belongings, and a small desk with a terminal. "Cozy," Sean said, setting his bag down.

"Not designed for comfort. We have shared showers at the end of the hall. You'll be allotted time each morning from zero six hundred to zero six ten for its use," McCleever said.

Not much time, but that was pretty standard protocol in barracks with tight quarters—something Sean had been lucky to avoid in his career path. It would take some getting used to. That didn't stop Sean's mind from wondering about the important aspects of the mission. "If it normally takes that long to train someone, what's going to happen?"

McCleever's face betrayed some hesitation. "We're going to employ some new technological techniques that are classified. You'll receive more information on that tomorrow, in your briefing from Dr. Morgana."

A doctor meant that there would be medical procedures involved. He'd been informed of plastic surgery, but if it were in conjunction with the intelligence aspect of the mission, he wasn't sure what to expect. There were people out there who had memory chip implants that attached to brainstems to retain information, but those were rare. It took a certain body chemistry to be able to adapt to those biological modifications, and he'd read far too many stories about rejection that often led to painful seizures or brain damage. If this Dr. Morgana were to propose shoving one of those into Sean's skull, he wasn't sure how he'd react. "Sounds good," Sean said.

McCleever nodded. "Very well then. I'll meet you in the briefing room at that time. Ah, meals. There's a food dispensary that provides rations here, but they're limited. You are allowed to go off base when you're not on duty, at least until you have your Aryshan look."

Sean chuckled. "It'd be a bit hard to fit in with the locals with that."

McCleever broke into the hint of a smile. "Pretty sure off-base meals aren't comped, but it still gets my recommendation. See you tomorrow, Lieutenant." He saluted.

With Sean's return salute, McCleever departed. The door shut behind him.

Sean slumped into the chair in front of the terminal. The shuttle ride had been long, and he was tired. But still not tired enough for sleep in a new, cramped environment. He poked around on the net, at least on what few secure information sources that a base like this allowed, which weren't much. As he was a temporary guest, his access was restricted to information pertinent to his mission. Aryshan culture, history, famous individuals. He stopped on a file of a Chavi Ny'aet di Aresh, First Speaker of the Aryshan people. Ny'aet was a little over fifty years old by Earth standards, but Aryshans tended to have longer lifespans than humans. He came to prominence when the Aresh tribe rose to power. The Aryshan people had been decimated at that point. No information ever came out about how it happened, other than that it was tied to an economic collapse. That was when the Aryshans pulled back from their galactic involvement, becoming more isolationist.

Sean noticed himself yawning. And his stomach grumbling. The jet lag was getting to him after all. He would have to eat now or he might go into hibernation for the next week. He turned off his terminal and headed for the door, back down the corridor where he'd come in through the shuttle bay. McCleever hadn't shown him how to exit the base to get one of those meals out in the city. He resolved to find someone to ask.

The Scenario Room doors were open when Sean passed by. Curious, he stopped to take a look inside. The walls were dark, covered in holographic display material. Several odd-shaped consoles and terminals were being constructed inside. Two engineers were huddled over it, wearing protective gear. One had a blowtorch in his hand, welding metal together.

"You heard about what we're doing here?" he asked his companion.

"Yeah. They recruited someone to actually go into Aryshan space. Crazy," the second man said. He lay on the ground, connecting different tubes at the bottom of the console, a safe distance from the flames. "Couldn't pay me to take a mission like that. I heard the last spy they sent was caught in three days. The bowl-heads got some weird telepathic sense. Can tell if you're not one of them or disloyal. It's not right to send someone else."

"Must have been someone who washed out of the service," the first engineer said.

Sean froze where he was. He'd understood this would be a dangerous mission, but these details weren't given to him. Was that something he could verify in the databanks? His throat dried and his palms became sweaty. He ducked back into the hall so he could listen more without the potential for the engineers to discover him.

"Don't know, but he's gotta be expendable. I guess it's worth a shot. If they can get a little information out of the Aryshans and commed back here, it's worth someone's life. Yeah? Might save thousands or millions." The sound of the blowtorch stopped.

"You're right. Wish there were a better way to do it, is all. I bet they didn't even tell the poor sucker he's bound for a suicide mission."

The stress became too much for Sean. He'd lost all of his appetite and desire to leave the base. Instead of continuing, he retreated toward his quarters. He'd heard enough.

Backpedaling, he almost ran into McCleever. "Lieutenant?"

Sean turned around. He saluted. "Sorry."

"You all right? You look pale as a ghost." McCleever returned the salute, but in a rote manner. "I'm headed off duty if you wanted to join me for a meal?"

"I'm fine. Was going to head out, but I think you're right. I may need sleep more than food. Rain check?"

McCleever smirked. "You're going to wait a long time. Cestus III is weather-controlled. It doesn't rain here. We have designated zones to collect water."

Sean saw the obvious attempt to lighten the mood, but he couldn't amuse himself with small talk. Not right now. "Sorry," Sean said.

"Don't worry about it. And don't be so nervous. Everyone is at first. Trust me, this is the most high-tech, professional installation in the galaxy. You're working with the best of the best here."

People who weren't expendable, as the engineers had mentioned. That's why they'd brought someone else in. Sean nodded. "Goodnight," he said, stepping around McCleever and retiring to his quarters as he originally planned.

18

Tamar woke from a vivid dream. Her comm unit buzzed. It had to be an emergency call or it would have been silenced. What hour was it? She rubbed her eyes and sat up in her bed, disoriented. Already, the dream faded in her mind as she focused on the comm.

"Lights," she said, activating the soft illumination of her room. She had it set so it wouldn't be overwhelming upon waking up, but gave her enough light to traverse the cold floor over to her terminal.

The display flickered on, prompting Tamar to accept the call. It came from the Ruling Committee's flotilla. She signaled for audio only. "Tamar here."

"Tamar. It's good to hear your voice," First Speaker Ny'aet said.

"Likewise."

"I'm returning your call from yesterday. I apologize for the hour. Life on the Ruling Committee does not follow military standard time. There's always something to do," Ny'aet said.

"I'm sure," Tamar said. Her head still had fog from recently waking up, a terrible time to talk to the First Speaker. She'd wanted to confront him, to be indignant, but she needed more energy for that.

"What did you need?"

Tamar rolled her shoulders back to get her body moving. She was a commander now, not one to give excuses, no matter the time of day. If she wanted answers, this was her opportunity. "I want to know why you put the *Issiana* on a patrol mission that keeps us away from any potential danger."

An audible sigh came through the comm. "Tamar, I can almost sense your aggressiveness even through all of this distance." Ny'aet chuckled, no doubt a persuasive attempt to lighten the mood. Nothing he did was by accident. Tamar had learned that much from dealing with him.

"I'm not a fool. This is the second time in as many weeks as you've kept me blind to what's going on. Do I not serve the Aresh faithfully?"

"Tamar, it's not about that," Ny'aet said.

"Then what *is* it about?"

A short pause. "You know what I'm doing, Tamar. You're far more valuable to Arysha than to risk you if some jumpy human decides to fire upon your ship while on border patrol."

Tamar shifted in her chair. "I don't want to be treated any differently than anyone else in the fleet. My duty is to the Aresh, and I have to serve faithfully. If you're trying to groom me for something, can't you see that holding me back in these situations stifles my growth? How am I going to learn to make the decisions necessary to lead if I'm sheltered from anything real?"

Another silence. "I see your point, but you have to trust me. The time will come when these small things won't matter, and we will not only need you, but we'll need the power of every ship like the *Issiana*."

That didn't sound good. Tamar cut short a breath in worry. "What have you heard?"

"The humans aren't backing off as we anticipated, but are emboldening. From their media, we've learned they're pushing war on all fronts."

Tamar wanted to scream that she had told him this was a terrible idea. Mynoan had wasted his life, and potentially wasted the lives of thousands of other Aryshans in the process. What had the Ruling

Committee been thinking? "Have you reached out to their leadership?"

"I'm afraid that would do no good, Tamar. Remember the Great Death. Our people showed weakness then, and look what happened. We can't repeat the leadership mistakes of the Anwii."

As quick as that, Tamar had let him push her off to a different topic. He wanted to protect her, for later. And she had accepted that. He was so manipulative, and that it worked bothered her even more. "I'll accept this assignment, for now, but when the time comes, I don't expect to be exempt from battle."

"You won't be. Your time will come soon, from all I hear. When it does, you'll wish you had more times of peace. Trust me," Ny'aet said.

Her comm flashed with emergency lights. A call from the committee chambers. Who would even be there at this hour? "There's an emergency. I need to go. Thank you for calling me, First Speaker."

"Be careful, Tamar. Ny'aet out."

Tamar quickly switched to the other channel, the call from Ny'aet disappearing on the screen. "Tamar here."

"Speaker, it's Intrei," the voice of the other female commander sounded on the comm.

"What's going on, Commander?"

"I'm sorry to bother you at this hour," Intrei said. "But I'm commander on call this evening for emergency hails."

A hail. So it wasn't onboard the ship. That knowledge made Tamar relax some. She considered who could be hailing them on this route, and realized she was overthinking. Intrei could answer her questions. "What happened?"

"It's the *Essix*. They've had an encounter with a human vessel who are arming weapons and are requesting nearby vessels to assist."

The *Essix* was also on patrol, their route taking them to more strategic systems along the human border. Tamar tried to visualize the map in the committee chambers. If she recalled correctly, the *Essix* would be about a system over from them. The *Issiana* would be the closest ship able to offer assistance. She stood up from her chair.

"I'm going to get dressed and I'll join you in the committee chambers. Have the auxiliary pilot plot a course to intercept."

Tamar let out a deep breath before rummaging through her closet for her uniform. Ny'aet had been right. She already wished she had a few more hours of peace.

19

Sean awoke the next morning in a full sweat. Though he couldn't recall anything he dreamed about, he must have had nightmares. The stress was already getting to him. He checked the wall chrono. It read 0600. He had to get to the showers quickly. There'd only be a few minutes left.

After rushing there and getting as clean as he could, he donned his uniform and headed for the food dispensary. A line had already formed as most of the base personnel readied for their daily work. Sean scanned his thumbprint, and a nutritional wafer spat out of the machine. It was flavorless but contained all of the protein and nutrients he would need for the morning.

After Sean managed to get the food down, he ran into McCleever, who brought him to one of the conference rooms. Two others were already present, a woman and a man, engaged in discussion about the Aryshan political situation.

The woman, lithe, with long brown hair which she had tied back, set a datapad on the table. "Last night came dangerously close to an open firefight. With our forces and theirs playing chicken in the border systems, something dangerous is going to happen sooner or later."

"From what I hear, the Aryshans are getting more aggressive. They know they have tactical superiority," the other man said.

"If that's the case, why haven't they tested it?" The woman looked up. Her eyes met Sean's. "Oh. Hello. You must be Lieutenant Barrows."

The two at the table stood. The woman wore an insignia designating the medical division. Sean guessed she was Dr. Morgana. The man had a commander rank. He saluted the two of them, and they returned the gesture.

"At ease," the man said. "I'm Commander Renoit." He motioned. "This is Dr. Morgana. We're going to be working with you during your time here to ensure you are as prepared as we can possibly get you for insertion into the Aryshan Navy."

McCleever smoothed down his uniform and slid around the table to sit beside Dr. Morgana. He motioned for Sean to take a seat across from them, which Sean did. "We've got slightly different roles here. I specialize in Aryshan military customs and current affairs, analyzing intercepted news broadcasts. Commander Renoit is more of a historian and sociologist. He understands their culture better than anyone. Dr. Morgana we brought in from DePino Research Facilities, where we have been running a joint project on information transmission and retention. They've come up with some pretty revolutionary stuff, which is highly classified."

"Brainstem implants?" Sean asked, guessing as he took his seat.

Dr. Morgana shook her head. "More of a nanotechnology specialist. We've come up with some— for lack of a better word— microviruses, which can write information directly into our cells."

"That sounds dangerous," Sean said.

"Don't let the term scare you. When it's commercialized we'll come up with something better," Dr. Morgana said, glancing at Commander Renoit, then back to Sean. "I won't lie to you. We're not at a stage where I can one hundred percent guarantee safety, but it should work based on the results of our limited trials. Some subjects have had psychological problems adapting to the written information. We'll do our best to make sure that doesn't occur here."

"And we'll do that by intensive training in Aryshan culture so your mind is already prepared for the information it's about to receive. That way it's more like helping you to retain information rather than writing information fresh," Commander Renoit said. "How much do you know about the Aryshans already?"

"Just what I've read in reports. I observed a couple in person at Palmer Station, and interacted with the captured saboteur. Not too much," Sean said.

"Better than nothing. Have you been following what's been happening at the border?"

"Aryshans gathered their forces; so did we. I heard you talking about a near firefight when I came in?" Sean asked.

"We think the Aryshans are waiting for an opportunity to catch us off guard. We have a few ships along the border, but it could be strengthened. Admiral Conley's first fleet is in retrofit at DePino shipyards on Toltair. They should be ready for action within the week," Commander Renoit said.

McCleever nodded. "That's why it's imperative that we get started and get you trained as fast as possible."

From that point, they discussed Aryshan history, geography, politics, culture, art, and language. The language training was the hardest, as Aryshan language didn't correlate well with the Earth standard. Hours went by and Sean wasn't confident he could ask the direction to the bathroom.

Eventually, McCleever checked the time on his datapad and nodded to the others. "I think we'll call it for the day. That's a lot for Lieutenant Barrows to process. We'll adjourn and meet here same time tomorrow," he said.

Dr. Morgana and Commander Renoit departed, leaving Sean with McCleever. Sean gathered his notes and belongings and stood. The stress in his shoulders had caused a knot in his neck, which he stretched to try to soothe, but irritating pain persisted.

"You did well today, Lieutenant," McCleever said.

Sean forced a smile. "Thanks. It didn't feel like it."

"It's always tough on the first day. We're also amplifying the amount of data that you're going to need to intake by ten times the speed we normally would for a new recruit," McCleever said. "But we'll get you up to speed."

Sean considered everything he'd heard last night and through the day. The intelligence division clearly didn't see this as a quick suicide mission if they were investing this much time and energy into his training. Still, it didn't sit well with him.

"What's wrong?" McCleever asked, apparently spotting his unease.

"Ah, nothing sir. Just tired," Sean said.

"I know that look, Lieutenant. You don't get into this line of work without acute attention to people. Something's bothering you, more than just the overwhelming amount of information." He crossed his arms.

"Just having doubts about the mission. If the Aryshans are so in tune to each other, it's about as dangerous a proposition as it gets to be hiding among them," Sean said. "What if it's just a suicide mission?"

McCleever considered Sean's question for a long moment, then nodded. "Of course it's dangerous, but we'll do everything in our power to make sure you have the ability to come out the other side. There's no guarantee, but you're the best hope for keeping human losses to a minimum. We wouldn't send someone if we didn't need the information badly. Commodore V'bosh has faith in you, and so do I," he said. He dropped his arms and made for the door. "Jitters are normal, too. Tell you what, I'll take you out to town to a nice restaurant tonight. My treat. Don't get used to it—I can't do this all the time." McCleever laughed.

Sean hesitated, but realized fretting did no good. McCleever was right. If humans didn't have the tactical information to be able to withstand the Aryshans, the ramifications could be catastrophic. Even if the odds of survival were low, he was a good choice for it. He didn't have a family, and was relatively replicable in his career thus far. It definitely didn't feel good to consider that, but if he were honest, that was fine. Making a difference should matter more to him than wanting a long, normal career, shouldn't it? Finally, he nodded. "Okay, I'll go," Sean said.

McCleever patted Sean on the shoulder and moved past him. "Good. Let's get you a good meal so you can focus on the work and not the fact that your last meals as a human are those wafers."

Sean laughed at that. The engineers last evening had a point, but McCleever and the others didn't seem to view him as expendable. Quite the opposite. As he and McCleever left the base for the city, that brought him some small comfort.

20

Tamar watched the display. The feed that the *Essix* had sent over was hours old, but the image loomed in front of her and the other commanders in the chamber. In the context of space, the human ship appeared as if it hung motionless, but any sudden movement could lead to a battle, destruction, and then death.

That's why the *Issiana* sped in its direction. The presence of two ships had to act as more of a deterrent than one, assuming the humans didn't have similar backup. But what if they did? The thought of the situation spiraling further out of control made Tamar's head feel like it was about to explode.

The others in the room projected just as much tension through the bondsense. She was Speaker. She had to be their calm, their rock to weather the storm. Tamar breathed in, but this time, she couldn't focus on space without seeing a human ship in her mind's eye.

"Fifteen minutes until we arrive in system," Tendell said. The glow of his console lights reflected off his face, intent on the task at hand. He would be managing the time windows.

Ever since their initial contact, the *Essix* had gone into comm silence in order to not betray the advantage the Aryshans would have if the human ship didn't back away from the zone. The only message they broadcasted was a warning for the humans, on repeat, that Tamar had filtered out of her communications scans hours ago.

Tendell hadn't intercepted any transmissions from the human vessel proper. If it was communicating, it must have been using some form of encryption they couldn't track. What were they thinking right now? Were they preparing for their assault? Awaiting orders from their government?

The more Tamar thought about it, the more she hoped a real incident could be avoided. The minutes passed slowly as she waited for the *Issiana* to drop from FTL into the system. Tamar found herself lost in her thoughts, imagining multiple scenarios.

"Entering the system," Tendell announced, snapping Tamar from her reverie.

She tapped on her console, switching the view to a current display of space. A gas giant illuminated the distance, with a standard flurry of asteroids and other objects in orbit. On the bottom left of the display, she could see the semi-circular shape of her fellow Aryshans' ship.

"There's the *Essix*," Neyral said. He cocked his head. "I don't see a human vessel, though."

Tendell tapped his console with a hard motion, betraying his own nerves in the process. His forehead wrinkled. "They're not coming up on scanners either."

"Should I stand down from battle alert?" Intrei asked.

"Not yet," Tamar said. Had the humans been scared off while they were in transit? "Contact the *Essix*. We should speak to their commanding committee."

"Aye, Speaker," Tendell said. He opened the channel.

A face appeared in front of her view of the system, opaque so she could still see a glimpse beyond, but there. "Greetings. Renall Artaya di Aresh, Speaker of the *Essix*."

"Chavi Tamar di Aresh, Speaker of the *Issiana*," Tamar replied.

"It seems the human storm has passed us by already," Commander Artaya said. He gave a smug grin. "Or should I say, the storm ran away."

"That's good news," Tamar said. She let the tension drop from her shoulders.

"It would be good, however, to have another ship on the patrol route for a few days, just in case the humans decide to come back," Commander Artaya said. "We would appreciate the backup if the *Issiana* is able."

Tamar glanced to her other commanders. The sense she had from them was that they would be happy to be alongside fellow Aryshans. Their path through space had been uneventful on this mission so far. Perhaps some fellowship would do them good. It would also help deter the humans from getting aggressive. "We will match course. With tensions so high, barring any other incident, would the commanders of the *Essix* wish to take leave and share a meal with us on the *Issiana* this evening?"

"Let me ask." Commander Artaya moved, his visage disappearing from the display. He returned a few moments later. "I've spoken with the other commanders. We accept."

"We'll prepare to receive you then," Tamar said.

"Speaker Tamar," Tendell interrupted.

"One moment, Speaker Artaya," Tamar said. She muted the signal from her console. "What is it?" she asked Tendell.

"I'm getting several scattered signals. Reports, transmissions from sector five-oh-three."

That was back by where the *Issiana* had reentered Aryshan space after departing Palmer Station. "What's on the signals?"

Tendell looked confused. He stared at his console. "There's too many coming through now, all over the fleet. Let me see if I can isolate."

The transmission came through garbled as the computer system made a mishmash of whatever was on line. "*Yitai* hailing...on alert... patrolling the sector...humans attacked. Weapons more powerful than we thought...assistance..." The transmission cut out.

"Unmute the *Essix*," Tamar said. It hit her how grave a development had occurred. The humans had fired on an Aryshan ship, and from the sounds of it, the *Yitai* might have been destroyed. "Have you been picking up the same signals we have?"

Commander Artaya nodded. "I have. Reports are flooding in now. It looks like we're going to have to cancel dinner."

"Perhaps another time," Tamar said. "We'll stay with you all the same, in case your recent friends decide to get aggressive with this news." Until other orders arrived.

The image blinked out as the *Essix* terminated their comm signal. If tensions had been high through the bondsense before, they were elevated to a level that made it difficult for Tamar to think clearly now. What would their next move be? She dreaded the wait. Orders would come soon enough, though. She could only guess what First Speaker Ny'aet and the Ruling Committee would have in store.

21

Several weeks of intensive learning passed quickly. In that time, the first firefights between Aryshan and human ships had occurred and not only made waves on intelligence channels, but also the interplanetary holovid news. No Earth ships were destroyed, but Sean hadn't seen such underlying dread in all of his time in the military, even in dealing with guilty subjects in Internal Affairs.

The good news was, something clicked about a week ago, where Sean found himself grasping the basics of Aryshan language. He could understand it far better when McCleever spoke it to him. Though some of the inflections still didn't sound natural from his own tongue, he could speak it as well as any tourist. Dr. Morgana had said she was impressed with how quickly he'd been able to pick it up. Sean posited that it might have been due to his attention to detail in his work, having to analyze, memorize, and compartmentalize facts quickly. Either way, his instructors voiced their happiness with his progress, which, in turn, made him more at ease than he had been during his early days at the base.

When he arrived in the conference room, only McCleever was present to greet him. "Morning, Lieutenant. We're going to be doing something a little bit different today. Commander Renoit believes you've made as much progress as possible, given the short burst of learning we're requiring. We've reached a point where we'll be getting diminishing returns on our efforts," McCleever said.

"I'm nowhere near ready for deployment," Sean said, taken off guard by the implication. Did they really mean to send him out this soon?

McCleever chuckled. "Don't worry about that. We're still a couple of weeks at least from wanting to send you out there."

That was all? Sean couldn't imagine that he'd be ready that soon.

"Calm down. You're going pale," McCleever said. "What I mean is, we're ready for Dr. Morgana's program. This is going to involve injecting you with the microvirus we discussed on your first day. It will solidify your Aryshan knowledge and, also, for lack of a better term, program more in you in detail."

Those words didn't comfort Sean in the least. He would rather be deployed than have that happen to him. He imagined little machines crawling inside of him, stripping away who he was, turning him into something new. He had never been the religious sort, but the implications of it were staggering. If people got wind of humans having their minds altered—and Sean hadn't been brave enough in his time here to ask the details of how much—they would definitely go crazy about it. And from what Dr. Morgana implied before, he might lose his mind, too. He wasn't ready for this. Not yet. "Is there any way to delay that a couple of days?"

McCleever shook his head. "You've seen the recent news reports. We've already waited far too long. Come on, Dr. Morgana's waiting for us in medical." He didn't wait for Sean to protest but brushed past him and down the corridor.

Sean had no choice but to follow. The worst-case scenarios played in his mind. What if this resulted in seizures and brain damage as Dr. Morgana had warned? Did she test him for any of the preliminary signs of that? He had so many questions, wanting to verify both what she knew about him and her methodology. He was only trusting that she was an expert in this field based on what the others had told him.

He wished he'd done more research on both her and this procedure, but Sean had spent all of his time—both working and free—in a desperate attempt to learn everything he could about Aryshans. Why did this have to come so soon?

They entered the medical bay together. Dr. Morgana was there, as well as a team of four nurses. A bio-bed had been prepared, instruments and panels all around it, with some additional lighting to shine down on the bed for her procedures. Dr. Morgana had gloves on, a smock, and a lab coat. She put some instruments down on a tray and looked over to them.

"Hello," she said cheerfully. "You're a little bit early. We're still preparing. You've told Lieutenant Barrows what's going to happen here today?" she asked McCleever.

"Just the basics," McCleever said. He stepped back. "I'll return to my duties and let you take over. See you on the flip side," he said to Sean with a nod, then a salute.

Sean returned the salute, and then turned his attention to Dr. Morgana. "What's the procedure entail?"

Dr. Morgana gave a trained smile. She motioned to the bio-bed. "You lay down, get injected with the microvirus, and when you wake up again, your brain has written memories of Aryshan culture, background, and language all stored in here." She pointed to her head. "This will change the course of espionage in the future as it will both help to avoid slipups and capture, and also help the agent if they happen to be interrogated."

Sean dragged his feet over to the bio-bed. It didn't sound terrible, but her words didn't reassure him either. From their conversation weeks ago, he understood this was an experimental operation.

"We would also like to begin the plastic surgery component of this transition while we have you under. That way, when you're recovered, we can get you right to the scenario rooms and ready for deployment when we find a window to transport you into Aryshan space."

Not only would he wake up with memories implanted in his head that he hadn't actually experienced, but he'd look different. That prospect didn't reassure Sean in the least as Dr. Morgana ushered him onto the bio-bed. He nodded all the same. It wasn't as if he had the ability to say no. He'd accepted this assignment, and this is where it would take him.

He tried to get comfortable, the nurses making him place his arms at his sides so they could strap him down. They did the same with his ankles. "Are these really necessary?"

Dr. Morgana didn't seem concerned as she moved to her instrument tray, working out of Sean's view. "The reaction could cause some involuntary reflexes. It's for your own safety," she said.

Sweat dripped from Sean's forehead. When did it get so hot in here? He tensed to the point where his stomach churned. He had to calm himself somehow. This would go fine. He would come out of this with more knowledge, ready to do his job, ready to make a difference. As much as he kept repeating that in his head, it couldn't ease his jitters.

Dr. Morgana walked back over to him. "Goodnight, Lieutenant Barrows," she said in a calming tone.

Sean's eyes went wide when she revealed what she had in her hands—the largest syringe he had ever seen.

22

Tamar still couldn't believe the orders from the Ruling Committee that flashed across her display. Not only was the *Issiana* going to be a part of important duty, but they had been ordered to go deep into human space, to a world that they called the Esare colony.

Intelligence had reported that they had a sizable military installation and training camp on the colony, much bigger than the civilian population that had been concentrated into a single city. The base was close to the city, but there was opportunity for a clean strike. The humans didn't have much of a planetary defense system. Esare's location, somewhat away from the border with the Aryshans, gave it an air of safety from the human perspective.

The plan would be to travel through open space, away from any potential human patrols, and effectively have a free shot at taking out an important ground troop and training installation for the humans. It sounded easy, but Tamar was still nervous. This would be her first real combat test as an officer—or a commander, for that matter.

The *Issiana* had stayed on course with the *Essix* for several days before receiving the orders. In that time, information arrived detailing their first real battle in the conflict with the humans. The

Yitai had been destroyed. Human information sources had pushed into overdrive, claiming the Aryshan ship had violated the border and refused to return to their space, which prompted a warning shot, and then fire back and forth. From the vids Tamar had seen, that was a lie. The humans had been the aggressors in this instance, and for the first time, she began to sympathize with the concept that the humans were expanding too far into space. Perhaps First Speaker Ny'aet had been correct in ordering the initial covert strike on Palmer Station.

Despite the human media sources pinning blame on the Aryshans, not all humans were on board with their militarization of the Aryshan border. More news reports came through, ones that the Ruling Committee was quick to capitalize on and send through Aryshan broadcasts. A human governor of an Earth province known as North America had stepped down from his post in protest to the Earth senate's actions with the military buildup. That surprised Tamar. She couldn't conceive of anyone dropping their post because of a government decision. It wouldn't be something one could do with the tribal bond. Aryshans were committed to each other, and that meant absolute trust. If there was something deceptive afoot, she would sense it, others would sense it. Human individualism was dangerous to not only Aryshans, but to themselves.

"Is something the matter?" Neyral asked from his station.

Tamar realized she had been shaking her head. "No, not at all. Just thinking about the mission."

"It's exhilarating, isn't it?" Neyral asked. He grinned, and he projected far too much eagerness through the bondsense.

She had to look away from him and focus on the star chart to keep that emotion from getting under her skin. "I wouldn't say that. It certainly has me alert, however." She tried to be as diplomatic as possible.

Through the translucent display, Tamar could see Intrei and Tendell. They were hard at work, focused on their own duties at their consoles. It was always Neyral who watched her every move, and the other commanders didn't seem to notice.

"You're off shift soon, yes?" Neyral said.

"I am," Tamar said, acting like she was looking down at her console.

"Me too. We could head to the rec center and get in a workout, or play a game of windstrike?"

It had been a long time since Tamar had thought about a workout or sports. Since this commander assignment she'd been fairly unhealthy, buried in work at almost all times of the day. Now was no different, plus she didn't want to spend time with Neyral in a casual setting. "As appealing as that sounds, I should go over the battle plans. Why don't you end your shift early? I'll cover if anything's needed." Tamar said. She flicked her eyes toward him and caught the disappointment in his face and through the bondsense.

"Sure," he said, smiling at her as if nothing happened. "Thank you, Speaker." He swiped at his control panel to lock it and stood.

Tamar looked at the time display on the upper right of her console. It was almost time for the *Issiana* to begin their assault. The FTL trip would take a couple of days, which meant the true action wouldn't begin until then, but the launch was still tightly scheduled and part of the plans. "Tendell, ensure that engineering and the pilots are ready. Intrei, have our fighter crew ensure their vessels and gear are ready. Check it and double-check it. We don't want to have a hitch with their launch."

The other commanders muttered their agreements with Tamar's orders. Technically, they were all of the same standing, but ever since Neyral had propped her into the Speaker position, Tamar felt as if she bore much more of the command responsibility than the others in the room. Tendell and Intrei had no desire to lead, which was odd to her. How had they achieved their positions?

It didn't matter. This was the command structure they had, and it had worked so far. In some ways it worked better because Tamar had no qualms about taking charge of situations. Her connection to the Ruling Committee gave her a certain authority that differed from other ships' commanding committee structures.

Neyral left the room while she was in her thoughts, the door shutting behind him.

Intrei looked up from her post. "The fighter crews are ready, Speaker." Her eyes bored into Tamar.

"Is there something else?"

Intrei clicked her tongue. "Just the aura between you and Neyral. He is interested in you, you know? Not just as a commander, but as a bondmate."

Tamar froze. She'd seen some of his inappropriate gestures to her, but hadn't considered it was that serious. "I see," Tamar said. Her tone was so cautious, even with Intrei. Didn't she trust her other commanders? They were Aresh just as she was. The stress of the pending combat must be getting to her.

Intrei's eyes widened into a look of understanding. "It is unwanted, then. That makes more sense."

By the Overseers, this made Tamar more than uncomfortable. She needed to end her shift and get her own rest. Two days. That's all she had to mentally prepare herself for the challenges ahead. "I'll be heading to my quarters. Inform me when we enter FTL, Commander Tendell."

"Of course, Speaker," Tendell said.

Tamar slid off her stool and moved away from her station. Intrei's eyes remained on her the whole way. She wanted to ask the older woman's advice, but what was there to say? Tamar didn't want to think about bonding with Neyral. She had no time for that, and her duties would only get worse. If she had someone, though, someone to be closer connected, to share everything with, would it ease her mind?

Those were thoughts she couldn't do anything about. She needed a meal, and then she'd get to studying more about the topography of the Esare colony.

23

It hurt like hell when Dr. Morgana injected him with that monstrosity. Sean couldn't hold in the scream for long. He pushed against his grips, but they held him firmly in place. While he expected there would be an anesthetic for the process, he hadn't explicitly asked for any—and now he wished he had.

The pain was immense, first in the vein that Dr. Morgana jabbed the needle into, and then shooting up his spinal column, into the base of his neck and skull. A splitting headache followed, one that blinded him.

That's when the lights flooded his vision.

Sean couldn't think, couldn't react. His body disappeared. Whatever the microvirus was doing completely enveloped his reality. The universe shattered into thousands of light splinters, travelling faster than any FTL ship in multiple directions at once. Sean's body seemed to coalesce in on itself a moment later, but he still didn't see the room. Streaks of vibrant color shot past him, toward him, through him, and all around him. It didn't dull the pain in the least. The microvirus tore away his insides.

The lights slowed to a grinding halt, leaving Sean hanging, weightless, in the middle of nothingness. For a moment, he had lost himself, who he was, where he'd come from, but with the freeze in time, he came back to some semblance of identity.

Did this mean his brain had overloaded from whatever the microvirus did to him? Was he trapped here in this vast universe of nothingness, unable to return to any normalcy? What of the mission? What of his life?

The light faded into blurriness, as if he had a concussion and couldn't see straight. That bright light was in his eyes, hurting his eyes. He wanted it to go away so desperately, but he couldn't move his hands to shield his face from it.

Then he recalled where he was. On an operating table. A bio-bed. But he still couldn't see around him. He tried to move but restraints had him secured in place. Three shadows hovered over him, staring, poking and prodding. Were those doctors? Sean tried to call out for help but his vocal cords wouldn't react.

The shadows in front of him moved in closer. They had sharp instruments, and they were going to pierce him with them. The plastic surgery, that's what this was. That's what this had to be. Sean just wanted to be back in reality, wanted to feel like he was human again. Why had they done this to him? He couldn't live the rest of his life like this.

As the shadows moved, he caught a glimpse of their heads. These weren't human doctors at all. These were Aryshans. They knew who he was. They'd found out that he was a spy. They were going to pick him apart as an experiment until he gave them all of the information he had on humanity. And then they were going to kill him.

Something jabbed into his arm again. Another pain like the needle before. This time, the whole world disappeared into a vast darkness.

～

"CHU CALLA MON THRWARTEE?" a voice said.

Sean opened his eyes. His head still hurt, but this was the reality he'd been used to. After what he'd seen, what he'd experienced, could he be sure this was real? He winced at the pain in his head, his eyes barely able to withstand the light in the room. What was it the person had just asked him? Sean processed it and knew what was said: *Welcome back to the land of the living.*

"*Mi rahhk,*" Sean said. Thank you. What were these words, and how did they come from his head and mouth so naturally?

When his eyes regained focus, he saw a human standing in front of him. A man in his thirties, dark hair, heavy five o'clock shadow. McCleever was his name. But why was he with humans? Why did that bother him so much? He was human, too, wasn't he?

The man continued speaking to him in the Aryshan language. "Do you remember what happened? You went into the procedure. It seems to have taken root."

Sean thought back to the last things he recalled. The bright light. Nothingness. Ego loss. Before that, though, he'd been in a medical bay, having trained for several weeks to learn as much about Aryshans as he could. "I remember," Sean said, speaking Aryshan still. "But I have other memories, too."

"That's part of your new identity. Retai Aeveron is your name."

Retai. That referred to the province on the southern continent of the first Aryshan colony world, Wynfal. That's where he was from. No, he was from Mars. That's where he'd grown up. Suddenly, he had two conflicting sets of memories. He tried to shake it out of his head.

"You no doubt have a lot to process still. I won't bother you, but Dr. Morgana said you should have someone waiting with you to make sure you're okay. If you have questions, I'm here to help," McCleever said. He had been standing but resumed a seat in a small chair across from where Sean lay.

Sean looked down at himself. He was still in a bio-bed, covered in a light blanket, but no longer strapped in. An IV line protruded from his arm, attached to a sack of clear liquid. "How long was I out?"

"Almost five days," McCleever said.

"Five days?" Sean went into a panic. The whole universe could have changed in that time. He had to get back to work.

"Don't stress yourself, Lieutenant. There'll be plenty of time for that later. We need to get you back to full health and make sure your head is situated with the microvirus programming. They've been drained from your system so you don't have any strange organisms lingering inside you, in case you were worried about that." McCleever chuckled.

Sean pulled down his covers. It was difficult not to stare at himself. He lifted his hand. Though faint, instead of the pink tone his skin had before, it now had a silver hue to it.

McCleever snorted, then covered his mouth. "Sorry. It shouldn't be funny. Your reaction is classic. You should see it." He snapped his fingers and stood, moving to a nearby cart and fumbling through the items there. He produced a hand mirror. "Actually, you can."

Sean wasn't sure he wanted to see himself, but he would have to sooner or later. For whatever reason, though his skin tone had initially shocked him, it settled within him now. It was the right way for his body to look; something inside him understood that. He took the mirror from McCleever and held it up.

His face reflected, not all that different than he remembered. His hair had turned black, and his eyes had been filled by his pupils, dark and foreign. Then there was the crown-like bowl that surrounded his head that marked the Aryshans, and the small protrusions that looked like flattened horns. "I make a pretty good-looking Aryshan," Sean said.

McCleever laughed. "That you do. Pretty amazing. Same with the fact that you've been speaking to me in their language through this entire conversation. Who would have thought you'd sound so natural? I'm impressed with Dr. Morgana's work already, and we haven't even delved into the deeper conditioning."

"Like what?"

McCleever considered. "Who are your parents?" he asked.

"Were," Sean corrected. "Rentai Tella and Rentai Maquiz. They died in a transport accident ten years ago." He blinked several times. "I know this, and I mean actually *know*. It's not just from having read a dossier and memorized it. I can visualize the memories. They're faint, but they're there."

"That's good. It means the nanites worked. It's not a complete safeguard against interrogation or slipups, but it's much closer than we ever could have done in the past. It looks like Dr. Morgana has a very lucrative technology on her hands." He glanced out the infirmary door, as if expecting to see Dr. Morgana there. Then he stood and refocused on Sean. "We're going to get you into scenario training in a couple of days. Rest up, keep studying, and get yourself fit again. There's not that much time to go."

Sean nodded as well as he could. He could hardly focus on the conversation at hand. His thoughts kept returning to his Aryshan life, the one that had been implanted in him. He could recall his family, his schooling, the salty smell of the air in the seaside town he grew up in. It was all there, and all fake.

24

The *Issiana* dropped from FTL. The ship slowed to a near-halt at enough distance so they wouldn't alert the humans. The idea had been that this target was far enough away from their border that the humans wouldn't be ready for the assault. And their plan worked flawlessly.

The orbital defense of Esare might act as a deterrent for pirate raiders, but against the full force of an Aryshan warship, they were more like the grass-gnats of Chavi, swarming and nipping at a full-grown Aryshan, than they were any real threat.

Tamar watched the multi-view display at the center of the committee chambers while the weapons officer corps went to work disabling the human defenses. Missiles launched from the two tips of the pincer-shaped vessel, plasma cannons following. The plasma hits would strike first, despite being fired after the missiles, weakening any shielding or armor plates that the human defense platforms might have.

After only one barrage, the human's planetary defense was reduced to rubble. "Too easy," Neyral said, conceit in his voice.

"Our assault has only begun," Tamar reminded him, her tone coming across chiding so he wouldn't let his arrogance lead to mistakes. Underestimating an opponent was the best way to lose to one, in Tamar's estimation. The humans weren't stupid or weaklings, despite the way much of the *Issiana's* crew talked about them. Tamar never scolded that sentiment as commander, since that kind of talk did much for morale, but she wouldn't engage in it herself, and she didn't need the distraction from Neyral in the middle of battle.

"Of course," Neyral said, sounding defensive. He looked down at his console. "All personnel still working at peak efficiency."

Tamar refocused herself on the task at hand. "Are there any more orbital defense platforms?"

Tendell scanned the area. "None on this side of the planet. There is one in orbit that is projected to be in range within the hour."

"Keep watch for it. We don't want it honing in on any of our fighters." The planet closed in on the display, a pretty world, with land of a soft purple-red hue, and murky green waters that looked striking from orbit. The main city of Esare was easy to spot, even from this distance. It was built out, with a glow of lights. "Are the fighters ready to deploy?" Tamar asked.

"They're standing by," Neyral said.

"Launch."

Neyral input the command. Dozens of single-pilot fighters launched from the *Issiana's* center docking bay. They would be able to penetrate the atmosphere and return again. Most importantly, they could strike small, precise targets, unlike the *Issiana's* broad stroke weaponry. That would avert civilian casualties and allow the Aryshans to maintain the moral high ground in this war.

The display switched to a bifurcated view of the fighter squadron leaders. The squadrons dipped into Esare's atmosphere. In some ways, Tamar was envious of the fighter pilot's experience. She fondly recalled a parade for the Ruling Committee where a squadron performed an overhead fly-by. The roaring sound of the fighters descending had been exhilarating. Just like she imagined the experience of herself flying one would be.

But that wasn't her calling. She didn't have the reaction times in the academy to be recruited for that path, and she needed to use the gifts she had for the good of the Aresh. Those gifts were in analytics and leadership. Those had been identified early in life. How they came up with the proficiency tests, Tamar had never researched, but they had surprising accuracy rates.

The best she could do now was watch her lead pilots through their transmissions below the clouds. The features on the ground moved, appearing a blur on the display.

The leader of Thunder Squadron fired his plasma cannons. Destruction plumed from the bird's eye view of the planet. The Lightning Squadron fired their volley soon after. The humans hadn't even been able to mount their defenses. A flitter launched from their base, but the rear pilots of the Lightning Squadron were able to shoot it out of the sky. They had nothing. If all human targets were this easy, this war would be over before the *Issiana* could get back to Aryshan space.

The two squadrons looped around opposite each other to make another pass. This time, there was some surface-to-air fire. The humans must have made it to their stations. She'd heard their reaction times were much slower than Aryshans, but this was the first Tamar had seen it in action. After the second volley of plasma cannon fire, the human military base had been reduced to rubble. No building left standing. Perhaps Neyral had been right in his conceit about the attack. Tamar was content to remain vigilant all the same.

The view of their city was somewhat disturbing. The damage they'd caused was more than they intended. That meant there would be some civilian causalities. Tamar imagined the people who had nothing to do with this, in their homes, their workplaces. One moment they had a normal day, the next, laser fire destroyed everything around them. Despite herself, she turned her head away. She didn't want to think about the innocent lives, and she couldn't afford to. No one in her position would be able to do the job they needed to if they dwelled on that.

"Attack run complete," Neyral said. "All targets obliterated." Pride dripped from his voice. "That was majestic."

"None can stand against the power of the Aresh in battle," Intrei said. The pride was contagious through the bond.

"We'll see how many more of these raids the humans will take before they back off our space and leave us in peace," Tendell said.

"Indeed. Ensure the bay doors are closed and we're ready to launch the moment the fighters have returned," Tamar said. "We don't want to wait around until the human fleet gets wind of this and brings their ships into the system. That fight wouldn't be so easy." She stood from her seat. "I'm going to head to the bay and personally thank the pilots who risked their lives for the tribe and for our people. Anyone who wishes to join me is welcome."

Tendell nodded to that, as did Intrei. For the first time since her tenure as Speaker began, Tamar felt something new through the bond, something positive coming from all of the other commanders. Respect.

It brought a smile to her face. Her first victory was a sweet taste, indeed. If the *Issiana* could maintain this level of work in combat, the war would end soon, just as Tendell had said. That could only be a good thing.

25

Smoke filled the chamber. Sean worked frantically to find the automated shutoff valve via his console. The ship's systems weren't complicated, but he hadn't worked with Aryshan designs before. He glanced to his side, where several other young operations officers monitored their own systems.

The controls, with their different shapes and symbols, were foreign to Sean, yet familiar. The two different memory patterns conflicted in his head and caused him to mentally stutter. He used his instincts to navigate through a couple of screens and found the air vent that caused the problem. He isolated that vent, flushed the system downstream, and closed it off.

The smoke stopped flooding into the room, the ventilation return pulling what was left of it out. Sean smiled to himself. Mission accomplished.

Then all hell broke loose.

The ship rocked. The station next to him exploded, sparks flying in the face of the officer standing there. The officer spun and fell to the ground in pain. This place was going to blow apart at any moment.

Sean bent down in front of the officer next to him to see if he could help. The man stopped moving. Flames engulfed the control panel. Heat flickered toward Sean. He righted himself and rushed over to the fire extinguisher rack, unlocking the device and spinning around. When he looked down at himself, he saw his hand was bleeding.

He couldn't be bleeding. At least he couldn't let it be seen, but he had more pressing matters at hand. Sean rushed over to the flaming console. He sprayed the chemical onto the display, putting out the fire.

Other officers approached through the haze of both leftover smoke and the flame retardant. Sean did his best to hide his bloody hand. He rubbed it against his side pant leg. The dark uniform concealed any potential hazard from it.

The officer stopped in front of him. It was McCleever. Disappointment dripped across his face. "You're bleeding, Lieutenant," he said.

Sean bit his lip. He tried his best to hide it, but what else could he have done in this situation? He couldn't have wrapped his hand or it would have been worse. "I shouldn't have gone for the fire extinguisher. Too much stray metal around to catch myself on."

"That won't save you if the Aryshans see your red blood," McCleever said. His eyes shot toward the ceiling, or rather the hidden cameras there that the intelligence analysts were monitoring. "End simulation." He returned his attention to Sean. "You did incredibly well for a crisis, to be honest. Finding that vent shutoff was no easy task, given your limited knowledge. I just hope our dated knowledge of Aryshan systems is a close enough approximation for what you'll expect on the military vessels."

Sean nodded in agreement. "Thank you, sir. It still amazes me how much I *know* about all of this."

McCleever chuckled. "Us as well. I wish we could control the little things like bleeding. Would make me rest easier."

"I don't intend on bleeding if I can help it," Sean said. He was just as scared as McCleever about the prospect, but he had to stay positive. He couldn't work under the assumption that his different circulatory system would cause problems.

"Good, because you're going to have to head out sooner rather than later. We've found a transport that's been slated to go from Drenite space into the Aryshan Empire, to a drop off point at Sirdanse Station. It's leaving in a couple of days, which means we have to get you out of here almost immediately. There's no time for more simulations."

Sean froze mid-breath. So soon? He had only been doing the simulations for a week. McCleever had told him there'd be significantly more time. They were at the mercy of the Aryshans and outside transports.

"You have a full cover story being implanted into the Aryshan nets and, fortunately, we timed this well enough with an Aryshan personnel transfer request that was put in by a ship a little over a month ago. Are you good with the details on how to transmit information to our satellite pods in Aryshan space so as to not be detected?"

"Yeah, I got it," Sean said.

"Then that's all we can do here." McCleever held out his hand. "It's been a pleasure working with you, Lieutenant. You're one of the best who have come through here. Be safe, you hear?"

Sean shook McCleever's hand firmly, despite the blood on his own hand. "Thank you. I'll see you in a few months' time?"

McCleever grinned. "Let's go with that."

The simulation bay doors opened and one of McCleever's staffers came in. McCleever gave the staffer some orders to escort Sean to medical to patch up his hand, and then take him to the hovercar that would drop him off at the Cestus III spaceport.

26

Tamar reclined in the chair in her bedroom. Ever since the *Issiana* had reentered FTL, on the way back to Aryshan space, she hadn't wanted to be around the crew. Too many of them had formed a conceited attitude about the humans, a brashness in her mind, one that their surprise assault shouldn't have created. The humans were still dangerous. When they were prepared, they wouldn't provide such feeble resistance as the Esare colony had. She had studied their interactions with the Drenites and seen how overconfidence shaped the outcome of that war. And the Drenites had more of a certainty that they had the moral high ground.

The more she thought about it, the whole conflict still felt wrong. It wasn't outright aggression on the Aryshan part, but she couldn't help but feel a nagging sense in the back of her mind that they should be working on accords with the humans, not making eventual peace harder. She recalled an Aresh philosopher who said differently, though, that one could not compromise until an enemy had been subdued. Who had that been? It'd been so long since she studied philosophy.

Her door chime rang.

Tamar stood and stepped into the reception room, unsure who would be visiting. She received very few visitors, barring emergencies, and usually then it was someone calling over the comm. She tensed, considering that Neyral might be here to make another advance. She couldn't hide from that, but she was prepared to tell him to go away. "Door open," Tamar said, triggering the door mechanism's release.

It opened to reveal Intrei. That gave her more surprise. Tamar stood.

"You don't have to get up on my account," Intrei said, stepping inside Tamar's quarters. She scanned the small room. "You keep things clean, not many personal effects."

"I don't spend much time on personal matters."

"Mmm," Intrei said, somewhat flatly. What did she mean by that?

"Can I help you?" Tamar asked.

"Ah, yes. We're returning to Aryshan space, and then to Sirdanse Station. I thought I would let you know personally that I intend on departing once we arrive."

Tamar had just been getting comfortable with this commanding committee set up. Intrei, while not as vocal as the two men, provided a grounding element to their decisions that required a vote. Tamar didn't like this at all. "Intrei, we need you here. I'm certain that, after our success, the Ruling Committee will place us on more assignments, harder ones. We all like working with you and we respect your input."

Intrei waved at Tamar to stop her. "You flatter me, though I do feel through the bond that your words are earnest. But my tour of service is complete." She paused, eyes flicking to Tamar's sparse room. "And let's say that I want to focus more on a return to personal matters the fleet doesn't allow."

Tamar couldn't help but have a sinking feeling. What would the new commanding committee look like without Intrei? "Is there nothing I can say to change your mind? We can give you leave, personal time?"

A tug of unease came through the bondsense. "I won't hide anything from you, Speaker. I don't have the sense that this war effort is something I want to participate in. I would prefer to keep that between us, but since my commitment to the fleet is complete, it makes a good time to bow out before matters get worse." Intrei shrugged. "There could be a draft if they do get worse, and you may see me back."

That sentiment shook Tamar. Enough that she couldn't conceal her own emotions through the bond.

"You feel the same way," Intrei said.

Tamar nodded. "I will do my duty and trust in our tribe," she said, even though the words sounded flat and dispassionate to her own ears.

Intrei nodded, her expression grave. She reached into her satchel and produced a datapad. "Here is my complete resignation form, and my recommendation for a replacement. She is a medical officer, Maela, and has been due for promotion for some time. I've already secured permission through the personnel division. It is, of course, up to the rest of the commanding committee to approve her, but barring you having your own preferences, I think she would do well."

"We'll take your recommendation with heavy weight," Tamar said, taking the datapad from her hand. "Thank you for coming to me. And thank you for everything you've done. I don't know how I would have handled my first days as a commander without your guiding hand."

"You did well." Intrei smiled. "Better than most on their first assignments. I see what First Speaker Ny'aet sees in you."

"Thank you for the compliment."

"It was earned." Intrei dropped her smile and returned to a formal tone and manner. "It was a pleasure serving with you, Speaker. Thank you for your time."

"The pleasure was mine, Commander Intrei," Tamar said.

The other woman turned and exited, leaving Tamar alone with the datapad. Tamar pulled up the profile of medical officer Maela and reviewed it. Stellar marks on all fronts, a prodigy and younger officer for advancement, much like herself. She had no preference of her own to replace Intrei, and Maela seemed a fine choice.

Tamar returned to her bedroom, plopped into her chair, and let out a sigh. So many changes, so quickly. She hoped she would be able to keep her head on straight through all of them.

PART III

27

Sean stared in the mirror, touching the crown that circled his skull. Even after the transit time into Aryshan space, he still couldn't believe how real his Aryshan features felt. They were even sensitive to the touch. His whole complexion had changed.

Throughout the journey on the large cargo ship, Sean hadn't mustered the bravery to step outside his quarters. He hadn't felt ready to speak with others in his new Aryshan form. No matter how he felt, he would have his trial by fire soon.

Even though McCleever had told him he was as ready as they could get him in the short time period, Sean would have liked more study, more trial runs to ensure he would be safe aboard an Aryshan vessel. It would be difficult enough, blending in among those who had their tribes, though from the intelligence gathered, a tribe only comprised about fifty percent of any given crew on average. Enough to assert dominance when situations required it, but also allowing for the intermingling and workings of other tribes, or the uncommitted, to work among them. The uncommitted were under pressure from the various tribes at all times to join their ranks, but committing to a tribe was a permanent decision, something Sean found difficult to relate to. Not that he was disloyal by nature, but he liked having options.

The bondsense concept confused him to some degree. How would the Aryshans not sense he was out of place? The intelligence trainers assured him he shouldn't worry. They claimed there were enough uncommitted among adult Aryshans that he wouldn't be too out of place. In theory, he should be perfectly safe and fit into their military structure with no problems. Theory didn't assure him as much as it should have.

To make matters worse, tensions had escalated even further between Earth and Arysha during his weeks-long roundabout journey into Aryshan space. The full might of both fleets had been deployed to the border following the attack on the Esare colony—not clustered together, but spread out in a web across the border region. Any one of those ships interacting with the opposite side could set off a chain reaction of devastation.

The concept of putting a fleet out in space to defend a border was an antiquated representation of two-dimensional battles from ancient times. It was impossible to defend open space like that. There would never be enough ships. Each side still managed to assemble enough of a line of ships to create heightened conflict.

Smaller conflicts sprang up regularly on the border worlds, despite the bolstered fleets. Humans had been interned on Nan-Vega, the only shared planet between the species. Now, both species laid claim to owning it. Ownership hadn't been an issue before, as the world was primarily occupied by a more moderate Aryshan faction. A fight broke out in a commerce district, which led to Aryshans taking hostages. Diplomatic talks had done nothing to secure their release. In turn, Earth and its various colonies demanded the deportation of all Aryshans from its space, similar to the proclamation Sean had seen back on Palmer Station.

Sean had been lucky that the cargo ship that transported him to Aryshan space had been allowed through the Drenite side. A real disaster could have occurred if they had been able to trace his path of travel back further. Every thought made him jumpy. He needed to calm down if he were to succeed.

The journey provided him some time to study his assignment for his new Aeveron identity. He was going to join the junior officer corps in operations aboard a ship called the *Issiana*. After doing some digging, Sean found that it had been the same ship that visited Palmer Station while he was there. A cursory scan of the personnel bios brought him to a picture of a woman he would never forget. She had been sitting in the restaurant that evening when security apprehended the saboteur. It wasn't just the jarring moment that allowed him to recognize her—it was that her face had been so striking in and of itself. Her silver skin shone so blemish free, like the digitally edited actors in holomovies. For a while, Sean stared at her picture, fascinated. Then he looked at her information. Chavi Tamar di Aresh, commander and Speaker of the *Issiana*. She would be his ultimate authority.

That was dangerous. What if she recognized him? It would be a long shot, especially with his recent body modifications, but it still posed some danger. His curiosity still lingered about her. Tamar had familial connections in the highest of Aryshan circles, and she had interned for the First Speaker of the Aryshan Ruling Committee. That was why they placed him on her ship. They must have hoped he might learn more than just basic Aryshan ship systems.

He would have to get close to her for the mission. Which didn't sound all that bad to him. Or was he convincing himself of that because he found her so physically captivating? Those sorts of emotions hadn't stirred in Sean for a long time, since his academy days. He'd always been on the move, never in one place for long during his tenure with Internal Affairs. He'd focused on work, never considering what building a lasting relationship of his own might be like. It's what jarred him somewhat when Reyna had been so forward on Palmer Station. She would have been a better fit for him than this Aryshan commander.

What even prompted him to think about this woman in those terms? He stood and paced around his cramped cabin to try to clear his head, but it did very little good. When he returned to his console, Sean shifted the view away from Tamar's profile to an exterior view of the cargo ship. A modular station grew in the distance, lighting the darkness of space with thousands of tiny specks shining into the night. That meant they were approaching his destination. Soon, he would have to report to the *Issiana*. If only there were a few more days in transit for him to study, to grow more comfortable in his Aryshan skin. He regretted not conversing casually with some of the other passengers and crew.

Sean stared at the station a while longer before lying down on his mattress. Even at this distance, the ship wouldn't dock for hours. It might prove his best chance for a good sleep for the next several months. From here on out, he would be living afraid, surrounded by the enemy.

28

Tamar glanced over her manifest. The *Issiana* would arrive at Sirdanse Station shortly, and she liked to be familiar with at least the officers among the new crew. It still brought her discomfort to think of Intrei leaving, but the older woman didn't seem to have any regrets or indecisiveness regarding the matter. Intrei kept working at her station and maintained a cheerful attitude. She would be missed.

Tamar turned her attention to Neyral, who was also busy in his own work. He apparently sensed her eyes on him and looked up, giving her a small smile. She quickly averted her gaze, lest he get the wrong idea. What would Neyral think when the command structure shifted? He didn't seem worried; nor did Tendell, for that matter.

Which meant she shouldn't worry either. Commander Maela, Intrei's replacement, was part of the tribe. She would desire the same positive outcomes as Tamar and the others. It wasn't so much the personal elements that bothered her, but more the new face in the scope of such danger with Earth.

The overall strategy still didn't make sense to Tamar. The humans could be called overly-aggressive in their expansions toward Aryshan space, but the crisis level had escalated overnight because of Speaker

Ny'aet's decisions. What did he desire? A master plan to solidify his leadership? The other tribes spread rumors through their media channels, and they were distrusting, not falling in line. And if Ny'aet had made a mistake and fell out of power, where would that leave her? Would she even maintain this speakership without his influence?

Neyral finished a conversation across from her, removed his earpiece and headed for her station, then leaned on her console. "Speaker, do you have a free moment?" he asked.

"Of course, what's on your mind?" Tamar sensed ease from him. His operations work would be rote while they docked, most of the work being done station-side as they would slave the ship's controls to Sirdanse's to bring in the *Issiana* securely.

"We're a day out of Sirdanse Station. Repairs are scheduled, supplies ready to ship, and we have our personnel changes to address," he said.

"I was just looking those over myself. Would you like to compare notes?" Tamar asked.

"That was my thought."

"What have you found on our new officers?" The marines and enlisted would be handled by the officer corps themselves, but what Tamar worried about was the officers' management skills. In future battles, they had to be even more efficient than they'd been at Esare.

Neyral smiled. "I haven't looked much into the marines or fighter pilots," he said, echoing Tamar's own thoughts. As much as he irked her personally sometimes, he did have similar thought processes for leadership, which had made the commanding committee a smooth operation thus far. "I've spent the most time on Commander Maela's profile." He glanced over in Intrei's direction. "With such a strong recommendation from our current commander, perhaps it would be unnecessary, but I like to know who I'll be working with directly. She has accolades in her record from prior assignments as one of the better medics in the fleet. She was last assigned to a military hospital on Trytarr, where she worked in a managerial capacity over other doctors. That leadership credential is likely what garnered the Ruling

Committee's attention to get her this assignment. I have actually had the pleasure of meeting her personally at a conference a number of years back. She's quite capable."

"I believe we have as good a replacement for Intrei as we could possibly get, not that she can be replaced," Tamar said, giving a nod in Intrei's direction.

Intrei returned the gesture.

"Next on my list for review," Neyral said, "is Lieutenant Tol. He is listed primarily as a pilot, but he also has a background in physics and technological maintenance."

"Versatile," Tamar said.

"Indeed. We have an opportunity to maximize his potential. He does have warning marks on his record because of his, and I quote, 'prolonged and unwanted tinkering.' There weren't details listed, but the commander's tone in the marks did not seem positive. My personal opinion is that a voice with unorthodox ideas to make the ship operate more efficiently can only be a benefit to this crew."

"Perhaps that tinkering interfered with his primary duties?" Tamar asked. Bad marks on a record made her nervous, even though Neyral seemed to ignore the prospect.

"I looked into that. His hours logged in piloting duty were as near perfect as one gets. I think we may have found a hidden gem here."

"Good work," Tamar said, hopeful he was right. She ran her finger over the console, sifting through more records. They had more than a dozen other personnel being added to the roster, though none she could see involved in key positions like the ones Neyral had mentioned. Except for one, listed as a new officer in the operations department. "What about this one?"

Neyral leaned over for a closer look. "Junior Lieutenant Aeveron. An operations, diagnostics, and forensics specialist. His name was placed on the list from command without any of our input. I researched his background and found his qualifications didn't match anything on our current manifest. If his background holds true, he will certainly be another crewman of interest to me."

To me as well, Tamar thought. The Ruling Committee had

assigned him directly? That gave Tamar red flags. Was it someone else First Speaker Ny'aet thought to stack the ship with for some secret assignment? She would have to watch for this Aeveron. "Thank you for the detailed information, Commander," Tamar said, signaling Neyral's dismissal.

Neyral smiled and hovered back over to his station. He immediately went to work on his console and didn't look up at Tamar when he spoke. "Do you have any plans for our couple days' reprieve on the station, Speaker?"

Tamar tensed. He was fishing for personal time, as he always did. "I'm going to be reading over tactical reports. We all need to familiarize ourselves with the details of the border situation so we can be prepared. We're bound to be deployed for something important again soon."

"Of course," Neyral said. His eyes pierced her with intensity. "I could assist you in your research if you'd like. I don't have other plans."

"No," Tamar said, a little more defensively than she meant to be. Her aura must have been off-putting, as the other commanders inclined their heads toward her. "I study best in quiet and solitude." And she needed that now. "I think I'll walk the ship for a visual inspection—make sure there's nothing our repair crews might have missed in their planning."

If Neyral seemed deterred or even hurt, he didn't show it. He still held his gaze on her with hard intensity. "Very well. Let me know if you find anything."

Tamar left her station and made for the door without another word.

29

When Sean stepped from the airlock into the corridors of Sirdanse Station, it was late by standard time. The station dimmed its lights to give the artificial sense of time. A cool color reflected off the metallic walls. Unlike the human equivalents, there were no open space areas to relieve the cramped sense of being in a metal can. The walls were also much thicker than those he had seen anywhere in Earth's jurisdiction, causing the corridors to feel narrow. His original cultural dossier had mentioned that the wall thickness was used to dampen the effects of the Aryshan bondsense between sections, in order to give a sense of privacy.

The hallway itself was sparsely populated, Sean being one of the first out of the transport. He had wanted to get out of the cramped transport, but found himself feeling equally confined as he had been.

He had to forget Sean and become Aeveron, the low-level officer with a history in operations rather than investigations. A track record of diligent, hard work. The background would allow him access to key ship systems without drawing much attention. He only hoped he had learned enough about Aryshan operations to be able to fudge the position. Everyone had a learning curve on a new assignment, right? With technology over the last several hundred years coming from an assortment of species, mixing and refining over time, it wasn't all that different from the systems he'd seen on human ships. But there were specifics the intelligence community wanted him to find out, to analyze and improve their tactics, and hopefully avoid repeats of the thus-far disastrous engagements between the humans and Aryshans.

The corridor wound until it came to a series of guest registration consoles. The check-in terminal required an identification crystal scan: his first test to see whether Aeveron's credentials would work. Thinking about it gave him pause. A couple of the other passengers from the transport brushed past him to scan their own identities. None of them seemed worried. He didn't want to stand out.

Sean stepped to the console. What if it didn't work and station security pounced on him? That would be a quick end to his mission, *and* his life. But the time for worrying about that had long passed. He was here now. There was no turning back.

He scanned the crystal.

The console light glowed blue—the Aryshan equivalent to green —and the check-in terminal took his information, flashing it on the screen in front of him. His quarters wouldn't be ready for another few hours, but he had access to all non-secure clearance areas.

Another passenger had finished scanning his own crystal at a neighboring terminal. Sean asked for recommendations for a first-time traveler to Sirdanse Station. The man pointed him to a bar on the same level, three sections over. A purported hotspot for transients and a good place to socialize.

Sean followed the directions and found his way to the bar, an open area cut into the wall of the corridor that formed into a half circle, its design feeling similar to a cave structure. The bar top itself was thick as the walls, as were all the tables. Dozens of people sat, consuming food and drink. Strange atonal music played in the background just below the conversation noise.

He took a seat on a barstool, glancing at the digital menu that had been imprinted into the bar top. Truth was, he wasn't familiar with Aryshan beverage choices. There would be a lot of gaps in the cultural imprinting that the nanites had provided him, gaps that existed within the intelligence community. He would have to learn and improvise on the fly and act naturally in the process. A bartender bot came by, asking Sean to make his order by selecting on the bar top. Sean pointed to one at random.

An Aryshan seated next to him noted the choice. He looked up at Sean and smiled. "You have good taste," he said. "Ruy'ach Oti is not a drink for soft stomachs."

Not for soft stomachs? Aryshans had much heartier systems than humans. This order might prove a mistake, but as Aeveron, he had to act like he knew what he was doing. He smiled in return. The bot placed a full glass in front of him. Sean lifted it toward the man next to him, then took a sip.

He nearly gagged on the liquid in his mouth. He couldn't describe anything about it other than it tasted like *burn*. When he swallowed, it felt like someone had taken a torch to his throat.

Despite himself, Sean maintained his smile instead of choking.

"Amazing, isn't it?" the Aryshan asked.

"That's one word for it," Sean said, barely able to choke out the words. He turned to the server bot. "Perhaps some water as well?"

The Aryshan didn't miss a beat, laughing. "My name is Lieutenant Eridel Tol di Aresh," he said. He swirled the liquid in his own glass and dropped back his own concoction with ease.

"Retai Aeveron," Sean said in return.

"Uncommitted?"

Sean nodded.

"Huh," Tol said, his expression unreadable. His eyes brightened a moment later. "Are you from the station? No, I suppose you wouldn't be if you're in the transient lounge. I'm newly assigned to the *Issiana*, which should be docking here soon. Piloting and special projects."

What luck, meeting someone who was transferring to the same ship. If he could make an inroad with Tol it would be a boon for his assignment. Contacts and allies were the most important things an agent could acquire. That line had been told to him several times during the last few months. "What a coincidence. I'm transferring to the *Issiana* as well."

"From where?" Tol asked.

This was another test for him, a moment he should have spent practicing while aboard the cargo transport. Now he had to produce his newfound memories as if they were real to someone who would be serving with him for the duration of his assignment. "Just a home-world base assignment. Nothing exciting," Sean said.

"Ahh, to be back on homeworld. I miss how alive one feels with so many tribemates around. Though I suppose you wouldn't have experienced that. To be as one with so many..." he paused and exhaled. "It's exhilarating. I miss Eridel some days, but this is where we signed on to serve our people." Tol stared vacantly into his drink, then shook his head back to reality. "Sorry, it's a rare treat even to think about. I've been on deep space assignments these past couple years."

It sounded as if he wanted to vent. Which was good. Sean had passed the small personal details test so far well enough to blend in. Then again, he had been told that Aryshans were inherently more trusting than humans of their fellows because of their tribal bonds. He shouldn't have to worry, but it would be difficult not to be on edge until he returned safely to human space. Already, he wished this assignment would be over. "Assignments, plural? I didn't know pilots moved that much."

"Not typically, no. Commanding committees rarely wish to lose a person who knows a ship well. All ships are different, with their own quirks, even if it's similar design."

"Then why—?"

Tol signaled the server bot for another drink. "I mentioned special assignments. I like to create. It's difficult to explain without going into each instance individually. Anything that requires electrical or mechanical engineering is of great interest to me. If you have a moment later, I'd be happy to show you my quarters here. I've amassed quite a bit of work."

A pilot with a side of engineering? Tol must have been a valuable asset. Sean brought his glass to his lips again, pretending to take another small sip of that vile liquid. "Different commanders are clamoring to have you aboard?"

Tol laughed, though bitterness came through with it. "Not exactly. You see, they often can't wait to get rid of me. It's sometimes made me wonder if I would better off serving the Aresh in another way. If you look in my file, they call me a liability."

Now Sean understood. Despite being a different culture, this was the military. He hadn't seen many commanders who respected creativity or allowed their subordinates to work to their strengths. Commodore V'bosh had been one of the few to be an exception to the rule, which may have had something to do with his being Tralos. Aryshans with their bonds had to have been even more susceptible to group-think than even Earth's military had been. Sean realized he had been quiet in his thoughts.

"Did I say something to offend you?"

"Offend? No, not at all. I was thinking that your prior commanders must have been short-sighted. Am I wrong?"

Tol gulped down his new drink and leaned in toward Sean. "I won't question their decisions to that degree. I am loyal and serve the Aresh as I can."

"Of course," Sean said, uncertain what else to say about that declaration.

Tol appeared contented with Sean's affirmation. "Good. To spare you time and detail, I started working on a wearable device that creates a field around an individual. It phases a person out from our dimension so that a person both is rendered invisible to the light spectrum and doesn't appear on heat-sensing scanners. The user is half in what I call a null-space and half in real existence. I tested the phase device, but there's a drawback. It drained an inordinate amount of the ship's power. My last commanding committee called me into their chamber, sat me down, deliberated, and told me in no uncertain terms I was doing far more than I was assigned and that was detrimental to the perceived safety of the crew."

Sean wasn't just dealing with someone with a talent for tinkering with systems; this man was a scientific genius. And an unrecognized one. What could this phase device do if it were properly harnessed by a military that understood the magnitude of what Tol was saying? How could the Aryshan commanders have missed this? Just by going to a bar, Sean had struck gold. This was information he could use, but he didn't want to overplay his hand and appear too eager at the same time. Tol sounded used to having his ideas shut down by others. While he wouldn't go that far, he had to stay cool. "That sounds like quite the device," Sean said.

"If I can figure out the power drain situation," Tol said.

Sean glanced around the rest of the transient bar. No other patrons seemed to pay attention to their conversation. "How many people know about this device?"

Tol shrugged. "Not many. I wanted to provide something of use to my tribe, and I never let my side work interfere with my duties, but the others don't see it the same way."

"If you don't mind, I'd be interested in seeing it." He tried to sound as flat as possible, not hungry for information. Set the hook, reel in the fish.

"Really?" Tol's eyes lit with an intense energy. "I'd be happy to show you." Then he frowned. "Except, I'm not sure I can requisition enough energy usage on the station to power it. Storing enough energy could take days, or even weeks, even for a few moments of use."

"It's okay. Do you have anything else that's interesting?"

Tol pursed his lips, then reached into his pants pocket and pulled out a small, translucent tube about the size of the finger he held in the air.

"What's that?" Sean asked.

"It's an odor modifier. Not your typical air freshener: the solution it carries holds nanotechnology that merges with foul particles and removes them completely, using that same principle of null space. You're left with a sterile olfactory environment."

"Handy in crowded bars."

Tol sniffed.

Sean did the same. Body odor from someone at a table nearby was quite ripe. He'd been too nervous to notice it when he first entered, but it trickled through the otherwise filtered air, distinct.

Tol brought the small device to his mouth and blew softly.

The odor depleted. Tol was right. It wasn't like any air freshener Sean had encountered before, nor was it similar to a gas that was pumped into station or ship environmental systems to send pleasing scents. The air around them was devoid of smell. Eerily so. He couldn't help but draw a long breath in through his nose. "An odd sensation, almost a sensory deprivation."

"Isn't it? I haven't found a way to show its usefulness yet. Most who have tested it have found it unnerving."

The Aryshans at tables behind them grumbled about the station's environmental system malfunctioning.

Sean glanced toward the complaining table, and then back to Tol. "Do you focus on manipulating senses with your devices?"

"Never thought of it that way. I haven't analyzed myself too deeply, truth be told. I do enjoy creating new things," Tol said.

That gave Sean an idea. Perhaps he could find a way to further blend into Aryshan society through these devices. "What about a way to block the communication through a bondsense? Have you tried anything with that?"

Tol shook his head. "I couldn't imagine anyone wanting to do that. It would erode all trust within a tribe if someone could switch their aura on and off."

"Not necessarily. Sometimes it can be good to keep feelings private."

"How?" Tol sounded befuddled.

Before Sean could answer, several station maintenance members came over to the bar. They asked a couple of tables about complaints about the environmental systems. At least they provided a quick reaction to potential threats to people's safety.

Tol took note of them as well. "I think it's actually best if I go. In my experience, trouble only follows from unauthorized demonstrations of my work."

Sean took his full glass and raised it to Tol. "I look forward to serving with you aboard the *Issiana*," he said.

30

Tol watched his screen eagerly. Perhaps it was a little presumptuous for him to have researched the location of Aeveron's quarters, found his comm signal, and called him to tell him about his latest breakthroughs. But Aeveron had seemed interested. More eager than anyone else Tol could remember speaking to about his projects. It made him smile, and that smile remained when Aeveron answered his call.

The lights were off in the quarters on the other end of the display, with a glow illuminating Aeveron's face. He looked haggard, with drooping eyes.

Tol had rehearsed what he'd say to the man. "Morning, Aev—" He paused. "Is something wrong?"

"Do you know what time it is?" Aeveron asked with a raspy, dry voice.

"Yes. Oh-four-hundred. I've been up for an hour and a half. I had this idea that was too good to wait. I think I'm onto something, but more than that, it's amusing." He took a deep breath to steady himself. He was talking too fast, too excited. Aeveron needed him to start from the beginning. "What I mean is, I've just had an incredible breakthrough. And since you seemed so interested in my work last night, I took the liberty of looking up your comm code."

Something smelled. Tol sniffed.

Aeveron narrowed his eyes on the other end. "Is that smoke behind you?"

Tol turned around. It was smoke. Rising rapidly and filling his quarters. His eyes widened. "Thanks for the warning, Aeveron. Come over soon. I may need help with this. I'm in section Blue Four, unit thirty-five. Comm off." He heard the sound of the comm unit powering down as he scrambled for his flame retardant.

He didn't use the standard issue stuff, not for his experiments. But he couldn't recall where he left his homemade extinguisher. His eyes darted from corner to corner, searching, when something in the station systems triggered. Water shot from the ceiling, drenching everything within the room. Circuits shorted, his notes were soaked, and sensitive experiments were all systematically destroyed. There was nothing he could do but watch. He hovered over an open circuit board attached to a compressor, using his body to attempt to save some semblance of his null-phase device. All it accomplished was to soak the back of his shirt through to his skin.

"No, no, no!" he shouted at the pipes that lined the ceiling above. The sprinklers ceased their bombardment of his quarters within moments, the last drops of water dripping over his head. All his hard work was lost. He was almost at a place where he could prove his worth to his new commanding committee. He swore it wasn't going to be like his last assignment. But what could he do now with so many expensive components in ruins? It'd take months for the Aresh requisitions department to approve his additional need for replacement parts, unless he had help.

In the immediate term, he had worse problems. Sirdanse Station security was bound to respond, and they would inform his new commander of this incident. He would be an outcast before even setting foot on the *Issiana*. Why did the Overseers hate him so? Hadn't he been faithful?

The door to his quarters opened, and the remaining smoke

rushed out toward the hallway. Tol tried to slide to the doorway and block the view of the catastrophe behind him. Smoke alarms flashed in the hallway beyond. The sprinklers in the hall engaged.

If he had been in trouble before, now it would be devastating. He hadn't just spoiled his private quarters with his carelessness, but the hallway beyond as well. They would have to close off this whole section in clean up.

Fortunately, it wasn't a security officer who greeted him at the door, but Aeveron. Smoke wafted into Aeveron's face before those sprinklers drenched him. He rushed inside and pushed past Tol. "Ugh!" he said.

"Aeveron!" Despite the situation, Tol was happy to see him. It impressed and humbled him that Aeveron would take the time to come see his experiment so quickly after he called.

The water outside stopped, and the doors to his quarters shut behind Aeveron. Tol took a step backward and frowned at the chaos around him. "The null-phase device isn't ready anymore. There seems to have been a malfunction. I'm sorry," Tol said.

Aeveron looked past him. At first, anger filled his eyes, but he shook his head and his expression changed to a humoring, wry smile. "At least I wasn't in here when it caught fire. What happened anyway?"

Tol picked up a piece of dead circuitry. "I thought about our conversation yesterday. About the bondsense and creating a sensory deprivation. And it occurred to me how to make my null-space device consume less power. To spare you technical details, I needed to trick it into thinking null space and reality aren't connected." The device was soaked now, metal burned and oxidized. "I must have crossed wires somewhere."

Now that the smoke had stopped, his quarters looked like a bomb had exploded inside. His mechanical fluids covered the floor, wires rested exposed, and much of his equipment was burnt out in addition to his experimental device. He had hoped to present a better first impression of his workspace to Aeveron, but it was much too late for that.

Aeveron's eyes searched the room, but they didn't appear to cast judgment. "Does this happen to a lot of your experiments?"

Tol felt small, like a *twivvie* herd animal. "Unfortunately," he said.

"We'll have to find a way to be more careful in the future. You wouldn't want to start fires on a warship like the *Issiana*."

Tol blinked. The man cared about his future social standing, and they had just met. It felt better than he'd been treated by many of his bonded tribemates. He had assumed his newfound friend would react like everyone else had when they saw him fail. The thought was almost enough to make Tol forget the scrap heap all around him. He nodded with determination. "I'll try to be more careful next time."

"Next time what?" Another voice came from the door. This one was not nearly as understanding.

Station security had arrived on the scene. The lead guard had a fire extinguisher in hand, ready like a weapon.

"Thank you. Ah, we have everything under control now," Tol said. The security guard was not Aresh. Tol couldn't sense anything from him in earnest, but his anger shone through all the same. At least his own nervousness wouldn't project too far.

The security guard held out his hand. "Name and identification, please. Both of you."

Before Aeveron could speak, Tol stepped toward the security guard. "He wasn't involved. Lieutenant Aeveron was passing by when he saw my slight issue and offered to help." Tol reached into his pocket and produced his identification crystal.

The security guard grunted, taking Tol's crystal. He unhooked an identification scanner from his belt and ran the data. "Your record shows a history of damage to both military and civilian property. By Sirdanse Station law, non-flagrant actions that may cause fire or breach are punishable by compensatory fines to be ascertained by our engineering crew. These will be processed by your closest requisition office and invoiced against your need-share. There could be further detention punishments if the magistrates deem it necessary." He then eyed Aeveron. "If you were truly not a party to this?"

"I wasn't," Aeveron said.

The security guard nodded. "Then you are free to go. Please remain on the station for the next several hours in case we require a statement. Your name should be enough to find you if we need to contact you."

"I accept full responsibility," Tol said, hoping that would be the end to the discussion.

"I need to process you and this incident. If you'll follow me," the guard said, motioning for Tol to vacate the quarters.

Once in the corridor, the security guard pushed Tol ahead. The floor was damp, its fabric swishing under Tol's feet. He looked back over his shoulder to see Aeveron heading the opposite direction. Even with the coming punishment, he worried more about the impression he had left upon his new friend, and hoped he hadn't ruined an opportunity.

31

A holo of the daily news flickered in front of Tamar. She relaxed into a soft cushion at a little-known café on the upper level of Sirdanse Station. The adjacent chair held her ryshbeast-skin handbag containing her tablet, a small tasegun, and her other personal effects. Despite receiving several messages that two of her new officers were involved in a security breach on the station, she was on leave for the next day. It'd been over an hour, and she hadn't bothered to look.

A few sips of hot tea later, a nagging sense of duty overcame her. She grabbed her tablet from the bag to look at the report. The names listed were the very ones Neyral and she had discussed in the committee chambers: Aeveron and Tol. Perhaps they would be names to watch in more ways than they had discussed. But why would First Speaker Ny'aet have assigned them to her if they had such propensity for trouble?

"Tamar," came a distinctly masculine voice from behind her. Speak the names of stormwraiths and they shall arrive.

"First Speaker," Tamar said, sitting up straight and readying herself to get to her feet and salute him. She kept her emotional aura masked the best she could and noticed that Ny'aet did the same.

He crossed around the table in front of her and motioned for her to remain seated. "You're off duty; don't get up on my account. This is a casual visit." His features had aged since she'd last seen him in person. Most considered him handsome for an elder statesman, his crown bone shaped in a regal manner, tight curves that gave a sense of strength to his elegant horns.

At the same time, nothing Ny'aet ever did was casual or a matter of happenstance. He'd planned to meet her here. That's why the personnel requisitions were approved so quickly after their last mission. "What brings you to the station, First Speaker?"

"Ny'aet. You can call me Ny'aet," he insisted. "You are like a daughter to me, Tamar." His voice was deep and poignant when he uttered her name. "I thought you would like to discuss my plans as you seemed so keen on getting the details over interstellar comm."

Tamar bit her lip. Yes, even with secure encryptions, she should have known such communications were unsafe. Though the words chided her, nothing came through the bondsense. Had he become that good at control? It startled her.

"Our sources tell us that the Earth's senate is about to declare formal war on Arysha," he said. "The pretense of conflict is over. Their fleet will be engaging us soon."

Tamar raised a brow. She wished that news surprised her. "Congratulations. That's what you wanted, wasn't it?" she asked.

Ny'aet inclined his head. "Yes. That was the original plan."

Anger welled inside Tamar, but she pushed it down into her gut. She couldn't let Ny'aet sense any lack of control. Intrei had the right of it, retiring to avoid serving in an all-out war. But Tamar was just beginning her career. She was trapped in Ny'aet's plans, whether she liked them or not. The missions up until this point made much more sense now. She only wished she'd been wrong in her concerns. "Hasn't there been enough death already?"

Ny'aet frowned, forming lines under his chin. "The Great Death was caused by humans, Tamar. All we've done is much like our fire rescue teams back home. We set controlled blazes, so that if the storms pick up, and the wind blows fiercely, it doesn't devastate whole regions. Yes, this will result in a small number of casualties, but if we take no action, what will happen this time when their culture trickles through our borders and invades our worlds? The death of all of us and not just a single tribe?"

Even saying it had been a single tribe was an understatement. The Anwii had been both the most powerful and most populous on Arysha and the inner colonies. The suicides that occurred with their leadership triggered so many more in the lower ranks. Tamar hadn't been born yet, but Ny'aet had seen it with his own eyes. "You can't know the humans are responsible, father. Mistakes were made. But we can control what aspects of their individualistic culture impact our greater whole. The Anwii's demise led to the rise of the Aresh by the same means you say leads to destruction. I don't mean to sound callous, but what if it is simply the forces of evolution?"

Ny'aet laughed, but without the sound of joy. "I wish I could be a youthful idealist, but this is why I work so hard to protect you. You believe in our people strongly. Let me put it for you another way, however. You've seen what happens when we encounter viruses from other worlds. When we don't have a resistance, it causes devastation. We can't control the humans as you say. They can't even control themselves. I am the one responsible for our immune system, you have to remember."

"You mean we," Tamar corrected. Stranger still. He sounded more like a human than a member of the Ruling Committee of the Aryshans.

"Of course."

Tamar tried to process the events of these last few months. "You saw the *Issiana's* firing on the human transport as a boon, even though you removed the commander for having such a happy trigger finger."

"We had to present a certain public face. We couldn't allow it to look like we condoned the actions."

"Even though you authorized small attacks in order to provoke Earth into disproportionate response," Tamar said. "What you did was create political solidarity within the Aryshan people, focusing Earth as an enemy."

Ny'aet's gaze became one of pride. "This is why I'm training you for leadership, Tamar. You understand. It's not that I don't believe the humans are an imminent threat, however, but if we control the context, the timing of the battles, we will come out stronger than if this all escalated naturally." He shifted his eyes to the news holo, which had turned to talking about a recent human seizure of an Aryshan supply transport.

Tamar followed his glance there, frowning. "I can see the argument that they're dangerous. But I'm not sure the threat was as imminent as you say." Yes, humans were strange, and she didn't understand them. Her interactions, however, had only involved them attempting to do the right thing. Had she been misled or blinded? She recalled herself following that one human several months ago, so angry that Mynoan had been arrested. She'd blamed him for it and wanted to attack him personally. Could that be a microcosm of how Ny'aet was reacting?

"When this is all over, we'll celebrate," Ny'aet said. "Earth, however, is still moving more slowly than I anticipated. But as soon as they officially declare war, we'll have all of the Aryshan Empire secure and behind us."

"In the meantime, their delay gives us time to prepare."

"Exactly," Ny'aet said, his face showing another flash of pride. "Our analysts have made a list of targets which will disrupt Earth supply lines and tip the balance of power in the region in our favor. We will be conducting a number of surgical strikes to ensure that we will be victorious, and at minimal loss of Aryshan life and Aresh resources."

This was the real reason he was here to talk with her. He wanted to deliver a mission without fear of its being intercepted. "I presume the Ruling Committee wants the *Issiana* to lead one of these missions?"

Ny'aet reached into his shirt pocket and produced a data crystal.

He slid it across the table toward her. "The mission we have in mind for you is relatively simple. It'll be both reconnaissance and a covert operation. You'll send a small crew aboard a shuttle, something that will allow them to move through a planet's security grid undetected, and they'll plant explosives in the proper place. Earth won't know what hit them until it's too late. The briefing is enclosed." He motioned toward the data crystal. "Again, we want to ensure minimal loss of Aryshan life. This isn't like the Esare strike where the humans weren't prepared."

Tamar nodded. "I like this plan better than a frontal assault, as well." It was more elegant and had much less risk of danger.

"Personnel decisions will be up to you. Use your discretion wisely."

Tamar took the data crystal and deposited it into her handbag. She thought about the mission, and it bothered her. "Why wouldn't you just use spies for this purpose?"

"Our spies are information gatherers, and we would like them to remain in place without outing themselves. The humans will see a shuttle come and a shuttle go, which will take the pressure off any internal hunt. We already have Earth ship signatures, access codes and topographical information. I do recall a young commander on border patrol who was eager to get into the thick of the action and planning... this will be your test," Ny'aet said.

Tamar watched him. No matter how much older she became, no matter the accolades she received for her work, she still had to prove herself. Would it always be that way? "Thank you," she said, regardless of her perceived slight. He didn't mean it that way. He never did. It didn't take the sting off, however.

Ny'aet took a step back and bowed his head slightly toward her. "No, thank you, Tamar. These are exciting times. I look forward to a bright future for both you and our people. You will do the Aresh proud."

"Take care of yourself," Tamar said.

"You as well." Ny'aet turned and departed, making his way through the café toward the exit.

The café had become a lot busier during their discussion, littered with Aryshan Naval uniforms, many with Aresh insignias. The bond-sense became a cloud, too dense to pick out any individual auras, though it teemed with excitement. People recognized Ny'aet and some stopped him to shake his hand on the way out. Tamar wished she had that naïve excitement about meeting her leadership, but she'd learned by being around them for so long that they were simply Aryshans, same as anyone else. There was nothing mysterious about them, and they had their moments of brilliance and made mistakes just like her.

While she watched Ny'aet leave, she failed to notice that two dark-haired men approached her. Tamar placed that hair tone as natives to the southern continent. "Speaker Tamar," one man said.

Tamar smiled, recognizing the faces but unsure from where. They both had a familiarity about them. One had the Aresh insignia, but the other had none—uncommitted. "Hello," Tamar said.

"We are new members of your crew. I'm Lieutenant Tol and this is Lieutenant Aeveron," Tol said, gesturing to his companion as they introduced themselves.

These were the two members of her crew she and Neyral had discussed, recently in trouble with station security. She hadn't had time to read the specifics of the report, but now she was more curious. Tol projected an aura of nervousness. He likely was worried about her scolding him for making a ruckus on the station.

"Nice to meet the both of you," Tamar said. She recalled that Tol was a pilot, and a reputable one at that. A perfect choice for Ny'aet's mission. "I'd actually like to speak with you when we board the *Issiana*, Lieutenant Tol. You've got some trouble on your record, and I have a mission that, if you perform, will give you a chance to redeem yourself."

Tol's eyes brightened as if he'd received a great gift. "Yes, ma'am. Thank you."

Aeveron stayed quiet. He would have faded into the background if Tamar hadn't been so observant, but he watched her closely. She met his eyes briefly, and he shifted his gaze away from her.

"Very well," Tamar said. "I hope you enjoy the rest of your leave before we board." That would signal they were dismissed. She liked her solitude and time of reflection when she could get it.

The two men said their goodbyes and let her be.

32

Sean couldn't help but glance over his shoulder at Speaker Tamar. On Palmer station, when he had seen her for the first time, he'd thought she had a captivating element. Upon seeing her again he couldn't bring himself to look away. Those thoughts were dangerous. He had a mission to accomplish, and any distraction would have been bad enough, but he couldn't let himself get caught up in his commander, of all people.

It was a good thing that he'd found himself dumbfounded enough in her presence to be unable to speak. He turned to follow Tol, keeping his head fixed forward so he wouldn't be tempted to stare again.

Sean had been so lost in Tamar that he'd almost forgotten his whereabouts. He'd met up with Tol after his friend had been released by security. They were fortunate that Speaker Tamar hadn't mentioned Tol's security problems, or even appeared irked about the matter—though she had dismissed them quickly. Sean glanced at his companion, deciding he wouldn't bring up the negative topic. If Tol wanted to talk about it, he would.

Tol dropped back to walk by his side, grinning at him, no concern in his face at all. He craned his head back in Tamar's direction, all too obviously. "Interesting. I don't think I've ever seen someone's pheromones have so direct an impact on him before. It may merit further study."

"How did you know—?" Sean asked, mouth hanging open.

"Besides the fact that your eyes haven't moved from her since we've arrived? Even though you're not part of the tribe, you're broadcasting emotions so intense that they'd be felt across a whole planet." Tol chuckled.

"I'm not sure if I should be offended."

"Don't be. You've given me an idea for my brainstorming notebook. A cologne that stimulates desirable pheromones. Perhaps if we get the chemical mix right, you can try it out on her and see if she notices you in the same way. I'd ask you to log your observations so we could study it scientifically, of course," Tol said.

Sean wrinkled his nose. "You shouldn't make fun of me, Mr. Arsonist." He immediately regretted those words after uttering them. They hadn't been acquainted long enough for Sean to be joking like that. Did Aryshans even rib each other in the way humans did? Tol's teasing implied it, but Sean feared he went too far.

"No need to be rude. I was just offering to help with my inventions. I really think you should try it," Tol said. "Besides, that's all buzzing through the groundwater now."

Some phrases didn't quite translate, and even though Sean had learned the language, his nanite-driven memories didn't come with a complete list of idioms. It reminded him to be careful about using human terms. He wouldn't want to have to explain things he regularly said, like *striking out* for instance. The good news was, though Tol didn't understand the humor, he didn't appear too offended. Bullet dodged. "Maybe later." He had to change the topic. "A special mission already, though. That sounds exciting, doesn't it?"

Tol turned a corner as they walked, his forehead creasing when he considered Sean's words. "She must have heard of my piloting skills."

"I thought you said your former commanders posted negative reports on you?" Sean asked.

"Those were because of my side activities. I've always been a good pilot. My record there is impeccable, but the commanding committees are never able to separate my on-duty and off-duty matters. I hope the *Issiana* will prove different." His words sounded bright and optimistic.

"I think she is," Sean said absently.

"She?" Tol laughed.

"I meant the commanding committee." *Dammit.* She really had done a number on him. He had to maintain his focus. Any slipup could be too dangerous to recover from.

"You're thinking far too much. It's against regulations for a commander to fraternize with subordinates," Tol said. He paused at his doorway. The carpet had already been cleaned and there was no sign of the earlier experimental failure. An efficient station to say the least.

"It is?" Sean asked, stopping along with Tol.

"Oh, Aeveron. You're far too gullible. I'll have this to hold over you forever. Thank you. Without your friendship, I'm not sure I would have been able to power through the storm of these last hours." His smile was wide and earnest. "Yes, there are regulations, but when chemistry happens, it happens. When two become entwined, nothing can break them apart."

Entwined. That word jolted Sean. He'd heard it before. It was an Aryshan word for marriage. He forced a smile. "I don't think we'll have to worry about that anytime soon."

"Especially with someone like Speaker Tamar. She's First Speaker Ny'aet's protégé. A lower-level officer like you or me would find trouble catching her attention. Many higher-ranking officers will be courting her, if she hasn't already pre-committed."

Sean frowned, though he quickly tried to hide the expression. Why did the conversation keep coming back to this? He didn't want anything to do with a relationship with any Aryshan. Their physicality, their anatomy... There were too many variables that would lead to one result: his being caught and executed. Tol wasn't helping matters.

"Don't look so upset," Tol said. "It's all in good fun. I need to salvage what's left of my equipment and move my belongings to the ship. Let's talk after my meeting with Speaker Tamar. Maybe I'll have good news."

"Yeah, you're right," Sean said. "I look forward to hearing about it." He waved a goodbye, and Tol disappeared into his quarters. Sean walked down the hallway, still unable to purge Speaker Tamar from his thoughts.

33

The corridors of the *Issiana* glistened with pulsing holos of the Aresh symbol. For the uncommitted that might have seemed oppressive, but for Tol, it reminded him he was home among compatriots.

Tol never had a knack for aesthetic designs. Everything he constructed thus far had been a jumbled mess of protruding wires, welded scrap metal, or parts that appeared as if they had no place in the unit. In many ways, he was envious. What a rush it must have been for the designers to have conceptualized such a high-quality ship. He would never progress so far into design, even if he were given the opportunity to engineer such a vessel. Such a big engineering project required immense payments. It didn't lend itself toward trying new things.

Then again, he wouldn't have imagined Speaker Tamar summoning him for a special piloting mission either. If he had extra bounce in his step, and he did feel much lighter—though that could have been the gravity plates on the ship instead of the station—it would be because he finally had a commander who believed in him.

Lost in far too many thoughts, he ran his fingers across the plating on the wall in front of him. The finishes of the *Issiana* were so sleek, so perfect. Perhaps with a little extra effort, he could make his own inventions shine like the ship. Was that how he could demonstrate value to the commanding committee? The ship wasn't all show. It had raw power and ability.

As would his null-phase device, when he completed it.

Tol weaved his way through the halls toward the committee chambers. When he came to the door, he saw a petite woman coming from the opposite direction. She was short for an Aryshan, dark hair flowing down to the small of her back. She had perfect proportions for her shape and was healthily toned. Worse, he knew who she was.

His stomach felt like it dropped out of his body.

The woman turned, facing him. She tilted her head coolly, instant concern radiating through the bondsense. "Tol?" she asked. Even in uttering one word, her voice sounded like music.

"Maela," Tol said, trying to keep his voice steady. "It's been years." All of his thoughts of missions or strange devices disappeared. All that was left was her. What was she doing here?

His fear must have been overwhelming to her. She averted her eyes toward the floor. The bondsense swelled with regret from the both of them. "I didn't know you were coming to this ship."

"I didn't know you were either," Tol said. He wanted to reach out and touch her, but dared not. He remembered her skin like it was yesterday. So soft, something he could never forget. They'd come very close to entwining. Close didn't count in such things, however. He did notice a rank insignia different than his—commander. She wouldn't just be his crew mate; she would be leading him. He tried to dampen his nervousness. "I've been assigned as a pilot."

Maela met his eyes once more. "You're one of the best pilots there are," she said, as if sensing his lack of confidence. She gave him a reassuring smile, seeming in that moment as if nothing had happened between them. "How is your mother doing?"

Tol shrugged. "I've been off-world on various assignments for some time. I don't speak to her that often. What about you? How's...?"

The question went dead on his lips. Had she entwined with another man? If she told him the answer and it was yes, how would he handle meeting with the commanding committee? He'd fall apart long before he entered the door.

Maela didn't seem fazed. She maintained her smile, much better with communicating than he was. "It'll be good to have a friend aboard, yes? If you're not too busy later, perhaps we can meet in the mess."

"That would be great." Tol pointed past her. "I should get going. A meeting. With the commanding committee."

She quirked a brow. "You mean me?"

"Oh." Tol grimaced, having momentarily forgotten her rank. "After you, then." He motioned her to go in front of him.

When she turned and the door opened ahead of her, the tension in Tol dropped. Something about having her eyes on him was more than he could handle. He wished he didn't have to have a meeting on a mission with her there.

"You need to work on shielding your emotional aura," Maela whispered when she moved. She headed into the circular chamber and took her place behind a vacant station. Three other commanders stood at their respective stations: Tamar, and two men that Tol recognized as Neyral and Tendell from his preliminary assignment package.

Shielding emotions was harder than it looked. Tol had never been good at that. It was another element that unnerved his fellow officers and commanders about him. In this room, and with Maela as one of those judging his performance, this couldn't go well. His mouth went dry. His palms sweated. Just when he'd thought he'd had a reprieve.

"Lieutenant Tol," Speaker Tamar said. "Welcome to the committee chambers. I see you've been introduced to our new personnel commander, Maela. As a physician, she'll do well looking after your and the rest of the crew's health."

Tol nodded. "I have no doubt of that, Speaker." He caught Maela's eyes once more, careful to look away before he became lost in them.

He recalled how Aeveron had acted around Speaker Tamar and wanted to laugh at himself for mocking him. If Aeveron could see him now, how much more of a fool would he look?

"Let's get to the mission," Speaker Tamar said. The lights dimmed and a world appeared on the room's center holodisplay.

34

Tamar waited for the other commanders to situate themselves. Tol was wide-eyed and shaking, projecting nervousness through the bondsense, almost a little too much for a mission like this. Had she chosen the wrong person? It would look odd, but she could reassign him.

No, the nervousness was directed elsewhere. Tamar peered through the holodisplay at the center of the room at the new commander Maela. The other woman was doing everything she could not to look in Lieutenant Tol's direction. Did these two have a history? Interesting.

"We've been assigned to send a small task force to Cestus III, across the border into human territory. Our objective is to destroy a military supply depot that is crucial to Earth's border region," Neyral said. He brought up a pointer that highlighted the supply depot's location.

Tol scrutinized the map, but it was impossible to see what he thought. He finally nodded. "Will this be a solo mission then?"

"We've allocated three other personnel for the mission," Maela said. "Two marines in case of altercations, and you may choose one person from available operations personnel to assist you."

"We understand you are new to the *Issiana*," Tamar said, "but this mission is time-sensitive. We will drop you at the closest border system, but from there you'll be on your own. We have intelligence that the humans are deploying sensor nets to detect our warships, but our researchers believe that a small shuttle can get through the nets undetected. Engineering has already prepared a shuttle for the launch, and you'll need to be ready to move as soon as we arrive."

"This is an opportunity to do the Aresh great honor," Tendell said. As he remained silent much of the time, his voice carried a great gravity to it. It made Tamar believe in this mission a little more. Disrupting supply depots would spare Aryshan lives, at the very least.

Maela tapped on her console. "I'm transmitting you a list of operations personnel so you can make an informed decision."

Tol waved off Maela's suggestion. "No need, Commander. I already have a person in mind. I would appreciate if Lieutenant Aeveron were assigned to support me."

Neyral shook his head. "I do not think this is a wise idea. First, these are two officers who just came aboard the ship. We don't know either of their capabilities."

"I respectfully disagree," Maela said. Her eyes focused on Neyral, challenging. "I know Tol's capabilities quite well."

The room fell to silence. This was a division that hadn't existed when Intrei was commander, but Tamar could already sense that Maela and Neyral were going to butt heads over more than just this. In some ways, the tension refreshed Tamar. She could use an ally for when he became aggressive. But at the same time, she didn't want a commanding committee divided. "There's no quarrel here. Neyral's first concern is noted. What's the second?"

Neyral turned his attention to Tamar. "You recall our discussion before arriving at Sirdanse Station? If something goes wrong…"

He must have not wanted to say more with Tol in the room. This wasn't intended to be a suicide mission, but it was extremely dangerous and would require a lot of things to go right for those involved to come out unharmed. On the other hand, if they were on Neyral's list of potentials to watch, wouldn't that make them the type to do well on a difficult mission? And if they hadn't fully integrated with the crew yet, they wouldn't be losing synergies if something did go amiss.

Tendell didn't seem to want to chime in on the matter, and Maela had already said her piece. Tamar was the Speaker, however. It was incumbent upon her to break the silence in the room. "I believe Lieutenant Aeveron is an exemplary choice. From what I've read of his bio, he will do well on this mission with you."

"With Speaker Tamar's endorsement, I see no reason to contest her judgment," Tendell echoed from his station.

Neyral looked as if he were about to explode. He projected quite a bit of frustration, but that was quelled within moments. "Very well," he said.

"I approve the requisition of officer Lieutenant Aeveron for this mission. Do well on this mission, Lieutenant Tol. For the glory of the Aresh."

"For the glory of the Aresh," Tol repeated, and bowed his head first to Maela, then in a larger act to the whole committee.

"You are dismissed. We'll transmit more information when we have it available," Tamar said.

Tol turned and departed the room in silence. Though Tamar still had misgivings over this whole war, this mission had settled fine with her. Tactically, it made sense, and carried minimum risk. But here in the room, watching as the other commanders went about their business, Tamar saw that she would have work to do to ensure that the *Issiana* ran at peak efficiency. Such was the duty of leaders.

She returned to the mission briefing on her console, planning the perfect point to drop off the shuttle and launch their attack.

35

Sean rested on his cot, staring at the ceiling in his cramped quarters. If he had been claustrophobic, these quarters would have been a complete nightmare. On the other hand, he was glad that the Aryshans didn't stack multiple people into a bunk unit, but provided thick walls for everyone so they could maintain their individual sleep without having the bondsense interfere. They held a value of personal time and privacy that actually surpassed the humans'.

A red glow flashed from his terminal, brightening the room with each pulse. Sean pushed himself off his cot with a grunt and took the single step to his workstation. He flicked the display on with the swipe of a finger.

Tol's face appeared above the terminal in holo form. He struck his thought about Aryshans valuing privacy. It didn't hold true to all of them, apparently. If Tol had the opportunity move into this small space with Sean, he was sure he would. Tol was a nice enough fellow, though, despite minor annoying habits.

"Hello, Aeveron," Tol said. It was a recorded message this time. For that, Sean was thankful. "I have good news. I've been assigned to an extraordinarily important mission that requires an operations officer. I've volunteered you to join me. If we're successful, we could show ourselves as adding much value to the Aresh. Come to my quarters to discuss further when you have time. I've transmitted my unit number into your personal files."

The holo disappeared. Sean let out a tired sigh. He rolled his shoulders back a couple of times to loosen up. The last thing he wanted to do was search for someone else's quarters, but he couldn't leave this idea of an important mission until later. He had hoped to settle into this new job in the operations corps, get an understanding of the workings of the ship, gather his data, and remain quiet. It sounded like Tol had the opposite plan and intended to bring him along into the open. Perhaps he hadn't made a great choice in friends to begin this assignment.

At the same time, Tol was his best information lead. He had access to newer technologies that could be useful to Earth. A true cutting-edge pioneer. Sean slipped on his shoes and headed out the door to go find Tol's quarters.

When he arrived, the doors opened without having to chime. Tol had already set up lab experiments in his new quarters, much more cluttered in the small space compared to the station's setup. It made it difficult to walk around. Sean didn't dare touch anything. Even as tight as this was, the dimensions had to be twice as large as Sean's own quarters. "How'd you manage to get this room?" Sean asked.

Tol popped his head up from under a large metallic device that emitted a blue electrical field. "I put in a requisition request early. I'm sorry about the mess, but there's not much I can do. There's a chair over to your left. Have a seat."

Sean did at he was told, moving some metal bits from the chair and placing them carefully on the floor beside him. "Maybe I should requisition a larger room, myself."

"You have need? I didn't know you were working on other services for the Aresh. You're uncommitted. Unless you're saying you're going to commit?" Tol asked, sounding hopeful as he ran a sensor instrument over the machine's field.

"Never mind. Tell me about this mission you called about?"

Tol didn't bother looking, but kept working away, and then logging his readings manually into a tablet that rested on a side table. "We've been assigned to take a couple of marines over the border to the Earth colony, Cestus III. The mission involves destroying a military supply depot. It's dangerous but could be invaluable."

If Sean hadn't been seated, he might have fallen over. Cestus III was where he'd trained for this assignment in the first place. Tol couldn't have known it, but he had volunteered him for a mission to attack his own people. He had to get out of it somehow. "I'm not sure I'm the best person for this job. I'm not really qualified for away missions of this magnitude."

"I can't think of anyone better. You'll do well to keep me grounded. Though Speaker Tamar asked me to assemble the team, I'm counting on you to lead it. I'm just a pilot, and I can wire explosives if need be, or figure out another way to accomplish our task. Dealing with marines, though—that's not my strength. You're better with people," Tol said. "When we succeed, it'll show our dedication, and perhaps even get us on a command path."

"This might be too dangerous for me. I don't think I'm cut out for command." To say the least. Though the more Sean thought about Tol's harebrained idea, it did give him a chance to contact Earth without prying eyes. If something went wrong, he could be safely on Cestus III. The only issue he had was finding the time to uncover information worthwhile to report. His orders were to engrain himself in the ship's crew, not to make any sudden moves or do anything suspicious until he'd settled in. That way he could get himself into crucial systems and get files that he wouldn't otherwise be privy to.

On the other hand, a supply depot would be a fairly bloodless target. He could alleviate future suspicions by doing good work on something like this. It was something to consider. "If you think it would be best, I'll defer to you. But ask me next time before you volunteer me for a mission like this."

"Great!" Tol said. He looked back at Sean, all smiles and enthusiasm. A test tube to his left boiled over and made a piercing, high-pitched noise. Tol's eyes widened, and he lunged for it, stumbling over some of his machinery. His scanner fell from his hand and hit the floor with a clank. "I'm sorry. This might all be too distracting for me. I need to fix this. You'll like it when I'm done."

"Do you need help?"

"I need you out!"

The piercing noise intensified. Sean didn't waste any time, but covered his ears and ran out the door. It closed again behind him, leaving him in the relative quiet of the corridor. Tol acted like this mission meant very little, but to Sean, it was something almost too big for him to chew. He had to think about this whole Cestus III mission more and what he would do. Tol's enthusiasm was enough to calm Sean in the moment, but he had too much more to consider.

In their training sessions, McCleever had told him that matters like this would come up. In deep cover, one had to ignore certain things and focus on the task at hand. His real goal was to bring the military tangible information on Aryshan ship systems and personnel protocols for Earth's engineers to identify a weakness. Risking himself over Cestus III wouldn't help toward that end. But going on the mission was risking himself in another way.

He longed for his easy days back in Internal Affairs—days that seemed hard at the time. All he had to worry about then was getting fellow officers too mad at him, which would result in a thorough chewing out. Now, any wrong move could mean his death.

Sean's stomach grumbled, perhaps from the stress, but also because he hadn't eaten since coming aboard. He tapped on one of the corridor logos, which brought up a ship map, and headed for the mess.

36

The hunk of re-moisturized meat in front of Tamar didn't look appealing. She usually enjoyed the chef's preparations, but sometimes she missed being on a planet and having access to something a little fresher. In truth, the taste was fine. But her mind had been spinning far too much for her to be hungry.

The committee was filled with strife. Maela and Neyral couldn't stop their bickering over small items, ones that could have been resolved quickly. The problem was that Tamar, as Speaker, broke the tie in votes, so her word either emboldened or enraged one or the other, depending on the situation. With each passing day, she lost more control of her ship, and of her life.

Then there was this war, a heavy weight putting multiple worlds' pressure on her shoulders. This mission that was likely to cause further escalation, even if it were the right thing to do. Who knew what First Speaker Ny'aet had up his sleeve after that? She suspected there were a number of his people here on the ship with the purpose of watching her, but she would have to identify those and extract information from them. If she didn't go mad and paranoid first.

Her eyes had defocused, and she shifted her gaze to the door to give her something new to look at. Lieutenant Aeveron made his way into the mess. Unlike most of the other new crewmen, she kept hearing and seeing more of his name. How was he ingratiating himself to the crew so quickly? Was he the one working for Ny'aet? There was the odd way his name had appeared on their roster. She'd been involved in too many political machinations over the years to think of it as a coincidence. The strangest part was that he remained uncommitted. That was rare in someone so ambitious.

He was odd, to say the least. The way Aeveron scanned the room, it almost appeared as if he had never seen a mess hall before. He looked lost, or at least that he was looking for something—or someone. His eyes settled on Tamar.

She didn't waver in her gaze, but met his with the firmness one might expect from a commander. If this Aeveron were some sort of political plant or ambitious fellow, he wouldn't be intimidated, but he would see her strength.

He reacted strangely again, averting his eyes, falling into line to retrieve his food tray. Tamar watched him. Why was he so uncomfortable with her? As she thought back to their prior meeting, he had been at that time as well. She might have found the Ruling Committee's spy after all.

The line for food dwindled, and Aeveron exited with a tray in his hand. He gave her one more surprise by heading directly for her table. The crew traditionally left her alone to have her meal. She'd been standoffish enough with them to garner that respect. Her emotional aura was always well-guarded, and that also signaled that she desired privacy.

Aeveron stopped in front of her table. "Hello, Speaker. I saw you looking at me when I entered and that you're eating alone. Thought you might like some company." He gave her a weak smile.

That smile came across as innocent, if not downright cute. Despite her earlier misgivings, she might have been wrong about him. If he were working for the Ruling Committee as some observer of her behavior, he wouldn't likely be so brazen. And something about the way he spoke, or perhaps about his face, seemed familiar to her. She couldn't quite place it. "You may, Lieutenant," Tamar said, though she typically would have turned a crewman away. If he could be surprising, why couldn't she?

He set the tray across from her and slid onto the bench. "Thank you." Instead of looking away, his eyes seemed to bore into her. He seemed to forget his food. "Being new, I don't know many people aboard."

"Lieutenant Tol?"

"He's occupied," Aeveron said. Something in his tone sounded almost amused by that.

Tamar could only imagine. "And so you chose to sit with the Speaker?" She hated being so blunt herself and wasn't quite sure why she was dedicating so much of her own prying as to why he wanted to join her, but she couldn't stop thinking about it.

"Is that inappropriate?" he asked. He reached for his utensil, but his eyes remained on her. It took him a couple of tries to find the piece.

Tamar almost shivered. What was it about him? She caught herself frowning, and immediately straightened her face. The last thing she wanted was to invite questions as to what was wrong with her. She might have to open up about the stresses of command, and that wouldn't do at all. "No, not inappropriate. Just unusual. You're uncommitted." That was a non sequitur. But she wanted to know more about his reasons for keeping from joining a tribe.

He looked down at his food then, taking a knife into his other hand and slicing some of the re-moisturized meat methodically. "I am," he said, giving her nothing.

The others around them noticed their socializing. No one ever sat with Tamar in the mess. There'd be rumors going around later, though she didn't care much about that. "I see," she said. Why did this conversation feel like both of them were hunting prey? And what were they hunting for? "Tell me about yourself."

Aeveron set down his knife and met her eyes again. His were dark, strong. She hadn't noticed that before. "What do you want to know?" he asked.

"How you came by this assignment? I am well-connected with the

Ruling Committee, you know." Her words sounded like gaudy posturing. What did she hope to accomplish with that?

For the first time since he'd joined her, she saw hesitation in his eyes. He could be intimidated after all. "I'm not certain." He shrugged. "I received the notification via my comm unit."

"From whom?"

"An officer from the personnel department."

"Anyone in particular?"

Their eyes locked again. Tamar saw that he understood he was being grilled, but he wasn't going to back down. Something about that stilled Tamar's breath.

"I don't recall," he said, his voice lowering to a near whisper. "Did I do something to upset you, Speaker? I'm only here to serve."

Those were the right words. And it was also the right tone. Nothing about him appeared deceitful. Maybe it was his uncommitted nature, but something irked her. He was *too* familiar. He had to have come from Ny'aet. With such heavy confidence, this man acted like he had another authority that could usurp her. It would be best to refocus the conversation to duty. "Forgive me, Lieutenant," she said. "It's unusual someone chooses to dine with me, as I said. I'm perhaps not the best company." She leaned back against the wall. "You were briefed of our special mission, yes? Lieutenant Tol advocated for you on the assignment."

"Cestus III, yes?"

"That's the one. It's of vital importance that this mission goes well, and overseeing the preparations has been taxing on me," Tamar said. Why did she volunteer that to a subordinate?

"I won't fail you." Those dark eyes fixed on her again.

She shivered. It jolted her like a mega-lightning storm from back home. Tamar narrowed her eyes, dissecting him. He wouldn't fail her, and he meant personally. What was this about? She couldn't tell if she enjoyed this exchange or if she hated it. He was making her head cloudy; that was for certain. "I'm sure you won't." Those words came out rushed. "Lieutenant Tol believes in you. I look forward to seeing the results of your efforts. I should get going though, if you'll excuse me."

"You haven't finished your food." Aeveron motioned to her plate.

"I have to be somewhere. I get limited time, you understand," Tamar said, covering for herself. What was wrong with her? She didn't need to explain herself to him. She stood and maneuvered around the table.

"It was good talking to you, Speaker. I hope we can share a meal again." He cocked his head back toward her.

"Of course." Tamar met his glance one final time before she had to pry herself away. She departed hastily and didn't look back.

37

S ince the away mission began, Sean spent most his time in the shuttle's cockpit with Tol. He had little experience in piloting, but that didn't deter his Aryshan comrade. The shuttle itself was larger than Sean had expected, with individual compartments for up to eight people, lined with the thick, Aryshan-style walls that he had become accustomed to in the last several days. The two marines stayed toward the back, apart from them.

The launch from the *Issiana* had been smooth, though his stomach did curl in the brief switch from the ship's gravity plates to the shuttle's. The transition was supposed to be seamless, though Tol explained to him the mechanics of how it would have been far more uncomfortable to have both sets of plates pulling on them at the same time. This minor glitch was a blessing.

Several hours into their journey, their identification signature was keyed so that others would view them as a private cargo vessel owned by DePino Starliners, with the designation DPC-7223. So far, they'd received neither contact nor harassment from Earth. Sean hoped it would stay that way.

It had been quiet for a couple of hours when Tol looked up from a tablet he was reading. "Have you had any more encounters with Speaker Tamar?" he asked patronizingly. A wicked smirk crossed his face.

Sean chuckled, though the question did make him shift in his seat. "What brought that up?"

"I was reviewing my projects list. Came across the phere-cologne we spoke about. I think you should try it."

"You should probably test on animals first before going to trial on sentients. What if I have an adverse reaction?"

"Animals?" Tol blinked several times. "That'd be cruelty."

"And it wouldn't be cruelty on me?"

"Of course not. You'd give your sentient consent."

"I'm definitely not giving my sentient consent." Sean couldn't help but laugh. Some may have found Tol's incessant pestering about his projects obnoxious, but he found it amusing. Didn't Aryshans have senses of humor about these things? Now that he considered it, they might not.

"You still haven't answered my question," Tol said, showing no signs of amusement himself.

Sean shifted to the side of his tight cockpit seat. "The answer is yes. I happened to join her in the mess hall a day before we left for the mission."

"Really?" Tol's question held genuine interest. "I didn't think you had it in you."

"What's that supposed to mean?"

"You stood frozen last time we met her. How did she take to it?" Tol cocked his head curiously.

"I'm not sure, to be honest." Sean recalled the day. They'd gone tit-for-tat, and though each of them stared at the other for a little more than was proper, he didn't know enough about Aryshan inter- actions to have a good comparison. Something about the encounter worried him that she might recognize him from Palmer Station, which had turned him into a recluse until his mission departure.

"That doesn't give me much information. How can I diagnose a fix if you won't give me the specs?" Tol asked.

Sean felt his face getting hotter, though his flushing wouldn't show through the skin complexion that the nanites had given him. "I don't know. She is definitely on edge, paranoid even. Perhaps the stress of being a commander. But she did say we could share a meal together again."

"She has a right to be paranoid, with you uncommitted." Tol tapped his fingers in a rhythmic manner on his armrest. "It does look strange, both with you aboard such an important vessel, and then trying to spend time with her. She likely believes you to be working for one of the other tribes. You're not, are you?"

"Of course not." Sean tensed.

Tol nodded, apparently satisfied. "Honestly, if you want to understand and get close to her, I recommend you commit to the Aresh. You'd be able to read her emotional aura and know fairly soon whether you were compatible. In theory."

"Why in theory?" The theory of the Aryshan culture had been one aspect of his assignment that made Sean nervous. They were so well attuned to each other that coming in as an outsider with little knowledge of how their physiological bonds worked could have been disastrous. So far, he'd managed to dodge any of the complications.

"In my brief interactions with Speaker Tamar, she was particularly adept at masking her emotional aura. I think anyone must be, in her position. But let me ask you a question. You've obviously worked with the Aresh long enough to be assigned to a prestigious vessel, and now you've even taken a hard liking to the heir to our Ruling Committee. Why won't you commit?"

Tol was pressuring him a little too much for Sean's liking. Even though he couldn't physically commit as Tol wanted, it still irked him. He glanced toward the back of the shuttle. The main corridor was empty. The marines must have been in their bunk or the small workout facility where they'd hidden for most of the journey. He was alone with Tol, an Aryshan who loudly highlighted his differences from the rest of the crew, and it was dangerous. At the same time, Tol didn't appear suspicious of his true identity. Why should he be so frightened? "You've put me on the spot, Tol," Sean said after considering how to respond.

Tol nodded. "I understand. I won't bother you about it too much, but you are one of my closer friends, and it would be nice to have you as a part of our tribe."

It sounded like a deep compliment, so Sean took it as such, turning back to Tol and smiling. "Thank you, Tol. I appreciate that sentiment."

"When we get back, I'll try to see if I can uncover any information on her through the bondsense. For now—"

The shuttlecraft controls beeped. They were almost at Cestus III. Sean looked out the cockpit window and realized he hadn't been paying attention. A planet grew in their view. He could see the various buildings cropping up across the red surface. In a lot of ways, it reminded him of home, not only because of his recent training there, but also because of its similarity to Mars. His stomach sank as he considered that he might never truly return to either world.

"Aeveron, let the marines know we've arrived. I'll transmit the landing codes. They should open the outer dome for us as soon as they receive, assuming these are correct," Tol said.

Sean pushed himself out of his seat, ducked below a beam, and headed to the back of the shuttle. He heard Tol's tapping of the codes, and paused to look back at the buildings in the distance. If the codes were wrong, they might not be granted landing, or worse, they could be shot out of the sky. Space traffic controllers had to be on alert these days. Sean held his breath.

Laser lights guided them to the spaceport, and the shuttle descended toward the landing bay. He released his breath and continued back.

The marines were seated, playing some variation of a card game that Sean hadn't had time to analyze. "We're almost here. Pack up the supplies."

Both the marines stared at him in the most uncomfortable manner, as if he were an alien. It didn't make it easier that the two of them could rip him in half with little effort. Regardless of what they thought, they moved about their tasks, setting their cards down and packing.

Sean sighed in relief and returned to the cockpit.

38

Stars lit the display of the committee chambers with a view of outside space. It had been more than a day since Lieutenant Tol's shuttle had departed for Cestus III. He hadn't reported in yet, but then, Tamar hadn't expected him to. She couldn't help but have a sinking feeling about sending her crew into enemy territory. The potential of harming someone in the tribe grated on her, along with the potential of losing Aeveron, whom she found herself unable to keep out of her thoughts these last few days.

She didn't have time to think about it. The rift with Maela and Neyral grew wider by the day. If one suggested something, the other almost always took the opposite opinion. Even on little things that didn't matter at all. Why couldn't they just get along?

Tendell hadn't been much help. He was content to stay out of the friction between the other commanders. The nice thing about him was that he deferred to her judgment. In the way he avoided conflict, it was easy to see why he turned down the idea of being Speaker when she first came aboard.

But friction between commanders, especially within the tribe, would be a disaster for a ship long-term. She had to do something to put a stop to it before the crew fell into different camps. They couldn't afford discord in the middle of a war like this.

That didn't even begin to touch on her misgivings about the war, which she hadn't felt comfortable vocalizing to anyone. Neyral was so blindly adamant about following the Ruling Committee in this, which was correct for an officer. Tamar couldn't risk any political problems of her own with her fledgling speakership. She was too young and didn't have enough of a track record to be perceived as questioning authority.

Neyral looked up from his display. His eyes sparkled with hope. He knew she was thinking about him.

Tamar cursed herself silently. She'd become sloppy in her agitation, projecting far too many emotions. She needed some space from Neyral's prying mind. Tamar turned to Maela. "Commander Maela, I need to make my rounds of the ship. Would you care to walk with me?" she asked.

Maela raised a curious brow at her. Tendell frowned. Had she been projecting that loudly? The problem was that an inspection typically would involve Neyral. He handled more of the controls and systems of the ship in the separation of duties between commanders.

"Of course, Speaker," Maela said. She finished work on her station, then stepped from behind her console. If she had any concern about the irregularity, she didn't show it.

Tamar led the way, not making eye contact with the others before leaving the room. It shouldn't have been as painfully awkward as this to exit, but with the bondsense, tension levels had a habit of escalating and spiraling. That's why control of emotions was so important, especially to command.

The two women walked through the corridors of the ship, winding through different departments. Dozens of her people sat working at their stations, some rising in respect as they saw their commanders. Tamar and Maela acknowledged them as appropriate, walking in silence. They moved through the ship until reaching the environmental systems mechanical room, filled with giant air compressors and filters that kept clean air circulating through the ship. A soft noise of fans blowing covered the area, and Tamar didn't sense any of her other people nearby.

"Did you want to talk, Speaker?" Maela offered when they reached a remote area. She craned her neck to survey the large room, up to the pipes above them. The computer terminal at the entrance controlled everything, with a backup outside of the room in case of an issue. Those redundancies were necessary to keep the crew safe.

Tamar stopped, turning to Maela. The question now was whether she could she trust the other woman, as she had Intrei in those final days with her in Maela's position? She couldn't be sure. The bond-sense didn't give her any illumination but that Maela had respect for her. The only way to see for certain would be to feel her out. "Are you well acquainted with anyone on the Ruling Committee?" Tamar asked.

Maela shook her head. "I haven't spoken with any of them much personally. Why?" she asked, projecting confusion. There was no sign of deception from her.

Tamar's opening question hadn't exactly been haphazard. She wanted to test, through Maela's reaction, her feelings on the Ruling Committee. The question hadn't gleaned as much as she'd hoped, but that meant that Maela's passions weren't particularly strong on the subject, or she was good at hiding them. But did she risk going further with this new commander? She needed someone to talk to. If anything, Maela would see through the bondsense that her own intentions were for the benefit of the Aresh tribe, and she only had concern about the good of their people. "I've been thinking a lot as of late. As to whether our recent actions with Earth are actually going to be for the good of our people. The truth is I'm not sure."

Maela's eyes went wide in surprise. She stifled a breath. "I actually feel the same. I wouldn't have brought it up, given your history. And I can't talk about it in front of the others, especially Neyral. He is almost blindly loyal."

Relief overcame Tamar. She could breathe easily again. "He can be rather zealous, but the Ruling Committee isn't infallible. With the changes to personnel lately, and all these strange, secret missions, I've needed someone to talk to. Confidentially."

"I keep my confidences, Speaker Tamar," Maela said. Those words had weight and pride. The bond was strong in that.

This had gone far more easily than Tamar had anticipated. She'd been so worried, but now with a small admission, she felt as though she finally had a friend aboard the ship. A friend Intrei could have been if she had stayed. Maela was handpicked by the former commander. Perhaps there was more purpose to that than Tamar realized. "Thank you. It means a lot to me," Tamar said. She motioned with her head to carry on, and the two women continued walking.

"The transition to this ship has been a little difficult for me, I must say," Maela said.

Tamar sympathized with all Maela had to deal with in Neyral. Though the bickering was certainly two-sided, Maela seemed the more reasonable of the two. And then there was that other matter. Tamar recalled how tense Maela appeared when Tol had entered the committee chambers. "Do you have an issue working with Lieutenant Tol?"

Maela winced, the bondsense tightening with fear. "I should have disclosed that Tol and I were previously in a relationship. We very nearly entwined. His presence can prove somewhat...distracting."

It should have been disclosed. Though it likely wouldn't have made a difference. For now, it didn't matter with Tol on assignment off the ship, but it could impact performances later. It was rare for someone to get so close to entwining, then break off the engagement. Once to that point, there was such a level of trust, especially if both were already committed to the same tribe. "Does this mean I shouldn't trust him?" Tamar considered reassigning Tol after this mission. His record did have a number of black marks to it.

"Oh no, that's not the case at all. He's very trustworthy, caring even. It can get in the way of his duties at points," Maela said. "We served together before my promotion. It's embarrassing, what happened. Our Speaker actually ordered our break up, claiming that

Tol's thoughts for me were causing errors in his judgment and clouding the minds of the rest of the crew because of their strong aura. I saw this as my duty and ended the relationship cleanly, for the good of the Aresh." She bit her lip. "It had a worse effect on Tol, though. He became depressed and had to transfer, because seeing me proved too much for him. I couldn't face him at the time. I felt terrible."

Tamar frowned. "That was foolish. If you were entwined, the emotion could have been channeled properly. Did your Speaker not understand that?"

Maela's emotional aura held more pain than if she had snapped a bone. The strength of it almost overwhelmed Tamar. "I could not disobey an order," Maela said. "I think he may have wanted me for himself, looking back. Now I'm uncertain how I feel."

Tamar frowned. "I'm sorry, I should have been more delicate in my questioning."

"No, honesty is best. I may have to reconsider. Tol's interest in me has not waned." They passed through the ship's food stores and processing.

Tamar walked along with her for a little while in silence, until they returned to the central corridor. With so much emotion being projected from Maela, it was time to stop the conversation—let her reflect and settle down. Otherwise, it might impact the rest of the crew. "Thank you, Maela, both for confiding in me and listening. I hope we can have more chats like this in the future," Tamar said with a nod, signaling her dismissal.

"Likewise, Speaker," Maela said. Her voice went soft, meek compared to the rest of the conversation. She nodded and turned toward the personnel quarters.

Tamar kept walking through the ship to give herself some more time to think. She clasped her hands behind her back as she walked. She saw nothing wrong in a potential relationship between Maela and Tol. If they were this fervent about each other, calming that would only benefit their performances. But that was getting ahead of herself. Maela didn't voice that would be her wishes. Yet. Tamar had seen too many friends in such a state to think that it wouldn't happen soon.

Alone with her thoughts and emotions, Tamar closed her eyes. She wondered if the Cestus III mission was going well, and whether both Tol, and this Aeveron who kept trickling into her own thoughts, would come back safely.

39

The sun descended in the Cestus III sky before Tol sent his signal to the local informant. It was a simple code, a prerecorded delivery notification message. The briefing he downloaded on the way over stated that the informant would switch the security cameras around the supply depot to ensure their safety.

The Cestus III spaceport was controlled by Earth's military. They wouldn't have to pass any guard stations upon making their delivery. The humans assumed everyone had proper clearance and had been checked via the codes they sent upon descent. Everything was going according to plan.

In many ways, humans deserved pity. Without a bond, without a tribe, they flailed in the wind, alone. They could never truly have trust in the way that he had for his fellows. He glanced to Aeveron. The uncommitted could be considered human-like, but Tol would convert Aeveron to the cause eventually. The Aresh was all that mattered.

"Okay," Tol told Aeveron and the marines. Aeveron was supposed to be the one to deliver the orders, but he had convinced Tol that being Aresh gave him more respect. Tol wasn't sure that was true, but he didn't mind. "There's five points where we are to set the explosives.

I'll show you how to wire the first one, and then we split up and hit each of the other four to save on time. Our orders are then to rendezvous back at the shuttle. We will be taking off at oh-one-hundred local time, whether you're here or not, so come back swiftly. The explosives are set to detonate at oh-two-hundred, once we are clear of the domes. Any questions?"

The others shook their heads. Tol had never given orders like this; it was exhilarating. He tried to suppress his excitement so the marines wouldn't get overwhelmed, but it was difficult.

Tol led them down the ramp and onto the loading bay. The bay was on a concrete strip, with the first right turn leading to their target. The timing was such that they would be able to enter and exit in between security sweeps, as long as they worked in a perfect rhythm. Which, of course, they would. They were Aresh, excepting Aeveron. Pride swelled within him, which was met with an agreeing nod by one of the marines.

For some reason, Aeveron looked nervous. This mission was out of his element. But the Overseers willing, Aeveron would retain his calm.

The team walked down the strip, passing crates, hovercars, and lifts along the way. Several crews moved and unloaded cargo. No one paid Tol's team a second glance. It helped that each of them wore long, hooded clothing that concealed their features. The dark of the moonless night obscured their skin tones. From a distance, they would pass as human.

They passed a warehouse where they would have to turn toward the supply depot. A security patrol wrapped up their rounds, just as Tol had been informed. Violent anger swelled in the bondsense. The marines wanted a fight. Tol tried to quell that with his own feelings of calm, hoping that would be enough. Engaging the humans would be the death of them.

The patrol turned the corner and Tol led his team briskly toward the warehouse. Aeveron produced an access crystal from his pocket and scanned it against the door. It opened. The four of them rushed inside before anyone else could see them.

Tol reached into one of the marine's packs and grabbed night vision goggles. He slipped them over his hood, and suddenly he could see everything as if it were daylight. The others followed his lead, putting on their own goggles.

"Everyone ready?" Tol asked, glancing between them.

The marines nodded.

"Good to go," Aeveron said.

Tol led his crew to the first explosive drop point, taking one of the packages from one of the marines who carried them. He carefully planted the device in between boxes, an inconspicuous square that looked like it should naturally be there. The others kept watch, ensuring that no humans would stumble upon them. When all looked clear, they gathered around him.

"This is your last reminder," Tol said, popping the lid. "See the current-putty inside? For our safety in carrying them, it was disconnected, but we need to connect them individually as we plant the devices. Like so," he said, embedding a metallic connector in between the two putty pieces. "Simple. This should go quickly. Any questions before we split up?"

Each shook their heads no, and the marines divvied the devices between the four of them. They had gone over the maps and knew where to go. Each headed to a different point in the warehouse.

40

S ean hustled away from the others, trying to give himself enough distance to fall out of earshot. He rustled through his jacket and grabbed a small comm device, inserting it onto his ear. Audio only, as he didn't want to carry a larger device. This was already dangerous enough. He had preprogrammed the frequency and dialed.

"Papa Emilio's pizzeria. May I take your order?" A female voice answered through the comm.

"Depends. Is your pepperoni fresh?" Sean asked. The emergency code had been drilled into him by both repetition and the microvirus memory. He would never order a pizza the same way again, if he ever got back to somewhere that made pizzas.

"Fresh as can be, imported straight from Earth. Is this line secure?"

"It is," Sean said.

"How can I assist you, Lieutenant Barrows?" The agent must have cross-referenced his voice print with the code.

"I'm on planet. Cestus III," Sean said. He still had misgivings about contacting the people from intelligence. "Is Commander McCleever there?"

"He's off shift right now," the agent said.

Sean glanced around him. The others weren't anywhere nearby. He had a charge in hand, and placed it up against one of the cargo containers, as Tol had instructed him. If someone from the team came back, he didn't want to look suspicious. "I want to alert you to something. The Aryshans are here, on planet. They have an informant embedded within the military. They're targeting one of the supply depots with explosives. I'm not sure if you want to blow cover and extract now or if there's a way to minimize damage, but I'm reporting in. Awaiting orders."

A pause came from the other end of the line. "I'm going to contact Commander McCleever. Stand by."

Sean wasn't sure that he had the time to stand by. He popped the top of the explosive box, connecting the putty as Tol had shown them. If he truly wanted to minimize the damage, he could have stopped right here, sabotaged his own sabotaging and called it a day. But he'd spent weeks being conditioned to follow through with his role, no matter what the cost. Even contacting his base was risky.

He waited longer than he expected for a reply, glancing at his chrono. It was already 0030. At this rate, he would have to run back to the shuttle. The others likely had already planted their devices and been back to the front of the building. They'd come looking for him soon.

"Lieutenant Barrows?" The voice returned.

"Here."

"I spoke with the commander. We appreciate the information and will act accordingly. We're going to make sure personnel are not in the area but will allow your mission to proceed. We will monitor outgoing transmissions and watch for the informant. Thank you for this tip. You have done well. Do not break cover. Return to your primary mission. Those were his exact words," she said.

"Copy that," Sean said. It filled him with pride to hear that Commander McCleever thought he had done well. Still, part of him hoped that he could leave the Aryshans. Go back to normal life. He hadn't provided his team with the information they needed yet.

"Pizzeria out." The line went dead.

Sean took off running toward the door. There was little time to spare. He rounded a corner stacked high with crates and nearly collided with Tol.

"Aeveron, where by the Overseers have you been?" Tol asked. For once, he sounded angry.

"I..." He had to think of an excuse, and fast. What could have taken him so long? His directions were clear and simple. It was a quick connection with no variables.

Tol opened the door to the outside. The streetlights were enough to need to take off the goggles. The goggles. That gave him an idea.

"My goggles went haywire in there," Sean whispered. "I couldn't see where I was at. Made it difficult to plant the device properly. Maybe something was loose?"

The marines looked at him as if they were unimpressed, but said nothing. If he shared a bondsense with them, Sean's lie would have been seen through and discovered. Being a human had its advantages.

Tol nodded, seeming to buy the excuse. "We need to get out of here. I'll take a look when we get back. Keep up," he said.

Sean grimaced, remembering that Tol had a knack for tinkering with devices. The excuse could come back to bite him if Tol prodded too far. For now, Tol had a good lead and Aryshan strength propelling him down the strip. Sean ran as hard as he could back to their shuttle.

41

The committee chambers were quiet, each of the four commanders preparing their mission reports. The Ruling Committee would be hailing them soon, and all of them felt a deep tension that hung in the bondsense like a cloud.

Lights flashed with the incoming communication signal. Tamar looked up from her station, glancing toward Neyral. "Commander Neyral, please open the connection with the Ruling Committee."

Neyral tapped a command. The lights in the room dimmed, first displaying an image of the Aryshan flag before shimmering into the visage of the four members of the Ruling Committee. All four of them were on this comm—a rare honor for a simple military vessel. In some ways, even though it made the rest of the room even more tense than before, it gave Tamar a sense of safety. She half expected to have a call alone with Ny'aet.

The First Speaker was there, his desk facing toward her in the center display that wrapped around. Each Ruling Committee counterpart was projected in line with the commander across from them. "We all appear to be connected," Ny'aet said. "I hope your journey finds you well, Commanders."

"Our mission is complete and is a success, Speaker. Our officers have returned safely to the *Issiana*," Tamar said.

From a side view, she could see another member of the Ruling Committee nod. Enrei, a woman who had met Tamar for the first time when she was a little girl. Though her working relationship had been much closer with First Speaker Ny'aet in recent years, Tamar had known Enrei for far longer than she knew most others. Enrei used to have such bright energy, confidence that was inspiring, but her skin no longer sparkled in its tone, and her eyes drooped with age. "The mission is complete, we agree," Enrei said, "though there was a major setback."

Tendell glanced at his console. "According to the report our officers made, they didn't mention a setback. All of the devices were planted and the team returned unharmed."

"Yes," Enrei agreed. "First Speaker?"

"The explosives detonated as planned. However, it appears that our intelligence regarding where the crucial supplies were stored was wrong. Unfortunately, we accomplished little other than destroying some foodstuffs and spare ship parts."

"The intelligence was faulty?" Tamar asked. Anger welled within her. They had sent her new crew on a dangerous mission like this without confirmed evidence of what they were doing? Her concerns for the recent actions of the Ruling Committee grew again. Such erratic behavior. This was why they had a committee and not a single leader in the first place.

"Faulty is not the right word," Enrei said. "We believe the supplies were moved shortly before our strike team arrived."

"A coincidence?" Tendell asked.

Ny'aet shook his head. "No, not a coincidence. We believe that our agent was compromised. Shortly after he reported the mission a success, he went offline. We believe he was captured."

"Overseers," Neyral cursed under his breath.

"Yes, it's bad," Ny'aet said. "He was one of our top informants. We have a blind spot on our intelligence side, and Earth is on alert. I've learned they've finally shifted their resources to this sector, and are deploying their full fleet power along the border."

Tamar remained silent, listening. Wasn't that what Ny'aet wanted? Why did he sound like it was a tragedy? He couldn't be falsifying his tone; Enrei would sense it, as she was Aresh as well. But she deferred to him, as did the other two committee members.

"As I expected," Ny'aet said. "We will have no choice but to do the same. I believe if this comes to all-out conflict, we will be victorious."

Pride for the Aresh swelled in the bondsense. Ny'aet was playing reluctant leader. That was his game. No one else seemed to care that this would result in a large loss of life on both sides. Was that the price to pay for security? "What does that mean for our next assignment?" Tamar asked.

"An excellent question, Speaker Tamar, and that is the reason for our discussion," Ny'aet said. He beamed at her. Despite her misgivings, sometimes the First Speaker could be fatherly. "The failure at Cestus III means both that the humans are alert and that their supply lines won't be crippled as anticipated. Though we know we still have the advantage, it is our goal to minimize Aryshan loss of life and end this conflict swiftly."

"As such, we understand that Earth will be sending their famous strategist Admiral Conley to the border as an intimidation tactic. If you recall the name, this is the same Admiral Conley who broke through the lines and overcame the Drenites in Earth's last war of aggression. The Ruling Committee agrees that the opening volley of this conflict should be to take out Admiral Conley's ship and strike a demoralizing blow to Earth before they have time to prepare an assault."

"How many ships will be in the envoy for this?" Tamar asked.

"Just one, Speaker Tamar," said Enrei.

"Tamar," Ny'aet said, "before you speak, I understand that it will be difficult, but as I said, the goal is to save Aryshan lives. That's why we have decided to use your strike team that was so effective in their infiltration of Cestus III. They can use the same codes, act as if they're delivering supplies, and plant explosives on Conley's vessel. Another simple mission."

"That may have worked on a colony where they're receiving shipments by the thousands, but to a single ship? They'll be able to tell who's approaching by simple observation. That's a suicide mission!" Tamar said. She found herself slamming her hand on her console. It chirped a dreadful tone at her, signaling that she'd hit too many conflicting commands at once.

"I'm inclined to agree," Maela said with an inclination of her head toward the Ruling Committee.

Ny'aet frowned. "We have already discussed this matter at length and have reached a unanimous decision," he said. "What the humans will expect is a full assault. A small shuttle may be able to penetrate their border unnoticed, as it did before. Commerce rules the minds of these humans. You don't understand how they think. At worst, you may be right. Our team may have to sacrifice themselves for this mission, but the ends are for the good of the Aresh, and for the Aryshan people."

The others in the Ruling Committee muttered their agreements. Tendell and Neyral showed no signs of dissent either. What struck through the bondsense was that Maela's objection was more than rational. It was personal. She feared for Tol's life. Could Tamar have been wrong in her judgment? The pressure was overwhelming for her to defer. Tamar had to fight for her crew, however. "With all due respect—"

"We are not going to debate this matter with subordinates, Speaker. Remember your place," Ny'aet said, his tone scolding. "You have your orders. The Ruling Committee has other matters to attend to."

The image shimmered out of existence as the transmission ended. Tamar cursed under her breath. It was tense in the room, with the male commanders looking at her like she was a crazed stormwraith. Maela appeared stunned.

If there had been division in this room before, this call had only amplified that to a startling degree. Tamar had to maintain her leadership and the committee's unity, or this ship would fall into disarray. The Ruling Committee appeared so docile in their following of Ny'aet. Something was wrong there, very wrong. She couldn't quite put her finger on what or why, but it spelled danger for Arysha. The worst part was there was nothing she could do about it. "We have our orders," Tamar said, despite her misgivings. "Let us begin preparations so we might find a way not to get our crew members killed."

42

Tol crossed his arms, surveying his incredible progress, grateful for the amount of time he'd had to work on his inventions upon his return from human space. Protective gear adorned him, including goggles and a breathing mask. He had been soldering two pieces of metal together on his workbench across from his cot. Requisitions had approved his equipment and tools orders, and those filled the quarters far faster than Tol had anticipated. Though the space was tight, Tol had a method to his tools placement, allowing him to move with the flow around his device as he worked. His terminal calculated that he was nearly complete, with a potential solution to his power-draw problems through the use a crystal powder catalyst that he'd ordered from homeworld.

The door opened behind him. Tol spun around to see who would be here at this hour.

Maela stood in the hallway, cocking her head at him with her special inquisitive adorableness that melted his body down to his soul. "I'm sorry, I used my commander's access crystal. I probably should have chimed," she said.

A surge of warmth pushed through the bondsense toward him. Interruption or no, nothing else mattered. Tol motioned her inside.

He did his best to project warmth back to her, and a sense of welcome. No words were necessary.

Maela smiled at him, stepping across the door's threshold. She moved carefully, ensuring she wouldn't step on anything important. The door closed behind her. "I wanted to talk," she said.

There was no regret coming from her this time, no wall between them. She was completely open to him. Tol had dreamed of moments like this since they had parted that first time. He nearly reached out to take her hand, but stopped himself. While lost in his own thoughts, he stumbled over some components, which *cracked* under his foot.

He didn't fall but, instead, his arm was steadied by Maela. She supported him, keeping him upright. They locked eyes. "I hope that wasn't important," she said.

"I'm certain it's replaceable."

"I'll make the requisition if you want. As a commander, I may have more pull."

"Thanks. It's fine, really."

If warmth existed in the bondsense before, it flooded through now, almost overwhelming Tol. She wanted him to touch her. He could feel that now. He tenderly moved his arm around her, placing it on the small of her back. Her body was so foreign to him, but nothing felt righter. How had he existed without this?

Maela responded by pulling him tightly toward her. She nuzzled against his cheek. He could feel her hot breath on his face. In that moment, Tol realized he'd been holding his own air in, and he gasped in a breath.

Their lips met.

The world became lost to him, his quarters all but disappearing in a kiss. Her aura pulsed all around him, the barriers breaking between them. Her lips parted for him, and their tongues greeted for the first time, as if this had been the most natural thing in the world.

Maela guided him through the cluttered room, pulling him hard by the shirt. All those parts on the floor lost any semblance of meaning. She pushed him onto the bed, her body pressing against his and pinning him there. She broke the kiss to breathe.

"Was this what you wanted to talk about?"

Maela chuckled. Her eyes cooled, filling with sadness. "I made a mistake before, Tol. I thought breaking away from you was for the good of the Aresh. Seeing you again, and then being without you so soon, with you on a mission you might not come back from—it was too much for me. Can you forgive me?"

Tol shivered, barely able to speak. Their eyes locked with intensity that he'd never experienced. "I live for you," he muttered.

Those words, while intense, seemed to surprise Maela. She nodded to him, glancing to the side. "I don't want to be apart from you again, Tol. If you mean it, I want us to become one."

Entwine? Tol's eyes nearly bugged out of his head. He couldn't believe this was real. It was so sudden. His mind made all sorts of excuses as to why they shouldn't, but why was he so nervous? This was foolishness. She was all he wanted. "What brought this on?" Those words came out all wrong. He wanted to tell her yes, he would do anything for her. Why did he have to jinx it?

The question did just as he feared. It made her project a lack of confidence. Had she erred? He could feel it so strongly, and wanted to tell her that she'd done anything but. Maela slid off him and cast her eyes to the side. "There's something I need to tell you. More than this."

"Huh?" Tol asked, confused.

"I just came from a meeting with the Ruling Committee."

"Is something wrong?" Her tone told him the answer to that question, but he asked anyway.

"There's going to be another mission. One that's possibly more frightening than the last," she said. She bit her lip, then looked over at him, sadness and fear written all over her face. She told him what was to come.

43

—————

Tamar inspected the entirety of the ship five times over the course of the evening. She'd barked at a crew member she'd thought was running too slow, and that had been a mistake. Taking her frustration out on the crew wasn't going to help anyone. The problem was with this new mission. Tamar could see clearly that the Aryshan fleet was on a course for destruction. She hated it with every fiber of her being.

She stopped at the lift, ready to call it quits and retire to her quarters. In truth, she shouldn't have been prancing about the ship with her emotional aura so imbalanced; it would only cause ripples among the crew. Her body didn't listen, though. It kept telling her to keep moving. If she confined herself to quarters, she'd go mad. Idleness was akin to death.

The lift door slid open, and Lieutenant Aeveron emerged. He froze in front of her, inadvertently blocking the lift. He was nervous. Had one of the other commanders informed him of their recent orders? "Speaker," Aeveron said.

Tamar felt for him. She truly did. These recent missions were a lot of pressure to put on an inexperienced officer. He'd had little time to acclimate to the ship, or to the crew. It must have felt like going from one foreign environment to another. And yet she had been worried that he was spying on her on behalf of the Ruling Committee. That seemed absurd now. "Is all well?" she asked.

"Huh?" His eyes shifted. "Oh, I'm well." He stepped out of the way of the lift. "I'm sorry. I didn't mean to slow you down."

Tamar stepped forward, her arm brushing against his. She couldn't help but feel an odd tingle from that, and stifled a breath. This was a feeling she couldn't allow herself to indulge in, or even think about. The way he'd joined her in the mess before his mission...it had warped her mind. Few others had such audacity, such confidence. Was that what scared him now? The thought brought a smile to her face. Despite her own misgivings, she turned around. "Lieutenant," Tamar said.

Aeveron had made good time down the corridor in front of her, but stopped in his tracks, looking back at her from over his shoulder. "Yes, Speaker?"

"Where are you headed?"

Aeveron frowned in thought. "Off duty."

"I did promise you we could share a meal again sometime. How about now?" Tamar asked. Her insides fluttered. This was a terrible idea, but why couldn't she help herself?

He hesitated a moment, but then made his way back toward the lift, where the doors kept trying to shut despite Tamar holding them. "I would like that," Aeveron said. He joined her.

Tamar keyed in the command to the top deck.

"That's not the way to the mess," Aeveron said.

"No, it's my quarters. It was odd enough sharing a meal last time with prying eyes. It would be nice not to have a tribe peering in on everything I do." The lift engaged.

Aeveron simply agreed to her statement, though she had hoped to get a little more information out of him as to why he hadn't committed.

They moved to her quarters, and Tamar opened the door. She hadn't allowed the crew much access to her quarters, preferring to keep her personal life rather quiet. In fact, Tamar couldn't think of a time since Intrei had left the ship where she'd allowed someone inside. At least with Aeveron uncommitted, she wouldn't have to worry about any spiraling through the bondsense while they were inside. She would feel nothing from him, and would be able to talk to him in peace. The prospect sounded pleasant.

Aeveron looked around and moved to the port side view of the reception room, a window out into space beyond. The stars streaked past them as the *Issiana* traversed through space. "Our crew quarters don't have windows," Aeveron said. "And they're much smaller."

"The theory is that I might need to entertain dignitaries. It gives me a reception room like this with my bedchambers beyond," Tamar said, pointing past to another door. "I requisitioned a Tuuko River spicefish before we left port. It's in my personal stores. Figured you might like a change from re-moisturized meats."

Aeveron grimaced.

"You don't like spicefish?" Tamar asked, maneuvering around toward him and the view outside the vessel.

"No, it's not that," he said.

"We're off duty now. You don't have to be afraid to talk to me," Tamar said, trying to encourage. She clasped her hands behind her back. What worried him so much that he stared outward, away from her? She had to admit she was intrigued.

Aeveron rubbed his hands together. "I'm not sure. I didn't expect to be asked to your quarters."

Tamar couldn't help but laugh. "I didn't expect to ask you."

He glanced toward her, a little smile crossing his face.

"You're stressed about the missions since you've arrived," Tamar said. She found she particularly liked the look of him smiling.

"You got it," he said.

"That's normal, you know. I remember when I first was commissioned as an officer. It was a stationary assignment, a base on Arysha proper. Have you spent much time on homeworld?"

Aeveron shook his head. "I'm from a colony world."

"I miss it, I have to say. It's not really my intention to spend my life out in the stars like this," Tamar said. She hesitated, realizing she'd said far too much, something she shouldn't be saying to a subordinate. But he'd made her comfortable by his own admissions. Were their thoughts the same? Tamar eyed him.

He met her gaze ever so briefly before turning back to the window. "Me too," he said simply. Why didn't he talk as much like he did that first time? When he'd seemed so confident? What had changed?

"I should call the chef and make sure our food is going to be delivered," Tamar said, breaking what could have been an awkward movement. She moved to the terminal and contacted the mess, communicating her order.

Aeveron joined her at the table soon after. Tamar didn't often consume libations, but she had a bottle of Ruy'ach Oti that someone had given her when she took the assignment, still unopened. She popped the bottle, asking Aeveron if he would like some. He hesitated but agreed once she had it in hand. They talked about their past, schooling, where they grew up, very standard pleasantries. Tamar found herself disappointed, hoping for a deeper conversation, but she wasn't certain how to broach the subjects. It had been far too long since she had had any casual conversation worth considering.

The chef's assistant delivered their spicefish, and it was perfect. It gave her an aroma of back home, a bitter pepper, but in a pleasant way that mixed well with the citrusy sauce. They ate, and talked more freely. The most amazing part of the evening was that he made her laugh, and several times at that. She couldn't remember the last time laughter permeated her life. Tamar had a couple of drinks herself, despite the fact that she didn't typically enjoy alcohol. She didn't like the feeling of losing control. Yet something tonight kept pushing her to do just that.

"You did well in your last assignment," Tamar said. "Even though the objectives weren't completed because of outside forces, people see that you are a person to get a job done."

Aeveron set his utensils down. "Thanks. I..." he paused, as if searching for the right words. "I intended to stay in operations, aboard ship. That kind of assignment really isn't for me."

Tamar peered at him curiously. "Too dangerous?"

He locked his attention on her again. "Too violent."

"I understand," she said. And she did. Perhaps that was what Tamar had been bothered with these last few months—the violence of it all. She had to think of the attacks, the loss of life, both Aryshan and human. Should she open up to him about her concerns? She already had with Maela, and that had gone well. She couldn't talk to everyone. But even Maela hadn't been quite a confidante of the sort that she felt she could have in Aeveron. This was different. Perhaps it was the drink getting to her head, but it made sense to her to bring him into her thoughts. "This war...it disturbs me sometimes," she said in a low tone.

Even without a bondsense, she noticed Aeveron become much more alert, tense. "How so?"

Had she made the wrong move by talking to him about this? Tamar became concerned. She couldn't appear weak before her crew, not with the committee so split as it was. "Violence, like you said."

Aeveron frowned. "Yeah."

Tamar leaned back against her chair. He hadn't taken offense at her thought. "I'm not sure what I can do about it, however. We have our orders, and must do what we can for Arysha. Being a captain is difficult. All decisions come from higher above. We're just expected to execute orders."

Aeveron chuckled softly.

"Was something I said funny?"

"No, nothing like that. It's just that I had this conversation with someone very different several months ago. Surprised me to hear it from you," Aeveron said.

What was that supposed to mean? Tamar could never quite read him. There was something so different about him. It bothered her, in both a good and bad way. "Did you come to any good conclusions?"

"No," Aeveron said. "I just listened."

Their eyes met again. And this time they lingered for a long, silent moment. The hum of the ship's engines took over in the background, and Tamar felt as if her body were lifting in the air. Or was it the alcohol? "It's different when you're committed, you know. You follow orders out of a sense of duty, but what I have comes from within me." She touched her chest. "It's something chemical, telling me to protect my tribe." She frowned. "Perhaps it was foolish of me to commit so young. There's just so much pressure to do so."

Aeveron reached a hand across the table toward her. "You don't have to regret decisions. War is hard on everyone."

What should she do? Should she offer her hand? Tamar hadn't been in a situation like this before. Physicality was dangerous, she understood that—yet with the way her whole body pulsed, she wasn't sure she could resist. She let her hand fall to the table and brushed her fingertips against his. That contact, light as it was, felt incredible.

He took her hand into his. "You're in a position where you'll be able to enact change. Remember that. It may not be now, but it could be tomorrow."

It took everything in Tamar not to panic and pull her hand back. She found herself liking his touch far too much. He was right, though. She would have that opportunity and might have more leverage now than she thought. Tamar squeezed his hand. "When I talk to most people, I stay on guard. It's usually something to do with the fleet, or someone trying to get to me because of my favor with the Ruling Committee. I don't sense that about you."

"I'm here for you," Aeveron said, his voice soft and deep.

This was getting far too dangerous. In that moment, Tamar understood that she had wanted to hear words like that for months, ever since she came aboard the *Issiana*. Tamar pulled her hand back and stood. Aeveron watched expectantly. She moved around the table toward him, his head still cocked upward toward her. And then she did the unthinkable.

She leaned over and kissed him. It was a soft kiss, and quick, but something she'd never even dreamed of allowing herself do with a man aboard her ship nonetheless. She'd kept herself away to keep herself safe, when she'd needed the opposite. And it felt good.

Aeveron had a look of shock about him, but that changed quickly. His eyes told her we wanted more.

Tamar pushed her hand softly against his chest to keep him from getting too many ideas. "Thank you, Aeveron. You've given me a lot to think about, and your loyalty means a lot to me."

"Thank you."

Straightening herself, Tamar grabbed on Aeveron's arm and gave him a gentle tug so he could stand. "I need to review some reports before turning in for the evening. We have a difficult mission ahead and it requires my attention," she said. It was true, but it was also an excuse to remove him before matters became too intense for both of them.

"Is it something I can help with?"

"No," Tamar said. She paced to the table, picking up the dishes and placing them in the bin for her sonic cleaner. "It's something you're going to be assigned to, actually. I know you dislike the violent missions, but the Ruling Committee wants both you and Tol to handle this because of your success on Cestus III."

Aeveron cocked his head. All his former tenderness had drained from his face, and he appeared concerned. "Can you tell me?"

"I suppose there's no harm in telling you early," Tamar said, moving toward her door to usher him that direction. "We're sending you to sabotage the Earth Admiral Conley's vessel, the *Reykjavik*, and destroy it."

"Admiral Conley?" Aeveron stumbled over his feet.

"You know the name?"

"No. I mean, yes. I think I've heard it. It's just...a big mission." He straightened his uniform.

Tamar reached out, taking his hand once more to give it a soft squeeze. "I'll do my best to find a way to complete this mission without making it too dangerous for you."

Aeveron didn't respond to that gesture. His entire mannerism had changed. "I should be going. Thank you again," he said in a hurried tone before turning for the door.

Tamar watched him as he left. The door shut behind him. She didn't want to tell him how she thought this was far too dangerous a mission herself. How could she send him into one so soon after they'd kindled...whatever this was? And so soon after he'd returned from his last excursion? His reaction was understandable, though too panicked without knowing the details she did. He was an odd one, but Tamar liked him, and she would do what she could to make sure he survived.

44

Sean worked throughout the night. He hadn't been listed on any of the active duty logs, but the news Speaker Tamar had brought him made it impossible to sleep. If the mission went through, it meant all the hard-laid plans would be gone. He'd have no hope of obtaining ship information, transmitting it, or learning about fleet movements. How had he gotten himself into such a mess, where they kept assigning him to missions off-ship?

Worse, this was Admiral Conley they were talking about. This wasn't like last time, a supply depot, where he could justify that he wouldn't be partaking in anyone getting hurt. He had only destroyed supplies. This new assignment meant killing—not just people, but a hero at that.

It also spelled a new escalation in the war. There had been a couple tit-for-tat strikes by both sides so far, but nothing to this degree. The destruction of the *Reykjavik* would propel the fighting to another level.

All of this was troubling enough, but then there was the whole personal situation with Speaker Tamar. She'd touched him, and not in a merely friendly way. If he hadn't been too hyped to sleep over all the mission and moral dilemmas swimming around in his head, she would have been enough to make him need a cold shower.

Looking back, Sean regretted every move with her. She had drawn his attention back on Palmer Station, and he'd been unable to get her out of his head since that time. Stupid. It put his entire life at risk. He should have never accepted the invitation to her quarters.

Yet he longed to be back there. More than anything. He had to concentrate on getting at least some information from the ship's databanks before he took off with Tol again. And he had to figure out what he was going to do when that happened. McCleever had ordered him last time to maintain his cover, but was this situation over the line? Was he trying to justify staying in cover now so that he could stay with Tamar? Sean didn't trust himself to make this decision. The worst part was he had no one he could talk to about it.

Sean tried to keep his troubles off his mind while he sat in Operations Controls, scanning through information. He found defense capabilities, ship design for boarding parties, shields, and weapons capabilities, and downloaded each of them onto his data crystal. He had been given a small interstellar comm beacon that was solid enough to go through the *Issiana's* trash receptacle. The thought was to dispose of the information when the trash was jettisoned to a nearby star, and transmit after the ship was on its way to another destination. That would minimize any risk of exposure. Sean hoped the plan would work. The operations terminal blinked while the information transferred.

The night had gone like a blur of the stars through FTL viewed through Tamar's reception room. He couldn't help but picture her across from him, her sparkling silver skin, those wide eyes that gave her the most innocent quality...

Sean couldn't remember the last time he had conversation that clicked into place on so many levels, even though he had been quiet to try not to divulge too much information and get himself into hot water. Tamar was smarter than him, more sincere, funny, interesting. Perfect. Despite all his inadequacies, she still chose to confide in him. She still chose to kiss him.

He subconsciously touched his lips with his fingertips. Her lips were so soft, and he hadn't kissed a woman in more than a year. He didn't take that encounter lightly.

For the sake of argument, Sean pondered what would happen if he did go through with the mission of destroying the *Reykjavik*. It would be a turning point in the war, this war in which he still didn't understand Arysha's objectives. Would they continue to press an all-out offensive on Earth? They appeared aggressive. Though at the same time, people like Tamar didn't seem to support pursuing this to its extreme conclusion.

He shook his head, wondering why he was even considering this. She had gotten inside his head, and he was panicking—something he couldn't afford to do.

The doors to operations controls opened behind him. Sean froze. No one was supposed to be here this late. He turned.

Commander Neyral stood in the doorway, frowning at Sean in confusion. He didn't look pleased. "Lieutenant Aeveron, I believe you're not supposed to be on shift for another three hours. What are you doing here?"

Sean leaned back against his console, blindly reaching for the data crystal. Once he had it, he slinked his hand back to his side, keeping the crystal hidden from Neyral's view. "Commander," Sean said, trying to sound deferential. He needed an excuse and fast. "I couldn't sleep, sir. I wanted to get ahead in my duties."

"Ahead? Why?" Neyral raised a brow, circling around him and looking over Sean's shoulder at the console.

The display didn't have anything incriminating on it. Sean had cleared most of his research from the screen proper before inserting the crystal.

Sean maneuvered himself so the crystal wouldn't accidentally come into view and slipped it into his pocket. What would make a good excuse? "The coming mission, sir. I know I'll be leaving my post for a long time. I figured I would take initiative."

Neyral craned his head at Sean. "Who told you about that?"

"Speaker Tamar," Sean said.

Neyral considered, staring at the screen for a long moment before nodding. "It will be a difficult mission, true. I commend you for your additional work, Lieutenant. You make a good example to the rest of the crew." Neyral stepped back from the console. "Tell me, have you considered committing to the Aresh? It would help advance your career considerably if you keep working like this."

Sean exhaled in relief, trying to let the air out slowly so that he wouldn't show more of his loss of tension than he had to. "Every day. It's not a decision to make lightly, sir."

"True, it's not." Neyral's eyes glimmered with respect. "Carry on. I'll see you come shift time." He turned on his heel and walked out, boots clicking on the floor behind him.

Sean reached into his pocket and gripped the data crystal once more. It was still there. He was safe. But that had been close. Too close.

_____

45

When his duty shift ended, Tol called Aeveron to his quarters to work on his phase device. Tol was contorted in an uncomfortable position on the floor, sealing in one of the energy storage arrays, when his quarters door opened. Grease and other chemicals covered him, but it didn't bother him. Such was the price to pay for getting work done. "Aeveron, can you hand me a wrench? I need to tighten one of the bolts."

"Don't you have a bot that can do this sort of work?" Aeveron asked. Tol heard the sound of metal moving, as Aeveron fumbled through his tool box.

"Don't get anything out of order. It looks messy, but there's a method to my madness."

Something under the device made a buzzing noise. Tol knew what that meant. Overload. He turned off the phase device and righted himself before moving over to his terminal. Once there, he made some notes while Aeveron stood behind him with the wrench.

"Does this sort of thing impress your lady-friend—what was her name?"

"Maela," Tol said. "And I don't need to impress her anymore. We're entwined."

"Really? Just like that?" Aeveron dangled the wrench down in front of him.

"I might not need it after all," Tol said, waving the tool off. It was time to end the small talk. He had to focus on the task at hand. He tapped in some commands, adjusting the energy input from his new power supply. It worked. The buzz became more of a hiss, and the air in the room changed.

It was hard to describe. It felt like a wave of pressure went through him. Tol stumbled back, looking at the device. Nothing in the room appeared different on the visual spectrum, but when he glanced back at the terminal, all the data calculations were gone.

"Whoa, what was that?" Aeveron asked, steadying himself against the wall.

Tol's eyes went wide. "It's working."

Aeveron blinked a couple of times and backpedaled to the front of the room. "It is. I can't see you or the device. You must be in the field."

"I tried to keep it within a couple of meters of the device," Tol said. He reached a hand out. "Do you see my hand? It should extend the field around me as long as the majority of my bulk is in its range."

Aeveron shook his head.

"Reach over, in front of the terminal console. Try to touch me."

Aeveron hesitated, but then moved over. He reached his hand toward Tol and the most amazing thing occurred. Aeveron's hand went right through him. He was out of phase with this dimension. Incredible!

Tol stepped away to make sure that he wouldn't accidentally come back into phase with Aeveron's hand inside his body, and then tapped the control on the device.

"Huh," Aeveron said, his eyes going a little wide when Tol appeared. "That's incredible." Something churned in his head, Aeveron could see it. "I was just told about a mission. Do you know about it? This could be the very thing to keep us from getting killed."

"You understand!" Tol grinned. "If we install this device in the shuttle, and with a big enough power supply pack, we can get out of phase with Admiral Conley's ship, drop the bomb, and be back in phase before they ever see us. We'll have to use a different shuttle than the Cestus III mission, something more compact but with the same power regulators. We'll probably need to draw power from several systems including environmental. Which means we'll have to have fewer people." He pointed back and forth between Aeveron and himself. "Two would be optimum."

"Hold on. This is your first successful test, right? It's great but how do we know it'll work in a larger capacity?" Aeveron asked.

"Trust me. I've done all the calcs," Tol said. He was proud of his device. "Now let's go." Tol trudged toward the door.

"Where are you going?"

"The committee chambers. We'll have to inform them about this." He moved past Aeveron and jogged toward the door. This was it. The first time one of his devices would be put to use for his tribe, for Arysha. He'd finally succeeded, and now he would tell the world.

46

"Y ou think you can install this device into a small shuttlecraft and have it operational within the next few days?" Neyral asked.

Tamar watched Neyral interact with Tol. The logistics of the phase device was more his territory. The bondsense was flooded with optimism from Neyral, as well as the other three commanders. She could hardly help but feel hopeful. If this device worked, it dramatically increased her crew's probability of surviving. Increased Aeveron's probability of surviving. She sneaked a glance at him.

Aeveron caught her look and gave a small uptick of his lips. Tamar turned her attention back to the situation at hand.

"I do, Commander," Tol said, broadcasting pure pride.

"This is quite the achievement," Tendell said, scrolling through specifications on his console. "If this can apply to our larger vessels, it could change everything."

"I sense we're all in agreement and therefore can vote unanimously to allow Tol and Aeveron a few days to install this device onto one of the shuttlecraft?" Tamar asked.

The other commanders muttered their agreements.

"Excellent. Then we will proceed," Tamar said.

"We'll do the Aresh proud," Tol said.

That set eyes on Aeveron, still uncommitted in the midst of this. How uncomfortable it must have been for him. What did he think of the tribe? Tamar would have to find out later. It would do no good to put him on the spot. "You two are dismissed. Thank you. Lieutenant Tol, you can be assured that we will forward our commendations to the Ruling Committee."

Tol's smile was impossible to hide as he bowed his head toward her. He bounded out of the room, followed by Aeveron, who glanced over his shoulder toward her.

Tamar's heart rushed at the look. She tried to get back to reading her reports and not react. But when the two left, Tamar sensed a tension from her fellow commanders, emanating from Tendell across the room. She looked up at him.

"There's another matter I believe we should address before continuing with mission preparations," Tendell said. He sounded unsure of himself, and that resonated through the bondsense as well. Neyral nodded to him.

"What's that?" Tamar asked.

"Over the last several weeks, Commander Neyral and myself have noted some peculiar disturbances through the bondsense. Most have centered around you, Speaker. With all due respect, you've had an aura of fear, paranoia, and anger. Regulations allow for the commanding committee to hold regular votes on a Speaker's ability to lead a vessel. Both Commander Neyral and I have discussed these recent emotional indiscretions at length and have concluded it would be a good time to have this vote. These coming weeks will be difficult and we need to ensure that we have a strong speakership that is fully in control of the ship," Tendell said. His face was cold and stoic, and he blocked his emotions through the aura.

"I've heard reports of you fraternizing with Lieutenant Aeveron. He is doing well for one uncommitted, and it wouldn't be right to have his record tarnished with personal issues," Neyral said, equally as cool as Tendell. "I believe your interactions with him may also be the source of these uncomfortable projections."

Uncomfortable projections? The audacity of him. Neyral's motivation had little to do with the ship, and everything to do with her rejecting his advances and his ambition. This whole call to vote incensed her. Tendell had to realize this, but why was he going along with it?

She had to control her emotions now more than ever. This was their whole argument, that she couldn't keep control in the most important of situations. She had to project calm. The void of space. Tamar envisioned the darkness and the stars. *Breathe.*

"As I understand it, the removal of a Speaker requires a unanimous vote from the other commanders," Maela said. Her anger pierced through the bondsense as quickly as Tamar had quelled her own. "I do not believe there is sufficient evidence to warrant Speaker Tamar's removal. Moreover, private relations are a part of a vessel. They are none of your business, Commander Neyral. I have seen nothing improper from Speaker Tamar. I have, however, noticed that your interest in her may be viewed by some as improper."

Neyral glared at Maela with all his fury. His fist clenched so tightly onto his console he was liable to pop the top off it. "Can't you see the real problem here? She is questioning the authority of the Ruling Committee. Even though she's favored by them, she is an affront to our harmony in a time of war. We need real leadership!"

"That's enough, Commander Neyral," Tamar said. "It appears you're the one who has lost emotional control, and under the stresses of these recent assignments, it's understandable. What I'm going to order is that you take these next few days off to relax and ready yourself in case something happens that calls the *Issiana* into direct conflict with the humans. We will need you at your best then." She tried to keep as respectful a tone as she possibly could, but it would do no good as long as Neyral stayed angry.

Neyral huffed a moment longer and released his console, smacking it with his fist. "There is still the matter of Aeveron himself. I found him in Operations Controls early this morning, acting strangely. I believe we should consider reassignment."

Jealousy. That's all this was. Tamar could sense it clearly now, and

Neyral had dropped any semblance of trying to shield his emotions. She caught Tendell's eyes and saw that he noted it as well. "That won't be necessary, Commander Neyral."

"I can speak with Aeveron to make sure all is well. I do have a medical background," Maela offered.

Tamar shook her head. "If there's something wrong with him, I'll speak with him. He is likely nervous about this assignment, and it's understandable. I have his trust."

Neyral's whole face tensed, but he said nothing. He turned toward the exit and stormed out of the room.

All of Tamar's fears so far about this war, and about this committee, had come true. She hated being right. She hoped Aeveron's promise that she could effect change would hold true.

47

___

Sean let himself fall backward onto the cot in his quarters. It had been a long day's work in preparation for his next journey. God, he was tired. Ever since Neyral found him in Operations Controls, he found himself looking over his shoulder, paranoid that everyone saw him as a spy. If only he had chosen to return to Mars, to continue with his prior career track, then he wouldn't be in this mess. And mess was an understatement. It was on the verge of being a catastrophe.

The door chime to his quarters rang. He rubbed his temples. "Not now," he mumbled to himself and pushed back to his feet.

It had to be Tol. Again. As fun as it was to see a new device that worked, each subsequent demonstration became far less exciting. And that was without considering what it represented: a looming plan to kill Admiral Conley and thousands of other humans aboard the *Reykjavik*. How could he be excited about that?

Instead of commanding the door open, Sean stood and moved to tap the control manually. He readied himself to block entry to Tol and shoo him away before he could get too caught up in conversation.

When the door opened, Sean couldn't believe his eyes. It wasn't

Tol standing there at all, but a much more pleasant sight—Tamar. She gave a gentle push on his chest, forcing him to backpedal inside. The door closed again behind her. Before he could speak, Tamar had pressed her firm body against him.

Even though he'd seen her many times, Sean found it difficult to believe the perfect, athletic tone of each one of her curves. She felt so good against him. Sean leaned his head in and kissed her.

Their lips locked and refused to part. She tasted so sweet, a soft coolness to her breath that tickled him when their tongues met. She was perfection, just as he had envisioned in those moments when he was on the edge of falling asleep, every night since he arrived on the *Issiana*.

Sean wrapped his arms tightly around her, his hands eager to explore every inch of her, and she followed his lead. He fell back on his cot, and Tamar fell atop him, breaking the kiss for a moment to giggle softly before she reengaged with even more fervor.

He worked to undo her tunic, and found Tamar grabbing him by the wrist a moment later. She broke the kiss again and looked at him. "We can't. Not yet," she said, her voice soft as a purr.

Those words dashed his hopes. Sean wanted her so badly, more than anything. He wasn't sure he could contain himself with her on his lap like this. Then he remembered. Aryshans were monogamous to an extreme. They couldn't engage in sex without creating some sort of bond that paired them for life. Entwining, it was called. That hardly mattered here. He wouldn't be able to entwine with her, as a human, would he? But then, she didn't know that. To her, he was Aryshan. One of her crew.

"Don't look so sad," Tamar said, nuzzling against his neck. "You're uncommitted. You understand what it means to take your time before such a big change. Besides, it wouldn't be wise to entwine right before you leave on a mission like this. It's too dangerous."

Sean frowned. "Maela and Tol entwined."

Tamar's eyes widened. "They what?"

"Tol mentioned it to me."

Tamar slid off his lap and onto the cot beside him. Apparently, this news had broken her mood. "What is she thinking?"

"Have so little faith that we'll return?" Sean asked, cocking his head toward her in what he hoped was a cute manner.

Tamar kept her eyes on the floor in front of her. "This isn't the easiest of missions, Aeveron." She leaned against him. "I wish I could tell you otherwise. But this device—it gives some hope. It lifts a heavy weight from my shoulders."

She looked so beautiful. All Sean wanted was to wipe that worry off her face—bring back that moment of pure pleasure they'd shared a moment prior. She cared about him; shouldn't that stop the way his heart felt like it was being ripped out of his chest by the mere act of being apart from her? How did he even let it get this bad?

Back at the academy, Sean had been very close to a Michael Walens. He wasn't sure what happened to the guy. They'd gone their separate ways after Michael fell for a second-year student. All the time that he and Sean had spent together evaporated overnight. It was strange losing a friend so fast. Sean had never really allowed his emotions to overwhelm his duties, or even his personal life like that. Until now, a point where these emotions could mean life or death for him. What a time to fall in love.

And yet, even understanding what was happening, all Sean wanted was to tell Tamar not to worry, that they should entwine anyway. To lie to her and tell her there was no problem. Yet he couldn't bring himself to speak the words.

The even more ridiculous part of this was the lie of his entire existence with her. She didn't know who he really was. Part of him wanted to open up to her, to tell her everything, but he fell short of doing that. The nagging red flag in the back of his head told him it was a terrible idea.

Tamar looked over at him and forced a smile. It was a weak one, but beautiful on her nonetheless. "I appreciate you being here for me. I wish you didn't have to go."

"Me too," Sean said.

With that, she stood. She laughed to herself and shook her head. "This was foolish of me. I'm sorry."

"Don't be sorry," Sean said. "I'll come back. I promise."

Her bright eyes caught his again. They told him that she wasn't so sure about that. "You do that, and we'll continue where we left off. Okay?"

Was she insinuating that she wanted to entwine with him? It sounded like it, and she certainly didn't look like someone who wanted to play it slow. Those words, the expression on his face, it destroyed every preconception about his purpose here on this Aryshan ship. Sean couldn't help himself anymore. His mission, all of this, it didn't matter. Tamar was everything. "Okay," he said.

PART IV

48

Since the officers had left in their shuttle, the committee chambers had been fairly quiet. Worry loomed in the bond-sense, mostly projected from Maela, but amplified by Tamar. She didn't bother trying to quell it. Her fear was far too strong, and too rational, to be helped. In some ways, it was better to be on edge. It made her alert, ready for action in a moment's notice. This is why the bondsense had evolved, for those moments when violent megastorms threatened the existence of entire tribes.

And this committee was a storm of its own. Her control dangled by a thread—Maela's loyalty to her. Her fellow commander was preoccupied with the fact that she had foolishly entwined with Tol before he left for a dangerous mission. Tamar couldn't chastise her. It would do no good at this juncture. What was done was done. Though if Tol didn't survive his mission, it left Maela in danger of becoming incapacitated. Tamar's command would be tenuous if that happened. This could all spiral so quickly for her, and for this ship.

Tamar had seen firsthand what a severed bond could do to a person. Her grandmother had gone into shock and died immediately after her grandfather passed. Older widowers rarely survived their entwined's death.

At least Tol had developed his phase device. If anything would keep them safe, the device was their best hope. It would be strange if they did return, as even with the device, no one on the committee appeared to expect it. She couldn't believe she had promised Aeveron she would entwine with him. It was too soon. They hardly knew each other.

Love had never been on Tamar's mind like this. She'd never acknowledged it as a possibility. But she had found it. He was difficult to stop thinking about, even when she had work to do. It didn't help that she had sent him away. She needed to focus on something else. "Commander Tendell," she said, "how are the personnel handing our emergency status?"

Tendell glanced toward her, his face shimmering behind the center holographic display. "I've run three efficiency drills so far, and the crew is operating within standard parameters. I have little doubt that should we have a confrontation with the humans, we will be fighting with peak efficiency."

No specifics, but Tendell wasn't the type to talk in too much detail. It didn't give Tamar anything new to work on while they waited. This away mission was going to be the death of her as much as her crewmen, if only because of her worry.

Before she could consider her other options on how to pass the time, Neyral entered the chambers.

He was frantic. No, he was beyond frantic. The feeling was so thick in the bondsense that it nearly knocked her from her chair. The others felt it, too, and focused on him. Whatever he had on his mind would be difficult to contain.

Neyral held a sealed bag with a data crystal inside. He waved it in front of the other commanders, his arms shaking from anger. He stood for several moments without a word.

"Commander Neyral," Tamar said. She tried to keep condescension out of her tone, in spite of the fact that she was still quite angry at him from the outburst the other day. The irony of his projecting such fevered emotion so soon after accusing her of being unable to control herself didn't escape her. "Please, try to contain your emotions. It's difficult for us to see what you want with such a cloudy projection."

"There is a traitor aboard," Neyral said. "This was found in our waste system by our environmental engineers. It was about to jettison into space. It was transmitting our ship's specifications."

That caught the attention of all three of the other commanders in the room. It was far more disconcerting than most other matters Tamar had worried about. The worry amplified within the others. "It couldn't be one of the Aresh," Tamar said.

"No, it could not," Neyral agreed.

"Perhaps one of the others? Is there a tribe dissenting against the recent Ruling Committee actions trying to gain power?" Tendell asked.

"Not to this degree," Neyral said. "The Aeryl would stand to gain the most if something happens and the Aresh fall out of favor, but I cannot fathom that they'd go to this extent. If this were happening, and one was working with the humans, wouldn't the others sense something that was wrong in any tribe?"

Maela frowned. "It depends. That level of deception is extremely rare. Of course, if all of them are in agreement that this is the best for the tribe..."

Tamar let out a sigh. Then that would mean they have even bigger problems. She hadn't considered a civil war. Conflict on that level hadn't existed within the Aryshan people for hundreds of years, since before the Anwii came to power. It would be hard to keep something like this from another tribe member. The committee couldn't rule out an insurrection of that scale, but it was unlikely. "Our primary suspects must be the uncommitted," Tamar said.

Tendell tapped on his console, and looked down at it. "Approximately twenty percent of the crew matches an uncommitted profile."

Neyral let out a little laugh. "No need. I've already determined who the traitor is."

"Who?" Maela asked.

"Aeveron."

Tamar froze. That accusation had been about as far from what she expected as anyone else Neyral could have accused. "No," Tamar said. "It can't be."

Neyral met her eyes, challenge written all over his face. "I'm certain of it."

"Do you have any evidence?" Tendell asked.

"Not as of yet. Aeveron was acting strangely before he left for his mission, and this. The information he transmitted would be data he was privy to in the operations department."

"But anyone could obtain that information," Tamar said. She didn't back down, didn't peel her eyes from him. He would blink first, she swore to herself. "And of course he's acting strangely. We just sent him on an extremely dangerous mission for the second time since he's arrived. He's not even had time to orient to the ship." Her words sounded defensive. Of course they did. Tendell frowned at her, disappointment on his face. Tamar found herself not caring about what he thought anymore. This was preposterous.

"I'll second that," Maela said. "Tol spends a lot of time with him and says he is one of the most loyal individuals he's ever met. He is certain that Aeveron will be committing to the Aresh soon."

Tamar was certain of further than that. He would soon entwine. To her. A sense of warmness ran through her body at the thought, though she couldn't voice it now. She'd never been that adamant about anything before. It had been more of a question mark to this point. How was it that it took such a crazy accusation for Tamar to let her full emotions come to light in her own mind? Odd how a psyche worked.

"I believe we should monitor him nonetheless, assuming he returns," Neyral said. He finally did turn away from her. "You'll find that I'm right, I'm certain."

Tamar wanted to claw at him. Even thinking about hurting a member of her tribe set off an instinctual reaction that made her stomach churn. She would get very sick before she could act in such a pre-meditated fashion against him—the saving grace of having a tribe. If he hadn't been of the Aresh, Tamar wasn't sure she'd stop herself.

It was reassuring to have the Aresh. None of her loyalists could possibly be the one transmitting this data. Even so, she would have to tighten security at the very least. It created the problem of getting the crew suspicious and making everyone tenser than they already were with this war looming, the last thing anyone needed. On the other hand, they couldn't risk inaction.

"Let's discuss the measures we're going to take to make sure we don't have any more information leaks," Tendell said.

Tamar nodded and refocused herself.

49

S ince Sean had departed the *Issiana* with Tol, he found he felt
more at home with the Aryshans than he could have imagined. The two of them had conversations that reminded him
of an extended trip he'd taken with his friends, back before his military career had gone into full swing. They would head off to a lake or
to the mountains, a nice retreat from a technology-driven life. Sean
found he missed those days. The last several years he had been so
alone.

In the whirlwind of his time in Aryshan space, all that had
changed. Or had it that much? He kept noticing that he found ways to
justify his enjoyment of being Aryshan. Which, in turn, justified his
attachment to Tamar. It jeopardized his mission, his life, and now he
grew comfortable in the thought. Soon, he would have to make difficult decisions.

He still couldn't be sure whether he would be able to let this
mission proceed. What happened on Cestus III had been an easy call
in retrospect. He probably hadn't needed to contact the intelligence
agents at all, though it did provide them some assistance.

This was different. Lives would be affected, ended. Did his
personal feelings cloud his considerations of those very real conse-

quences? Commander McCleever's training still stuck with him. He should never break cover, no matter the cost. Guilt simmered inside of Sean all the same. Because that was not his primary motivation.

It always came back to Tamar. Even the brief thought of her quickened his breath, stirred energy inside of him. Because of her, he found himself considering spending his life as an Aryshan. That could help humanity as well, couldn't it? She would be a political power, and he could influence her to work for change, to stop this war. Tamar had voiced that she was leaning toward that viewpoint. If he gave it a nudge, how many more lives could he save compared to the ones who would lose theirs on the *Reykjavik*?

But what would happen when she found out he wasn't who he said he was? Would she still love him?

Tol interrupted his thoughts by making a loud clanging noise in the back of the shuttle. He had been hard at work ensuring his phase device would be compatible with the shuttle's systems, and the energy draw for this size wouldn't pose a problem. He had written Sean's worry off as part of mission jitters, as if Sean had the same mechanical concerns he did. It made it easier on Sean to have time to think without having to conceal his worry.

They'd had some good talks as well. Sean learned a little bit more about what it meant to be entwined. It wasn't a simple marriage like humans had. The Aryshans shared a deep telepathic bond with their partners. Tol claimed each partner gifted part of their souls to the other. It was yet another thing Sean wouldn't be able to provide for Tamar, and he wished he could.

The last several hours, Tol had been engrossed by his device, poring over technical manuals on his datapad. Sean made the mistake of asking him if there was anything good to read, and his question had led to a half-hour explanation of crystal data and energy storage and how it could be used to open whole worlds of possibilities. Sean certainly liked the use of technology but had never been much one for taking things apart and figuring out how everything worked.

"Don't you have anything else to read?" Sean called to the back of the shuttle. He should have uploaded something to his own datapad, but his nerves had the better of him before the trip.

"You should get used to my manuals. I could really use your help," Tol said, not looking up from his work.

Sean took that as a signal to get up from his seat in the cockpit. The shuttle proceeded along on autopilot, not requiring much live reaction for this trip. He moved toward the device, and that's when he stumbled over a tool Tol had left on the ground.

He fell face forward, and he had to stop himself lest he crack his head on the phase device. In desperation, Sean reached his hand forward to brace himself. His hand descended on a piece of sharp metal protruding from a corner of the device.

The metal pierced his hand.

For a moment, the pain didn't register. Memories of his training sessions flooded back to him. A single drop of blood could break his cover, ruin his mission. He froze, looking over to Tol, keeping his hand in place. He had to get Tol to look away somehow and buy some time to cover his tracks.

Despite Sean's attempts not to exacerbate the situation by moving, blood drizzled down the corner of the device. A single drop grew in size, and then gravity took hold. It trickled through the air and splatted a crimson stain on the floor.

Worse, Tol stared directly at it. "What's that?" Tol asked.

Sean jerked his hand back, ripping further into his skin in the process. Only then did the wound sting. The metal had been sharp, jagged. It was no small cut. Sean cradled it with his other hand.

Tol moved over to examine the blood, confusion all over his face. "That's not a lubricant. Aeveron?" He stared at him, pale, eyes begging for an answer.

"I..." Sean had no good excuse. He couldn't think of anything that would make sense. Of course, Tol would immediately put two and two together. Aryshans didn't bleed. Nothing Sean could say would quell his curiosity either. There was only one thing he could do. He looked his friend in the eye, and hoped his friendship with Tol was as strong as he believed. "Tol, I have something important to tell you."

50

"Very funny. With your facial expression, I almost believed you!" Tol laughed as hard as he could remember. Aeveron couldn't possibly be a human. All those times they'd spent together...

Tol considered back to their first-time meeting on Sirdanse Station. He'd been odd compared to most people Tol had met. Come to think of it, Aeveron hadn't known minor details like what a standard drink was. He'd followed Tol's order, and then reacted very poorly to the taste.

He also took all too keen an interest in Tol's progress with his phase device, something that could have immense military value. A lump grew in Tol's throat.

Aeveron stood silent, and even though he wasn't of the Aresh, he broadcasted immense fear. He cleared his throat. "I'm serious," he said.

Silence fell over the shuttle again. Tol watched him. It couldn't be. All those weeks, their friendship, had it been a ruse? Tol stumbled back from his chair and bumped against the sidewall. He fumbled for one of the side panel compartments and produced a plasma pistol.

Then he leveled it at Aeveron's face. His hands shook. He didn't want to point this weapon at his friend. "Traitor," Tol said under his breath.

Aeveron lifted his hands above his head in surrender, careful in his movements. Tol wondered if he should make a move to shoot him immediately, but the other man didn't appear to be threatening him. If he was a traitor, wouldn't he attempt to sabotage the mission? No, he would wait until Tol was asleep or incapacitated. Which he already had been. This was so confusing. It made no sense. Or maybe it did. "Did you lure me out here in a shuttle alone to deliver my device to one of your admirals?" His eyes went wide. Aeveron's plan seemed obvious now.

"I know it looks bad, but you have to believe me. I'm not here to turn you over to the humans," Aeveron said, his body still as the night sky.

"Then what are you doing here?" Tol asked.

"I won't lie to you. I was assigned to the *Issiana* to gather military information. But I'm not here to hurt you, Tol. My goal is to end the war."

"The humans could end it by backing off our borders. You don't understand the devastation you cause," Tol said. He was so angry he felt like he was aflame. He had never considered that someone could be a fraud. Why would he? In the Aresh, such things were impossible.

"You're right. I don't think we do understand. That's why our peoples need to talk and figure out the best way forward. This isn't good for anyone. Can't you see that?"

Tol frowned. He wasn't going to let this human deceive him further. Nothing Aeveron said could be trusted. That strange red liquid still dripped from his hand. Tol didn't know how to handle this situation, but he could tell Aeveron was in pain. It didn't matter. "I follow my orders," he said, and then motioned his plasma pistol toward the sleeping compartment. "Get in there."

Aeveron glanced to the compartment, then nodded slowly. "I'll do as you say, Tol. Believe me. We should talk. I'm not here to harm you." He moved over to the compartment and ducked inside, allowing himself to lay down. Once again, he cradled his hand.

Tol moved over to the wall terminal and sealed the compartment shut. The door descended and Aeveron didn't move at all. At least it was true that he wasn't planning to attack him. All the same, Tol had to think and consider what to do.

He couldn't abort the mission. This was too vital, and it was assigned directly by the Ruling Committee itself. He had a real chance to take down one of the enemy's most prestigious vessels without any loss of Aryshan life, without direct confrontation. It would do wonders for his people if he were to succeed.

With several taps to the controls, Tol engaged a lock. Aeveron would be trapped inside the sleeping compartment with no possible way out, at least without slicing into the shuttle's security systems from the inside. From what he'd seen of Aeveron, the man did not have those kinds of skills. But he had managed to fake an identity and insert himself into the Aryshan navy. Tol had so many questions.

The most important ones were internal. He needed to be alone, to think about what he could do next. He could hardly trust Aeveron in going through with the mission. Aeveron's nervousness took on a whole new meaning. Tol thought it was fear for his ability to accomplish such a vital mission, or his insecurities about mechanical knowledge. It hadn't been such innocuous things. Aeveron was nervous because he didn't want to go through with being a traitor to his own people.

Tol settled himself into a chair and stared at a bulkhead across from him. Aeveron was right, it was clear he had meant Tol no harm. He'd had many opportunities to take control of the situation, or to lock Tol in the sleeping compartment himself. He hadn't taken those opportunities. The likelihood of Aeveron waiting until the last moment to try to wrestle control of the ship from Tol and turn him in to his human admiral was low.

Could Aeveron have meant to go through with the mission? He was a spy, but his actions didn't make sense in that context. Tol did need help if he was going to install his explosive device on the human vessel. It was a true two-person job. Having a human familiar with their vessels could only help that. It warranted considering continuing the mission as if he hadn't learned anything about his companion.

The most rational explanation was that Aeveron was being earnest. But why? Something had changed in Aeveron. Only one variable made sense: Speaker Tamar. It was obvious, the more Tol thought about it.

Aeveron had acted a fool around Tamar since they first had met. The way someone completely love-struck does. The way Tol reacted whenever he was around Maela.

Warmth filled him, and some that wasn't his own. It was the part of Maela that lingered with him always. He could feel her, even at this distance. The bondsense was faint, but there. She was nervous that he was away, but happy that she had him. He echoed that sentiment. Even all the way across star systems, they would never truly be apart.

Tol considered the hypothesis that Aeveron was so smitten with Tamar, he lost all sense of duty to his people. If that were the case, he could probably trust him, at least with the mission. This mission would prove a good test for his loyalty and could justify the decision later.

He blinked. Did Tamar know of Aeveron's false identity? If she didn't, that could pose further problems. This whole matter was just like digging into a ship system. He could open a compartment and see problems on the surface, but once he peeled back the layers below, there might be even worse problems.

It wasn't something he could control. What was between Speaker Tamar and Aeveron was their personal matter. If she accepted him, it would reshape some of his thoughts on their whole situation. In truth, he'd never considered humans much before and never come across one personally. It was fascinating from an educational perspective.

Tol nodded to himself, resolved. He had to be vigilant all the same, in case Aeveron had other plans. For the time being, he went back to work on his device. He'd let Aeveron stew and worry for a few hours, and then they could have a talk.

Hours later, Tol completed the next portion of his device's integration to the shuttle's systems, stood, and surveyed his work. It was going better than he had expected. Ever since he'd discovered the resolution to his power issues, it was like everything had fired on full cylinders. It was a great thing, and it reminded him that he'd left Aeveron in the compartment for long enough.

He moved over to the terminal and tapped in his security code. The sleeping chambers door unlocked.

Aeveron had used the chambers for their intended purpose.

Tol prodded him with his elbow. "Wake up."

The human rolled over, almost to the edge of the compartment, before his eyes opened halfway. Dazed from just waking up, it took him a moment to process Tol in front of him.

Just in case there was some underlying deception he missed, Tol revealed his plasma pistol, keeping it trained on Aeveron. "Don't worry. I have no intention of shooting you. Yet," Tol said. He moved over to the chair on the opposite side of the room and took a seat.

Aeveron righted himself, hands on the edge of the compartment as he let his legs dangle over the ledge. He stared at Tol. "You believe me," he said, sounding relieved.

"I don't know," Tol said. "I believe the part where you don't want to harm me, but you're going to have to earn my trust."

Aeveron nodded. "Whatever it takes."

"You can start by telling me your real name."

"Sean Barrows," Aeveron said.

Tol mouthed the words. They sounded ugly to him. It was going to be difficult to think of him as something in that strange, human tongue. "You're going to have a hard road ahead of you. Do you really think that Speaker Tamar will be as understanding as I am? She is primed to become one of the leaders of our people. When she finds out what you are..."

"I know," Aeveron said, casting his eyes downward. "I don't know what to do about that. I only hope that she loves me as much as I love her."

Those words sounded sincere as anything Tol had ever heard. It reaffirmed his earlier conclusions. Aeveron was love-struck. The poor soul. He couldn't imagine being torn between that kind of emotion and loyalty to his tribe. It would be impossible. His physiology wouldn't permit anything like that. It would kill him first. "I don't know if there's anything that can prepare her for what you have to tell her, but I will think on it."

"You're going to help me?" Aeveron asked, cocking his head at Tol.

"If you prove yourself first." Tol turned his weapon, setting it on a small table next to his chair. "This mission does require two people, and I'm going to need your help. You'll have to see this through."

"There has to be another way," Aeveron said.

"There's not," Tol said before Aeveron could get another word in. "We have a duty to do. I don't care what your past has been, but from this point forward, you work for the good of the Aresh. If you want any real relationship with Speaker Tamar, you will have to do that."

"Are you sure this is the best course for the Aresh? Tamar isn't so certain," Aeveron said.

"Oh?"

"She has strong opinions that this war on Earth is wrong. You talked earlier about how dangerous humans were to your kind, but what if that assumption is false? Have you considered that?"

"There was a lawful vote by the Ruling Committee. It's been commanded," Tol said. He didn't like how this conversation was going. He'd never had cause to question his orders before, and he wasn't about to be disloyal now.

"People can't make mistakes? From all I've seen, it sounds like the Ruling Committee erred in judgment." Aeveron's eyes were pleading. He truly cared about this as much as he had anything else he had said.

Tol shifted in his chair. "You make it sound so simple."

"Because it is."

"No, it's not. Your words sound right, but I'm not certain I can fully believe them. This is why we have committees in the first place, and not single rulers like your kind. It protects against those kinds of mistakes. It balances the scale."

Aeveron lifted his head. "We do similarly. It's called *checks and balances* and a *separation of power*. We're not that different, and humans aren't going to be the cause of any problems for Arysha. As we all grow in this galaxy, we need to work together."

"Hmm," Tol said thoughtfully. He'd never considered anything of the sort. This was radical talk. It tugged at his bond, almost like a betrayal of the Aresh.

"If it's not error, then it's possible your leaders aren't looking out for your people."

"Impossible," Tol said. "You don't understand our bonds."

"I do," Aeveron said. "I've seen how strongly you care about your people, and even more how you care about Maela. I get it. And I'm jealous. I wish I could be so sure of everyone." He chuckled.

"What's funny?"

"My whole prior assignment had been monitoring our military, making sure there weren't any violations of rules or insubordination. We call the department Internal Affairs. I suppose the Aryshans have no need for that sort of thing."

"Of course not," Tol said. His words sounded defensive. This questioning had unsettled him far too much. It shouldn't. He was confident in the Aresh, in his commanders, and in the Ruling Committee. Why should Aeveron's words ring like they did? "If your suggestion is true, then there's a traitor within the Ruling Committee."

"And what if there is?" He paused. "No, traitor's not the right word. What if it's someone looking out for his or her own self-interest and putting that above your people? I only know a little of your history from my training, and then some from interacting with you. My theory is, since the Great Death, your people have all fallen into a trap where your second sense has taken over, become stronger. I don't see how a society could even function without questioning its leadership."

"What you speak of is an impossibility," Tol said. "Let's suppose you're right though. Say this is some internal power issue causing a wrong course of action. What would you do about it?"

Aeveron opened his mouth, but stopped immediately as an alarm sounded at the front of the craft.

Tol scrambled, leaving his plasma pistol behind. He leapt into his cockpit chair and acknowledged the alarm on the display panel. "This can't be right," Tol said, tapping the controls to make sure the screen read correctly.

"What's the matter?" Aeveron came up behind him, glancing at the controls from behind the seat rest.

Tol narrowed his eyes at the screen, and pointed to the sensor-reading display. "Look. If this is correct, the *Reykjavik* is here. It's violated our border!"

"We're at war. Maybe my people are going on the offensive," Aeveron said. "Does he detect us?"

"Not yet. I managed to get the phase device operational before I woke you, and it's providing a sensor mask."

"What do we do?"

The question was ludicrous. All this did was move up their timetable. Tol looked over his shoulder at Aeveron. They didn't have time to delve further into whether this war was a mistake. They had to act in good faith on the Ruling Committee's orders. Soldiers didn't make decisions; they could only pray to the Overseers those decisions were correct. "We follow our orders," he said.

Aeveron grimaced, but he didn't contest Tol's decision. He couldn't, not after the clear directive Tol had given him.

Tol turned back to the cockpit and set the display to track how long it would take to reach the human vessel. He dropped the shuttle out of FTL so that they could approach at a more natural pace. With the phase device on, it shouldn't register on the humans' end. This was quite a trial run. It invigorated him.

A power warning flashed on the upper right of the display. "Storms," Tol said under his breath.

"What is it?" Aeveron asked.

Tol took in a deep breath. This was bad, very bad. "It looks like I didn't work out all the power issues after all. We're about to become visible to the humans."

51

Neyral passed through the committee chambers doors. His presence had unnerved Tamar ever since his attempted coup of the commanding committee. He had single-handedly brought paranoia to the entire ship, between that and his relentless search for a traitor. It created a looming sense that something was about to go dreadfully wrong.

Instead of heading to his station, Neyral stopped in front of Tamar. She inclined her head when he arrived. "May I help you, Commander?" she asked. His aura didn't help with the tension in the room. "Does this involve your investigation?"

Neyral nodded. "It does. Forensic tests of the device came up with very little. The device had already been soiled from being in our waste disposal unit. As far as personal investigations, we've been careful so as not to risk alerting the traitor. Our analysis of all of the uncommitted aboard ship has come back negative thus far."

That wasn't good news at all. It only created more suspicion that Aeveron was indeed the culprit. Tamar still couldn't believe that, not after the time they'd spent together. Not after his work on these special missions. "Very well. Make sure your team continues their search, just in case they missed anything."

"Of course," Neyral said. He bowed his head respectfully and moved back to his station.

Tendell motioned to Tamar. "Speaker?"

"Yes?" Tamar asked.

"A shuttle has arrived in the system and requested to dock," he said.

That was odd. They weren't due to rendezvous with anyone. She glanced at the time on her display. Tol and Aeveron weren't going to be back for at least another couple of days, if they did manage to return from the mission. It couldn't be them. "Did they give any indicators who wants to dock with us?"

"Yes, Speaker," Tendell said. "It had the Ruling Committee's code."

Tamar felt a knot clinch in her shoulder. "Why didn't you say so in the first place?"

Tendell shrugged. "My apologies, Speaker. I thought it best to inform you of the docking first."

"Is it the whole committee?"

Tendell tapped on his console. "No, it appears to be solely First Speaker Ny'aet."

Neyral cleared his throat. "I highly recommend keeping this visit contained. We have a potential traitor aboard and the security risk to the First Speaker is too high."

Tamar nodded to that. "We'll have double the standard security detail placed on him."

The other members of the committee muttered their agreements. At least she could still manage to get consensus on simple operational matters. It was a start. She couldn't let Ny'aet see her committee as anything but a unified front.

"I hope that we can put our recent issues to rest and be on our best behavior for the First Speaker," Tamar said, those words aimed toward the two men in the room.

Tendell nodded, but Neyral stared at her with calculating eyes. "We'll do what is best for the Aresh," he said.

Which didn't mean what was best for her. She couldn't let herself be goaded into losing emotional control, not now. It would only further Neyral's goals, whatever they were. Perhaps she could use this visit to turn the tables on him and get him reassigned. Wouldn't that be quite the turn of events? Those plans would have to be left for later.

Tamar glanced at her uniform to make sure it wasn't bunched in an odd manner, and moved toward the exit. "I'll be headed to the shuttle bay to greet our First Speaker."

The others followed her lead, falling into line behind her.

Why did Ny'aet have to come now of all times? She had too much going on as it was. Did this mean that they were about to be assigned to yet another secret mission? It was beginning to feel like she had no command at all, and that the *Issiana* was the Ruling Committee's personal errand ship.

She shook her head and made her way for the shuttle bay.

52

Despite the shuttle having more than adequate artificial gravity plates, Sean couldn't help but grip his seat. Tol had made several tight maneuvers in the last few minutes and the plates had compensated for the inertial forces without issue, but some nervous habits were impossible to quit. "Can't we go any faster?" Sean asked.

A missile pummeled into their aft shielding. The display in front of them blinked red. A couple more hits and there wouldn't be enough left of the shuttle craft to grip.

Tol frantically tapped the piloting controls. "I'm doing what I can," he said. He kept his focus in front of him. "In FTL, it's like trying to outrun a storm. The human warship is a long-range vessel and designed for these faster speeds. This shuttle is medium-range. But we have to try to get to the *Issiana*. If we don't, they'll get away with whatever they're up to."

The *Reykjavik* had been jamming their comm since the moment their phase device failed. Sean had first argued that Tol should be working on getting the device back online, but Tol was a much better pilot than him. If he hadn't assumed control, they might not have made it this far. At these speeds, Sean would more than likely have rammed them into some interstellar object. "There. An asteroid field in the next star system. Can we make it?"

"Not if they keep firing at us." Tol frowned. "Our hull isn't rated for higher speeds, but they do build in some leeway into the ratings, don't they?"

"I wouldn't know," Sean confessed.

Tol spared a quick glance. "Right."

Another missile narrowly missed them.

"If another one of those connects, we're dead anyway. Go for it!" Sean said.

Tol overrode the safeties with blinding speed. Sean couldn't even see some of the commands he input. The console erupted with safety alarms, but their speed increased. The gap between them and the *Reykjavik* widened but quickly closed again when the human pilots made their adjustments.

"Ten seconds until we're out of FTL," Tol said.

Sean hoped another missile wouldn't come in the meantime. Conley had been frugal with his use of weapons so far, as if not wanting to run out before a real battle in Aryshan space.

The stars slowed from their streaking pattern. They'd dropped out of FTL without any problems. Sean pointed. "Asteroid, dead ahead!"

Tol didn't panic. He calmly maneuvered the shuttle upward and around the rock, keeping it between them and the *Reykjavik*. Rocks of varying size dangled in space in front of them, the smaller ones pelting against the shuttle's shielding.

"Will our shields hold through the debris?" Sean asked.

"Yes, much better than being hit with the human missiles. Hopefully they won't be able to find a way to target us through the field." Tol said. He set the controls back to autopilot. "The computer will handle maneuvering around the debris much better than I could manually. I've set the parameters to keep larger asteroids between us and the other vessel."

Sean checked the comm system again. The field didn't help with the comm signals, and Conley still had his scattering signal on. They couldn't contact the *Issiana* and get help. "No luck on the comm," Sean said.

Tol frowned and adjusted the autopilot controls. "I'll put some more distance between us and the human vessel. Maybe we'll get lucky and they'll stop pursuing us."

The display read the *Reykjavik* staying put at the entrance to the field. "Doesn't look like it." Sean let himself slump in the co-pilot's chair. "I thought we were going to die back there."

"Still might happen," Tol said, focused on the controls, even though there was nothing to do. The computer adjusted course around a large oblong asteroid. "We have to come up with a plan soon."

Sean considered. They couldn't get a signal out to call for help, and they couldn't leave, or they'd be blown to bits. The longer they waited, the more likely it was that Admiral Conley would find a way to destroy them through the field. "You haven't gone back to look at your device."

"No, I know what happened. The power converter overloaded. We won't be able to run the device without draining the shuttle's power. It'd leave us helpless."

"But we're in Aryshan space. All we need is enough power to disappear long enough for Conley to give up the chase. If he thinks we're gone, he'll break off, or at least drop the comm scattering field. Then we can get a message to the *Issiana*." Sean was optimistic for his plan. If Conley didn't break off as he expected, then they'd be in even bigger trouble. But Conley had to be here on some sort of mission, and if that were true, why would he spend his time lingering to investigate a vanished shuttle? He would have to presume they'd found a way out of the field.

Tol pushed himself up from the pilot's chair and moved to the back. "Good idea, Aeveron. It just might work. I'll bypass the power converter. I'll need you to shut down engines and any other system you can think of that requires power."

Sean pulled up the power consumption screen on his display. "I'll keep on the comm unit, environmental, and shielding." He made the adjustments. "Oh, and I'll drop gravity to fifty percent. Everything else should be off."

Tol went to work in the back. Sensors had been turned off, leaving Sean blind to what was in the field beyond his direct vision. He hoped they wouldn't drift into a large asteroid, but it was a risk they'd have to take if they wanted any chance of getting out of this alive.

Part of him was relieved for more than just the chance of survival. It was as if the universe had allowed him a way out from being responsible for a human vessel's destruction. He hadn't had to plant an explosive. He could remain loyal to his people *and* to Tamar, at least for now.

Even though they weren't out of the woods yet, that small victory was enough to give him energy to keep going. Sean set the comm unit to repeat attempts to connect with the *Issiana*. If Conley did break away, they would know immediately. Assuming the *Issiana* answered.

A few minutes later, Tol returned from the back of the shuttle. "The device is ready."

Sean tapped the controls to bring power to the device. The lights dimmed immediately. He looked back at Tol. "Was that supposed to happen?"

Tol shrugged. "I told you there was considerable power drain."

"How long is this going to be able to last for anyway?'

"A few minutes."

"A few minutes?" Sean stopped himself from popping from his seat. That might not be enough time for the *Reykjavik's* crew to notice they were gone. "That would have been nice to know before we did this."

"It'll work. Have a little faith," Tol said.

A few moments passed. Sean waited, staring at the console. Finally, the comm unit *bleeped* to alert him to their signal going through.

Tol moved to the front of the ship. "I told you not to worry. Ah, the *Issiana* is responding." He reached over to acknowledge the connection.

"Shuttle One, this is ill timing. Aren't you supposed to maintain comm silence?" asked a voice from the *Issiana.*

"Our situation has changed," Tol said. "We are in Aryshan space, transmitting our coordinates. The human vessel has crossed the border and spotted us prior to engaging. We require assistance."

The voice on the other end paused. Sean looked over to see if the connection was still open and saw it was.

"Sorry about that, Shuttle One. I have transmitted the message to the commanding committee. This is bad timing, but they agree this is an urgent situation. Maintain your position and we will be in the system soon."

The lights in the shuttle flickered again, this time dimming for a long moment before coming back to life. Sean looked to Tol expectantly.

"We'll be here," Tol said.

"*Issiana* out."

Sean moved to the console to turn off the device. He looked at the power reserves. Fifteen percent. That was barely enough to keep environmental going. "I think we're in trouble," he said.

"Hopefully they arrive soon," Tol said. He didn't seem worried, but instead moved back to check on his device. His faith and focus were amazing, but then again, it wasn't as if they had anything else they could do while they waited.

Sean couldn't help but worry, as the power percentage changed on the display. Fourteen percent. How long did they have left, that they could survive out here? And worse, without sensors, they could have the *Reykjavik* tracking them down for their destruction, with nothing they could do.

53

Metal clanged against metal, and the sound reverberated throughout the shuttle bay. Tamar's crew unloaded cargo, secured airlocks, and transported large crates onto hoverlifts. At least Ny'aet had brought supplies with him.

The shuttle bay itself was one the largest areas of the ship, with enough space to fit both the *Issiana's* away shuttles, a fighter squadron, and room for small visitor vessels. A long, sleek shuttlecraft currently occupied the first visitor landing bay. A ramp extended and its occupants proceeded outward. Four soldiers, adorned in traditional Aryshan honor guard tabards, marched down the ramp, followed by Ny'aet.

The First Speaker was dressed in formal grays, walking with the trained step of a statesman and carrying himself with a royal presence. Tamar still had no clue as to the looming question—what was the purpose of this visit?

She waited along with the other members of the commanding committee, all standing at attention for their leader.

Ny'aet greeted her informally, with open arms, clasping his hands just above her elbows. "Commander," he said.

"First Speaker," Tamar replied with cold professionalism. Her whole body was tight, weary, but she tried her best to mask that with protocol and an impassive face.

Ny'aet stepped backward, nodding to acknowledge the other three commanders with Tamar. The honor guard on both sides looked on, staying at attention. "If you wouldn't mind, Commander Tamar, there are matters I'd like to discuss with you alone," he said. The other commanders fell back to allow them space, good soldiers following the orders of their First Speaker. "Walk with me," Ny'aet said to Tamar in a low tone, before stepping past her and heading for the shuttle bay exit.

Tamar followed. Ny'aet's honor guard broke into formation behind them, giving them adequate space, pausing when Ny'aet and Tamar reached the door. The bay doors opened for them, and soon they were alone in the corridor, with nothing but the echo of their steps to disturb them. "Your visit is unexpected," Tamar said.

"Of course," he said, spinning to greet her with a warm smile. "You've done well here, from the reports I've heard."

Reports? Could those have come from Neyral and Tendell? Unlikely that those two had good things to say. She couldn't read Ny'aet, even with him standing next to her. He masked his aura far too well. It was as unsettling as his visit. "I pride myself in my work," Tamar said.

"Good, because as you might guess, I'm not here for an inspection," he said and continued around a corner. "Please, let's head somewhere we can talk."

"There's a conference room two doors down," Tamar said. She pointed, and then led the way.

When the two of them arrived, they settled into the room and the door closed behind them. Ny'aet paced in a nervous manner around the center table. He met her eyes. "I'm here to take personal command of this ship."

Tamar froze. She couldn't have expected that at all. Her heart sank at the same time. "You just said I was doing a good job."

"I know that you just received word that Admiral Conley has

crossed the border into our space. This requires direct action," Ny'aet said.

That didn't ring true to Tamar. Was this some power game he was playing? But how could he lie to her without her sensing it? Perhaps she was becoming paranoid, finding problems where there were none. They had just received a transmission from Aeveron's shuttle hours ago. Ny'aet couldn't have planned his trip around that. As a commander, however, it was her job to do her duty. "As you wish, sir," she said, but she couldn't keep all the anger or disappointment from her voice.

"Thank you, Commander. I need you to inform the committee they will be deferring to my decisions. We will have a strict communication blackout while we deal with this matter, save for my direct orders."

He had to have been planning an attack the entire time, something over the line that he wouldn't be able to garner approval for. But why would he do that? That wasn't the Aryshan way. Tamar didn't like this in the least. Ny'aet was acting, for better or worse, like a human. Individualistic, and therefore narcissistic. All the same, from her position, there was nothing she could do. "Yes, sir," she said.

Ny'aet nodded. "Good. As I said, you've done very well. You're a good soldier, and you'll make an even better leader one day."

Tamar didn't know what to say about the compliment, as little as she understood the situation. This behavior was erratic, and she wished she had someone to voice her discomfort to. "We need to retrieve our crewmen," she said. "I hope that's our first order of business?"

"Yes, yes," Ny'aet said, appearing distant, distracted, as if he hadn't considered that. Another reason he likely shouldn't be putting himself in charge of the vessel. He'd been in command before, but it had been prior to Tamar knowing him that he had such a post. He moved for the conference room door. "I'll get settled into guest quarters and we can talk over dinner."

His words made Tamar frown. "Wait," she said, even though it violated protocol.

Ny'aet stopped himself. "Yes?"

Tamar took a deep breath. "Did you expect this result of their mission?"

Ny'aet nodded. "I presumed the chatter of an indirect attack on the human vessel would draw the admiral into our space for a more direct confrontation. He thinks he can avoid the trap and catch us off guard, but we are ready for him."

Now the mission made more sense. Tamar had wondered why it had been assigned this way. The official story of the desire to minimize Aryshan loss of life didn't jive, and it proved a ruse. Which meant he knew there were traitors in the Aryshan fleet and information being transmitted from the committee across space was not secure. There were always deeper machinations with him; she had to remember that. Those implications were frightening enough, but a human destroyer was in Aryshan space. Even in the midst of all this flurry of Ny'aet's presence, she would have to prepare her crew for battle.

"I'll be speaking with you soon. Inform me when we're about to retrieve your crewmen. They should have the honor to meet their First Speaker after embarking upon such a daring mission." Ny'aet nodded and left the room.

Tamar hoped that she could trust Ny'aet in everything that would come next.

54

Twelve percent.

Sean stayed in the co-pilot's chair, watching the screen in front of him. The power status bar dwindled. All but emergency lights were powered down, with everything except the necessary environmental systems offline. In their last-ditch effort, Tol had completely turned off the artificial gravity in the shuttle, making for awkward movements when Sean did want to move from the seat. Hopefully their power would last a little bit longer.

At least the phase device had been disengaged, which slowed the drain. They could feasibly go several more hours. Sean briefly turned on the sensors, which showed the *Reykjavik* to be nowhere in the system. Conley and his crew had to have continued to whatever mission brought them into Aryshan space in the first place.

It didn't mean that he'd survive this trip. They still had to get out of the asteroid field for the *Issiana* to pick them up. That required power to maneuver even after the warship arrived.

Tol didn't appear nearly as worried as Sean, or maybe it was that Aryshans were better at concealing their emotions. With the way their bondsense worked, it would make sense for them to be a little less reactionary.

"Should we engage our engines?" Sean asked.

Tol frowned at the display from his pilot's chair. "I don't see the humans, but our sensors are limited, especially in the field. I can't guarantee it's safe to come out."

"It's not safe to stay here," Sean said.

"I agree," Tol said, tapping the controls to activate the shuttle's thrusters.

Ten percent.

"How did that happen?"

"Engine start up." Tol shrugged. He didn't seem concerned, but they were cutting it very close.

Tol glided the shuttle through the field. They didn't maintain their repulsor shields, which would keep the small debris out of the way.

The first of the debris hitting the shuttle came as a shock. A larger piece hit the vessel, rocking them. Fortunately, Sean had strapped himself into his chair or he might have gone flying in the lack of gravity. "Tol," he warned.

"I'm doing all I can. This is a thick part of the asteroid field. We'll be through in a moment."

"What if something cracks the hull?"

"It won't."

Sean wasn't as certain as Tol sounded. More debris clanged against the outside, making Sean cringe every time he heard it. If one did happen to penetrate, it wasn't as if there was much he could do about it anyway.

He hadn't watched the power status bar in several moments. It read seven percent. "Our power's dropping fast," Sean said.

"A few more seconds and we can coast the rest of the way out of here," Tol said.

The sensors didn't show any sign of the *Issiana*. How far off was the larger ship anyway? He had no way of telling.

The crackle of debris hitting the shuttle stopped. They'd made it back out to open space.

Tol leaned his head back into his chair, letting out a deep breath. "Success," he said.

Six percent.

Instead of waiting for Tol, Sean reached for the center console and shut the engines down. That should buy them a little bit of time. "How much longer do we have with minimal environmental systems and nothing else with these power levels?"

"Four to five hours," Tol said, frowning. "Hopefully the ship makes it in time."

He sounded so matter of fact about it that Sean wanted to strangle him. They'd had so much stress on this mission that it was amazing they hadn't fought more. Tol hadn't pressed the issue about Sean's humanity, despite the fact that they hadn't been able to complete their mission.

Tol's Aryshan features seemed more pronounced in the low emergency lighting. The large flattened horn structures to the sides of his head gave a real sense of prowess that Sean hadn't noticed before. He wanted to talk to Tol more, ask him if everything was truly repaired between them—and, more importantly, to ensure that he wouldn't turn Sean in upon return to the *Issiana*. Tol hadn't said anything and was typically very direct, but Sean still had some concerns.

He closed his eyes, trying not to worry about what he couldn't control. If Tol wanted to turn him in, he would. It wasn't like Sean could escape now, with no power left to the systems. He'd had his ability to take control and flee earlier, before his confession. Now he was at Tol's mercy.

By the same token, he didn't want to press his luck by bothering the Aryshan and reminding him of their differences. He hoped the friendship they'd had before would be bond enough to keep his secret.

55

Ny'aet had all but taken over Tamar's station in the committee chambers. If Tamar had been uncomfortable in the room before, now she felt useless. All she could do is stand back and watch, arms folded, and provide assistance when she was asked for. It was like the old days on homeworld when she interned for him. He would be hard at work on whatever he did, and she would bring him food, drink, whatever he required. It wasn't glamorous work, but it had built this connection she had with him that allowed her the speakership role.

It felt hollow now.

Her console displayed tactical readouts of the sector: planetary defenses, the locations of other warships—all in an effort to trap Admiral Conley and his human ship.

"He has to be headed for our crystal production facility on Treil," Ny'aet said. He pointed to the map.

Tamar peered over his shoulder. "That would be a logical place to strike."

"Are we within sensor range of the shuttle? Is there any sign of the human vessel in that system?" Ny'aet looked up and across the room at Tendell.

"Unless they're masking sensors somehow, I don't see anything on the scanners," Tendell said.

"Mm," Ny'aet muttered with disappointment.

In some ways, Tamar was relieved. She wasn't certain that the ship was ready for a one-on-one conflict with an Earth warship, let alone one with such a track record of excellence in battle. This allowed them to pick up Aeveron and Tol while readying an assault with better resources and planning.

Ny'aet turned back toward her. "Relief?" he asked, his question directed at her emotional aura.

"If we are going to battle, I wish to be as prepared as possible," Tamar said.

"Preparation can only help so much. With how this war is going, we need to be ready to engage the humans at any moment. One never knows when they'll strike."

Tamar nodded to that. She still would prefer to have the battle on her own terms, or at least on Ny'aet's, if it would happen. They were only speculating on the human ship's mission in their space. The humans could be anywhere.

"We will be entering the system with our shuttle soon," Tendell announced.

"Excellent. I will take a brief leave," Ny'aet said, stepping aside to allow Tamar access to her own console. "Have your operations department see if there's any way they can track where the human ship may have gone. I know it's difficult to triangulate the signatures of crystal drives, but we need more information. And when our people are retrieved, please notify me." With that, he stepped from the station and made his way for the exit.

Tamar watched the others at work, none of their stations having been invaded like hers. She kept a mask up, a firm wall so she wouldn't broadcast how irritated she was through the bondsense. Her concerns seemed petty, and it would do no good to vocalize them to the rest of the committee.

The good news was, she would have Aeveron back soon.

Maela looked over at her as if she had similar thoughts about her entwined. Tamar gave her an understanding nod.

56

They were going to die out here.

Sean couldn't have imagined this would be the way he'd go. In a lot of ways, he'd been prepared to die, to sacrifice himself for humanity. It wasn't a comfortable thought, but the risks had been made clear when he'd accepted this assignment.

However, in all the worst-case scenarios playing in his head, a passive death by lack of power in a shuttle had never occurred to him.

He laughed like a madman.

Tol looked over at him, wary. "Don't breathe in too deeply. We need to conserve all the air we can once we run out of power."

"It won't matter," Sean said, the laughter still on his lips, though he settled back into resignation. It had been funny for a moment, considering how he'd exposed his identity to Tol, and yet that hadn't been his undoing. "We gave it our best shot."

"We still have one percent," Tol corrected, pointing to the display. The lettering could barely be seen with minimum power. In the darkness of the craft without any other light, it illuminated enough to give an impressionistic feel to the other objects in the craft.

With a *bzzzzzzooo*, the power went out.

The air that they had in the cabin was all they'd get now. And Tol was right. Every breath meant one closer to their last. Even though the carbon dioxide inside hadn't reached toxic levels yet, Sean's throat constricted as if he were suffocating. He tried to breathe shallowly all the same.

Both knew better than to speak. They'd discussed that hours ago, when the prospect of the *Issiana* arriving in time still seemed attainable. When they still had hope.

Minutes passed. Or hours. It was impossible to say. Sean recycled the same thoughts over and over. How he had expected to die. What life would have been like with Tamar. Could he even have a life with her? With Aryshan entwining, Sean wasn't sure what could or would happen, should they push their physical relationship further. The training he'd received had a rather glaring omission in that department. He assumed Aryshans made love the same way humans did. Their bodies looked remarkably similar. There would only be one way to find out, and he'd have to live through this in order to learn.

It became harder to breathe in earnest. Two people could consume the oxygen of a room relatively quickly if there was no outside replacement. His extremities didn't quite feel right, and he felt himself growing weary. This is how it would end.

"Tol?" he asked, daring one last conversation.

"Yes?"

"I'm glad I could be your friend," Sean said. It was true. Of anyone he had ever met, perhaps Tol had been the kindest and most loyal. To have accepted him despite their differences, despite the deception that Sean had to have for his mission, spoke a lot about the man.

"I'm glad I could be your friend, too," Tol said.

They said no more. Sean waited several more minutes in silence. His eyes grew heavier and, finally, despite his every attempt, he couldn't keep conscious any longer.

SEAN AWOKE to someone shaking him. His eyes fluttered open to see Maela hovering. "Huh?" he asked.

"He's alive," she said, looking back at someone else.

Several nurses gathered around inside the shuttle. They hovered over him, but all he wanted was space.

The last thing Sean remembered was having far too tender a moment with Tol before drifting back off to sleep. He thought it would be his final rest but, apparently, the *Issiana* had been close enough to retrieve them before they had become too oxygen-deprived.

"Where's Tol?" he asked.

"He's fine," Maela said. She undid the straps that had him secure in the co-pilot chair. "He's awake and being assisted to the infirmary. We weren't sure you were going to make it."

It had been close. A sobering thought. Sean tried to push himself out of the chair, but his body was weak.

Maela braced him. "Be careful," she said. "You'd best not exert yourself for a while."

"Tamar," Sean said, as if by instinct. It was improper, and he sensed that immediately from the way a couple of the nurses stared at him. She was the Speaker; he shouldn't be referring to her so informally. A mistake. He winced.

"I'm here." Tamar's voice had never sounded so sweet.

There she stood, at the back of the shuttle craft, the most beautiful view Sean could imagine. Lithe, athletic, silver skin, and tied-back hair that showed the crown and horns that made her Aryshan. She was breathtaking, and it was all he could do to push himself farther toward the back of the shuttle.

Her eyes lit up upon seeing him, and she jogged into the shuttle, careful to maneuver around Tol's phase device.

Sean stumbled toward her, his legs not complying with his will. But he managed to reach her. A moment later, they embraced.

It was more public than Sean would have expected, but the shuttle did provide some shielding from anyone who might have been looking on. The nurses had moved out of the shuttle, leaving the two of them alone with Maela.

Tamar pulled back. "I'm glad you made it alive."

Sean offered a small smile to her, still in a daze. He almost didn't believe he stood before her. "I'm glad, too," he said.

Maela scooted past them as if trying to dodge out of their reunion without notice. She was unsuccessful. Tamar turned almost immediately.

"Commander," Tamar said.

Maela stopped in her tracks and glanced back. "Yes, Speaker?"

"Do you require this patient for any further monitoring or examination?"

"No. He's not showing any signs of oxygen deprivation. It looks like we retrieved him just in time. I would recommend against heavy physical duty for the next three days, however," Maela said.

Tamar nodded. "Good. Thank you."

The other woman departed then, leaving Tamar and Sean to themselves. "This was supposed to be my sleep shift," Tamar said. It made more sense as to why she would return the gesture of being so informal with him.

Sean nodded and slipped his hand into hers, squeezing it gently. There was so much going on, so much to think about, but he didn't want to process any of it now. The thrill of a simple touch from Tamar was enough to push those other thoughts aside.

She gave his hand a squeeze, and then released it. "We can talk more about your mission in my quarters," she said and sauntered away.

Her hips moved in a way that stilled Sean's breath. It took everything in him to peel his eyes from her long enough for him to follow.

They walked down the ramp, out into the shuttle bay at large, where several technicians were already running their diagnostics on the shuttle's systems, the craft used and abused by their voyage.

Sean saw that he was dragging a little behind Tamar and jogged to catch up.

57

The doors to Tamar's quarters *whooshed* open. She turned around and saw Aeveron standing right there. When the doors closed again she lost all control. It'd been hard enough with these last several days of him gone, her fretting over whether he would come back again. As much as she'd thought Maela's entwining Tol had been a mistake, the other woman had been much more at peace than she had been. There had been other frustrations going on simultaneously, but this lingering sense that she had missed out on something she would never be able to get back—it had nearly crushed her in its weight.

Aeveron responded just as voraciously as she did, pawing at her. His hands slid over her sides and her back as he backpedaled toward the wall.

Tamar pushed him hard against the wall, having no qualms about any of his touches. She'd never wanted to let herself go so much. Overseers, he felt good. Good enough for her to think about Overseers in the first place, which she hadn't in years. Where had that come from?

It didn't matter. Nothing mattered. Only her. Only him. Together. She writhed against him, trying to feel every portion of his body with every portion of hers. Their lips came together and locked. His tongue sought hers and they connected again.

Tamar lifted Aeveron's tunic. Her fingers ran curiously up his torso, exploring every hard muscle along his stomach up his chest. His skin had a little darker tinge to it than hers, a signature of Aryshans originally from the opposite side of the planet. He said he had been born on a colony, but that didn't matter. No matter how far apart that was, they were here together. And they would come together as one.

She had to break the kiss to force his tunic the rest of the way off. And he took the opportunity to push hers upward, exposing her breasts. In a moment of shy modesty, Tamar squeezed her arms around herself. She laughed, unable to help it. It was so ridiculous. He would see much more of her soon enough. Why would she worry about this?

Aeveron didn't seem to mind. Her quick act of modesty grew the fire within him. She shivered at the way he looked at her, his eyes hungry, like twin storms ready to overwhelm her shores. He pulled her clothes the rest of the way off and tossed them aside.

Tamar gripped onto Aeveron's pant line, pulling him backward as she stumbled herself. They moved together like in a dance. Aeveron kept her pressed against him. She took each step with faith that he was guiding her, moving back into her bedroom. Her legs met with the bed and she fell back onto it. He fell atop her.

Their lips met once more, with more heat than at the doorway, if that were even possible. Tamar wrapped her legs around him. This was everything she ever wanted. She felt a little electric pulse through her, her body telling her that this was the moment. She was ready to bond with this man in a way that she had never considered before. For the rest of their lives. For eternity.

"Take me," she whispered to him, not even certain that the words were audible.

Aeveron didn't need the encouragement. He kissed her hard, hot breath moving down on her face, to her neck, collarbone, and then to her breasts. Her nipples hardened and she felt her stomach tighten as the pleasure erupted in her.

She heard him undoing his belt, watched his clothes drop and his hands move to her pants.

The lights were already dim. He looked so beautiful in the soft illumination the room provided. Strong, yet tender. Everything she'd ever wanted in a man.

The minutes and hours passed with more pleasure. He took it slow enough to arouse her to levels she could have never dreamed possible. All at once, Tamar understood why people focused so much attention on entwining, on finding that one mate for life. She could barely take how intense it was and lost all semblance of thought when they made love.

Tamar reached out with everything in her, mind, body and soul. And she felt his soul in that moment. It had walls like she'd never experienced in her life. None of the other Aresh had anything like the amount of shielding that he managed to have over his emotions. Was it because he was uncommitted?

As they engaged themselves physically, Tamar's spirit reached out, pushed harder to penetrate those walls. She would overcome this distance between them. Nothing would separate them. Never again.

Then it happened.

It was like a sun went nova in that room. Everything erupted at once. Everything changed. Tamar was one with him. Everything he felt, she felt, and in the moment of pure ecstasy that only amplified. Neither of them had thought, only passion for the other. It reverberated and amplified within them as they fed off one another.

The moment settled all too soon. And though a strange sense of peace overcame her, she wished she could return to it more than anything. She locked her mouth with his once more, and let him kiss her tenderly. He wanted it too. She could have never imagined how wonderful it was to be loved.

And so strange at the same time. There was another thought, another voice there suddenly. She could almost see through his eyes. It wasn't exactly jarring. Being committed as she was to the Aresh, she understood the emotions of the tribe. But this was something much stronger, much more vivid. It was incredible.

I love you more than anything.

He didn't say it, but he thought it. She pulled back, nearly losing her breath at that thought. *I love you, too,* she thought in return. She met his dark eyes and saw that he heard her words as much as she had heard his.

And then he had concern. Something was wrong. He shouldn't be sensing things like this. But why? Tamar watched him, fear overcoming the beautifully intense love and joy from a few moments before. Not her fear. His. *Why?* she inquired in that internal voice that only he could hear. Something she would have to get used to now that they were entwined.

Then his thought returned to her. She wasn't in the least bit prepared for what she heard. "No," she said aloud. It couldn't be true.

58

This couldn't be true. It physically couldn't happen, could it? He was linked with Tamar in some sort of telepathic bond that he couldn't get out of his skull. It was disorienting, to say the least. He could barely tell where his body ended and where hers began. It resulted in a loss of control.

When she pushed him away from him, it hurt worse than it should have. He had a sinking feeling that was almost inexplicable. It hadn't come from him. Oh no.

"You're human." Her voice cracked, her tone frightened. She scampered back on the bed, away from him. Still naked, she brought her knees to her chest to conceal herself. "How could you? How could we?"

The sense of betrayal that he felt, through what he could only perceive as her thoughts, jarred him. Instinctually, he wanted to flee. He found his pants and hopped to try to quickly squeeze his body into each leg. This couldn't be happening. "I-I'm sorry," was all he managed to say.

But she was still there. He couldn't change that, couldn't get her out of his head.

I loved you. How could you?

Those words burned into him. He still loved her. It shouldn't matter, but it did. Worse, he couldn't hide from her. Was this what it felt like to be committed to one of their tribes? Would the thick walls of the Aryshan ship give him the space he so desperately needed to figure things out?

Tamar watched him in complete shock. It didn't help to have those eyes boring into him like that. So many conflicting emotions running wild in her head, and in his own. He wanted to pound his own brain out of his skull.

Moments later, he had his pants and tunic back on, and he looked at her. She still stood there, shell-shocked, silent. "Say something!" Sean yelled at her.

He immediately wished he hadn't. She was hurt, and his anger hadn't helped. It only exacerbated the problem.

Instead of saying something else, he grabbed her clothes and tossed them onto the bed. It wouldn't do to have her naked like that. It wasn't right. A few moments prior and he would have been staring at her, going over her every curve as if trying to memorize some holy book, but now...

Now he had to get out.

It's what she wanted as much as what he needed to do. He could feel that much from her. He turned from her, ashamed. His whole world had been turned upside down so many ways these last few days. What did he even want? What should he do? There was no one there to answer these questions for him. Even with her swimming around in his skull, he was more alone, more isolated than he'd ever been.

Sean hurried out of her bedroom and through the door. The hallway was empty. This was the night shift, which meant more of a skeleton crew. They would have more people at battle stations than usual, but Aryshans still needed their rest.

Sean looked both ways down the corridor, disoriented. He hadn't been on the ship very long as it was, and hardly remembered where his quarters were. Tamar was still there, in the back of his mind, and her thoughts actually guided him, with a little annoyance in having to think it.

The walls wouldn't be enough to push this bond away. Sean cursed under his breath. What was he going to do?

Before he could even begin to think of an answer to the question, which was far more complex than it should have been, several Aryshan security guards appeared farther down the corridor. They moved in a well-trained military manner, and they weren't just making patrols. They came right for him.

He wanted to run, but where would he go? Fear filled him. And a sensation of concern—Tamar—also welled within him. The competing emotions impaired his ability to act. They were so strong. He had to get a handle on this. How did other Aryshans get anything done while having these intense emotions escalating within them?

The Aryshans opposite him had no problem acting. Before he could blink, they were on him. One held each of his arms while the other two kept plasma pistols trained on him. Another Aryshan strode down the corridor behind them. Commander Neyral.

The commander was practically beaming with glee, his steps slow and confident as he approached the scene of his security officers securing Sean.

"Ah, Aeveron. Or should I say, human traitor?" he said.

Sean didn't bother to struggle. With the Aryshan strength he'd already encountered before, it would just get him hurt. "I don't know what you're talking about," he said, though he didn't have nearly the confidence with which he said those words.

Neyral produced a laser cutter. "There's one easy way to tell. His hand," he said, motioning for the guard to extend Sean's arm toward him.

Sean couldn't help but try to squirm away, to no avail. The guard nearly ripped Sean's arm from his socket, forcing it forward and holding it in place with very little effort. Sean tried to move, but he was stuck.

Neyral activated the laser cutter, bright energy protruding from the device. He brought it down toward Sean's hand with the precision of a surgeon, slicing into his skin. Within moments, red blood pooled in the wound, trickling down the back of his hand and dripping. Neyral cupped his own hand beneath it in order to stop it from hitting the floor. "We wouldn't want to stain the ship, would we? Not like you did the flooring of the shuttlecraft."

That was how he figured out to look for Sean. It made sense. In the flurry of the last mission with Tol, Sean had forgotten to make sure to scrub everything in the shuttle and make sure there was no evidence left behind. When he'd cut his hand on the device, it had been his undoing. Stupid. He should have known better, but then he had spent most of his time on that mission thinking he was near death anyway.

Neyral drew back, keeping his laser knife trained on Sean. "I knew there was something off about him from the way he acted. He used our Speaker to gain access to confidential files and manipulated her emotions to sow dissension through the ranks." He lifted the laser knife and pointed it at Sean's face. "Take him to the brig!"

The guards who held him tugged him backward, and Sean was dragged back down the corridor in the opposite direction he had been going. He went limp rather than resisting, not sure what he could do on an alien ship, with a crew who knew he was an impostor spy, far away from any allies. Even if he managed to free himself from the guards, where could he go? There was no way he could recover from this.

Neyral followed behind them, his laser cutter still activated. The way he grinned sent a shiver down Sean's spine.

PART V

59

Silence filled the committee chambers. The tension cut thick through the bondsense. Tamar wished she could be anywhere but here, and more, wished that she could get this human out of her head. Panic filled him, like a trapped animal, and it made it impossible for her to concentrate.

Tendell and Ny'aet worked together, crafting fleet movements over at their console, with a focus on trying to find the human Admiral Conley's trajectory. He would strike soon, and they had to be ready.

She hadn't told anyone that she had entwined Aeveron, or whatever his name was.

Sean.

She shook her head, trying to clear the stray thoughts from reaching her, but to no avail. His thoughts wouldn't stop coming. Though, by the same token, it was impossible not to project all her troubles to everyone else. They understood that something was wrong with her, and it made the others wary.

Not that anyone said anything to her directly, but the way Ny'aet kept close with Tendell left her out of the planning discussion. Maela's voice was requested at times, but never Tamar's. Right now,

Maela was in the infirmary assisting the doctors with a few marines' wounds from a battle-readiness training exercise.

The only one missing was Neyral. He had other matters to attend to—which meant torturing Aeveron. His actions were very clear through the bond: keeping Aeveron in near darkness, frightening him in a silent room while Aeveron lay on the cold, hard floor. The real interrogation would begin soon. Both Aeveron and Tamar understood that. She wanted to rush to his rescue, but Tamar tried her best not to react. She didn't want to give herself away.

Did they know that she was forever tied to this impostor? No. They couldn't have more information than the base emotions that she sent to them. The amount of information from the tribal bond paled in comparison to what she had with Aeveron.

A moment later, Aeveron's projections went dark. Blank. Was he dead? Tamar stifled a breath. No, from what she understood of entwining, the break of such a bond would have crippled her. She wouldn't be able to stand from the pain, let alone have clear thoughts as she did. He must be unconscious.

Without Aeveron swimming in her head, she tried her best to get back to her own work. This ship had to be running at peak efficiency as never before, especially with all the personal problems happening. Her crew would need to make up in their performance for the odd situation in the commanding committee.

Minutes went by, and she still managed to stare at her display, accomplishing little. Her heart felt like it was continually being ripped from her chest. She couldn't work like this.

The chamber doors opened, revealing Tol, who gave his proper salutes to the committee.

Ny'aet, by proxy, had taken over the speakership role. He lifted his head from his work with the fleets to acknowledge Tol. "Lieutenant," he said.

"First Speaker." Tol bowed his head low.

He was nearly as panicked as she was, and far less adept at shielding his emotions. His broadcasts pushed everyone to an additional level of fear. "Say your piece, Lieutenant. We all sense your urgency. You have nothing to fear from us," Tamar said. She hoped that much was true.

Before he could speak, the door opened again.

This time Neyral came in. He projected sadistic joy, and it interrupted the flow of so much nervous tension from the others. Tamar wanted to vomit. How could he have been chosen for a commanding position with such a twisted streak about him?

Ny'aet chuckled. "I see all of you could use some leave and meditation training as soon as possible. I've never been in a committee chamber with so much emotion flowing through the bond," he said. "I understand these are difficult times. But they will be over soon, and we will have a great victory for Arysha."

Neyral nodded. "For Arysha and the Aresh."

The others muttered agreement. Tamar was silent. This still didn't feel right to her. And she still felt nothing through the bondsense when it came to Ny'aet. It was as if he were disconnected somehow. He couldn't possibly maintain so much control.

"Do you have a report to make, Commander?" Ny'aet asked.

Neyral brushed past Tol and made his way to his station. "I do. Our engineering crew found human DNA in the recent mission shuttlecraft."

Tol shrank where he stood.

"We tested Lieutenant Aeveron, finding that he exhibits internal physiology consistent with humans. He is an enemy spy." Neyral rubbed his fingers together. "Their blood is quite messy and sticky. Difficult to clean off. I'll need to check myself for infection. Who knows what kind of strange bacteria humans could carry?"

Tamar wanted to be anywhere but here. Her body urged her to run away. Instincts took over. Deep-seated instincts of her ancestors heading for the caves deep within the rocks when the megastorms approached. But she had nowhere to go.

Tol felt it, too. He projected it worse than her. But why should he be worried? He wasn't the one entwined to Aeveron. Or was he worried he would be implicated?

Neyral cocked his head at Tol. "You performed a brave service,

Lieutenant Tol, going on a mission with that human alone for several days. You couldn't have known it, but you were in immense danger. It's something worth commending on your record."

"Th-thank you," Tol said. He glanced at Maela as if to wish for a way to hide behind her.

"Excellent news," Ny'aet said. "It was troubling to find out we had a human spy among us. It's almost reason enough to make sure that all our service members are bonded to a tribe. It'll be something I'll discuss with the other committee members later. But you and your crew have done a great job. Tell me, Commander Neyral, have interrogations begun yet?"

"He has been placed in a holding cell," Neyral said.

"Ah. I would like to take a hand in the interrogation. Such events are very rare, and it would be best to obtain information first hand," Ny'aet said.

Neyral grinned. "I would be glad for your assistance, First Speaker."

The room felt like it was spinning around Tamar. It clamped down on her in the way the bond prevented her from actively trying to hurt one of her own within the Aresh. The entwined bond was much more intense, and it could prove fatal. She would experience anything they did to Aeveron, and her body reacted to the prospect. She stumbled away from her station. "If you'll excuse me, I need to check on some personal matters," Tamar said.

Ny'aet tilted his head, concern on his face. "Of course. Rest while you can. We'll need all of us at our best when we discover the location of the human vessel."

Tamar slipped by Lieutenant Tol and rushed out of the room.

60

"It did not go well," Tol said, pacing in Maela's—soon to be his—quarters. The room was much bigger than his own, which had barely enough space to contain all his tools and experiments. Once he moved in here, he'd be able to organize his work in a much more functional manner. The south wall would make for a perfect work bench, and...

And he had to stay on task. His long-term work mattered little if Aeveron was going to be held in the brig, tortured, and then executed. He finally had a colleague who at least somewhat understood his eccentricities, and he was taken away.

Tol had envisioned a situation where Aeveron would confess his humanity without this whole debacle. It would have been in private, with Maela present, of course. She would be interested from a purely scientific perspective, likely never having encountered human biology up close. Tamar would have been there, too.

Maela jolted him, her hands gripping his shoulders tightly. "Tol? I've asked you the same question three times and you were in some sort of walking trance. You worry me when you're like this. What do you mean by 'it did not go well'?"

"Oh, sorry. I'm still getting used to what gets through in the bond and what doesn't. In the committee chambers today. You saw the tension with Neyral, Ny'aet, and Tamar, yes?" Tol cocked his head at her.

"Yes, but that's why I asked you what happened," she said. She gave a knowing smile that showed her patience and her care for him. Her love reverberated through the bondsense.

It was an intoxicating feeling, in which Tol could lose himself and never come back. He'd be happy to, but they had trouble. "Aeveron was identified as the traitor. Speaker Tamar is devastated," he said, frowning.

Maela pursed her lips. "That is shocking news. He was your friend."

"Still is."

She surveyed him for a moment. "I see that. You knew about this beforehand?"

Tol nodded. "I discovered it while we were en route to human space. He was loyal to us despite the fact that he's human. I believe his love for Tamar to be earnest."

"That complicates matters."

"It does." Tol backed away from her and paced around the room. In his nervousness, he misjudged and bumped into the corner of a table. It didn't hurt much, his thick skin absorbing the shock before it could do any real damage. The opposite of what may have occurred with Aeveron. With their circulatory fluids so close to the surface of their bodies, it must be perilous simply being one of them. "I am not certain Speaker Tamar will maintain control of her emotions through this. It's not my place to judge command structures, however."

Maela stepped into his tracks, placing her hands on his shoulders when he paced back in front of her. "Stop doing that. You're making me nervous."

"Sorry."

Her hands slid slowly off him, down his chest, as if she savored the touch as much as he did. "Would you like some ye'tai?" She moved over to her kitchenette to open a cupboard, from which she produced a bottle of blue liquid.

Tol shook his head. "No, thank you."

Maela poured herself a glass. "Sorry I don't have any Ruy'achi Oti. That stuff will burn a hole in your digestive tract."

"I'm careful," Tol said, unable to help but smile from her concern for him. Entwining had been the best decision he'd ever made.

"Correct me if I'm wrong," Maela said, sipping her drink. "You trust Aeveron, and you don't like that he's been detained."

"It's sensible to check him out for security purposes now that they know, but the interrogations that Neyral and Ny'aet discussed sounded much more like torture." He shook his head. "I can't condone that. He doesn't deserve it. He's been helping us."

"Mmm," Maela said, her tone non-committal. "You're certain he can be trusted?"

"Yes. I've thought about it and I believe he can be. He's smitten with Speaker Tamar, and that's real."

Maela chuckled. "It's amazing what love can do."

"Yes," Tol agreed. "You're willing to help him?"

"If you say he's worthy, then I trust you." She finished her drink and set the glass down. "The first thing we need to do is to calm Speaker Tamar. She needs a clear head to get through this, and with the way Tendell and Neyral were meddling with command before, she'll need to stay extra focused."

"Should we go to her quarters?"

Maela's eyes shined, sparkling with not just her overall typical radiance, but with love. It pressed through the bondsense, warming Tol in ways that nothing else could. "I think I should go alone. We have a kinship that I don't think you've quite developed. I want her to be at ease."

"Of course," Tol said.

"We'll see if my calm will be enough to cut through." Maela brushed past him, bringing her hand to Tol's face, teasingly tracing his jawline before turning toward the door.

"You're always enough for me," Tol said.

She turned, looking over her shoulder in a way that made Tol melt completely. "Because I have you to ground me, my love. I won't be long."

61

Tamar had her face buried in her pillow when the door chime rang. She didn't respond. She was unable to move. If only she could stop breathing and surrender herself to the void of death. It would be far easier than being entwined to an enemy, while her whole life fell apart around her.

The betrayal stung. How could Aeveron have gotten so close to her and been lying the whole time? She hadn't understood some of society's underlying prejudices about the uncommitted before, but it made perfect sense now. If someone couldn't commit to a tribe, to be open and honest with their own kind, then there was something wrong with them.

The way he looked her in the eye and told her he loved her. How he manipulated her into laughing at his brazen behavior at times. Even his talk about how he hated this war! It was all a lie. The human enemy was insidious, intoxicating. They pushed boundaries until there were none left. Ny'aet was right. All humans wanted was to twist every culture into their own way of being.

Phony.

And that still wasn't the worst part. He still lingered in the back of her head, buzzing like an insect that wouldn't go away. She could never escape it.

In this moment, Aeveron experienced intense fear and pain. Her biology compelled her to be empathetic for him, and on the flip side, bile rose in her throat because that sympathy was detrimental to her tribe. Two warnings, both providing her anguish, and both pulling her in different directions. Those emotions would rip her apart.

The door chime rang again. Whoever stood outside was persistent. Who could it be? Ny'aet? She didn't want to speak with him right now, not when she was like this. Neyral to gloat or attempt to relieve her of command? Either way, Tamar didn't want to answer.

It rang a third time.

Tamar rolled onto her back and sighed. "Come in."

The door's automatic opener made its whooshing noise and was followed by footsteps. "Speaker, I wanted to check on you," came a soothing voice. Maela. Perhaps the only person on the ship who would be here out of concern for her personally.

"I want to be alone right now," Tamar said.

"If you were in my position and could sense your emotional aura, you wouldn't allow that," Maela said.

Tamar sat up on her bed, letting her legs dangle over the edge. Maela was right. She projected a calming sense of true care for Tamar. It had an impact, even though nothing could console her completely.

Maela sat down next to her. "I heard about Aeveron."

Tamar tensed. Even mention of him bothered her far more than it should. Was she worried about an accusation? No one could question her loyalties. At least, Maela wouldn't. Who knew what Neyral would do with his ambitions. "Humans are craftier than we gave them credit for. Endearing a spy to someone so close to the Ruling Committee," Tamar said.

"Tol doesn't believe Aeveron means any harm to you," Maela said.

"I know he doesn't."

Silence hung in the room for a long moment. Maela turned to her. "You *know*?"

Tamar met Maela's eyes, and took a deep breath. "Yes. We are entwined."

Maela's mouth hung open. "The implications of this are staggering on a scientific level. It could imply a shared ancestry."

"I hadn't really considered it," Tamar said dryly.

Maela bit her lip. "My apologies. My background is in medicine and biology. It's not the time for that. But it also means that some of the fears that our people have, about our cultures being incompatible —they have to be wrong."

"Mm," Tamar muttered. It didn't particularly comfort her.

Maela patted her arm sympathetically. "He followed orders, went on missions that were detrimental to his own people for you. It means that he has some loyalty to you. You have to be able to feel that if you're entwined."

"Tricks," Tamar said.

"Maybe, maybe not."

Tamar let her head fall onto her hands, propping her elbows on her thighs. "It doesn't matter now. He's human. We're in a war, and he's going to be interrogated. No matter how much it hurts me."

"Does Ny'aet know that you're entwined?"

"Of course not."

"Hmm," Maela said. "We should at least make him aware that any tortures to Aeveron will have adverse effects on you."

"And what will that do to me? I'm forever bonded with one of our enemies." Tamar lifted her head again and balled her fist. "My career is over, at the very least." Up until now, she'd taken for granted her career, her advancement toward the Ruling Committee, how fast she progressed through the naval ranks. It was all over now. Others would find out, and there would be nothing she could do when it all came back on her. Aeveron had ruined her on top of everything else he'd done. It made her so angry. But Maela remained calm. She trusted Aeveron, and so did Tol. She considered. "Tol trusts him," she said aloud.

"Yes."

"That means he knows."

"Yes."

Tamar turned back toward Maela. "How?" The word came out sounding so accusatory. Perhaps she meant it that way, but she wasn't sure. What did it matter what Tol knew?

"He found out when they were out on this last mission, not long before it was discovered," Maela said.

Tamar frowned. Tol trusted him, and Maela trusted his instincts implicitly. The way it all felt, Maela wasn't worried about having a human aboard in the least. They had both discussed their feelings toward this war, how it was an overreach. Was it even worse than that? Were they being the aggressors? Tamar reached out with her new sense, seeing that Aeveron was still asleep. Whether that was chemically induced or not, she had no idea. She found herself missing those first moments of being entwined with him, when it was filled with such immense joy, love beyond anything she'd ever experienced. "Even from the first time we met, Aeveron looked at me differently than the way everyone else did."

"That's how Tol's been with me. Since the very beginning," Maela said.

"If he loved me, in earnest, why would he hide it from me?"

"Well, how have you reacted to the fact that he's a human?" Maela asked.

That was a valid point. Even uncovering the news now, she had lost all sense. But, was that more because he was human, or more because he'd deceived her? The fact that he could lie to her, even by omission, struck her like lightning. The most painful part was that she still cared for him. She couldn't deny that. "I need to think about this more. Thank you for being here, Maela. I don't know what I'd do without you."

Maela leaned over to her and gave her a hug. "We're here for each other. That's what the Aresh is about at its core."

Pride stirred within the bondsense, and Tamar felt it, too. It drowned out much of the pain she'd felt moments earlier. "I don't know what to do yet, but we won't act in haste. We'll return to our duties, and see what we can do to sway the others. If we can convince key movers that the humans are indeed kin to us in some way, we might be able to save lives. We can't let our actions be dictated by fear."

Maela stood and smiled at her. "Yes, Speaker. Spoken like a true leader."

Tamar returned the smile. "For the good of the Aresh."

62

A lone security guard stood outside the translucent, electrified bars of Sean's cell. He'd found out about the shocking aspect of the bars the hard way. The cell itself was just as efficiently laid out as every other section of the ship, a cramped space for the prisoner. On the right corner of the wall was a sink with no mirror, a thin drip of water being the only luxury he was afforded.

The guard, a fit Aryshan man with plasma pistol in hand, peered inside, watching him.

Sean did his best to maintain a smile, to appear as if he couldn't be broken. He hurt, to be honest. When the guards dragged him into the cell the first time, they hadn't been gentle. He'd been hit with batons, pummeled, and given several blows to the head. His skull pounded. He didn't want to think too much on his pains. Judging from inabilities to move in certain ways, he probably had several fractures and perhaps worse. It wasn't as if anyone would give him medical attention anyway.

The Aryshan guard acted as if Sean was beneath his gaze.

As much as it amused him to get a reaction out of the guard, a precious small victory in a spot where he had very few, his thoughts turned to other matters. *Entwined* matters.

What had originally stirred him from a drug-hazed sleep, courtesy of a tranquilizer that had been jabbed into his arm, was Tamar's rage. The sensation had been so intense that it felt like he'd been physically shaken. It filled him with an overwhelming desire to quell her rage, to protect her. It was almost as instinctual as the fight-or-flight response in dangerous situations.

For the last hour or so, Tamar's rage had faded. It became sorrow, lethargy. All it did to Sean was allow him to focus on his wounds. The pain throbbed in an ebb and flow, in an almost rhythmic manner. He clenched his teeth when it flared again.

The guard watched him from the corner of his eye.

"You know, I'm right here. You can talk to me," Sean said. Anything would be better than the silence and confusion of both his and Tamar's thoughts going through his head.

"I don't speak with human scum," the guard said.

You just did, Sean thought and wanted to say, but he opted not to tempt fate in teasing the guard. Instead, he sighed.

The sound of footsteps came from down the hall, followed by Commander Maela, who had a bag with handles draped over one arm. She approached his cell and stopped before the guard.

"Commander," the guard said with a slight bow.

"I'm here on the orders of First Speaker Ny'aet," Maela said, not even looking at Sean. "I'm to prepare the prisoner for interrogation. Please allow me a few moments with him."

The guard nodded and moved down the hall.

Maela tapped the controls outside the cell, deactivating the force field. She entered the cell and opened her bag.

"Maela," Sean said softly enough so it wouldn't be heard down the hallway. His hopes rose. Was she going to rescue him?

Instead of ushering him out, she produced a hypo and a vial of solution from her bag. She clicked the solution into place. "This is a relaxant. If you feel drowsy, or more like talking, you'll know why," she said.

"What? But—" Before he could protest further, Maela had the hypo to his neck, injecting him with the solution.

His neck burned. Sean grunted from the pain as he brought his hand to the wound. Aryshan injections cut deeply due to their physiology. Anything toward the surface wouldn't pierce through to their circulatory systems. It was pure torture for Sean.

In a surprising move, Maela leaned close to his ear to whisper. "I do what I must, but do not lose hope, Aeveron. I have spoken with your beloved. You are very lucky that she appears to care as much about you as you do her. Keep that in mind as you endure these trials. We will do what we can, when the time is right."

She pulled back from him and departed the cell before tapping the wall control to reactivate the force field bars. "We're done here," she said.

When the guard returned to his post, he had an older Aryshan man at his side. This man had a bag as well. Even from Sean's vantage point, he could see that the man had a charisma about him, statesman-like. There was something familiar about his face.

"Thank you for your work, Commander. I regret having to bring you down here to see this disgusting creature, but some things are best kept in the hands of the commanding committee," the man said.

Sean recalled where he'd seen that face before. It was one of the members of the Ruling Committee. He'd studied them while on Cestus III. This one was Ny'aet, the First Speaker. Leader of the Aryshans. He had to be hallucinating. Why would someone of that stature be interrogating him personally?

Ny'aet reached into his bag, and produced thin, white gloves. With a careful precision, Ny'aet slipped his fingers into those gloves, snapping them into place over his wrists.

The drugs hit Sean like the stutter of a crystal drive going into FTL. His eyes went wide. The cell seemed to grow to the size of a large conference room around him. Ny'aet filled his vision, the older Aryshan's head circling around in front of him. It was so funny watching his face in that swirl. Even funnier as words were barked at him.

Something new pricked his skin, but it wasn't worth noticing. He saw red on the floor soon after. Was that his own blood? It couldn't be. Not when the world was so joyous, so beautiful. The only thing that could make it more beautiful would be Tamar at his side. Where was she anyway? She was in his head; that was the important part. Still alive somewhere. Warm. Oh yes, so warm.

His vision blurred into unreality.

63

Tamar rushed into the committee chambers, thoughts awhirl. Aeveron's projections had become like a buzz in the back of her head, incoherent. Dangerous. It'd been like that for the last several hours, and it became increasingly difficult to ignore it.

The first thing she did to try to keep her thoughts at bay was make rounds. She went to the junior officers' hold first, inspecting the large semi-circle that comprised their stations. The mood was tense there, with much uncertainty, as was to be expected. They were the youngest of the crew. It wasn't to say they were undisciplined. Training programs took care of that, but no training could prepare for the rush that came from being so close to combat.

The looming sense of impending battle thickened. While Tamar had been grieving, plans moved forward. She hadn't talked to the rest of the committee before she started her inspections, but the work she saw on the holodisplays in front of her crew indicated only one thing: the *Issiana* was on the move. Did that mean they had found where the Earth ship had intended to strike? Or had they struck already? She should have had a clearer mind through all this and paid more attention.

If only her full attention had been possible.

She cut short her surveying of the junior officers' hold. There was only so much time left before they would be involved in something irreversible for the lives around them. More and more she was convinced aggression was not the best course of action for the Aresh, or for Arysha as a whole. Even if they came out victorious, the cost would be too high. What would they gain? Pushing the humans back? As long as they shared a border, these tensions would creep into the two species. What about the next time? If they didn't destroy each other now. From what she had seen of humans' tenacity so far, they couldn't be counted on to back down.

It was a miscalculation of human selfishness. The assumption of their behavioral patterns didn't appear based on fact, but on how Aryshans would act in a similar situation. The attacks they'd coordinated thus far hadn't worked in the way intended, and the vast majority had been successful. Why, then, would more be presumed to create a different outcome?

The other committee members watched the center of the room, where the main holodisplay had a tactical map of the adjacent sector of space. A light pulsed in the northwestern quadrant of the three-dimensional display. By the orbits of the various planets and moons around it, Tamar recognized the location. Palmer Station.

Ny'aet paced around the holodisplay. "After hours of interrogation, I received no information from the prisoner. It seems the humans have trained their intelligence officers well. All he does under our drugs and coercion is babble like an idiot," he said.

He took a moment to survey the other commanders present, inclining his head to Tamar. "However, the reason I called everyone here after shift hours is not to talk about the human saboteur. Minutes ago, Earth Admiral Conley attacked our outpost on Ygvar."

If the mood in the room had been somber before, it became downright grave. Even Tendell and Neyral projected unease.

"Our thoughts that he would go for Treil were incorrect," Neyral said.

Ny'aet nodded. "And we diverted most of the fleet there. The human admiral is a savvy one, and that left one of our supply lines vulnerable. His bombardment was brutal, but reports are still coming in. No word as to the state of survivors, as of yet."

Tamar had a friend from the academy stationed on Ygvar. Chavi Elyna di Aresh. She wanted to inquire after the other woman, but she sensed it wouldn't be the time. The last thing she wanted to do now was make waves, not until she was ready to take an action regarding this war, or Aeveron. She still didn't know what she wanted to do with him.

The holodisplay changed, displaying several Aryshan warships. The *Issiana* was there. The *Telv*, the *Ry'ielm*, the *Skyweyr*, and the *Enola*. Five heavy cruisers in all, each with its own contingent of fighters. Were they going to join a battle formation and take down the human attacker?

"It's clear to me after deliberation that Admiral Conley is meant as a diversion. The humans understood that he could penetrate our border and create chaos, hoping he would throw us into disarray and concentrate our forces inward. What this tells me is they will not be anticipating a strong counterstrike."

Tamar reflexively stifled a breath. She wanted to deescalate the conflict. "Isn't the intention to deter the humans from entering our space? Our actions so far have done the opposite. If we launch a heavy offensive with five warships—"

Ny'aet waved off her concern. "The humans have already shown they will not respond with reason. We have to play to their instincts and ensure flight is the only option for them."

Neyral and Tendell muttered their agreements. Maela shot a glance at Tamar that held as much concern as she had about the matter, but she said nothing.

"The plan is to take Palmer Station," Ny'aet said. "The station is Earth's closest outpost to our borders. This would push them back to Cestus III and give us an ample buffer from further assault. We can also use the station to resupply and repair, as it has the capacity to dock our five large cruisers."

Tamar stared at the map. The strategy was sound if a larger war were to be inevitable. But what had Aeveron communicated to Earth regarding their strategies and movements? The humans might be keener in their understanding of the way Aryshans reacted than Ny'aet anticipated. She couldn't voice any positive remarks about the humans, however. With the way Ny'aet reacted to them, it would draw further ire toward Aeveron. He already had enough pain.

"We will never again stand by, as the Anwii did, while we watch a Great Death consume us. No longer will we be idle when aliens over-reach. Arysha needs this buffer zone. It will send a clear message," Ny'aet said.

Neyral grinned. "I look forward to this new era of Aryshan strength."

Tamar wanted to shout about this foolishness, but Ny'aet's passion had stirred the others. Even Maela seemed pacified by his words. There was the possibility that Tamar was clouded in her judgment by compassion for humans. For one human in particular. Perhaps she was becoming unfit for command, as Tendell and Neyral had stated.

The talk continued. Ny'aet detailed the proposed ship movements and assured the others of the strengthening of defenses along the border worlds. Tamar didn't listen. Little had to do with her or the *Issiana*. The others could handle the logistics.

"Any further questions then?" Ny'aet said as he finished discussing the details of the attack plan.

"No, First Speaker," Neyral said.

Tendell shook his head, as did Maela.

"Very well then. Please, go and relay orders to each department. These matters are best spoken in person. Our strength will project through the bondsense, and the crew will need that," Ny'aet said. He motioned to Tamar. "Tamar, you stay here. We still need to speak further."

The others gave respectful bows of their heads and departed the committee chambers.

When the door shut behind them, Ny'aet circled around the

holodisplay to approach her. "There is still the matter of Lieutenant Aeveron."

Tamar stiffened. Aeveron's projections cluttered the back of her mind, incomprehensible. The effects of whatever interrogation drugs he was given overwhelmed him. But there was far worse that could occur. What did this have to do with her?

"The spy babbled, as I mentioned, but some of his words were disconcerting. Those words pertained to you."

This couldn't be happening in addition to everything. Tamar didn't want to believe it. She wanted to shrink away into nothingness, to hide, to be anywhere but this ship.

Ny'aet watched impassively, scrutinizing her. He still projected nothing, pure emptiness. Only her own fears filled that tribal bond. "He spoke as if he were one with you, Commander Tamar."

"He's human, not Aryshan," Tamar said. She couldn't lie, not with her emotions this strong through the bond, but she could make the implication that it would be impossible to bond because of physiological difference. She would have thought it the case mere days ago.

Ny'aet leaned against her console. "It shouldn't be possible. However, I'm actually rather studied on the finer biological elements of bondsense. It's a symbiotic relationship of bacteria within us that modify the empathetic synapses in our brains, combined with pheromones that we produce in stressful situations, which is why emotional moments amplify the connections. These bacteria can change and mutate, as anything else within us. Your entwining with Aeveron is very interesting. My scientists will love to learn more about it. When we have taken Palmer Station, I'm going to be sending you back to homeworld to study these effects."

"But I—"

"No buts. As I said, it's an interesting phenomenon. Our bond is both our greatest strength and greatest weakness. Your example may actually lead to some interesting strategies in the future with humans." He shrugged. "We shall see."

Tamar wanted to ask about her command, but she didn't want to appear desperate. It was bad enough that he knew about her and

Aeveron. The fact that he was so cold and calculating about it made it even worse. Anger she could have understood, but she couldn't predict anything that he was planning.

Ny'aet peered at her, as if trying to read her and react to the worry so heavy within the bondsense. "I am not going to pull your command, Tamar. You are one of the best in the fleet. Your loyalty is not in question."

"Thank you," she said, the only words she could manage to squeak out of her lips. She was completely at his mercy.

"I appreciate your work. No doubt it's been a struggle. You may not have realized this, but the entire Ruling Committee, not just me, took a keen interest in your development. We placed you into this position knowing that Tendell and Neyral could be difficult." Ny'aet inclined his head. "They certainly have voiced their opinions about you to me in private. Though what's interesting is they have a small amount of fear of you, a fear that translates into respect. It's a crucial part of leadership, I've found."

"Thank you," Tamar said again. Where was he going with this?

"Eventually, once you are fully battle tested and trained, I will be bringing you to the Ruling Committee, Tamar. A couple of the members are getting old, and we'll need younger blood with greater energy in these trying times ahead." He placed a hand on her shoulder. "What I'm saying is, fear not. After this, after my scientists do their research, we'll handle your issue with the human."

Tamar blinked. "If you harm him, it will harm me."

Ny'aet removed his hand and chuckled. "That's not what I meant. No, I mean that we will remove the bond for you."

All feeling drained from her face. A numbness followed, and it was impossible to contain the shiver that slithered up her spine. Removing a bond? She'd never heard of such a thing. Suddenly, she understood why she couldn't sense any projections from him. His talk of scientists, of research. He had found a way to remove or alter the bond. "There's no way..."

"There wasn't, until recently."

"How?" Tamar whispered.

Ny'aet paced the room. The holodisplay obscured him as he circled around. "Several years ago, I authorized a grant for a study into our bondsense. I was looking for ways to amplify it, to provide easier communication between our scouts and officers across star systems. However, upon testing, they uncovered something far more interesting. Yes, we've done something science has never been able to do before. Of course, we didn't let this information leak to the general public. Our entire society relies on commitment, entwining, the bondsense. If this information fell into the wrong hands..."

"...it could destroy Arysha," Tamar said. Their whole culture, every faction, not just the Aresh, was based on trust, on the warnings that the bondsense brought. Without it, they would be selfish, alone, lie like the humans. Did Ny'aet remove his bond? No, that wasn't it. She could sense that he was Aresh. But nothing else emanated from him. Nothing ever did. She had to find out more. "You performed this experiment on yourself, didn't you?"

"Yes. Though perhaps not in the way you think. These genomes are complicated. There are many layers. After months of research, we discovered a way in which to keep commitment intact, but in a manner in which a person would not be as physically bound to his or her faction. I can think, come to decisions without the weight of the Aresh bearing on me. It's made me think more clearly than ever before, though I still maintain my link to the others."

The news disturbed her almost worse than if he had been able to sever the bond completely. It meant he could lie to her, to anyone. Everything he said was suspect, yet he had perfect information about others. He was insane. Which meant she had to be careful.

Ny'aet stopped at her station again. "Very few are aware of this. Consider yourself part of the inner circle. We'll take care of you, and I won't harm Aeveron while you have this bond. When it's over, you'll transfer to the *Skyweyr*, and then head to Arysha. We'll tell the others you're on medical leave. No one will be more the wise."

This was the entire reason that leaderships were structured as a committee, not a single man. If there were a problem, committees could take care of it—override the ill judgment of one. With Ny'aet in such a position, where he didn't have to betray any of his emotions to anyone, where they thought he was strong in his emotional shielding, he could manipulate anyone just by sensing their emotions. And who knew what other psychological impacts modifying the bond would have? He certainly wasn't the Ny'aet she remembered interning for all those years ago. But now wasn't the time or place to fight this. She couldn't even do so with the rest of the committee, save Maela. They would take his side, perhaps write her off as the insane one. No, she needed a different way to deal with this. Something she'd need time to think about. "I appreciate being in your confidence, First Speaker," Tamar said, bowing her head respectfully.

"Make sure you're rested and ready for action. We'll be meeting with the rest of the fleet in a day's time, and we'll need everyone at peak efficiency," Ny'aet said, signifying the end of the conversation. He nodded to her and took his leave of the chambers.

Tamar stood alone, staring at the planned fleet movements. More than anything, she wished she had Aeveron's advice. A gentle tug in the back of her skull let her know that he missed her. She missed him, too.

———

64

Tol grabbed two trays from the ship's food processor in the mess. Maela was already seated at a table in front of a floor-to-ceiling window, the darkness of space beyond. He balanced a tray on each hand as he moved over, and set them down before him and his entwined. "How was the command today?"

"Better than I expected," Maela said, grabbing a hooked utensil. "First Speaker Ny'aet has a good sense for tactics and big plans. Perhaps your friend has correct ideas from his perspective, but I believe we're on the right course."

"Oh?" Tol was surprised. He took his own utensil, slicing and grabbing at the re-moisturized charnbeast mutton. It was one of the standard meals the chef prepared, bland but tolerable.

"Yes, though we should talk about this later when we are in more of a private setting," Maela said.

Tol considered, chewed his meat, and swallowed. "Of course," he said and changed the topic. "The senior officers' quarry ran so many readiness drills, I could probably perform my battle duties in my sleep now."

Maela laughed. "That's the point of them."

"Still, redundant."

"Not everyone's as quick a learner as you, Tol. You have to remember that."

Tol found himself lost in the way she ate. She chewed with precision, small movements which he found adorable. He could watch her for hours, much better than the display screens he stared at during combat drills. "I'd still prefer to vary my duties. These last months have been interesting, allowing me to work on my inventions, going on various extra-ship missions."

Maela smirked. "You're too creative for your own good."

"Thank you," he said, taking it as a compliment.

Another aura entered the mess, this one strong, with a sense of dread. It immediately made him lose his appetite. Tol set his utensil down and turned to see who had arrived.

Speaker Tamar made her way in with all haste. She scanned the mess. Did she realize how strong her emotions were? Tol considered standing and ushering her into private quarters, shielded by thick metal walls that would protect the rest of the crew from her agitation.

Maela did stand. She'd always been quicker to act than Tol in situations like these. Perhaps that was why she had a command and he didn't. "Speaker?" she asked.

Tamar spoke at a just above a whisper. "Matters are worse than I feared. I need you both to be on the ready to act on my communication. I cannot tell you more now, but stay vigilant. Every moment could make a difference." She immediately turned to leave.

Maela jogged after her. "What's going on? Should I come with you?"

Tamar stopped. "No. What I'm doing next I do alone. Just be prepared."

Tol sat in silence when Tamar left. He was no longer in the mood for a meal, too tense to be able to consider eating. He pushed his plate from him and focused on Maela.

She projected confusion, the same as his, but where her beautiful serenity typically radiated from her, Tol could sense only fear.

65

The drugs swam in Sean's system for what felt like an eternity. Slowly, the world reappeared around him. Everything up until this point had been a haze. He remembered seeing Maela, and then Ny'aet, and the guard, but he had no idea what they did or said after the drugs took effect.

His face pulsed. It had to be inflamed, even if he couldn't see it. Talking would probably hurt pretty badly if he tried, but it wasn't as if he had anyone to talk to. When he attempted to stand, he slipped on some liquid on the floor. His eyes widened at the pool of blood beneath him. Not good.

As soon as the pain welled within him, a wave of euphoria hit. The drug again. It wasn't completely out of his system yet. He couldn't worry about what was out of control. He just had to relax. He hummed an old song to himself. What was that tune? Something from when he was a kid. It felt good. Really good.

"Quiet, prisoner. Unless you want another beating," the security guard said. He still stood outside the cell, staring at Sean.

Sean felt too good to care. He grinned. "Don't you have anything better to do? Your leadership is about to send your fleet into wah-ahar," he said the last bit in a sing-song voice. Talking didn't feel so bad after all.

The guard huffed at him in return. "I hate truth serum," he muttered.

"Nice of you to stare then. You know, now that I think about it, they should be giving me a medal instead of, you know, torturing me in here." Sean giggled to himself. Even with the drugs, his laughter sounded embarrassing. He couldn't stop it, though.

He regretted his words in some way, but they were true. There was no reason to censor his thoughts. What more could they do to him? Dying wouldn't be so bad.

The guard held still, returning to ignoring him.

Sean squeezed his eyes shut a couple of times in rapid succession to try to shake the drug's effects, but it only made the world spin. "I'm glad they left me with a great conversationalist. You know, back Earthside, we wouldn't treat one of yours like this. We call it a war crime. There's a little joke back home that we give our prisoners an education, hot meals, a place to stay. We even got this prison planet where it's a nice temperate area, outdoors, woodsy. Gave it a number instead of a name. I can't remember exactly. Too nice if you ask me, it sounds like a vacation. Sometimes, it's better to be in there than out in the real world."

The security guard finally moved, taking a closer position to glower at Sean through the translucent energy field. "Our justice is swift. When we are no longer in a state of emergency you will be tried, you will be found guilty, and you will be executed." The guard smacked the electrified bars with his baton, and it fizzled in front of him.

Before Sean could talk back, a buzzer sounded. The guard moved down the corridor to answer it.

Sean stared straight ahead, letting his eyes drift in and out of focus as he experimented with blinking. Eyes were so amazing. He hummed a tune again. It'd been too long since he was able to listen to good human songs.

When humming lost its entertainment value, Sean took to

watching his foot. He twisted it back and forth in the blood pool on the floor, making an irritating squeaking sound each time it moved.

"Are you going to do that forever? It's making my ears ring," came a familiar voice.

It took all his energy to lift his head. He didn't need to see straight to see the absolute angel in front of him. Was this a hallucination? No. He felt her in his very core. Or maybe the weird entwining-bond mixed with the drugs caused her to appear in front of him. If this were part of his life flashing before his eyes before an eternal rest, he could live with that.

But if this was a hallucination, why was she shouting at him? Her words were completely lost to him, even though her tone was angry and erratic. The sense in the back of his skull told him she was frantic. He snapped from his drug-induced reverie and scrambled to his feet, slipping in the process. With his arms outstretched like wings, he balanced himself. The room swayed, but he managed to stay upright.

Tamar rushed to his side. The force field had been lowered. She grabbed hold of his waist.

"You're real," Sean said.

"Of course, I am," Tamar said. "I don't think we have much time though. We need to get out of here."

"Where are we going?"

"Escape pods. I'm going to get you off this ship."

"You're rescuing me?"

"Yes, you idiot human!"

Sean managed to watch her out the corner of his eye as they moved through the cell. He walked more slowly than she wanted, but that wasn't important. She was there for him. He almost couldn't believe it. Didn't she hate him for lying to her? "Why?" he managed to ask aloud.

"Because I'm an idiot, too, apparently," she said, her voice low. Even though the words weren't particularly romantic, they warmed him. Tamar moved an arm and pushed his mouth shut, forcing him to look her directly in the eye in his drug-addled state.

He grinned ear to ear.

"You're my entwined," she said. "I love you, and I will not allow harm to come to you while I live. Do you understand?"

"Mm hmm," Sean managed through his shut mouth.

Tamar released his face.

"I love you, too," Sean said. It felt so good to say it. "You know that, yeah?"

"If I didn't, I wouldn't be here. Let's keep going." Tamar dragged him forward, through the brig. He braced himself on her shoulder. Walking in a straight line proved difficult, but she compensated for him. She didn't seem to be averse to giving him as much help as he needed.

The rest of the brig was empty. Tamar had run a tight ship since he came aboard, and he couldn't recall hearing of an incident where this detention area had been used. If they would have gone into direct battle with the humans, with boarding groups, it might have seen a lot of activity with prisoners of war. It was something he didn't want to consider, given how he was treated.

When they reached the end of the row of cells, Tamar took her free hand to rustle with her access crystal, inserting it into the door lock. She waited a moment, but nothing happened. The system didn't change colors to give them access.

"Your key's not working," Sean said.

"I don't know why." Tamar gently maneuvered Sean against the door before removing the crystal and reinserting it with more force. "Maybe it's a—"

She was cut off by a holographic image appearing on the wall behind Sean's head. He turned to look at the bright light from the projection. "Commander Tamar," a deep voice said.

Tamar frowned at the image. "First Speaker."

"Uh oh," Sean said.

The image peered at them, giving a cold, disapproving *tsk*. "I must say I'm disappointed, though obviously I had planned for this contingency after our little talk. Your emotional aura was...not quite right, to say the least. You've thrown away my long-term plans, ones meant to bring you of all people to great prosperity. Though this is why I made sure Commander Tendell monitored your location."

Tamar's shoulders drooped. She looked—and felt—more defeated than Sean had ever seen her. Her eyes shone with moisture, but no tears fell. "I'm sorry," she mouthed to him.

What could he do? He could try to rework the panel so they could escape. Tol had taught him a little bit of how to work these kinds of systems, but he was no expert in it.

The image of Ny'aet grinned as if understanding their thoughts. "Do not try to escape. There's no way out of the detention area. The door is sealed and security is on the way. The more you resist, the more painful your future interrogations will be."

Sean desperately made for the access panel anyway, ripping Tamar's crystal away, and then pulling the face off it. Behind it was a strange bio gel system, much more complicated than Tol's makeshift projects or the explosives they'd used on Cestus III. Regular Aryshan technology was far too advanced. He ripped out the components anyway.

It sparked, but it had no impact on the door.

He cradled his hand, feeling the shock despite the drugs. "Dammit."

"This was a mistake," Tamar said. "I should have planned better."

"We're not lost yet," Sean said, trying to figure out something, anything. The air vents? He looked upward. When he did so, he noticed a strange citrus odor. "What's that smell?"

Tamar sniffed. "Oh no. That's a nerve—" Her eyes rolled back in her head and she fell limp.

Sean barely managed to catch her in her arms. His own arms felt like noodles. He was still under the influence of the drug, and now he'd breathed in this substance. A sleeping gas, or so he hoped.

Whatever it was, it seemed to have little impact on him. His physiological differences amounted to good for once. He tried to set Tamar down carefully, and went back to work on the access control panel.

The door began to slide open. Whatever he'd done had opened it.

After his brief moment of elation, he saw the truth of the matter.

Five Aryshans rushed him. They were in complete marine gear, with gas masks and shock-batons.

His flight instinct took over as he attempted to charge through the marines and get to safety. That failed, as the Aryshans formed up, shoulder to shoulder. A wall of strength.

The first Aryshan hit him in the gut with his shock-baton, while another hooked back of his legs in a tackle. Sean slammed face first into the floor. He struggled and squirmed away from them.

Within moments, he was surrounded. The marines jabbed their shock-batons into his back with no compassion or hesitation. Electricity pulsed through his body.

Sean could do nothing but scream.

66

"There has to be something we can do." Tol paced in his own quarters while Maela stoically sat on his couch. He still hadn't migrated his belongings over to Maela's larger quarters. There had been no time for personal considerations, with perpetual crisis in these last couple of days.

Maela stayed silent, her natural calm acting as the only clarity on the subject. She even remained calm on the inside. Tol both envied her and loved her for that.

They still hadn't made any progress in terms of what they were going to do. Neither of them was a tactical planner.

At the end of the day, he was a pilot, and a glorified handyman. His fighting skills weren't noteworthy. He'd barely made the marks in the academy to allow him into the Aryshan Navy in the first place. What he should have done was talk to Tamar earlier, and convince her to drop her foolishness. But he hadn't. He couldn't change that now.

Maela stood. "The only thing we can do is incapacitate First Speaker Ny'aet and take control of the ship."

Tol nearly fell over at that suggestion. It was unlike her to suggest such an outlandish idea. The fact that she could, without even flinching, meant that she believed, in full, that removing the First Speaker was the best course of action for the Aresh. It was the opposite of what she had been saying a few hours ago regarding the path that they were on. But her information had changed over the course of that time as well. Maela was a fiercely loyal person, which was part of what Tol loved about her. Her loyalty ran deep with Speaker Tamar.

"That'd be impossible," Tol said. "Think about the experience he has, and how we would be going at him alone. We'd end up in the brig, the same as Aeveron and Tamar."

"I'm so confused. After our meeting in the committee chambers, I was sure that Ny'aet had us on the right track. But to lure Tamar into such a trap?" She shook her head. "Something's not right. I don't know what yet, but Tamar does not deserve to be imprisoned."

Tol fidgeted. He didn't like this kind of stress. Political matters were beyond him. He just wanted to work on his ideas in peace, away from all this. Service in the Navy was supposed to be structured, routine, a way to earn his keep and be able to dedicate a few hours a day toward his passions. Since he'd come aboard the *Issiana*, life had been anything but predictable.

"Tell me," Maela said, "if these situations were reversed, what would Aeveron do?"

"He would fight to free me, I'm sure," Tol said with a frown.

"We owe him the same. That's what loyalty is. He's one of us, even if he doesn't share our physical bond. If he is entwined to Tamar, it's as close to Aresh as he can get without being one." She reached her hand out to take his. "What about your tinkering? Is there anything you could think of to help?"

"I wish teleportation was possible," Tol said with a frown. "We could shoot Aeveron off to some distant world and not worry. If I had time, I could experiment with some of the principles of the crystal drive and see if there's a way to bend space."

Maela squeezed his hand. "How long would it take you?"

"Years. If it worked at all." Tol shrugged.

"We don't have that kind of time."

Tol thought about everything he'd attempted to create. Of everything he'd made so far, only the phase device had any tactical use. But the device was so large, and the power it used would pose a problem. He considered. Perhaps if he could program the emission field to only capture a limited space, he could make the power packs last for long enough to sneak in and sneak out of a room. But they'd have to carry the large device. "I may have an idea."

"What is it?"

"We have to get to the shuttle bay. I'm going to need some help carrying some tools, and we have to move quickly. Where did you put my welder?"

Maela stared at him blankly. "What's a welder?"

Tol mimicked the device with his hands in the air, contorting his arms into what he hoped looked like the shape. "It's got a nozzle at the end that gets white hot."

Maela laughed.

"What?"

"You look ridiculous."

"Come on, we don't have time for jokes!"

"Okay, but you need to calm down some, too. You're projecting nervousness like I've rarely felt. If it's unsettling me, it's going to arouse suspicion in others."

Tol moved over to a cabinet and grabbed his tool. He held it in his hand like a weapon. "Let's go."

67

The drugs wore off, leaving Sean wide awake.

Though he was more tired than he could recall being ever in his life, he couldn't sleep. His head pounded with each pulse of blood. His body throbbed, and though he'd never broken a bone before, he was pretty sure that some bone had cracked in his leg. It hurt like it, at the very least.

Unlike the last time he awoke, he wasn't in a cell. He lay on some slab or table, staring into a bright light that gave him no sense of space. A couple attempts to squirm confirmed that he was strapped down. Something held him along his arms, wrists, waist and ankles, giving him no opportunity to move. He couldn't even shift to find a more comfortable position for his aches and pains. His current bonds might have been a more effective torture than anything else the Aryshans had done so far.

Sean twisted his neck to the side as far as it could go, unwilling to accept being blinded. To his left, he was surprised to see Tamar. She lay strapped to a metal table, in a similar manner to him. Unlike him, she had a pillow under her head. He reminded himself to complain about the service later.

Tamar had a breathing apparatus covering her face and nose, and appeared to be unconscious. Vapor rose from the holes in the mask with each exhale of her breath. Drugs to keep her incapacitated?

Her being incapacitated was actually an odd sensation. He had grown used to having her presence in the back of his skull. She'd been awake and alert while he had been thus far. Even when she had been asleep, he sensed strange elements of her dreams. There was nothing now.

Tamar's elegance, even in this state, moved Sean. He couldn't help but admire her. There wasn't anything else he could do anyway, pinned down as he was. These could be his last cogent moments for all he knew. He might as well enjoy them as much as he could.

Voices caught his attention. Sean lifted his head to try to see, but his eyes lost focus with the intense light pulsing on his face.

"Are you sure we should be doing this? We should at least notify First Speaker Ny'aet," came the voice of Tendell.

"You'll never be seen for the full glory you can offer the Aresh if you don't take initiative. You wish to move up to fleet command someday, yes?" the deeper, more calculating voice of Neyral said.

"Yes, but—"

"But, if we extract information from the human spy pertinent to our situation, we will be heroes, regardless of the means. You understand?"

"I understand."

"Let's proceed, then."

A strong hand gripped Sean by the neck and squeezed, forcing his head up from the table. He looked directly into Tendell's eyes. "Hello, human. Have a good rest? We've been ordered not to kill you, for the sake of Speaker Tamar and our own. But those who gave the orders aren't here right now. I'd hate to have an accident where you bleed out and leave one of our own catatonic," Neyral said.

Sean tried to resist, but his body only rubbed against his bonds, which burned his skin. His heart thudded, and he could feel adrenaline course through him.

"What my associate here is trying to say is that if you cooperate with us, we can make at least what's left of your life more comfortable. If you don't..." Tendell left the end of his words hanging in the air.

"If you don't," Neyral said, "we will ensure you experience such pain that it very well may cause a Great Death within humanity."

Neyral dropped Sean's head, which smacked against the table. The back of his skull reverberated with pain.

"Tell us, Aeveron," Neyral said. "How did you dupe Speaker Tamar into believing you were in love with her?"

Something in Neyral's tone of voice caught Sean. This question wasn't of any impact to the Aryshan military efforts. This was personal. Neyral was jealous of him. That made this situation all the more dangerous. "I didn't dupe anyone," Sean managed to say, though his jaw still hurt from whatever had been done to him in the interrogations. His mouth was dry as well, which didn't make speaking easier. "I do love Speaker Tamar."

"Liar!" Neyral growled.

"Let me go. I'll prove my loyalty to her," Sean said. He tried to sound as earnest as possible.

Something sharp stabbed him in the leg. "You will answer our questions, human," Tendell said. "Do you understand?"

He could hear the squish of flesh as Tendell twisted whatever he had stuck in Sean's leg. Sean screamed.

Neyral grinned, looming over the area in front of the light, a shadow crossing his face. "Let's continue. What process did you use to entwine Speaker Tamar? Is this a new trick the humans have learned?"

"Nothing. I didn't even know it could happen," Sean said between short breaths. God, his leg burned.

"You expect us to believe that?" Tendell asked.

"It's the truth," Sean said.

"What else do humans know about our bonds? Anything weaponized?" Neyral asked.

"I don't know anything, I swear. I'm here for Tamar—that's all."

"What's going on here?" the voice of Ny'aet boomed from across the room.

Tendell pulled the sharp object out of Sean's leg, and the pain flared anew. He wasn't sure how much blood he'd lost over the last day or so, but it couldn't have been a healthy amount.

"First Speaker," Neyral said, stepping back from Sean's table.

"We were questioning the prisoner, ensuring that the humans don't have a biological weapon that can prey off our bonds," Tendell said.

Hard footsteps fell on the floor of the lab, echoing off the metallic walls. Ny'aet's face came into the periphery of Sean's view. "I ordered all interrogations to be conducted with my input." He stared at Neyral. "I sense that your personal influence in this is already troublesome."

"My apologies, sir," Neyral said.

"You're both dismissed," Ny'aet said without hesitation.

"But—" Neyral said.

Tendell cut him off. "Come, Commander. We should work on more combat preparedness drills for the crew. There's little time before we are to rendezvous with the fleet." Two pairs of footsteps walked away.

The room fell quiet again, with Ny'aet looming over Sean. "Don't expect leniency from me, human. You stole one of our best, my protégé, and perverted her mind. What you've done is unforgivable and may have destroyed years of planning. I won't allow her to come to harm from foolish aggressive officers. But you will get your due, in proper time."

Ny'aet walked away, leaving Sean with real worry for his own survival.

68

A marine armed with a plasma rifle stood in the shuttle bay, directly outside the craft Tol and Aeveron had taken on their last mission—the craft where Tol's phase device still resided. Tol hesitated when they reach the entrance, which drew a glance from the marine, as well as a squeeze of his shoulder from Maela.

"I believe in you," she whispered to him.

Determined, Tol marched through the bay over to the marine, tool box clutched to his chest. Maela followed behind him, projecting calm through their entwined bond.

"Sir?" the marine asked.

"I'm going to need unfettered access to the shuttle. There are necessary modifications that need to be made to my phase device," Tol said, careful not to lie. The guard was not Aresh, which was good, because he wouldn't be able to sense Tol's nervousness.

The marine glanced at the shuttle. "I wasn't informed of anyone who was supposed to perform maintenance on the shuttle."

"Commander Maela here," Maela said, sidestepping from behind him. "He has authorization."

The marine nodded, then stood a little straighter at attention.

"Aye, ma'am. I'll escort you inside the shuttle. We can't be too careful with human spies aboard."

Tol side-glanced at Maela. They needed to be alone, at least when he completed his work on the device. Maela continued to project calm to him. She motioned the marine ahead.

The marine led the way up the ramp at the back of the shuttle. Maela slid her fingers over Tol's hand. She coaxed his toolbox away and took it from him. The guard disappeared inside. Maela took her free hand and pressed it against Tol's chest so she could go ahead without him. Then she followed the marine inside.

A *crack* and *thunk* sounded from inside.

Maela peeked her head out from the shuttle's rear entrance. "Are you coming, or were you going to stand and wait for another guard to show?"

Tol blinked, then hurried inside. Maela dragged the marine out the back and down the ramp, then jogged back up and inside. She tapped a command on the rear panel, and the ramp retracted, sealing them in the shuttle.

"He'll be out cold for at least a couple hours, in my medical opinion," Maela said.

"We have less time than that if we're going to save Aeveron and Tamar," Tol said, eyes settling on his phase device. He crouched, and Maela handed him his box of tools. Tol opened the box, taking tools in hand, and went to work.

The panel was welded together intricately. The gel system inside couldn't be jarred too much or the device might well not function, but he did have replacement parts for the capacitor that had fried on their journey before. That would help. Next was to make sure he had a portable charge system in place. He'd worked on some storage before, so the device wouldn't have to continually draw from the shuttle's power but, instead, could run off charge for a time. If only there had been time to test the new battery system.

He made sure the device was hooked up to the shuttle's power for now so it would charge the power packs. With so much current running through it, he had to make sure he was careful. After a few minutes' work, he had the device ready to split from the shuttle's power.

The programming was going to be a bit trickier. The field was amplified by the shuttle's debris deflecting system, and would have to be cut off, and then retooled to only expand around objects of his choosing. The programming for the field to sense two Aryshan-sized bodies was intricate. The calculations took a little bit of time, even with the computer's processing power. When he was ready, he stepped back and surveyed his work, proud of what he'd accomplished.

"Are we going to carry this thing the whole way? It looks heavy," Maela said.

"Not all the way to the biolab. There are hovercarts in the shuttle bay. I didn't want to bring one in here and alert the marine that something strange was going on. We'll have to carry it that far. Do you think you can manage?"

Maela nodded. "But won't others see us?"

Tol smirked. "You should know better than to ask that."

"Oh, we'll be out of phase and invisible. Right."

"All we need to do is stay quiet."

"What about the device? Does it make noise?"

Tol appraised the device. "Most of the noise comes from the power transfer from ship systems. I've just changed to its own power pack rather than the shuttle's crystals. Hopefully with the smaller field being generated, the power packs will last."

"How long do you think we've got?"

"An hour," Tol said.

Tol moved back to the control pad and flipped the phase device on. It whirred when it started, the power pack sparking when it came to full power. "We're online," Tol said.

A rapping noise came from outside the shuttle. "Anryl, are you in there? You didn't report during the last check point."

Tol glanced at Maela.

"The shuttle should conceal him from the entrance," she whispered.

The shuttle gave a chime and the ramp clicked into its slow descent, opening to the outside world. The marine outside glanced around the shuttle. He looked confused, and in a moment, he glanced directly at Tol.

The Overseers had granted them fortune—this marine was not Aresh. He wouldn't be able to sense all the fear radiating from Tol.

The marine moved closer. Tol held as still as possible. The marine reached out his hand, and it seemed to go directly through Tol. It was an experiment he'd wanted to try with the phasing, but never found a good way to attempt. If it failed, and something were to get caught inside him, it could be fatal. Good thing it worked.

Shaking his head, the marine moved back down the ramp, leaving Tol and Maela alone. Even if he found the first marine and sounded the alarm, Tol and Maela would be able to move through the ship as long as the phase device had power.

Tol picked up one end of the device, and it was extremely heavy. Maela managed to do the same. It would be a struggle to get it to one of the hovercarts, but they had to be tough. This could be their friends' last hope.

They carefully moved down the ramp and through the shuttle bay.

69

Tamar's eyes fluttered open, but she promptly shut them again when she was met with a bright light in her face. The light was strong enough to penetrate through her eyelids. Where was she? The last she remembered...

Aeveron. The gas. They'd been captured. Restraints held her in place. Did Ny'aet really distrust her this much? Something covered her face as well. A mask of sorts. It made the area around her mouth moist and humid. They had continued to keep her drugged after knocking her out. Why?

The explanation horrified her. They wanted her sedated so they could continue to torture Aeveron without inflicting psychological harm upon her.

Her mind reached out to Aeveron. He was nearby; she could sense that even with her closed eyes. Intense pain covered him like a blanket. What had they done to him? It was then that she sensed there was another in the room with them. No...three others.

"Tamar? You're awake?" Aeveron said, his voice faint and labored.

"Yes," she said. Her throat was dry. What she wouldn't give to have the mask off her face.

"I've been thinking. A lot. It's all I've been doing. When I'm not too drugged to think, that is." He sucked in a hard breath. A wave of pain came through their bond. "I just wanted to let you know, if we die—I love you. And I'm glad I was able to be entwined with you, even if it was for a short time."

Tamar shivered despite herself. His words rang so true, his love all-encompassing, radiating around her. This was what a bond was supposed to be like, what she recalled from their first night together making love. Though he had given up in defeat, it filled her with renewed energy. "I will not let you die, my entwined. You have my word," she said, almost for her own resolve as much as to comfort him.

She tried to open her eyes again, this time much more slowly. The bright light still irritated her, but her eyes adjusted soon enough. She turned her head as well as she could.

Aeveron's head was cocked awkwardly toward her, and he stared at her with hungry eyes.

"Hi," Tamar mouthed, and then tried her best to smile at him. She tested the restraints again, pushing against them, but to no avail.

Footsteps clicked from the other side of the room toward them. "Touching," Ny'aet said. He moved between them, glancing back and forth between the two of them. "I can feel the strength of your entwining. Our greatest strength as a people, and as you can see, our greatest weakness, as well. It's almost a shame that we'll have to biologically break the bond between you."

"Biologically what?" Aeveron asked.

"Don't listen to him," Tamar said reflexively.

"Ah. I'd hate to spoil the surprise. The rest of the fleet will be here within the hour." He frowned. "Tamar, I'm rather embarrassed for what you're projecting. You hold his good above the Aresh."

"They're not conflicting matters," Tamar said, gritting her teeth.

"You truly believe that, don't you? And worse, so many people have seen you attempt to rescue this spy. Oh, Tamar." Ny'aet reached out and touched her cheek with the back of his hand. "I put so much into training you. Into giving you a place and lifting you up above the others. I don't think you're going to be able to recover your image from this. It's too much."

As it had been in recent days, she could feel nothing from Ny'aet. This time, though, she didn't question why. She had the answers. This Ny'aet was not the person who led the Aryshan people when she was young, who took her in charitably to groom her for service. This was an entirely different, selfish monster. He was crazy, and the more he spoke, the more it was clear how much of a sociopath he had become. It became even more important to escape, if not just for Aeveron, but for all the Aryshan people.

"I'll think about what I'll have to do. I can't bear the thought of having you executed, even if you are a traitor to our people. But unless we can see a drastic change, and soon..." he let his words dangle in the air and he shook his head. Then he stepped away from her.

With Ny'aet out of the way, her eyes locked with Aeveron's once more. *Let me die, save yourself.* The words came from him, directly through the bondsense, clearer than anything else he'd ever projected to her. The words chilled her to her core.

She tried to clear the thought from her head. It was something she couldn't do. They were entwined. One soul, two bodies. Even if she managed to convince Ny'aet that she was willing to separate herself from Aeveron, she wasn't sure that she could physically go through with it.

Ny'aet let out a grunt. "What's going on here? Is this some sort of human trick?" He backpedaled between the tables that held Tamar and Aeveron. Then, he lost his footing, stumbling backward and crashing into an equipment rack behind them.

Tamar couldn't see beyond that. The light still shone in her eye, but she heard a loud *crack* behind them.

"What's going on?" Aeveron asked. Concern flooded their bond.

And there were more there. A presence. Two presences. They seemed faint compared to what she had with Aeveron—the Aresh tribal bond. What was going on?

"Ny'aet?" Tamar asked. This was all too odd. She couldn't help but be worried by it.

"I think I'm hallucinating," Aeveron said.

With the medical mask still on her face, Tamar couldn't be sure that she wasn't hallucinating herself. Suddenly, stepping from nothingness, came Lieutenant Tol. He appeared to split the fabric of space himself. "No hallucination," Tol said, with a confidence she'd never seen in him before. He grinned. "Just science."

Another figure appeared behind Tol. Maela. "I think we've heard enough of the First Speaker's delusions. It's my opinion that he's not working for the good of the Aresh or the Aryshans, and requires medical leave."

Tamar recalled Tol's phase device. But wasn't that something that required an immense amount of power? How did he make it work here? It was no matter. This was a miracle.

"Well, if you're real, I'm happy to see you," Aeveron said.

Maela reached over and pulled the restraints off her arms and torso. Tamar ripped the mask off her face and sat up. She stretched the best she could while she surveyed the room.

Biolab two. She recognized it now that the lights weren't blaring into her eyes. A holodisplay monitored their vitals and displayed statistics on the human circulatory system. Behind her, Ny'aet lay crumpled in front of the equipment he'd crashed into, supplies atop him and on the floor behind him from where they had fallen.

Tol had removed Aeveron's restraints as well, and he glanced around the room, a dazed look on his face. Maela worked Tamar's legs out of the remainder of her own binds.

"Tol, you've just involved yourself in what I'm sure will be considered treason," Aeveron said, bringing them back to a sober reality. "What are you going to do?"

Before Tol could respond, the door to the biolab whooshed open. Two security guards appeared, plasma pistols in hand. "First Speaker!" one of the guards shouted, eyes going wide when he saw Ny'aet on the floor.

"Tamar, look out!" Aeveron shouted as the other guard took aim at her.

Tamar scrambled off her table, rolling to the side, and using the slick floor of the biolab to slide toward the guard. She used her momentum to kick his legs out from under him.

Tol pushed forward and pummeled into the one who shouted. The element of surprise had done well. The guards had not expected much resistance. They crashed to the floor, both dropping their weapons in the process. The two guards scrambled to try to reach their plasma pistols.

The bondsense jolted her. The guard she had attacked was Aresh as well. It made her stomach churn as it caught up with her—that she had attacked one of her own. But her survival was at stake. It overrode any of her base instincts.

Maela saw one of the plasma pistols on the floor and kicked it across the room. The guard in front of Tamar managed to regain his weapon. Tamar grabbed him by the arm to try to keep it pinned to the floor. "Someone grab the weapon!"

Tol pushed himself off the guard he'd just tackled, regaining his feet and hopping over to the other side of Tamar. The guard struggled beneath Tamar's grip and weight, but he couldn't take on two of them. He managed to fire a shot, which ricocheted off the biolab's walls, causing the holodisplay to spark. Tol kicked hard at the guard's wrist. The guard yelped and his hands lost their grip on the weapon.

The guard tried to push Tamar off him, but by the time he managed to, Tol had the plasma pistol in his hand. "Freeze," Tol said, pointing the weapon squarely at the guard's head.

Both guards froze. The heat of battle filled the bondsense, both the elation of Tamar's side and the woes of the other. It was a strange intermingling of different sensations, but she focused on the void within herself and dampened the emotions to keep focus.

Tol wasted no time and delivered a blow to one guard's head with the butt of the plasma pistol. The guard thudded back to the floor.

The remaining security guard's eyes widened. "No, please don't —" he began to say, but it was too late. Tol moved over to him, and his gun descended upon the man's forehead. He went limp along with his companion.

Maela blinked at Tol's sudden gumption. "That's one way to handle it."

Aeveron gingerly stood, struggling to keep his balance. With the torture he'd endured, it was a wonder that he was awake at all. Suddenly, he jerked his head, bending over the table where he'd been restrained before. He gripped the table, and a chunky substance spewed from his mouth. The retch felt like it came from Tamar's own mouth. Ny'aet may have been right about the bond being their greatest strength and their greatest weakness.

After a few moments, when Aeveron had emptied everything in his system, he stood upright again and wiped his mouth on his sleeve. "The room's artificial gravity appears to have been fixed. It's not spinning anymore," he quipped.

As much as the joke wasn't all that funny, Tamar laughed with a little relief that he had the wherewithal to make light of the situation.

"Vendardre," Maela said as she observed Aeveron. "The truth drug. It must not agree with human biology."

Aeveron let out a small breath. "You got the phase device working on a small scale?" he asked Tol.

Tol nodded. "It always had. But with the size of the device, I didn't think it would have much of a practical application at this level. I may revise my thoughts on that matter."

The device was on a hovercart across the room from them. Aeveron moved over to it, cocking his head toward Tol's invention. "Will it conceal four of us?"

Tol shook his head. "No."

Aeveron glanced back at Tol. "That's not good. It's our only way off the ship without being spotted."

"Unfortunately, we don't have the battery power to maintain the field for two of us, let alone four. We almost reached the end of its capacity coming here," Tol said.

Tamar looked to the door and weighed the options. "We can stick to the maintenance corridors. I doubt there will be many out in the ship actively looking for us. At least until these three wake up." She motioned to the guards and Ny'aet.

"What do we do about the First Speaker?" Maela asked.

"For now, we leave him," Tamar said. "When we escape here, we take to the media and bring his ability to lead into question. There are enough witnesses to his erratic behavior. And I have information that will stun the people of Arysha." The fact that he'd modified the tribal bond would be shocking enough to anyone that it would bring his leadership into question. She had to count on people to trust that.

"Wouldn't it be better to take a hostage?" Aeveron asked.

The three Aryshans stared at him. He was human. He did not understand. "That's off the table."

Aeveron held up his hands in surrender. "Bad idea. Sorry."

Maela tapped her security clearance into the wall panel and opened the door. She stepped outside, then abruptly scurried back into the room and shut the door with another keyed command.

"What's wrong?" Tamar asked.

"Security," Maela said. "They're coming down the corridor."

70

Sean grabbed one of the fallen guard's plasma pistols and Tol secured the other. Adrenaline rushed through his veins, removing his weariness from all the interrogations he'd endured. A dull pain still throbbed in his leg where the Aryshan commanders had cut into him. He flattened himself against the wall by the door, pointing his plasma pistol toward it, and motioned for Tol to follow his lead at the other side. The two women fell in behind them, not having weapons of their own.

The doors to the biolab opened with a hiss, and two more guards rushed through. They had their weapons drawn. Both guards hurried over to their fallen companions, holstering their weapons and kneeling beside them. "We should call for medical help. The prisoners—"

Before the guard could finish speaking, Sean and Tol fired their weapons simultaneously. The plasma bursts drilled into their backs, eating holes into the guards' chests. The smell of burning flesh rose in the air. The bodies fell to the ground.

Sean's three Aryshan companions looked as if they were going to be ill. Through his bond with Tamar, he could feel the way her stomach twisted from the death of a fellow Aresh.

Tamar moved to the fallen guards, retrieving a plasma pistol from the holster at his hip. She frowned. "Reajnik and Sayal. These were good men," she said, bowing her head toward them in a moment of respect.

"There's little else we could have done," Maela said.

"I know," Tamar said.

An alarm sounded—a piercing, shrill noise, more than loud enough to stop any line of thinking or conversation. Strobes flashed within the room. The sounds repeated every three seconds.

Sean looked up toward the strobe. "There must be a ship-wide alert for us now," he said. "We need to move."

Tamar moved back toward the door, shaking her head. "No, this kind of alert wouldn't be for a lone prisoner. This is a battle alert."

"But we're just going to meet with our fleet?" Maela asked.

"We should be going quickly anyway, as Aeveron suggested," Tol said.

They hurried toward the biolab doors with Tamar taking the lead. The doors opened for Tamar, who paused in the corridor.

Something was very wrong. The sense came from the back of his skull, from Tamar's thoughts. She turned to face him, a look of horror in her eyes.

"Not so fast," the voice of Ny'aet came from behind them.

Sean turned around slowly, as did the others. Ny'aet stood not two meters from them, with a plasma pistol trained on Sean's torso.

Tamar hooked her foot around Sean's ankle and stepped in front of him. She bumped her rear into him to force him backward, causing him to stumble. "There's four of us and one of you, First Speaker," Tamar said. "Set the weapon down." She leveled her own plasma pistol at him, though her hands shook.

Ny'aet laughed, his voice fading into the alarm noises. He kept his weapon pointed at Tamar. "Oh, Tamar. I know you far better than that. You wouldn't be able to bring yourself to shoot one of your own, let alone me. Your loyalty is engrained in you, in your commitment to the Aresh. However, you've rightly outed yourself as a traitor."

"Speaker Tamar is no traitor," Tol said. "If anyone has betrayed the Aresh, it's *you*."

Sean had been extremely lucky to make such close friends with Tol before being discovered. If he hadn't, how would these events have gone? It might not matter, anyway. They couldn't take down Ny'aet without one of them getting shot first. And he may be right about their faction bond slowing their reaction, at the very least.

Ny'aet snarled at Sean, staring at him as if the others weren't there. "You spread disharmony through my ranks, human. Look what you've done to this ship, to my protégé, with your lies. This is exactly why we can't allow humans anywhere near our culture. Each word you breathe brings Arysha one step closer to division and death."

Behind Ny'aet, the two incapacitated security guards stirred. Time was running out for Sean and his friends to leave. He glanced to Tol then back to Ny'aet. "You're wrong. Humans have no interest in harming Arysha. I personally have a vested interest in your people," Sean said.

"How can you say that with a straight face? I saw the Great Death as a child and watched as we recused ourselves from the galactic stage. Human culture *still* trickled in despite our measures." He motioned wildly with his free hand. "At first it starts with trade, fashions, children's toys, music. It all seems so harmless until you bring your governmental reform and central banks, which is code for the human takeover. We've watched how you swept the Tralos into your empire, and our agents report that the Drenites are looking to sign a similar treaty. It's insidious, and Arysha is next."

"You're paranoid," Tamar said. Her arms still shook. "Whatever you've done to modify your bond has warped your mind."

One of the guards behind Ny'aet was getting to his feet. There was no time left to debate. Even though the risks were higher than Sean would have liked, no one else would be able to act. It was on him. "I'm sorry," Sean whispered into Tamar's ear.

"What?" she asked, turning back toward him.

Sean pushed her. She fell and hit the deck, losing her grip on her plasma pistol as she braced her fall with her hands.

Ny'aet pulled the trigger of his weapon, but Sean was already on the move. The blast missed, energy dissipating into the thick wall behind him.

Sean leapt to his left, firing his own plasma pistol several times at Ny'aet.

Surprise crossed the Aryshan leader's face. He stumbled backward into the biolab. His plasma pistol fell, and he brought his hands to the gaping wound at his core. He collapsed, reaching out toward Tamar as he did so. His lips quivered, but no words came from his mouth.

Tamar cried out, the pain of someone so close to her resonating through the bond, despite the fact that this man had proven her enemy.

Sean stepped backward, not sure how the others would react. Tol and Maela stood in shock.

The two formerly incapacitated guards moved toward the group. One dove for Ny'aet's weapon. He grabbed hold of it before anyone else could react, and fired quickly. A shot blasted into Maela's side.

Tol charged forward, firing several shots. His plasma blasts connected with the two Aryshan guards at point blank range. Nothing remained of them except ash.

Maela spun and crumpled against the corridor wall. She convulsed, bracing her side and howling in pain.

Tol dropped to his knees beside her, propping Maela against his chest. He held her tightly, but she continued to convulse. "No, no," he said.

Sean slid over to them, leaving Tamar for the moment. "Is there anything I can do?" he asked, with that looming sense that there was no way he could help. He had to ask anyway.

Maela stopped convulsing in Tol's arms. Tol turned her, and Sean could see the skin that had burned off her side and shoulder. The flesh smell filled the entire area. Sean tried to hold his breath.

Maela breathed shallowly, burying her face in Tol's chest.

"The blast didn't get through to her bones. She'll survive," Tol said, bringing a hand to his own temple. "The feedback from the bond—it's terrible."

"I know. I feel it, too," Sean said. He did. Immense and crippling hurt. It was odd that he would pick up on Maela.

He realized it hadn't come from her.

Tamar still lingered on the floor where he had left her. She shivered, tears streaking down her face. It was all he could do to crouch down and cradle her in his arms.

"Ny'aet, he was like a father to me," Tamar whispered. "Not recently, but before..."

"I'm sorry," Sean said. It was his fault that she felt like this, and the regret burned within him. He should have found another way, one that wouldn't hurt her.

Tamar wrapped her arms around him and squeezed. Sean squeezed back. They held each other for long moments, alarms still blaring in the background.

"I think I can walk," Maela said from behind them, her voice strained.

They couldn't take any more time to mourn. More security would be coming soon. Sean stood, gently pulling Tamar to encourage her to rise. She was on her feet a moment later.

He turned to Tol and Maela. "Are you all right?"

Maela nodded. "I'll make it. We should head to the shuttle bay."

"I need to find out what's happening first," Tamar said, motioning to the strobes that flickered in the corridor.

"How?"

"By asking. Word may not have gone through to the officers yet of what's happened." She trudged over to a wall comm unit and tapped in a command, calling the senior officer's quarry. "This is Speaker Tamar. I see a shipwide alarm has sounded. Report."

"Lieutenant Eytel here. Four large vessels have entered the system, set to intercept the *Issiana* in five minutes."

"Our fleet?"

"No, Speaker. Our fleet is here already. These ships are human in origin."

Admiral Conley had anticipated their plans. Their communications might have been intercepted. Sean wondered if he were the only agent that had been inserted onto Aryshan vessels. It made sense that there would be others. Conley must have struck his target and rendezvoused with others in the Earth fleet.

"Launch all fighters," Tamar ordered.

"Launching. All crew has reported for combat stations. Commander Tendell is receiving regular reports," Eytel said through the comm.

"Very well. Tamar out," she said, and clicked the comm off.

"This is bad," Sean said. There hadn't been a battle with this much firepower in the conflict so far. No matter what happened here, it would propel the Aryshan crisis to another level.

Tamar frowned. "No, this could be fortuitous. Our plan had always been to take a shuttle, but what then? The *Issiana* could blow us out of the sky under ordinary circumstances. Now they will be distracted."

"We could get lost in the fray this way," Sean said.

Tamar nodded. "If we're lucky and the other ships don't notice us."

Tol grinned. "I can make the shuttle telemetry mimic debris once we're launched. They'll never know that we're another vessel."

"Good. Let's get going," Tamar said. She led them down the hall and paused at an access hatch. She entered a command on the terminal and it popped open, revealing a small chamber with a ladder that led downward. "Maintenance shaft. This way we can stay out of the common corridors during the fight. Better if no one sees us."

They entered one by one, until all of them were on the ladder. They made their way down the metal rungs, one foot and then one hand. The alarms seemed to be louder in here, the sound echoing off the walls and bouncing back up again.

Something sparked above Sean. The ship rocked.

Sean gripped his current rung as tightly as he could to keep from falling. "What was that?"

"The *Issiana* must have engaged the humans," Tamar said.

They were running out of time. Sean couldn't think of many worse possibilities than dying in a cramped maintenance shaft. They moved down the shaft as quickly as they could and without further word.

71

The ship trembled once more.

"How much longer until we reach the shuttle bay?" Aeveron asked.

Tamar kept moving along each rung. "Not too much further," she said. Several more steps, and she moved to the bottom floor landing. "Here we are."

The others followed onto the platform. Tamar moved to the door and placed her hand to the scanner to open the hatch. Nothing happened.

"It won't budge," Tamar said.

Tol descended the final rung of the ladder onto the platform. Tamar stepped aside so he could take a look at the pad. He pressed his hand against the scanner. Still nothing.

"Huh," Tol said.

"What's the matter?" Tamar asked.

"It's not our access. The door won't open," Tol said.

"What do we do?" Aeveron asked. "This is our escape route."

Panic flooded Tamar through the bond. All three of their emotional auras swelled. They were too much on edge. They had to be calm.

Tol brought up programming language on the scanner's display, tapping in commands. He shook his head. "The sensor is showing a vacuum on the other side. It won't open because of the safety protocol. Do you want me to override it?" He turned to Tamar.

A vacuum. That meant one of two things—the shuttle bay was in use and fighters were departing, or the humans had blasted the shuttle bay to bits. Either way, this wouldn't be able to be used as their escape option. "No. The warning is probably accurate. We have to find another way out," Tamar said. She should have considered these possibilities before they climbed all the way down here.

"It's not your fault," Aeveron said, leaning against her. He sensed her thoughts. His warmness poured through the bond, soothing her nerves.

"Agreed," Maela said. "Now isn't the time to second guess yourself. Should we return to the committee chambers and try to retake command?"

All three of the others looked to her for the next plan. She was their Speaker, their leader. Maela's suggestion was a good one, but they would have an uphill battle trying to gain control over the ship, and the last thing she wanted to do was interrupt the flow of the battle between her people and the humans. One slipup could spell destruction for the whole ship. There was a better solution. "Escape pods," Tamar said. "It's dangerous. They have far less maneuverability than one of our shuttles, but that's our only way off the ship."

"Up to the junior officers' quarry then?" Maela asked.

Tamar shook her head. "Too high a probability of being caught by security. Everyone will be at their posts now. A comm signal is one thing, but being physically present might cause security to pursue us."

"Where to?" Aeveron asked.

As much as she had just ruled out the idea of retaking command of the ship, there would only be one place with easy access to escape pods that wouldn't mean going through dozens of her crew. Tamar resigned herself to it. "The committee chambers, as Maela suggested.

In theory, only Neyral and Tendell should be in there, which makes escape out the back pods easier. There are two pods outside the chambers, each meant for two people, the four commanders. It's our best option."

Aeveron let out a deep breath as he lifted his head toward the maintenance stairwell. "My legs are already burning from the climb down."

"Must be a weak human physiology," Tamar teased. She moved over to the ladder and gripped it. "Let's go."

The four of them climbed through the ship once more. It was a long journey, twice as far as the descent down the ladder. Tamar found herself winded by the time they reached the top. Aeveron's whole body resonated with pain to the point where it clouded their bond together, but he didn't complain during the whole climb. The ship took several more jolting blows. Tamar tried not to wonder how much time they had left. There was nothing she could do about it.

At the top of the shaft, Tamar climbed onto the landing, gripping Aeveron by the arm and pulling him the final distance to his feet. Maela and Tol hopped over after them.

Tamar turned to the hatch. "Weapons at the ready. In case we have trouble."

The others nodded and produced their plasma pistols. Tamar grabbed her own.

She twisted the lever, popping open the hatch into the corridor. Three security guards stood at alert, the committee chamber's last line of defense if the ship were boarded. Their auras hit like a plume of tension. They were on edge, as was her team. The bondsense looped those emotions into a feedback between them.

Tamar had to do something to diffuse it before violence occurred. "Speaker Tamar here! Hold your fire." Earlier, when she had called the junior officers' quarry, they had recognized her authority. Hopefully, news of her incarceration hadn't spread.

The guards looked at her and gave pause. "Speaker," one of them said respectfully.

The rest of Tamar's team stepped out into the hallway behind her. The guards kept their eyes trained on them.

"Why are you coming from the maintenance shaft?" another guard asked.

Maela stepped forward. "We were in a section of the ship that was depressurized. It was the only way out," she said.

All went well. The guards stepped aside to allow them passage. Tamar nodded and proceeded down the corridor. The others followed. The guards watched as they passed.

"Wait a minute," one guard said.

Tamar turned back to see the guard's eyes narrowed and focused upon Aeveron.

"That's the human spy! They're collaborating," he shouted, pulling his plasma pistol from its holster.

Before Tamar could figure a strategy to talk her way out of the situation, two of the guards had Aeveron pinned on the ground. Their knees ground into his back. Aeveron struggled for air.

Tol fired his plasma pistol at the third guard. A hole bored through him, and he slumped against the wall before falling to the ground.

The two guards atop Aeveron jolted from the bondsense resonance of a fallen tribesman. It hit Tamar, Maela, and Tol, as well, creating a brief respite as they all struggled for breath. It was as if the wind had been knocked out of them.

Aeveron pedaled his feet to scoot backward, away from the guards. The movement allowed Tol to take another shot. The blast rang in the echoing corridor and connected. A second guard slumped into lifelessness. The corridor filled with the stench of singed skin.

The one guard left alive backed toward the main lift. Tol raised his weapon toward that guard, but Tamar caught him by the wrist. "No," she said. "He's not fighting. He's fleeing. Leave him be."

Tol watched, keeping his arm steady, but he dropped it as soon as the guard disappeared from sight. "Thank you, Speaker," he murmured.

Tamar moved to assist Aeveron to his feet. When he stood, he came very close to her. She could feel the heat of his body, and it stirred her through her core. But now wasn't the time for more. Their eyes met briefly in understanding, but then she turned back toward the committee chambers.

"Should Tol and I lead? We're not known to be traitors and prisoners," Maela said.

Tamar shook her head. "Tendell and Neyral are committed to the Aresh. They will sense something wrong once the door opens. No, we go together and hope we don't have to have another firefight."

She couldn't pretend she wasn't nervous. Coming face to face with the men who had tried to undermine her command hadn't been in the plans. It was both embarrassing and enraging at the same time. She approached the chambers, pressing her thumb against the security pad. The codes still hadn't been changed. The door opened, and Tamar walked through with her team.

Tendell and Neyral were occupied, managing the officers and the battle. They didn't look up to see who entered the room. The center holodisplay had a map of local space, with ship camera views of the battle outside. A graph of ship's systems displayed below that.

The human destroyers loomed in space, circling to try to surround the Aryshan fleet. Fighters flew everywhere, painting a haphazard picture of plasma and missile fire. A smattering of voices came through the comm system.

"Hurricane Squadron wing five, got three human fighters closing in."

"I read you, wing five. Moving in for cover."

"It's a feint! Back off!"

Static filled the channel. Tamar tensed. Though the distance and hull prevented her from feeling the deaths directly, the awareness that so many of her people were in the midst of losing their lives overwhelmed her.

That moment of laxity in containing her emotions trickled through the bondsense and drew Neyral's attention. He jerked his head toward the door where she stood. He spoke through bared teeth. "You're supposed to be contained in biolab two."

"Plans change," Tamar said.

The others fanned into the chambers. Tamar pointed toward another doorway across the room. "That way," she said.

Maela led the others.

Tendell bent to the side to see what the commotion was. Angry eyes settled on Aeveron. "The spy!" he cried. He furiously tapped in several commands on his station. "I'm calling the marines."

It would be too late before anyone arrived, if anyone arrived at all. Tamar pressed through the chambers, circling around the main holodisplay on the opposite side from Neyral.

He didn't stay put at his station, but bounded over to cut her party off. "You're not getting off this ship," he said.

Maela was in front of Neyral. "Commander Neyral, reach out with the bondsense. There's more to what's going on than you realize. This war is not for the good of the Aresh, nor for the good of the Aryshan people."

The ship's lights dimmed. Power drained. Something had hit them. Neyral looked to the display. One of the large human battle cruisers closed in on the *Issiana*. The humans had too much firepower.

Tamar pointed to the display. "Look at this. This is the result of Ny'aet's hubris. The humans aren't something we can run over. Their Admiral Conley was ready for us."

"Because of Aeveron," Neyral said.

"Doubtful," Tamar said. "Think about the timing of this." She met his eyes, focused, determined. He had to see reason. "Ny'aet has broken the bond medically. He's insane."

"Lies!" Tendell said. His hand dropped below his console, and he produced a plasma pistol.

Tamar tried to position herself to block the others from harm. These were her people. This was her command. She had to take this responsibility.

Nervousness swelled in Tendell's face. It was difficult for him to point a weapon at one of his own tribe. Tamar could sense that.

She looked him right in the eye, hoping he would see a fellow compatriot, a fellow Aryshan in her. It had to supersede all their troubles and quell his rage. *We are tribemates first and foremost,* Tamar thought.

"Leave them be, Tendell," Neyral said. "Speaker Tamar is right."

She shifted her attention to Neyral, not sure she heard him right. Was he advocating for her?

"You can feel her aura. She is sincere," Neyral said. He stepped aside. "I don't like the way she acted as Speaker for this ship. She was too divisive, and her entwining to a spy is troublesome, but there is something amiss with the Ruling Committee. I cannot sense the same bond from First Speaker Ny'aet as I do from all of you."

Tendell held fast for a moment, weapon trained directly on Tamar. He let out a breath, as if he'd been holding it the whole time, and lowered the plasma pistol.

The *Issiana* shook. Sparks flicked from the center holodisplay screen.

"I need to manage this battle if we're going to survive," Neyral said. "Go. Do what you must for the Aresh." He returned to his station, not looking at Tamar.

Tamar wanted to thank him. Despite all her problems with Neyral, she would never have expected this. It was clear he still didn't like her, but he understood what was right for the tribe. Even with that, Tamar found it best to say nothing. She nodded to Tendell, silently wishing him in luck in the battle.

She headed toward the door on the other side that opened into a small landing area for the escape pods. The wall control panels displayed that the two pods were in place and ready to launch.

"You first, Speaker," Maela said.

Tol nodded. "Your life is most important in this. We're going to need to let the people know what's happened here, regardless of which side wins the battle."

Those plans could come later. She hadn't thought much about the future beyond getting off the ship, but it started here. Part of her wanted to assist Neyral and Tendell with the battle, but she couldn't risk staying aboard the *Issiana*. Aeveron had killed the First Speaker.

Even if she managed to convince some of the others on the ship that it had been necessity and in self-defense, loyalty would override rational considerations in the hearts of too many. If they were to make a difference in this war, for both of their peoples, it would have to be in another place and another time.

Aeveron clasped Tol on the wrist. "Stay safe, my friend," he said.

Tol returned the gesture. "You too."

"We have a lot of work to do before there's safety again," Tamar said, glancing between her three friends. She forced a smile. "Thank you all for believing in me. There may be a lot of trouble yet to come, but this is the right path for our people."

"Of course. We—" Maela started, but she was cut off as the ship swayed violently.

The lights in the corridor flickered. Part of the ceiling collapsed behind them. Tamar watched in horror. This ship, *her* ship, wasn't going to make it. "We have to go, now."

Tamar keyed the command to open the escape pod hatch, and Maela did the same for her own. An explosion sounded behind them. A roar of flame erupted from the committee chambers, the fire blasting toward them. Aeveron lunged toward her and pushed her into the escape pod. She fell into the cramped area, and Aeveron slammed his hand into the hatch control.

The door whooshed shut. The flames didn't reach the interior. Tamar barely had time to catch her breath before the pod launched away from the *Issiana*. Tamar forced herself to her feet so she could look back to the door. Through a small, transparent view hole, she caught a glimpse of the ship shrinking in the distance. Burnt damage and flames engulfed the vessel. The humans focused much of their firepower on it.

With such a small view, she couldn't see if Tol and Maela had made it out alive. But worse, how many other loyal Aryshans were about to lose their own lives?

Missiles and plasma fire focused on the center of the semi-circle that comprised the *Issiana*. It broke in two, metal crumpling and imploding on itself. The ship twisted and writhed as it met its destruction.

"So many deaths..." Tamar whispered. Her head throbbed. She closed her eyes and pressed her face hard into Aeveron's shoulder.

He pried open her clutched fist, entwining his hands with hers.

72

The small escape pod drifted through the vastness of a battlefield in space. It was set to a natural pattern, to appear more as floating debris than anything else. Sean had programmed the shuttle that way, unsure whether it would be best to attempt to be rescued by Earth forces or the Aryshans. Tamar would have to help him with that decision. It wouldn't be one he'd make alone.

She was still in no condition to make any decision. Since they'd entered the escape pod a couple of hours ago, Tamar spent her time staring at the floor, rocking back and forth. Her sadness hung like a weight in the back of his skull. It was hard enough for him to keep any focus on making sure they didn't accidentally veer into debris or an asteroid. The escape pod didn't have a robust protection system. It was meant for temporary use.

The Aryshan tribal bond had so many protections. Distance, thick metals could dampen the senses. But so much being cut off at once by death, by pain—it pierced through in a way Sean could only empathize with through his own connection with Tamar. This must have been how the Great Death had impacted them all. He'd read about that, but until now, he hadn't comprehended the reality of its reach.

Sean tried to hold her, reassure her, but nothing had worked so far. Eventually, he let her be, and he focused back on the controls. The display had a couple of options for viewing the outside world, but nothing robust like the cameras on a ship or space station. The tactical map of nearby objects didn't provide much information either, as the pod wasn't equipped with sensors that could detect the various states of the vessels.

Eventually, they settled into a pocket of some space debris which was just large enough to hide in, but small enough that they wouldn't risk crashing into something that could cause them trouble.

From the star charts, it looked like they were a little more than a light year from Palmer station. The Interplanetary Navy must have discovered the rendezvous point for the Aryshan fleet before they were ready for an assault. That added more weight to the battle. If the Aryshans did succeed here, it would put the civilians on the space station in danger. He wished there were something he could do.

Judging from the sizes of the objects on his display, it looked like the humans had a slight advantage in terms of numbers of large ships, especially after the destruction of the *Issiana*. That didn't guarantee the battle's results.

If they could find a way to contact Palmer Station when this was over, he could go back home. It was something he hadn't considered in earnest for a long time. He wondered if his family had given him much thought. It wasn't as if he went home or checked in much before this assignment. With his job in Internal Affairs, he had been busy jetting away to different systems on a regular basis. It made communications difficult.

He didn't fit in with them anyway. Oddly, he found himself feeling much more at home with the Aryshans. When he wasn't in their brig being interrogated, at least. He glanced back at Tamar. Her black hair was frazzled, and she was a mess, but she was still beautiful, even in her vulnerability.

Tamar lifted her head. "You've never mentioned your family before," she said.

"You could hear my thoughts, huh?"

She nodded weakly. "You need to learn how to calm your projections."

"I don't even know how to begin with that."

"I know."

Tamar leaned back against the side bulkhead, resting her head against it. "I've read that human family units are very much like a faction commitment," she said.

"Something like that. I guess I'm a little disconnected from my own. But even so, I would do more for them than I would for a lot of people. And you won't find much more of an ability to sense what's going on than with a human mother," Sean said, laughing to himself.

"I was never close with my direct family," Tamar said. "I was placed in advanced schooling for the Aresh at a young age. Speaker Ny'aet, until recently, was much closer to me." She frowned.

The hum of the escape pod's environmental systems covered a moment of silence. "I'm sorry," Sean whispered.

Tamar looked up at him, her eyes big, shining, full of love. She was everything that Sean ever wanted. "I'm glad I have you here," she said. "Now we have to plan for the future."

73

T he *Issiana* was little more than a speck of light through the back viewport. Smaller lights brightened and dimmed. The dot on the display disappeared. The size no longer registered on these woefully inadequate sensors. Tol shuddered, understanding what the reading meant.

The ship he had called his home for the past several months, the first place he'd found his home since he could remember, had been destroyed.

Maela watched from over his shoulder. She pointed to another dot on the display. "The *Skyweyr* is making a retreat," she said. "I can't believe the humans are winning this. I thought our fleet would do better."

"Our?" Tol asked, glancing back toward Maela, his face so close to hers. Hadn't they become traitors to the fleet? Could they really call it theirs?

"We are still Aresh, and still members of the Aryshan Navy in full standing," Maela said. "Even if I don't like this war, it would be better for our people not to lose their lives."

Tol wasn't sure what he thought anymore. The events of the last several days had been more than unnerving. He needed time to reflect and regroup his thoughts. "Of course."

"We should set our thrusters to intersect with the *Skyweyr*. They can bring us in if we time it right."

Tol thought about it. Were there any dangers in going to the *Skyweyr*? The only ones who could associate them with the spy Aeveron would have been Neyral and Tendell, and with the explosion coming from the committee chambers, it was unlikely they had made it out alive.

Maela was right about one thing—they did need to work within the Aresh. They still had their careers, still could make a difference. It wasn't nearly the same situation as Tamar. He didn't envy her. "What about Aeveron and Tamar?" Tol asked.

"They can handle themselves. I'm not certain from what I sensed that they have any intention of coming back to our people. Everything was such a flurry since we helped them from their bonds, though," Maela said.

Tol tapped in commands to set the thrusters of the escape pod. The tug of acceleration hit a moment later. Then he keyed in a distress signal, directing it toward the *Skyweyr*. They sped away from the battle. They still had much to do, and he had as much to recreate. A personal phase device that soldiers could wear on their back. Tol considered the potential.

74

T amar stretched and opened her eyes. Her body had shut down after running so hard these last several hours. Though it had been hard to get the sense of death and destruction out of her head, sleep overcame her. Resting had done her well.

Aeveron had fallen asleep next to her. He remained in a slumber, lips pouting as he lay on his side.

Careful not to wake him, Tamar stepped over to the main controls. The space was cramped, not giving much room for them to maneuver about within the escape pod, as it was certainly not designed for prolonged periods. She glanced at the main display at the front of the craft.

It was hard to get much of a clue as to what was going on in the outside world. It looked to her like the battle was winding down. There weren't as many large blips on the display—markers that would have shown larger objects like destroyers or battle cruisers. From what she remembered of the originally planned formations, it appeared the *Telv* and the *Ry'ielm* were still engaged with the humans. They weren't faring well. Hundreds of small human fighters swarmed around them like insects. Tamar frowned.

Aeveron stirred.

He pushed himself to an upright position, using his arms to keep him propped up. Seated as he was, the muscles of his arms flexed, sturdy, strong. He stared at her with the hot desire that captivated her interest in the first place.

Tamar's heart thudded, forgetting the battle. "Hi," she said.

"We're still alive," Aeveron observed.

Tamar nodded.

"The battle still going on?"

Tamar nodded again.

"Hmm," he said, glancing around the pod as if getting his bearings. He stretched his neck to look at the display in front of her. "I can't make heads or tails of that."

"It takes some getting used to," Tamar said. "It's what we had to work with in our academy training."

Without needing any further prompt, Aeveron moved on her. It was the first time they'd been alone since the one fateful evening when they had entwined. His hands ran up her sides, and Tamar melted into him.

She softly brought her mouth to his and nibbled on his lower lip. Even though they both hadn't time to get clean in the last several days of action, it didn't matter. They were the same. They were one.

Tamar grasped at Aeveron's back, gripping some of the fabric of his shirt and lifting it. She touched his skin. His back was hard, muscular, with just a hint of sweat. A thrill came over her, causing her to rush a breath.

Aeveron caught her open mouth and his tongue met hers. His excitement pulsed through their bond and made her lose all sense. She wanted to rub against him, to get as close to him as possible.

Her clothes were gone before she even could sense what happened. They bumped against the confines of their small space a couple of times, laughing about it with pure joy. Minor discomforts didn't matter. She had to be close to him.

They made love in the escape pod, and Tamar drifted off into the most peaceful sleep she'd had in days.

S<small>HE</small> <small>AWOKE</small> <small>AGAIN</small> to a clanking sound. Tamar scrambled awake, sensing that something was amiss. "Aeveron," she said, prodding him in the side.

He groaned and turned over, swatting at the air where her hand had been.

"Aeveron, I'm serious. You need to wake up. Now." Tamar hurried to get her clothes on. The escape pod jolted. She lifted her head to get a glimpse out the back viewport.

They weren't in open space anymore. No, this was a shuttle bay of some sort. A large metal room, at the very least. Equipment lay in the background, and the shimmer of a force field cut off an area behind it.

Aeveron finally sat up. "What?" Through their bond, he had a moment of panic.

"Calm," Tamar warned him.

He nodded, glancing around to get a sense for where he was at. He reached for his pants and pulled them on over each leg.

Men in helmets approached the back of their escape pod. They worked the panel outside. Fortunately, Aeveron had managed to cover himself.

The escape pod hissed as the back hatch cracked open, pressure equalizing with that of the larger vessel. These weren't Aryshan soldiers. They were in dark combat armor, a camouflage meant to blend with the vastness of space.

One of them shouted something in a language that she didn't understand.

Aeveron must have comprehended it. He placed his hands up, keeping his eyes on them. He stood slowly. He returned words in their language. Humans. They'd been pulled out of space by a human vessel.

The armored soldier and Aeveron conversed. The bond didn't give her any sense of worry, but the opposite. Aeveron felt at home here. He reached over to her and squeezed her hand to reassure her.

"It's going to be all right. These are my people," he said to her. "I love you."

The guards approached and grabbed her. "I love you, too," she said hurriedly as she was removed from the shuttle. She prayed that she could trust Aeveron's instincts with these soldiers who carried her away, but what choice did she have? For better or worse, they were entwined.

NEXT IN THE SERIES...

Sean and Tamar return in The Stars Asunder - Coming in 2020!

If you liked The Stars Entwined, please leave a review on Amazon!

ABOUT THE AUTHOR

Jon Del Arroz is a #1 Amazon Bestselling Steampunk author, "the leading Hispanic voice in science fiction" according to PJMedia.com, and winner of the 2018 CLFA Book of the Year Award for his novel, *For Steam And Country*. As a contributor to The Federalist, he is also recognized as a popular journalist and cultural commentator. Del Arroz writes science fiction, and comic books, and can be found most summer weekends in section 127 of the Oakland Coliseum cheering on the A's.

email: jdaguestposts (at) gmail (dot) com

ALSO BY JON DEL ARROZ

The Adventures Of Baron Von Monocle:

For Steam And Country

The Blood Of Giants

The Fight For Rislandia

The Iron Wedding

The Steam Knight Series

Knight Training

Guard Training

Spy Training

The Nano Templar Series

Justified

Sanctified

Glorified

Other Books

The Stars Entwined

Make Science Fiction Fun Again

Star Realms: Rescue Run

Graphic Novels And Comics

Flying Sparks Volume 1

Flying Sparks Volume 2

Flying Sparks: Meta-Man Special

Flying Sparks Issue #0

The Ember War

Printed in Great Britain
by Amazon

23684698R00202